Educated at Hampton Grammar School and the University of Nottingham, Graeme Roe had a marketing career working for major international companies.

He then founded and built an extremely successful advertising agency. At the age of forty he decided to take up riding and under David Nicholson's guidance gained an amateur National Hunt licence. His biggest success was winning the Ayr Yeomanry Cup on Dom Perignon.

He then took out a Jockey Club permit quickly followed by a full licence. Amongst his many winners were All Bright, Dom Perignon, Kitty Wren, We're In The Money, Le Grand Maitre, Fairly Sharp and Bad Bertrich.

Graeme now runs a corporate communications company. He has written two books on business. *Odds on Death* follows on from his highly successful first novel *A Touch of Vengeance*.

Other titles by the same author

A Touch of Vengeance
Dangerous Outsider

ODDS ON DEATH

GRAEME ROE

ROBINSON
London

Constable & Robinson Ltd
3 The Lanchesters
162 Fulham Palace Road
London W6 9ER
www.constablerobinson.com

First published by Roe Racing Ltd, 2005

This edition published by Robinson,
an imprint of Constable & Robinson Ltd, 2007

A copy of the British Library Cataloguing in
Publication data is available from the British Library

ISBN: 978-1-84529-584-4

Printed and bound in the EU

1 3 5 7 9 10 8 6 4 2

To Jean and Jessica
My best friends

Acknowledgements

The saying goes 'Everyone has a book in them' and I suppose I was lulled into a false sense of ease when I embarked upon *A Touch of Vengeance*. The saying may well be true, but I had no idea how hard it would be to translate the aspiration into reality. Since *A Touch of Vengeance* was published I have been amazed and touched by the reception and support it has received from so many people, both in and out of racing. To single out a few is difficult, if not invidious. Hopefully many of those who have been so kind and positive will forgive me for a lack of mention. This in no way means that their kindness is not greatly appreciated.

Those I feel must be recognized include – in no particular order – Adrian Pratt, Colin Hughes, Richard Dunwoody, Richard Pitman, Toby Balding, Rosie Lomax, Edward Gillespie, Mark Kershaw, Marcus Armytage and the many independent and multiple bookshop managers who have been instrumental in its success. To this list must also be added the press, radio and television managers and journalists who gave it so much positive coverage. Most important of course are the thousands of readers who have bought the book, and the many people who have met, written to me or phoned me with their kind words about their enjoyment. These have all been major factors in encouraging me to embark on *Odds on Death*. In particular Jonathan Powell, Bob Champion and Jilly Cooper have been most enthusiastic.

Over the years the Willesley Equine Clinic has helped keep my horses fit and running, and my thanks are due to them for this and many of the medical details in this book.

During most of my thirty years in racing I have been a member of the Turf Club. This has been a great source of enjoyment and countless stories. To all of those who have been kind and supportive I give thanks without reservation – in particular to the staff, who are all so friendly, efficient and long suffering with our oddities. Last, but certainly not least, have been the tireless efforts of my wife, Jean, and my secretary, Jane Amor, who have struggled with the details, my terrible handwriting and, very often, unreasonable demands. I hope for all concerned that *Odds on Death* will justify their faith.

Author's Notes

As I said in *A Touch of Vengeance*, horseracing has been, and still is, full of amazing characters from all walks of life, many fascinating, colourful and even eccentric. They come to racing from different backgrounds, with varying hopes and aspirations. Some come for the gambling, some for the spectacle, some for the excitement or just for the association with one of nature's most beautiful and bravest animals – the thoroughbred horse.

With over thirty years' direct involvement in racing as owner, trainer and jockey, I have met an extraordinary cross section of people who are captivated by this fascinating and exciting sport. As a result of that book I have met people I would never have met under normal circumstances. I have been amazed at their passionate love of horses and of the sport, yet some of them throw all caution and normal common sense to the wind in their aspirations to train, own or ride winners, or to land a huge gamble. Hope and, in many cases, unrealistic expectations, have resulted in both tragedies and unexpected triumphs, but at the centre of all this is the courage and magnificence of the thoroughbred racehorse.

The very best are nearly always supported by skilled and sensitive trainers, understanding owners and dedicated jockeys. On the other hand, the sport depends on the also rans and the less well known owners, trainers and jockeys who underpin the pinnacle of the sport in the same way the lower divisions of football support the Premiership.

Again I have tried to ensure that, with the obvious exception of personalities who are mentioned, I have not caused offence by describing people or horses who exist, and to whom I have inadvertently referred. This really is a book of fiction and all the horses and characters are no more than that.

Chapter One

The dining room was elegant but austere, like the facade of the Holland Park mansion – and indeed its owner. Three men and a woman were sitting at the superb eighteenth-century table which, at one end, was set out for a board meeting while at the other sat an interesting cold buffet. Wine, bottled mineral water and two salvers of thinly cut sandwiches, fresh fruit and a selection of ripe international cheeses promised a pleasant light lunch.

The board was an interesting and diverse group. The host, Victor Rainsford, the owner of the house, was a successful, rich entrepreneur specializing in property and the building sector. He was slightly overweight, but always immaculately dressed. He had initially seen racehorse ownership as a status symbol, which would allow him entry to a social group that had always excluded him. He made frequent trips abroad, but usually for only a few days at a time, enough to account for his suntanned appearance. He had a rather volatile personality, and a tendency to alienate people by driving unnecessarily hard bargains. More recently he had become more mellow, but was still a tough negotiator – one of the reasons Jay had wanted him on the County View team.

Next to him sat Howard Barrack, an equally successful businessman in the catering industry.

1

Born in the East End of London from a very poor background, Howard had been blessed with an amazing head for figures. Starting life as a bookmaker's assistant he had gone from job to job gaining experience, and making a huge circle of tough but successful friends. Loyal but tough, he was a good friend but a dangerous enemy. On his left sat Eva, a rich and glamorous South African in her early thirties, who was married to Jay Jessop, the fourth board member and one of the country's top National Hunt trainers. The group had set up a highly successful racing establishment in the Cotswolds, and each had invested a substantial amount of money in the enterprise. Jay had been an outstanding amateur jockey, as well as a leading publisher of scientific and technical magazines. For various reasons, the idea of co-operating in an innovative racing enterprise had been a strong enough bond to weld the four of them together. Victor had long felt the need to be recognized and accepted in the higher echelons of racing. Howard wanted a few really good horses but also to use racing to settle an old debt of cash and honour. Eva's father had been educated in England and at that time had become addicted to National Hunt racing. On his death his daughter had inherited a huge fortune and his dying wish was that she should accomplish in English racing the one thing he had yearned to achieve. Jay had grown bored with business but also accepted that he could not ride for very much longer. His dream was a challenge – to take on established trainers and beat them at their own game. He wanted to prove to them that he could take on the best and win. One of the interesting aspects of the group's strategy was that they seldom accepted already successful horses. They wanted it to be shown that their skill in spotting potentially good young horses, and conditioning them with skill and patience, could still have a huge and powerful impact on the sport. They required complete control of the horses' training and when and where they ran. They had accepted one or two already outstanding horses, but these were the exception rather than the rule. Simultaneously, they had gathered together an extraordinary team. This included Jed Larkin who had been a very good middle rank trainer but had had to slow down on doctor's advice. Joining Jay had eased the strain on his health and the move to the new establishment had given him a new lease of life.

The other key member of the team was Danny Derkin. He had been an outstanding young jockey before being badly injured in a racing accident. He had become a drug addict and had nearly been killed when trying to break with his supplier. Now completely cured, Danny was a vital member of the team, both because of his skill in spotting horses and the respect he commanded from all the stable staff.

The board meeting had been convened to review the company's finances. They were extraordinarily healthy for any racing yard in this competitive business. However none of the four were happy to leave things to chance so there was an informal review every month and a more detailed one – like today's – every quarter. The main topic on the agenda was to deal with any major improvements which needed to be made to the yard or facilities plus a review of the maintenance. It was at this stage that Victor surprised them all. 'I think we ought to buy a helicopter,' he said. The other three were stunned. 'Well, think about it – how much easier it would be for Jay to get around, to take his jockeys with him, plus getting from one course to another on the same afternoon. I think it makes total sense.' Howard thought for a moment and then slowly nodded his agreement. Eva looked less certain and Jay was weighing up the added convenience against the additional costs. At this moment Howard slapped his knee and said, 'I think I may have an even better idea. One of my business friends has a helicopter and a full time pilot. He also has an engineering business so the 'copter is maintained within an inch of its life. He's getting older and doesn't travel on business as much as he used to. I have a feeling there might be a lot of spare capacity there. Let me talk to him and see if we can do a deal. I can't believe that there would be many days when there would be a conflict, but let me look into it.'

There was general agreement around the table and the formal business came to an end. The sandwiches and drinks were handed around and the conversation turned to racing in general, the main objectives of the season, and also the relatively new and much discussed subject of exchange betting. Exchange betting was essentially a system whereby companies allowed and provided a facility for individual members of the public to offer odds and take and make bets against each other individually via the internet.

This was not restricted solely to horse racing but covered many other sports as well. The big issue here was that it allowed members of the public to bet against each other on horses losing, unlike betting with conventional bookmakers when win or place bets was the norm. There had been much media coverage, and indeed some serious enquiries on

4

large bets on fancied horses, and some of these bets had been made on these horses that duly obliged by running badly.

The opinions voiced around the table were lively but certainly not unanimous. However they were all agreed that the case for or against had not been fully made. On this note the meeting broke up with Victor going to his Aldwych office, Howard to his home in Surrey and Eva returning to County View, their training establishment in the Cotswolds.

Jay was staying overnight to see a bloodstock agent about possible young horses for the next season. The previous season had been one of spectacular success, with winners in several major races including the coveted Cheltenham Gold Cup.

Each time he approached County View Jay always had that feeling of almost not believing that they had achieved so much in such a short time. At the same time there was a steely determination to cap success with success. This would not be a flash in the pan. He had seen so many trainers and jockeys have one or two seasons of spectacular success followed by pure bad luck – injuries to horses resulting in fickle owners leaving like lemmings.

The fact that the four main partners, backed by Hal Bancroft and his American friends, controlled the overwhelming majority of the equine athletes, provided an insurance policy against horses leaving at short notice. It did not, however, safeguard them against the other trials and tribulations of training fragile creatures subject to injury and illness.

The following morning, as he drove into County View, past the security man who gave Jay a cheery wave, the young trainer felt his spirits rise as they always did when he got back to his home base with

5

an exhilarating day ahead of him. As he parked his car he noticed that Eva's was missing and assumed that she was on her weekly shopping expedition, so he walked across to the yard, where he found Danny and Jed in deep conversation.

'Everything OK here?' he asked.

'Absolutely fine,' came the joint reply. 'We were just talking about the schooling arrangements.'

'OK,' said Jay, 'I'd like to watch that. Come and get me when you start.'

As he walked away Jed called out, 'By the way, there was a telephone call from a young lady called Amanda who's a student at the Cirencester Agricultural College. She said she would call back at the end of the day when her lectures are over.'

'Thanks,' replied Jay and walked on without giving it another thought.

The morning went smoothly and Jay and Eva had a quiet afternoon watching racing on television until it was time for evening stables. Jay, joined by Jed, went round every evening and looked at every horse, checking their legs, looking for any signs of discomfort, their interest in their food etc. At the end of this daily routine Jay had barely settled down with a glass of wine when the telephone rang. A woman's husky voice enquired if she was speaking to Jason Jessop. 'Yes,' he replied.

'Oh, good evening Mr Jessop. You don't know me. My name is Amanda Lambert, and I am a student at the Royal Agricultural College. I am just wondering if it would be possible for me to ride out at your yard most days each week?'

'Do you have any experience?' asked Jay.

'Oh yes. I've ridden in a lot of point-to-points, and had five winners last season.'

'Well, that sounds pretty impressive,' replied Jay. 'You'd better come down and we'll have a look at you.'

'That would be great,' she said. 'I'm afraid that I am going away on a week's field work next week, but perhaps I could phone you on the Sunday and see when it will be convenient for me to come over. I will also know my lecture timetable by then, so I will be able to be very accurate about the days I'll be available.'

'That sounds great,' said Jay. 'We look forward to seeing you in the not too distant future.'

'What was all that about?' asked Eva, and Jay filled her in.

'Let's hope it's not a flash in the pan and that she just turns up a few times at her convenience,' said Eva.

'If that happens she won't be welcome here for very long,' replied Jay. With that they settled down to watch an old film on TV before having an early night. Jay was always up early to supervise the gallops, the horses going racing and a myriad of other activities that made up the normal day in a busy racing yard. Eva was seldom very far behind him and she rode out with at least one lot most days, both from enjoyment and as a way of keeping fit.

Chapter Two

An ancient Land Rover was parked beside an all-weather gallop just outside Lambourn, the centre of National Hunt racing. The grass was covered with a heavy October frost, looking almost like snow, which sparkled in the morning sun.

Eighteen horses cantering in pairs side by side swept past the vehicle. Some were ridden by men, some by women, and of very different ages. They all had one thing in common – the love of thoroughbred race-horses. One of the last two horses to come up was ridden by a rather grizzled-looking man in his fifties. Terry had been around racing all his life, as a boy in Yorkshire, as a young man in Newmarket, and later on at Lambourn. He had never been a good jockey, in fact he had only had a few rides and never ridden a winner, but he was nevertheless a very good horseman. He was head lad in this medium sized successful yard.

The horses went past at a good pace but not a flat-out gallop. The work that they were doing climbing up this steep incline was very strong and steam was rising from their flanks by the time they reached the top. Terry was surprised when the Land Rover did not follow. The trainer, Matt Jenkinson, was normally up at the top by now to look at his horses the moment they finished, but this time there was no sign of movement.

Terry looked at the Land Rover and thought, 'Oh God, it's not starting again.' The vehicle could be temperamental but this usually happened only in wet weather.

On his way back to his boss he noticed that there was a single tyre track from the Land Rover off towards the main road. This surprised but did not over-concern him. His relaxed attitude changed dramatically when he looked through the window. His boss, sitting behind the wheel, was covered in blood, and clearly dead. A bullet had taken off a lot of his head!

In a state of shock, he just sat on his horse who was becoming unsettled by the smell of blood. After a moment he dialled 999 on the mobile that he always had with him but had never expected to use in such circumstances. He explained the situation to the police and was told to wait near the Land Rover. Then he phoned the stable yard and very quickly a young man and woman arrived in another 4 × 4. He shooed them away from the horrific scene that had confronted him, put the girl on his horse and sent them back to the yard. Moments later two police cars with blue lights flashing drove up beside him. He pointed out the rapidly disappearing tyre marks of what he assumed, and the police agreed, were almost certainly those of a motor cycle. He sat in the back of the police car, by now in a glazed state of shock, and he told them the very little he knew.

TRAINER FOUND MURDERED ON GALLOPS

The screaming headline on the first page of the following morning's *Racing Post*, plus full coverage on page two, caused a sensation in the racing fraternity. Matt Jenkinson was a respected trainer in the highly competitive world of racing and nobody could think of any reason why his life should have been taken in such a dramatic and brutal way. It was so surprising there was almost no speculation as to the motive behind such a vicious attack.

Jenny, his wife, could tell the police nothing and neither could the stable staff. Preliminary police enquiries indicated that there were no financial problems, all the owners spoke of the dead man with affection and respect and nothing unusual seemed to have surrounded the normal routine of his life. He had had one telephone call that had made him angry but had told Jenny that 'it was some nutter', and left it at that. It had not been mentioned again. Tributes were paid to him by the racing correspondents of all the national newspapers, who described him as a likeable, highly competent trainer, who was always in the middle ranks of the prize money winners and very often pulled off major coups.

He was also recognized as a trainer who could regenerate enthusiasm for racing in horses that appeared to have lost interest in their game.

The funeral held at Baydon church had a huge turnout. The television and press coverage owed as much to the circumstances of the crime as it did to the reputation of the victim and the affection in which he was held by so many. The murder of a racehorse trainer caused a sensation. This was dwarfed when a few days later the media splashed the incredible story that Gordon Rowlands, one of racing's top television and newspaper journalists, had also been shot. He was found dead in one of the stables that he kept for the few retired racehorses that he always got from The Moorcroft Centre. This was one of a number of organizations that rehomed and rehabilitated racehorses when their racing days were over. He kept them out of sentiment, and also to provide him and his family with high class hacks.

By now, speculation was running rife, particularly when under mounting media pressure the police announced that not only was it murder, but ballistics had indicated that the same weapon had been used in both crimes. This had become such a high profile issue that Harvey Jackson – one of the most highly regarded detectives in the whole of the British police services – was drafted in to head up the enquiry. At the same time Giles Sinclair, the head of the Jockey Club security department, was also invited to join the team trying to solve these two strange, but apparently related, crimes. Rewards were being offered by newspapers, friends and owners for any information leading to the conviction of the murderer.

The police and the Jockey Club pooled their resources but could find no apparent connection between the two men or the incidents. Clearly they knew each other through racing, but were not perceived as close friends, and certainly there was no known animosity between them.

Bookmakers were interviewed, but there were no major gambles involving either victim and neither of them had a history of violence, criminal connections or any other suspicious factors. In fact the most surprising thing was that both of them appeared to be, as one person said, 'squeaky clean'. Both had reputations for complete integrity and rather modest lifestyles.

In view of the fact that both lived and worked close to the town of Lambourn, it was decided to set

11

up a major police operational centre in Newbury. The bank records, telephone calls and travel arrangements of both men were put under close scrutiny. Not only was nothing unusual found, there were also no apparent links between the two other than the normal contact between trainer and journalist at racecourses.

Chapter Three

Just as the interest in these bizarre murders was beginning to wane the media went wild again. Hank McMullen, the leading young National Hunt Jockey who looked certain to win the Conditional Jockeys' Championship, was found shot in a motel room off the M4 motorway. Under significant pressure the police disclosed that again ballistic experts had indicated that the same revolver had been used as in the previous two killings.

Jay Jessop and his assistant trainer, Jed Larkin, were sitting in Jay's office at County View. The racing yard was located in the Cotswolds. It had been a wartime airfield but had been transformed into one of the most sophisticated training establishments in Britain. This morning though they were not thinking too much about training. They were devouring the *Racing Post* and the other racing columns in the national press. They were in the same state of bewilderment as the rest of the racing fraternity. Confused and sad they agreed that they had better get on with the day's work.

They both returned to the kitchen, sat down and enjoyed the coffee and toast prepared by Eva, Jay's wife, and Cathy. She was Jed's wife and it was she who had persuaded him to slow down and join Jay. Like the two men the women were also stunned by the terrible news of the three brutal deaths.

Jay and Jed started to review the work that each horse would do that morning, and also the possible races for them over the next few days. Not only did they have enviable facilities but also some of the most truly magnificent hurdlers and steeplechasers in the UK. Their joint objective – although they seldom admitted it even to each other – was to become the champion yard, earning more prize money than any other training establishment in Britain. For a second year operation it was a somewhat extravagant ambition.

Entries were made at Stratford-upon-Avon, Worcester, Towcester, Sandown Park, Newbury and Chepstow, with prize money varying from £5,000 to £30,000.

Both men had a deep conviction that running horses too frequently shortened their racing life, and were fortunate that their owners accepted this when they sent often extremely expensive bloodstock into their care. Everyone in the yard knew that the long term objective was for a significant number of horses to win races at major tracks, and in particular at the Cheltenham Festival and the Grand National Meeting at Aintree. Overseas raids on France and Ireland were also on the cards.

However, there were other rich pickings to be had if the preparation and the planning was careful enough.

It took a really strong horse with an enormous amount of stamina to win at courses like Cheltenham and Towcester. Flat courses like Stratford-upon-Avon and Worcester suited horses that had natural speed and could get round sharp bends with

14

ease. All these factors had to be weighed in the balance.

As these decisions were being made the welfare of the horses came first, and loyalty to the owners not far behind. Whilst looking at the *Racing Post* columns and statistics they both had a considerable degree of satisfaction in seeing that they were placed third in the table, and not that many thousands of pounds behind the reigning champion trainer and his closest rival.

Having finished their breaks Jay and Jed went back into the yard and were joined by the head man, Danny. Freddie Kelly, the champion jockey, who was paid a retainer by Jay, was also present plus a young jockey called Paul Jenkins. Paul had been working for Jay for most of the previous season following a successful spell with him in the previous year. The morning's work was completed with horses on various schedules, some working short distances uphill very fast, others long steady canters, some on grass and some on all weather gallops plus a number of them being schooled over hurdles or fences.

Amongst their many charges were two horses that were really concentrating their minds: one was a grey mare called Pewter Queen who had turned out to be an absolutely outstanding young hurdler, and a more mature horse called The Conker. The other super star was Gold Cup winner Splendid Warrior who was having a long walk that morning with Eva on his back. Pewter Queen was being prepared for the Champion Hurdle and The Conker for the Grand National. They were due to work upsides at racing pace. Both were owned by Howard and the 'Queen' had started her career trained by Jed and ridden by Jay.

The mile and a quarter was run on the grass and all looked well as they flew past Jay and Jed. Waiting for the two to return the two colleagues chatted happily. As soon as the horses reached them Danny jumped off Pewter Queen, then turned and looked with obvious concern towards Jay.

'She's lame, Guv'nor,' he said. This was devastating news for Jay. She and Splendid Warrior, whom he had ridden to win the Gold Cup in his riding days, then trained to repeat the feat, were his two trump cards for Cheltenham. This was where the real prize money was available which could give him his greatest opportunity of overtaking the two trainers above him. He walked over and felt the mare's leg. There was warmth at the very bottom but no swelling. Jay heaved a great sigh of relief, even though the hoof itself was boiling hot.

'We may be OK,' said Jay. 'I don't think it's a tendon.' He sprinted back to his office and rang the vet, Chris Langridge, who said he would be there within minutes.

The maroon 4 × 4 drove quickly into the yard. The young, but well respected, vet got out.

A quick handshake and into the stable where the grey mare was standing. Clearly in some discomfort she was standing with all her weight on three legs. A pair of horrible-looking tongs were produced and the vet squeezed round the sole of the hoof behind the shoe from one side to the other. Suddenly the mare jumped. 'I think she's definitely got an abscess,' said the vet. He whipped the shoe off and made a small puncture hole in the sole of the hoof. Pus shot out. You could feel the relief all around the box, not least in the mare's own demeanour.

'This will need to be poulticed for a few days, until there is no discharge,' said the vet. 'I'll come back to see her in a few days' time. Don't give her too much to eat, and hopefully we'll have her shoe back on within a week.'

Chapter Four

Howard, Eva, Victor and Jay were once more sitting in Victor's sumptuous dining room off Holland Park, after a delicious dinner prepared by Victor's French chef. Victor had got the *Racing Post* open at the statistics page. Drinking his usual Black Label whisky, he tapped the page.

'Do you realize that you could easily be Champion Trainer this year? All we need is a bit of luck and perhaps an extra top class horse or two.' Howard nodded his agreement but Eva was less enthusiastic.

'We had always agreed,' said Jay 'that we wouldn't go out and buy success, we would make it ourselves. The only way that we could inject extra real prize money into the yard at this stage of the season would be to buy already proven horses.'

'So what's wrong with that?' asked Victor.

'It will undermine the whole reason that we started this,' responded Eva.

There was a pause before Howard agreed. 'Actually, I think Eva's right.'

Victor looked slightly disgruntled but eventually said, 'OK, but let's agree that anything we can do to win the Championship we should.'

Jay, for once, lost his cool. 'Do you really think that we're not trying to do that? Jed, Danny, Eva and I work every reasonable hour to make sure that the horses are fit and are placed in the correct races. Of course I'd love to be Champion Trainer and the champion yard, but you can't make it happen overnight.'

There was another pause. Eva put her hand on Jay's arm and smiled at the three of them. 'Come on all of us, it's such an amazing run, let's not fall out over something that may be just a year or two too soon.'

Eva and Jay stayed the night in his small Hays Mews house and left before 6 a.m. to get back to County View in time for that morning's exercise. On the way down the M4, as they passed Lambourn, they both thought of the triple murders that had slipped from the news as nothing new was reported. 'Have you heard anything at all?' Eva asked Jay. 'Nothing. The racecourse gossip hasn't lessened but nobody seems to have a clue why they were killed or for what reason. I feel so sorry for everyone involved but particularly for Jenny Jenkinson. She's trying to take up the reins but it's really tough and I wonder how loyal the Jenkinson owners will prove to be.'

'Let's go and see her,' suggested Eva, and after a moment's thought Jay agreed and they left the M4 at the next exit. Eva phoned Jed and told him the change of plan. The work schedule had been agreed the night before so Jed was quite able to sort things out with Danny.

They turned into the Jenkinson yard and Jay was not surprised to see that the horses were already pulling out with Jenny and Terry legging up the riders. The surprised look on Jenny's face quickly changed to one of pleasure as she realized who her visitors were. Although not close friends they had always got on well when they had met up at the races but it was obvious that Jenny was curious about why they were there now. A flash of concern crossed her face and Jay guessed that she was probably worried that he had come to tell her that horses was leaving her yard to join his.

Jay smiled at her. 'Hi! We've come to spy and see what you're up to.'

She chuckled. 'That'll be the day!'

'Look, I don't want to interrupt, but I really wanted to check if there was anything we could do to help. I know it must be tough and you must be missing Matt terribly.'

'That's very kind, Jay,' she replied. 'Actually we are coping quite well, and to be honest, having to work in the yard is helping to keep my mind off what happened. The police have been very considerate and have tried to keep me informed. Although they are working hard they haven't come up with any explanation for either Matt's or the other two murders.'

'Well, all I wanted you to know is that there may be times when something happens and you would like a second opinion, to share a horsebox on a long journey, or anything else. By the way, how are you off for spare boxes?'

'Fortunately no horses have left us yet and I have got four or five that I had hoped to fill, but as you can imagine, new owners are going to be hard to find in this situation.'

Jay nodded his understanding and then he surprised Eva with his next remark.

'I don't know if it's of any interest to you but we've got a couple of young horses recently broken in, and they need time. I wondered if you would be interested in looking after them for me for a few months. They would only need light work and it would free us up to get on with both our priorities during this really heavy part of the season.'

Jenny's face broke into a smile and, walking across to Jay, she gave him a big hug. 'That would be fantastic!' Turning to Eva she said, 'This is a really nice man you're married to.'

'I know,' agreed Eva. 'Most of the time!'

'I'll give you a call later on today and arrange a convenient time for us to get them over to you. By the way, don't hesitate to let people know that I have sent you a couple of our horses – it should also help give your yard staff some confidence. I'll also let the *Racing Post* know.'

'You're a brick,' Jenny said, and giving him one more hug she turned and waved them off before getting on with her morning's work.

'That really was kind of you, Jay, it's a great idea,' Eva told him.

'Will you ring the *Racing Post* and let them know what we're doing? You never know, one or two of the other big yards may send her a horse or two. That would at least help to tide her over at this terrible time.' Eva nodded in agreement.

Later the next morning Jed and Jay were talking over a mid-morning coffee when Jed gave Jay a hard look.

'Have you noticed that we're having an extremely good run of winners recently?'

Jay looked blank. 'Of course I have,' he replied.

'Don't you think there is something slightly un-usual about it?'

'No,' replied Jay. 'Our horses are well and they're running well.'

21

'I know that, but the truth of the matter is that a significant number of recent winners were horses we didn't expect to win.' Jay looked at him hard. 'What are you saying?'

'What I'm saying,' Jed replied, 'is that in a number of these races there was at least one horse that, on form, could beat us, and these horses have, at the last minute, not run for various reasons. Don't you think that's odd?'

Jay thought for a moment, 'I really hadn't considered it. What do you think we should do?'

'Two things,' answered Jed. 'I'd like to spend some time looking up horses that should have run against us but didn't, who trains them, plus any other information I can glean from the form books. The next thing is that you should go immediately to the Jockey Club and say that you are concerned with this odd situation.' Jay agreed.

As soon as Jay and Eva had had lunch he rang Giles Sinclair at the Jockey Club. Very briefly he explained that Jed had pointed out to him the strange coincidence of a number of horses being withdrawn very shortly before they were due to run. In all these cases, Jay pointed out, they would have expected the horses in question to give his horses hard races, if not actually beaten them.

There was a pause at the other end of the line. Sinclair was obviously thinking.

'Have any of the trainers spoken to you?' he asked. 'Do you know any of them well enough to ring and ask?'

'No is the answer to your first question, and I am only on nodding acquaintance with all of them.'

'Thank you for letting me know. Please keep me informed if you have any further thoughts on the subject and of course if you become aware of another incident.'

As a matter of courtesy Jay then phoned Victor and Howard. Victor was slightly sceptical about the whole thing, but Howard was concerned that this might in some way damage Jay's otherwise impeccable reputation.

Chapter Five

A police incident room had been set up just outside Newbury. Telephone lines and computers had been installed and technical experts were working alongside key police personnel. They were being helped as needed by a number of people from the racing authorities and the bookmakers association. So far they had drawn a complete blank. There was nothing linking the three dead men other than that they had all been involved in National Hunt racing as their livelihood. The young dead jockey had had a couple of rides for Matt Jenkinson and had had some brief conversations at the racecourse with the journalist. None of them had any apparent link with any bookmakers, and the police were becoming increasingly frustrated at the lack of progress.

It was at this stage that news came through that Jason Jessop had telephoned the Jockey Club to say that he was somewhat suspicious that a number of strongly fancied horses, running in his races, had suddenly been withdrawn. Immediately the trainers of these horses were visited by the police and racing officials. They were met with a stone wall of silence and, in many cases, apparent disbelief.

By this time the whole chapter of incidents had become an enthralling topic of discussion and wild speculation in racing circles. It was against this background that Eva, Jay, Jed, Howard and Victor met again in Victor's house. For once it was Jed who took centre stage.

'This just does not make sense,' he began. 'All the horses that have been withdrawn have come from relatively small yards. There had been no bets on them and nothing that we can find in terms of gambles on our horses. It can't be a coincidence. It must be suspicious in some way or other.'

It was at this moment that Howard jumped up and said, 'I think that this is when we call in Benny.'

Benny was a long time friend of Howard's who came from the East End of London. Along with his brothers and other close associates, he had been fundamental to solving problems for all of them in the past. Never actually breaking the law, Benny sailed as close to the wind as possible, and his contacts in the East End, across Europe, North America and the Far East were legion.

It was agreed that his involvement would be a sensible course of action and within minutes he had been contacted and a meeting set up between him, Jed and Jay in an East End boxing gym. This had been used in the past for a number of meetings connected with Danny's difficulties in Ireland in the aftermath of Howard's big gamble for revenge.

At eight o'clock the next morning Jay and Jed were collected from Jay's Mayfair home in an ancient BMW. The car's battered exterior belied the extremely powerful and perfectly maintained engine which purred beneath the bonnet. The glass and coachwork were all bullet proof. On arrival at the gym they were quickly escorted through to a small but comfortable office at the rear. The walls of this

25

were lined with signed photographs and action shots of boxers of the last twenty years.

'So what's all this about?' asked Benny.

Jay reminded him of the three murders and told him as much as he could about the background of each victim. He also said that the police could find no apparent connection between them, nor any motive.

'What's worrying Jed and me,' explained Jay, 'is that we are suddenly getting winners that we did not expect to have.'

'What's wrong with that?' asked Benny. 'This happens all the time in racing, particularly in National Hunt.'

'Not quite in this way,' replied Jay. 'Jed has been looking into it and in a number of races we have won we expected at least one horse to beat us. In a significant number of cases these horses have been withdrawn at very short notice and our horse has been left as the outstanding chance. It has not always won, but on the whole we have been successful in nearly all of these races. All of the horses have come from only a few yards.'

Benny thought for a moment. 'Any obvious gambles?'

'None at all,' replied Jay.

'The bookmakers have been extremely co-operative and there is apparently no connection whatsoever.'

'So what do you want us to do?' questioned Benny.

'Just quietly ask your friends and contacts if there are any whispers going on. There has to be some connection, but we haven't been able to find it.'

'There's another line you could consider,' suggested Jed. 'If you could get friendly with some of the stable staff in these yards, it would be interesting to know if there's an obvious reason why these horses were withdrawn, or if the yards were as surprised as us. In some cases a vet's certificate saying that the horse is not fit to run can be "arranged", but this is rare because most of the vets are totally straight. Try to find out if there seemed to be any sudden loss of form or other problems with the horses and, in particular, if this was common to a number of the yards concerned.'

'How many yards are we looking at?' asked Benny.

'Eight or nine. Some of these may have perfectly straightforward explanations.'

'OK,' said Benny. 'Anything else?'

'Not that I can think of, how about you, Jed?'

'No,' came the reply. Jay continued, 'If you hear anything at all, let us know. It might trigger a thought that would let us point you in the right direction.'

'Right,' agreed Benny. 'There is a decent little pub around the corner, let's go and have a drink before we all get to work.'

Chapter Six

Two days later Jed and Jay were sitting in the back of the Jaguar being driven by Danny. It was relatively unusual for the two of them to go to the races together. Jed had suffered a heart alarm when he was a successful middle level trainer and had thrown in his lot with Jay. Part of the deal was for him to go racing only on high days and holidays, or if they had runners at different meetings on the same day.

Today was rather a special occasion. Just over a year ago the Irish vet Jay used had phoned to say that he had seen a particularly nice three year old and thought it would be worth Jay's time to go over and have a look for himself. Jay had done so, had seen the filly and was completely captivated. A few weeks later, after being passed by the vet, she arrived at County View. That's when the fun began! She was a real madam, and was one of the most difficult horses to break in that either Jed or Jay had ever seen. She quickly won the stable name of The Bitch, but this was thought to be inappropriate for racing. It was therefore modified to Wot A B.

Once she had settled down it became clear that she had an enormous amount of natural ability. Always lively when first mounted, once she got to the gallops she really put her heart and soul into it

28

and there were very few of Jay's best horses who could master her.

Today was Wot A B's first race and Stratford-upon-Avon had been chosen for her racecourse debut. Stratford had always been one of Jay's favourite courses because the ground was invariably impeccably kept. The whole course was visible from the stands and the facilities for owners, trainers, jockeys and stable staff were all excellent.

Wot A B was travelling to the races in company with Up and Away, another ex-Irish horse who had run very well in point-to-points, but this was his first race in England under rules. The yard's third runner was Hopeful Return, who had been ridden by Jay in his jockey days and originally trained by his now mother-in-law, Fiona. He had come third in the previous year's Triumph Hurdle. Not the most robust of horses but one with exceptional ability, they all held their breath when he was running. In some ways this was a day of high expectations, mixed with acute apprehension.

As Danny drove into the car park there was, as always, a sigh of relief when they saw their County View horsebox neatly parked outside the stable block. Jay jumped out and Danny drove nearer to the grandstand to park the Jaguar in the space reserved for owners and trainers.

Producing his identity card Jay signed the register at the security office at the stable yard and was told in which boxes his horses were stabled. He strode round the corner and found his three with their heads over the stable doors, all looking relaxed and interested in the general hustle and bustle associated with a racecourse stable yard. He felt all his horses' legs, and trying in vain to relax he left to meet

Danny and Jed in the owners' and trainers' bar. Jed had already gone into the weighing room to make sure that the declarations had been made and that all was in order. 'I'm much more nervous before our horses run than I was before I rode in races,' confided Jay.

'That's not so surprising,' replied Jed. 'You don't have any contact once they leave the parade ring. It's all out of your hands.'

Their horses were due to run in the second, third and sixth races, which meant that they would be very busy in the short space between the second and third.

Danny was sent off to find the stable lad and lass who were responsible for those two horses, and Jed went off to find Freddie Kelly who was going to ride the mare in the last race and find Paul who was riding the other two horses.

From then on everything went smoothly. Jay and Jed each had a sandwich and a glass of beer and Jay then lit up one of his customary cigars. Jed, who had been instructed by his doctor to cut down on his enormous cigarette consumption, now occasionally smoked a cigar but normally not until the end of the day. He went off to the weighing room to collect the saddle, leaving Jay in splendid isolation with a cloud of smoke hovering over his head.

The first runner, Up and Away, was saddled and led into the parade ring. Minutes later the jockeys streamed out of the weighing room, had a word with the connections and were then legged up. Paul was led the short distance between the paddock and the racecourse, and they were on their way to the start. The sun was shining and the conditions looked perfect for National Hunt racing.

Jay's horse was a stayer rather than a sprinter which was why it was running in a two and three quarter mile race. The start was well to the left of the grandstand and young Paul the jockey took him down steadily although he was pulling hard for his head. The sixteen runners circled behind the tape and the assistant starter helped jockeys who needed a hand tightening their girth. As a conditional jockey it was mandatory for Paul to have his girth checked, but all was in good order.

The starter checked his watch to make sure the race did not go off too early. That would result in chaos for the bookmakers. He then walked to his platform and shouted to the jockeys to walk in, he pressed the lever to release the tapes and the race was on.

At Stratford-upon-Avon races are often run at a very fast pace because of the good ground and the fact that the course is flat. Today was no exception.

Paul kept Jay's horse in the middle of the field as they passed the stand for the first time and made the sharp left-hand turn round the bend.

Jumping the fence on the bend there was no significant change in the order, and Paul kept Up and Away in the middle of the field. As they lined up for the fences down the back straight, there was a sudden injection of pace and very quickly the field went from bunched up to strung out. Paul kept his head and allowed his horse to creep up bit by bit, and he passed one horse after another. Turning for home he was lying fifth and he and the four horses in front of him had drawn well clear of the rest of the pack.

Stratford-upon-Avon does not have the longest of finishing straights and at this stage Paul decided to make a move. A slap on the shoulder and his mount quickly passed the horses lying fourth and third.

The jockey on the second horse was already working hard but the leader looked very comfortable. Paul gave his horse one slap behind the saddle and was repaid by an immediate quickening that took him within a length of the leader. As they jumped the last flight there was a mere half length between them.

By now both jockeys were riding flat out with hands and heels and the occasional flash of the whip. They passed the winning post locked neck and neck and the loudspeaker announced a photo-finish.

As Jay trotted to meet his steaming runner, he looked up at Paul and panted, 'I think we lost it.' A few minutes later the announcement confirmed this. Although this was a slight disappointment, the fact remained that the horse had run extremely well. There was no hint of criticism of either horse or rider.

Jed was waiting in the weighing room to grab Paul's saddle the minute he jumped off the scales, having confirmed he was the correct weight for his next race.

This, of course, was Hopeful Return and Jay was very confident that this would be his winner of the afternoon. As soon as Paul had weighed out he and Jed walked quickly to the saddling enclosure and, between them, quickly got him saddled up. The horse was one of the last to be led into the parade ring. It had taken Paul longer to weigh out than jockeys who had not ridden in the previous race. On his way to the parade ring Jay was stunned to hear somebody call to him: 'OK, Jessop, you haven't been able to buy off your competition today.' He spun round to confront his accuser but was unable to see who it was. Jed gave him a startled glance as they made their way into the middle of the parade ring.

'What was that about?' he asked.

'You tell me,' replied Jay.

They were soon joined in the ring by Paul Campbell, Hopeful Return's owner. Before Jay had him the horse had been trained by Fiona who was Eva's mother so there was a long history of friendship and mutual respect.

'How do you think he'll do?' asked the owner.

'Well, he is the best horse in the field, but let's hope the weight's not too much.'

Hopeful Return was running in a handicap hurdle and was carrying a hefty weight as a result of his Triumph Hurdle performance plus many other wins. Nevertheless this was assisted by using Paul. As a conditional jockey he was able to knock five pounds off the weight and this race, though no walkover, was nothing like the quality of Cheltenham.

The normal preliminaries at the start went without mishap. As soon as the race started the twelve runners sorted themselves out and there were no mistakes in the jumping of this highly experienced field.

Another conditional jockey was leading the pack. Without the experience of the fully fledged jockeys, he was going at a pace that was clearly unsustainable. Jay and Jed watched intently as Paul kept Hopeful in the middle of the pack, but slightly to the outside to make sure that he did not get boxed in. Jumping the last down the back straight he had moved smoothly up to third, and remained there round the bend before facing the final two hurdles. At this moment Paul slapped him down the shoulder and was rewarded with an immediate response. He cleared the second last hurdle and-strode into the lead. He was soon two or three lengths clear of his pursuers. However as he went into the final flight, to Paul's amazement and Jay and Jed's horror, he took off a full stride too soon. He hit the top of the hurdle, staggered, and his nose nearly grazed the ground on the landing side. The young jockey sat as still as he could, thus allowing the horse to regain his balance and momentum.

However, by this time the second and third horses had closed right down on him. There was now real concern that his extra weight might tell on the run in, but once again the young jockey showed why he was gaining such a name for himself. One smack behind the saddle and he had drawn half a length clear. Then just using hands and heels, and occasionally waving his stick without actually hitting the horse, Paul maintained his lead and passed the winning post with half a length to spare to the delight of Jay, Jed, Danny and the owner.

They met Paul as he came into the winners' enclosure and the young man was beaming from ear to ear.

'You did absolutely brilliantly,' said Jay.

'Couldn't have done better myself,' remarked Danny, with a big grin, as he joined in with the enthusiastic back-slapping and horse patting. Paul Campbell rushed up to join in the celebrations. In the winners' enclosure photographers swarmed around the sweat-soaked horse and his excited connections. A beaming lass led the winner back for the mandatory dope test and then gave him a wash down prior to putting him back into his own stable.

Jay and Jed breathed a joint sigh of relief and exchanged big smiles. They then started concentrating on Wot A B. Although the performance by Hopeful Return was encouraging, the County View group were extremely nervous about the National Hunt Flat Race and how Wot A B would perform and behave. Jay had been somewhat unsettled by the remark made to him before the last race and had decided to keep a low profile. He and Jed went to the owners' and trainers' bar and, with cups of black coffee and this time a cigar for each of them, they waited until it was time for the preliminaries of the last race. One or two people came over and spoke nicely to both of them and offered congratulations. Although being polite, Jay was not too effusive. The time came to saddle Wot A B. Jay and Jed joined Danny in the parade ring in front of the saddling boxes. They were seriously worried about how she would behave.

To their delight and amazement she seemed to be somewhat bemused by her surroundings. Although she was showing some signs of nervousness, it was not the sort of uncontrollable behaviour that had sometimes been evident at home.

This time Freddie was on her and she showed no resentment when he was legged up. Her race was rather shorter so, leaving the paddock, they cantered past the grandstand before turning and going round to the start at the back straight. She was one of sixteen runners. There were two previous winners, three placed horses, four that had run before but without distinction, and the rest were like Wot A B, having their first time on a racecourse. This was where the advantage of having the Champion Jockey was so great.

Freddie kept her covered up behind some of the more experienced horses, and soon had her settled.

The pace was strong but not suicidal and passing the winning post for the first time the race seemed to be going to plan.

As the runners again went down the back straight, the field gradually got strung out, but Wot A B stayed in touch with the leaders.

There was a gasp from the crowd as, rounding the final bend, the fourth horse slipped and fell. Freddie had to pull Wot A B round the now prostrate horse and, in so doing, lost a good five or six lengths. The previous winners were several lengths ahead of her and both seemed to be going very easily. As soon as they entered the finishing straight Freddie slapped his mare on the neck. Jay and Jed could hardly believe their eyes – they knew that she was quick, but had not expected the surge of pace that the mare found. Within twenty yards she swept past everything. Freddie gave a quick look over his shoulder and, realizing that there was no danger, kept her at her work without doing anything extravagant. She cruised past the winning post, a good three lengths in the lead.

'I think we might have got another Pewter Queen here,' suggested Jed.

'You just could be right,' Jay replied.

They were standing in the winners' enclosure waiting for Freddie to jump off.

'This is something a bit special,' he remarked. 'I think that you could start looking for really good bumpers for her – the one thing I will say is that she wouldn't run on soft ground.' Again photographs were taken and reporters wanted to know Jay's plan for the afternoon's three runners.

'To be perfectly honest, it's too early to be certain. I want to see how they all come out of their races today and then make plans for each of them. The one thing I can say is that the two youngsters will have a good break before they run again, and the ground will influence when and where I run Hopeful Return.'

With that, and a big smile, he and Jed left the enclosure and went to the owners' and trainers' bar where they waited to be joined by Danny, Freddie and Paul Campbell, who insisted on buying champagne.

They had hardly sat down when Jay's mobile telephone rang with an absolutely ecstatic Eva on the other end. She had been watching the races on television and could hardly believe that they had had two winners and a second – particularly as the two younger horses had never run before.

'I think that we will all go out for a little bit of a celebration,' announced Jay to Eva. 'Can you reserve a table for us all at the Shepherds Rest tonight?'

On the way home Jed turned to Jay. 'You remember that remark made to you as you walked into the parade ring?' he asked. Jay nodded. 'Could it be anything to do with the mysterious withdrawals?'

Jay looked worried. 'Your guess is as good as mine, but it is a bit odd,' he mused.

The Shepherds Rest was an old, charming pub not very far from County View, and was almost a club for all the staff.

It was now a tradition to gather there after a winner or a particularly good day's racing. A large number of the stable lads and lasses were there, and the pub's speciality of sausage and mash was being dished out in enormous portions. Talk was about the day's triumph, but also of the expectations for the next few weeks. Almost as much excitement resulted from the vet's report on Pewter Queen. He was confident that she would be back on form within a few days.

As usual with these gatherings, it was brief as everyone had early starts the next day.

Chapter Seven

The next day Giles Sinclair of the Jockey Club telephoned Jay to say that something extremely serious had occurred, and could he visit the Jockey Club on the first day that he did not have runners. He also suggested that Jay should be legally represented. Jay was staggered. He, Jed and Eva put their heads together but could think of no actions taken by them that could lead to any serious accusations against them. As a matter of courtesy he telephoned Howard and Victor and advised them of the latest situation, which he felt might have some connection with Jed's concern.

Meanwhile work went on as usual at County View, and the next two runners produced a second and a fourth. The fourth was another young filly, Soulful Sound, having her first race in a bumper at Sandown Park, so the result was particularly encouraging. There were twenty-one runners, a number of whom had good form, and the race had been run at a fast pace. She had been seriously interfered with as she turned into the home straight but was running on very strongly up the stiff climb to the finish. She would almost certainly have come at worst second but for the unlucky incident. Freddie, her jockey, was very enthusiastic about her future prospects. This helped to take some of the gloom of apprehension out of the trainer's summons to the Jockey Club at their new offices in Shaftesbury Avenue.

Two days later, dressed in a smart grey suit, white shirt and a yellow polka-dot tie, he presented himself, along with Alex Johnson-Smith, one of the top solicitors with a wealth of experience in racing matters, particularly disciplinary affairs. They were ushered into a meeting room, and Jay was greeted by Giles Sinclair and Sir Christopher Pollock, one of the senior members of the Jockey Club.

'Please sit down,' invited Sir Christopher. 'Let me make it clear that at this stage this is an entirely informal meeting, but the situation is so serious that we thought you ought to have legal representation. I am now going to let Giles outline the situation.' Giles looked at both of them.

'Over the last couple of months we have heard one or two rumours that horses running in races where you have entered a good runner, have suddenly been withdrawn. You indeed brought this to our attention yourself. We then heard that at least two trainers had been offered substantial bribes not to run their horses.

'They completely denied this and we could find no proof. It became even more surprising when there was no record of any unusually substantial betting on your horses, or indeed any other aspect of these races.

'We were continuing our enquiries quietly until we received a telephone call from Harry Solomons (the Champion Trainer) to say that he had been approached by telephone and offered a substantial bribe not to run three of his horses against you at the next Newbury and Cheltenham meetings. As you know, the prize money at these meetings is very substantial indeed.'

Jay was absolutely dumbstruck.

Giles continued, 'We have been through his telephone records and nothing corresponds with any of you or your staff's telephone numbers.

'We have no reason to believe that this offer was at your behest, but clearly if this story gets into the press it is going to be very damaging to you, and indeed racing generally. We wondered if you had any comments.'

Jay paused and thought for a moment.

'All I can say is that Jed, my assistant trainer, was the first to notice that horses were being withdrawn against us, which is why I contacted you. None of my subsequent winners were heavily backed. None of the owners of the winners concerned are big gamblers, and I am sure you know enough about them to appreciate that they are men of considerable integrity, with impeccable histories in racing.'

There was an understanding nod of agreement from the other side of the table.

'I do not think that there is anything to be done at the moment. I thought this meeting would be useful to ensure that we have joint statements prepared should the story leak,' proposed Sir Christopher. 'I am suggesting that your solicitor sits down with ours, and with our public relations director, in one of their offices and they get something put together which we are all agreed upon. I am suggesting one of the lawyers' offices to try and keep this as low key as possible.'

The meeting was soon wrapped up and a very

subdued and thoughtful Jay was on his way back to County View.

On his return he took Jed and Eva into his confidence, then rang Howard and Victor. Both of them were amazed at this bombshell and Victor was clearly incensed. It was agreed that Jay would keep them informed of any other developments and also ensure that they both had copies of the agreed statement when it was completed. It was at this stage that Jed suddenly frowned.

'What about that abusive remark at Stratford-upon-Avon as we walked into the parade ring?'

'Damn,' said Jay. 'I'd completely forgotten about that.' He rang Giles at the Jockey Club and told him about the incident. There was a pause at the other end.

'Oh dear,' came the reply. 'That may mean that this is going to be more difficult to keep under wraps than we had hoped. Anyway, let's keep our fingers crossed and we'll meet again as soon as the draft has been prepared.'

That evening a carefully worded joint statement from the Jockey Club and Jay's lawyers was faxed through to him. It was essentially simple but made it quite clear that Jay refuted any such allegations. The Jockey Club said they had no proof that there was any substance to these stories to link them to Jay.

In some ways it was rather too bland but the Jockey Club had to ensure that the statement was not so emphatic that if future events proved there was any truth in the accusations they would look naïve or complacent.

No sooner had Jay finished reading this alongside Eva and Jed than the telephone rang. It was Benny from London. 'I would like to come down and see you in the morning, Jay, if that's all right – I think I am beginning to get some news.'

'Come,' said Jay. 'I'll see you late morning when the work has finished.'

Chapter Eight

The following morning Jay grabbed the *Racing Post* with trepidation, but there was nothing in it referring to him or these incidents. He, Jed and Danny supervised the morning's work, and at ten o'clock Benny's blue BMW drove into the yard. Jay left the other two to carry on and went into his kitchen where he remembered to offer Benny strong tea rather than coffee, after which they both sat down.

'So,' asked Jay, 'what's the news?'

'Well, there's nothing hard, but there are stories going around. Some of the bookmakers and a number of the serious punters are hearing that somebody is bribing a small number of trainers, and in some cases threatening them to ensure that horses do not run against you. But now there is a story that someone, and the whisper is that it's you, has tried to persuade one of the very top trainers not to run his horses against yours in some big up and coming races. The thing that the bookies don't understand is why, if all this effort is being made, nobody appears to be backing your horses in these races.'

'I know,' Jay nodded agreement. 'It's puzzling us and the Jockey Club. Now the police are starting to investigate this aspect, just in case it has anything to do with the three murders.' The phone rang. Eva answered it. 'Just a moment,' she said, putting her hand over the mouthpiece and whispering to Jay, 'Harry Solomons wants to speak to you.'

Harry Solomons was the leading trainer who had rung the Jockey Club. Jay paused for a moment as he was not sure that he should take the call. On reflection he thought that as long as he was cautious then why not?

'Good morning, Harry,' he said.

'Good morning, Jay. Look, I had to report what happened to the Jockey Club, but I want to tell you that I find it difficult to believe that you would be involved in any such activity, and I cannot see why you would want to.'

'Well, the fact remains that it has happened and it could be very damaging,' replied Jay.

'I realize that,' Harry agreed. 'I just want you to know that you and I have always got on well enough and this was not done out of spite. I just felt that I had to protect my own position.'

'I realize that, and I appreciate your call,' was Jay's reply.

They talked for another minute or two about a number of totally unrelated issues in racing and promised each other that they would have a drink the next time they met at a racecourse.

Jay looked at Benny and said, 'What can we do next?'

'Well, I guess that we could put the frighteners on one of the trainers, but that is a dangerous strategy and could result in us alienating the Jockey Club if it got out. What I would really like to do,' continued Benny, 'would be to follow two or three of them to see if they appear to have any unusual connections, or surprising meetings. We are already trying to make friends with some stable staff at the yards in question.'

This was readily agreed to and after finishing another cup of tea Benny returned to his car and returned to the East End.

Jay phoned Giles and relayed his conversation with Harry Solomons.

'Did he give you any useful information about the telephone call?' Jay asked.

'Not much, except it sounded like fairly good English with an Australian accent, but he couldn't be sure. The man was talking really big money by the way, enough to make most people listen carefully. Fortunately Harry is not like that and he doesn't need the cash anyway. Have a good day!' concluded Giles in a mock American accent and ended their conversation.

Early the next morning a maroon 4 × 4 pulled up in front of Jay's house and the familiar figure of Chris Langridge the vet got out. Chris, at the age of thirty-six, had already established himself as one of the leading equine vets in the country, and looked after more than one racing yard, plus some high-class eventing and show-jumping establishments. A little over six feet tall and with crinkly blond hair, Chris had the athletic, solid figure of a man who had played at stand-off for his county. A keen skier and scuba-diver too, he had the look of a man who spent a lot of his time out of doors. He was always tanned, and that accentuated his deep blue eyes. Walking into the kitchen, he grinned at Eva and pleaded for a cup of coffee. 'I've been up half the night with a mare with colic.' Turning to Jay and Jed, he continued, 'I have come to do those flu injections and to have a final look at Pewter Queen's foot – how is she?'

'She seems fine,' replied Jay. 'She's been led out

every day with a protective boot over the hoof, and has swum every day as well, so she shouldn't have gone back too much.'

'Great,' said the vet.

The three of them were soon on their way out to the yard where the first lot was already leaving for the gallops. The horses to be injected against equine flu (an annual racing requirement) were dealt with quickly. This meant that they could only be in light work for the next few days. Strenuous work that resulted in sweating would not be good for their general well being. Walking along to the beautiful grey mare's box they talked about everything except the rumours which were flying around. Eventually Jay decided to clear the air.

'You know all this talk about me bribing trainers not to run their horses is a lot of rubbish,' he said.

'Of course I do,' replied the vet. 'You can be sure that anybody who suggests differently will get a pretty bleak response from me.'

With that they entered Pewter Queen's box. She was happily standing four square. A quick examination proved negative – no warmth in hoof or leg, no reaction to pressure exerted with the tongs. 'Shoe on and off she goes,' said Chris. 'Make sure you let me know when she is going to run as I always love watching this mare.' Jay suddenly had a thought and asked, 'Can you spare me a minute?'

'Of course,' Chris replied as they walked into Jay's office. Quickly outlining what was going on, Jay asked Chris a question. 'Could you find out who the vets are who look after these trainers' horses, and how trustworthy they are? Some of those that were withdrawn had a vet's certificate and it is important to know if they are genuine. Big money has been offered in at least one case and I suppose even some vets could have a price.'

Chris promised to help but said it would take a day or two. Then he was on his way and Jed and Jay returned to the kitchen for another cup of coffee. After that Jay went back to his office and Jed returned to the yard to supervise the next lot and to hear from Danny what had happened during the first.

Jay was deeply into entries when Eva came in with the post. Giving him a quick kiss on his forehead, she turned as she walked out of the door and said, 'That young man is going to break somebody's heart, if he hasn't broken a lot already.'

Jay look puzzled.

'I mean Chris, you idiot,' she said. 'He's absolutely gorgeous. If I wasn't married to the most attractive man in Britain, I would fancy him myself,' she added with a wicked little smile as she closed the door on her way out.

Chapter Nine

The dramatic events of the previous few days started to fade a little as the team got back to concentrating on racing and, in particular, on the Chepstow meeting at the weekend. There was also a need to start planning for the big Christmas and New Year meetings.

My Final Fling was owned by a lovely Irish lady called Kate Harty, and had been placed in a very good handicap at Cheltenham the previous year. The Conker was in many ways the old star of the stables and his exploits included coming second in the Welsh Grand National, winning the Long Distance Amateur Race at the Cheltenham Festival and being a major player in the huge gamble for Howard at Towcester, that had also settled an old score. Although he often needed the first race to get fighting fit Jay had managed to get two racecourse gallops into him and the one thing they all knew was that you never had to worry about The Conker's jumping.

Both horses were in action at Chepstow. On the day of the race Jay, Eva and Jed set off early. They were joined by Howard, his wife Bubbles, and Victor shortly after arriving at the course. As always, Howard was in a great state of excitement and eager anticipation.

Mrs Harty had telephoned to say that she had not been very well and would not be able to get there, but assured them that she would be watching every yard on television.

The handicap hurdle was the first of the two races and young Paul Jenkins, who had ridden the horse at Cheltenham (and in all honesty had made a mistake which may have cost him the race), was being allowed to ride the horse again as Mrs Harty had taken a great shine to him, and he still took a few pounds off the horse's back.

The race was surprisingly uneventful. Nine experienced runners jumping cleverly and, on the whole, economically, streamed past the winning post for the first time in single file but closely bunched. Rounding the sharp bend at Chepstow there is a steep climb to the entrance of the back straight, and here three of the horses started to feel the gruelling pace. Soon it was down to six in contention. Paul kept his horse in fifth position and, as another of the horses started to come under pressure, found himself lying fourth without making any extra effort. They were all experienced jockeys in front of him and they knew that the long final bend at Chepstow was followed by a very testing climb to the winning post. Paul remembered only too well that at Cheltenham he had found his horse moving so well that he had taken the lead too soon, only to be caught on the line. This time he was not going to make the same mistake.

Staying in third place he jumped the last two hurdles before he made a move at all. At this stage he crept closer to the horses in front of him but did not make the mistake of trying to move past them too quickly. He sat just a length off them after the last flight. My Final Fling had a very quick rate of acceleration, and Paul waited until the last seventy-five yards before he pressed the accelerator. The response was immediate and he quickly gained a length. This he held on to in spite of the others desperately trying to get back to him, but it was too late.

Jay turned to Jed. 'That's the most mature ride that young man has given us yet.'

'I couldn't agree more,' replied Jed.

They met Paul on the way into the winners' enclosure and both stood with him as the photographers took the mandatory photo for the connections, all smiles beside the steaming horse.

Jay's phone rang and at the other end was a bubbly Mrs Harty. 'If only my husband had lived to see his horse do so well,' she mused. 'Still, I get so much pleasure from him, I'll do my level best to get over next time.'

'Do that,' said Jay. 'We love having really enthusiastic owners with us.'

'Well, I am sure that you need to start thinking about The Conker. Good luck with him and thanks again, Jay,' and she rang off.

He joined Harold, Victor and Bubbles in the restaurant. You would have thought they owned the horse they were so enthusiastic. A few moments later Jay's mobile rang and there was Mrs Harty again. 'Please tell Paul how well he rode,' she said, 'and buy him a bottle of champagne on me. Also give him a £100 bonus. Perhaps you would be kind enough to add it to my monthly account.'

They chatted for a few more moments then Jay politely explained that he would soon have to be saddling The Conker, but promised to telephone her the next day to reassure her that her horse was fine.

It was soon time to collect The Conker's saddle from Freddie. There was no need to talk tactics as the jockey knew the horse almost as well as Jay did, having won on him in the epic race at Towcester.

The Conker was an out and out stayer, and his greatest strength lay in his amazing jumping ability. Three and a half miles around Chepstow takes some getting and, although The Conker was capable of going at least another half mile, it had already been agreed that once the early part of the race was over he would lie in second or third place, then go for the line as soon as he entered the home straight.

The race ran exactly to plan. There were no fallers, no incidents of interference and The Conker was a length and a half behind the first two horses turning for home. Freddie gave him a slap on the shoulder as they approached the first of the fences, which he cleared like the proverbial stag without breaking his stride. He did the same over the next, an open ditch, and by now had drawn three lengths clear. Approaching the second last, his leap was again extravagant but completely safe. At this stage, barring a fall at the last, The Conker had the race at his mercy. Freddie steadied him slightly going into the last, which he jumped rather more economically than the others, but just as safely. A quick glance over his shoulder confirmed that there was no challenge, so he let The Conker slow down a little and pass the winning post a good ten lengths clear of his nearest rival.

As always Howard was ecstatic, Bubbles was excited and Victor, although slightly more reserved, was still extremely enthusiastic.

The afternoon was not yet over. Jay had permission to gallop Splendid Warrior, his double Gold Cup Winner, after racing. He would have See You Sometime, a very good three mile handicapper, to accompany him. As soon as the last race was over, the two horses made their way out onto the track. Paul rode See You Sometime and Freddie, Splendid Warrior. Starting well to the left of the grandstand, they set off at a brisk pace and rounded the bend into the back straight. Gradually increasing the pace they were soon round the second bend and facing the uphill finish. The two jockeys kept the two horses neck and neck as they flew up the rising ground and eased up as they took the bend after the winning post. When they were pulled up, they turned, trotted and then walked off the course. Jay met them as they came back. 'One race and this fellow will be ready for Kempton on Boxing Day,' said Freddie.

'My lad has never been better,' added Paul.

Jay thanked them both, gave each of the horses a pat and then rejoined Howard, Bubbles and Victor.

On their way back to County View in triumph and high spirits, Howard insisting on taking them all out to dinner. Jed was equally adamant that first of all they should return to County View. Jay agreed with him. They decided therefore to have a celebratory drink in Jay's house, but when they entered they were amazed at the scene that confronted them. The dining room was candlelit, and Cathy, looking very neat in a black dress and white apron, greeted them with a shy but composed smile.

'I thought we would eat at home for a change,' she said, 'so I have cooked something a little bit special.'

The little bit special turned out to be an avocado mousse to die for, followed by fillets of sole, beef

Wellington and a wonderful cheese board. Fortunately Victor and Howard had taken the precaution of booking two rooms at the Shepherds Rest, so for once they all stayed up a little later than usual. Jay arranged for one of the security guards to drive them back to the pub, and promised that they would be picked up at eight thirty the next morning, as Howard's Rolls Royce would be returning to the safety of County View rather than spend a night in a pub car park. Bubbles said she would settle for an extra hour in bed.

When they had gone Jed, Jay and Eva sat down and the men each enjoyed a cigar and a nightcap of brandy. They went to bed with a feeling that the world was not such a gloomy place as it had seemed to be earlier in the week.

The next morning Jay said goodbye to Howard and Victor and he was sitting in his office after morning work when the telephone rang.

'I think that I've got something interesting, Guv,' came Benny's voice. 'We've been following up the stable staff, and have established good relations with three from different yards. Each one is cautious so we are not pushing it. Once a real trust has been established, a few drinks will probably do the rest. However, we have found one interesting thing. In one yard a lad has gone missing. His name is Tim Finch but he is known as "Chirpy". He disappeared overnight and although his girlfriend is one of the other grooms, neither she nor anyone else has heard from him. What's even more interesting is that the trainer has not mentioned his disappearance to anyone nor has he reported him missing to the police.

'We managed to get his parents' address and, without revealing that he's disappeared, have gathered that they have not heard from him either. What is more this is the one trainer who has had a number of brushes with both the security side of the Jockey Club and the police. Nothing very dramatic, and nothing has been pinned on him, but he is considered to be unreliable.'

'Which trainer?' snapped Jay.

'Tom Flintlock. Do you know him?'

'No, but I'll talk to Sinclair and let him know what you have found out, which means I'll have to let him know a little of what we're doing.'

Jay continued, 'In the meantime it is interesting to note that of the nine trainers involved, our vet has already determined that one of the horses withdrawn was definitely lame and one other had a very dirty nose the day before it was due to run. Both the vets in these cases are known to Chris, and he guarantees that they are completely honest. This reduces our target yards to seven, which should help you to concentrate on the real potential threats.'

'Which are the two clean yards?' asked Benny and Jay filled him in.

'If you're talking to Giles Sinclair,' continued Benny, 'find out what you can about Tom Flintlock.'

'Good idea. I'll call you as soon as I have any information.'

He tried to ring Giles Sinclair but he was unavailable. However, his secretary promised that Mr Sinclair would be in touch as soon as possible.

Half an hour later Giles was on the phone and Jay passed on all the information he had.

'How did you get this?' asked Giles.

'Could I just say that I have my own contacts, and if you recall, they proved to be very useful a year or so ago with the drug dealer and when I was under threat at Cheltenham.'

'Enough said. I will find out what I can and come back to you.'

'Likewise, I will keep you informed of any developments at this end,' agreed Jay.

'Thank you, Jay. I'll talk to you soon.' The conversation ended.

Jay had barely put the phone down when it rang. It was Benny again.

'I don't know if this is relevant, or if it is a total red herring, but do you know somebody called Harry Clough?'

'Yes.'

'Well, I've heard a whisper that this guy seems to be extremely rich, is not particularly well disposed towards you, and has been saying that he bets the trainer in the rumours is you.'

'Well, that's no surprise,' said Jay. 'He and I fell out in spades a long time ago, and he didn't like it when Jed and I refused to train his horses after we had merged. As you say, he is extremely rich and, as you may have found out, is in the diamond business, but he is a spiteful man, and not one with whom we would wish to be associated at County View.'

'That's all I have at the moment,' ended Benny, 'but you never know, it might be useful, and if you are suing for a large sum of money I hope that I will get a finder's fee,' joked the East Ender.

'Thanks a bundle,' laughed Jay. 'Cheers!' and he put the phone down.

Later that day Benny was on the phone again.

'Another little piece of the jigsaw. My friend who is at Flintlock's yard has managed to win the confidence of Rita, the missing lad's girlfriend. He

56

genuinely believes that she doesn't know where he is. Evidently he did talk to her just before he left. He seemed really frightened of something, but all he would say was "The Guv'nor's up to no good and I think he knows I know." Then he said, "I'm out of here and I'm going to disappear for a while. When I think the coast is clear, I'll contact you." As much as she was pressed, she wouldn't add anything else, and we really do believe that she doesn't know where he is. Although he may have phoned her on her mobile, that wouldn't tell her where he is.'

'You're doing a great job, Benny,' said Jay. 'I'll let Giles Sinclair know this extra bit and will be discreet,' he promised. He rang Giles straight away, who after digesting the information, made a suggestion. 'I think it's time we shared all this with Harvey Jackson, and see if his police colleagues have come up with anything that might help us.'

'Let's do it,' agreed Jay. 'Will you make the arrangements?'

'Of course. I'll be in touch.'

Chapter Ten

On the next two days there were no runners, and the normal routine returned to the yard. The following day Jay had a runner at Worcester. Jumptoit was a five year old that had run twice and been second on both occasions – both races over hurdles. This was his first run in a Novice Chase. He had shown himself to be a good jumper, and Paul had done much of the schooling, so Jay had decided to let the young man have the ride.

Arriving at the small, but always well kept, course Jay checked that the declaration had been made correctly then went over to ensure that the horse had travelled well. He seemed completely peaceful yet interested in his surroundings.

A few minutes before the horses left the paddock the commentator told the crowd of the latest odds. Jumptoit was 16–1. On the way to the start his odds shortened, and the loudspeaker announced that Jumptoit was 'the springer' in the market and was now only 8–1.

'That's not surprising,' commented Jay. 'After all, his two hurdle races were pretty impressive in good company, and its well known our horses are all well schooled.'

The start for this race was at the beginning of the finishing straight. The first three fences were jumped uneventfully although with fifteen runners it was a big field for a Novice Chase. Going down the back straight Paul had his horse well to the outside so it could see the fences. As they started to pass the stable block a horse on the inside suddenly swerved violently across the rest, apparently trying to make his way back to the stable. He hit Jumptoit who, in trying to avoid further contact, crashed his way through the wing and fell to the ground. Paul was flung about ten yards from the horse, but was on his feet by the time the ambulance team arrived.

The horse struggled to his feet, and there was a gasp of dismay from those members of the crowd with binoculars who could see what had happened. The horse's front left leg was dangling, and it was clear that there was no hope for him. Within seconds a green screen was erected around the horse, nearly always a sign that the end had come. The vet was there quickly and the poor creature was put out of his misery. Jay and Eva were devastated. They had had accidents before, but this was their first fatality – apart from a horse that had been deliberately killed in his stable the year before.

Jay found the vet to sort out the necessary procedures in relation to eventually making an insurance claim. He then went and consoled the stable lass before he and Eva drove home in silence.

Eventually the empty horsebox arrived, and there is almost nothing more depressing in a yard than that moment. The girl was still in tears and Jed got Cathy to try and console her. After years of living with Jed and his racing yard in Sussex, she was all too familiar with this type of tragedy. After Jed, Cathy, Jay and Eva had a somewhat muted dinner, Jed suddenly said, 'Come on, we all knew that this was going to happen some time, let's go down to the Shepherds Rest and have a drink and start talking about what we do next.' This seemed a sensible plan. When they arrived in the bar a number of people had heard about the tragic incident and offered genuine condolences. County View was now a central part of the local community, who were proud to have such a high profile and successful sporting team in their midst. Fortunately the horse was one owned by the syndicate so Jay did not have the unenviable task of phoning an outside owner. Nevertheless, Victor and Howard were equally saddened by the news.

'Well,' mused Jay later when they had got home, 'things can only get better after this.'

How wrong he was. This was proved the very next day.

At six thirty the following morning he and Eva were having a cup of coffee before going out to the yard, when the telephone rang. It was Benny.

'Have you seen the *Racing Post*, Guv'nor?' he asked.

'Not yet,' said Jay, 'it doesn't get here for another hour.'

'You won't like it.'

'Oh God, what is it?'

'I'll read you the headlines, it's a big story, it starts on the front page and reads TOP TRAINER UNDER INVESTIGATION FOR TRYING TO FIX RACES.

'The *Racing Post* has heard that one of the top National Hunt trainers is being investigated for influencing other trainers to withdraw horses from races in which they have horses entered which would pose a major threat to his runner.

'At the moment the Jockey Club has no comment to make on this, and neither has any trainer approached by the *Racing Post*.

60

'However, rumours are rife, and a reliable source has said that both the Jockey Club security department and the police are investigating this seriously and as a matter of urgency.

'It is understood that the trainer concerned is one who is in contention to finish the season very high up amongst the prize money winners. No further details are available at the moment although there is much speculation. Giles Sinclair, Head of Jockey Club security, commented, "From time to time there are always rumours about improper behaviour or activities in horse racing. More often than not these turn out to be completely fallacious, but of course we will take any such possible situation seriously, and will investigate it thoroughly as soon as we have more information that will allow us to pursue our investigations if we feel that would be appropriate."'

Benny continued, 'Underneath this, Jay, you will see a list of the top ten National Hunt trainers, and a list of how much money they have earned this season, compared to how much money they had won at a similar stage last season. I will dig around and come back to you as soon as I have anything.'

Jay sat down and wondered what to do. Almost before he had finished his cup of coffee the telephone rang again, and this time it was Giles Sinclair. 'I think we ought to have another meeting, Jay. Clearly it's got to be very secure. Have you any suggestions?'

'If you could get to my old offices just off Mayfair, Hal Bancroft would let us have a room. There is nothing suspicious in me going to see him, as not only did I sell him my company, but he and two of his friends are shareholders in County View.'

'Oh, that sounds excellent,' said Giles. 'By the way,' he added, 'I tried to get an idea of who gave the *Post* the story. The editor tried to convince me that he did not know – but the media always protect their sources. However, I've always found that he is very co-operative if he feels the interests of racing are under attack. He also suggested it was highly unlikely that any of the top five trainers would risk all for such a venture.'

'Oh, I agree, but I wonder if Jackson would chat with him first in case this is all tied in to the murders.'

'I'll try, but don't hold your breath,' said the Jockey Club man. Jay rang Hal and explained the background. He was greatly concerned for Jay and readily agreed that he could have one of the conference rooms.

As had been arranged, Jay arrived at Hal's office at 7.20 next morning and Giles arrived ten minutes later. The meeting room had been set out with pads, a thermos of coffee, milk, orange juice and a plate of croissants. Having greeted each other, and had the orange juice and coffee, they got down to work.

'I fear that this may get out of hand, Jay,' began Giles. 'I am now beginning to feel that it is some deliberate attempt to discredit you. It has all the signs of being backed by an organization, rather than just individual petty jealousy or rumour mongering.'

'I understand that,' replied Jay. 'Jed, Howard, Victor and I have been talking about it a lot, but we cannot think who would want to do it. If there was a clear gambling element behind it then that would be understandable, but as far as we know the only two serious enemies we have are an Irish drug dealer who is in jail awaiting trial for murder, and a discredited bookmaker, who is out of the country, and anyway would not have anything like the sort of money needed to set up an operation like this.

'You know of them both!' Giles nodded as Jay continued. 'I am going to have a look into that all the same,' he promised.

They then had a long discussion on making a pre-emptive statement, though Jay's name had never been mentioned. They decided that unless Jay was contacted directly by a member of the media, the best plan was to say nothing. If this did happen, however, Jay was to dodge the reporter until he had had a chance to discuss the matter again with Giles.

As Giles got up to leave he paused. 'Thank God you phoned us in advance to tell us your suspicions about these horses not running, otherwise it would look far from good from your point of view.' Stopping on his way to the door he added, 'Let's go and have a chat at Newbury. We can exchange information and have a word with Harvey Jackson.'

'Agreed. You fix it and let me know when. Late morning or early afternoons are best from my point of view.'

'Done,' said Giles.

After he had left Jay thought for a moment and then phoned Benny.

'How do you fancy a trip on the London Eye?' he asked.

'Ah, I gather there is something you would like to talk about in confidence.'

An hour later they joined the queue but first thing in the morning it did not take them very long to find themselves in one of the capsules on their own.

'I want you to find out what you can about Frankie Johnson – where he is and what he is up to,' said Jay. Frankie Johnson was a crooked bookmaker who they had dealt with before, which had resulted in him leaving the country and eventually losing his money.

'That should be easy,' replied Benny. 'I believe he is still somewhere in France and, as you know, I've got very good contacts there.'

'I also want you to find out what you can about The Friend, and if he's operating anything from inside prison.'

The Friend had been a major Irish drug dealer who had nearly killed Danny, and had almost certainly been responsible for the murder of a bookmaker in Ireland. Jay, with the help of Benny and a small group of his brothers and friends, had been responsible for his arrest and eventual imprisonment. It might be that he still had connections and influences outside the prison. It was a beautiful morning and although they were in earnest conversation they were enjoying the spectacular views across London.

'Have you heard anything else?' asked Jay.

'Well, two totally different rumours – one is that there is a very powerful and rich Englishman somehow involved in this, and we are trying to establish if it really is Harry Clough. The other is that there may be a foreign element. That of course could be Frankie Johnson in France, or someone connected to The Friend in Dublin. Both seem a bit far fetched. Anyway, we are still working on it.'

'I know it's unlikely, but it would be great to have a clue about who tipped off the *Racing Post*,' commented Jay.

'Not easy,' replied Benny, 'but Angel has a drinking pal who works there. He's one of their tipsters so he might be helpful.'

'Let's hope so.'

None the wiser, and not particularly encouraged,

Jay eventually left, drove back to his little London house in Hays Mews, and then down the M4 to County View. The journey and the rest of the day were without incident, and Jed and Jay sat down to plan their runners for the next few days.

There was good prize money to be had at Newbury, so they decided to enter three horses there, plus one to go on the same day to Uttoxeter. The Newbury runners would be Hot Toddy, Paddy's Pal, and Bucks Fizz, and The Happy Banker would go to Uttoxeter. Jed would go to Uttoxeter, and Jay to Newbury.

Pointing to the statistics page in the *Racing Post* Jed mentioned that Jay was £250,000 behind the leader, and nearly £100,000 behind the second in the Trainers' Prize Money Table. A successful Newbury and Uttoxeter could make significant inroads depending on their competitors' results. Still puzzling on what could be behind all this the two men strolled round the yard, visiting each box, to reassure themselves that their charges were well. Then they toured the gallops and the schooling fences to check if there were any major maintenance jobs requiring urgent attention.

Chapter Eleven

A few days later the meeting with Harvey Jackson took place at the police incident room just outside Newbury. Although the number of staff involved had been scaled down as time had passed, all the information gleaned, plus a number of key players involved, were still there when Jay arrived. Giles Sinclair was drinking machine coffee from a plastic cup, and whispered to Jay, 'It's not up to the quality of County View.'

A moment or two later they were joined by Jackson and a young man dressed in civilian clothes.

'This is Peter Murray,' announced the policeman, introducing the young man who shook hands formally with both Jay and Giles. 'Peter is an IT expert, and has spent a lot of time tracing phone calls, bank transactions and betting records, which have been made available to us from all the leading bookmakers and exchanges.'

Jay and Giles filled the other two in on the progress they had made, and there were nods of understanding and agreement from both. Tactfully Jackson did not enquire into their sources, and probably assumed it was the Jockey Club security staff and perhaps a little racecourse gossip.

'We will certainly look into this,' said the policeman. 'I also think we'll put out a search for the missing groom and maybe have a quiet word with this Rita. It may be that she is more forthcoming in front of the law than she is with someone who is clearly digging around privately.'

At this moment Jay decided to reveal the gossip that Benny had given to him regarding Harry Clough.

'As far as I know he's never had any trouble with the law, but Eva says that her father was always surprised that he made as much money as he appeared to from his diamond activities. There's no doubt he did make money, but for the sort of operation he ran, his apparent wealth seemed out of proportion.' Jackson turned to his colleague.

'Pete, I'd like you to give priority to looking into this guy. We have contacts in the City and I'll put out feelers in that direction as well. Have you any idea how much his racing activities would have cost him?'

'No, but they'd certainly be pretty substantial,' replied Jay.

'I can find that out quite easily,' suggested Giles, 'unless he's got some horses running in a syndicate under another name. Even then, unless he is a sleeping partner, we would know.'

'That's pretty unlikely,' commented Jay. 'He has a huge ego, and I can't believe that he would want anything that he had invested in not having his name on it.'

Giles mused for a moment and then said, 'I'll tell you what I will do. I'll contact the overseas Jockey Clubs too, particularly in South Africa and the Far East, and see if there is any record of him owning horses there.'

'That's a hell of an idea!' enthused the policeman.

From then on the conversation was mainly going over old ground, and Jay and Giles rose to leave the office.

Peter Murray looked at his boss and then at Jay.

'I found something which may not be of any significance, but it is specific in the journalist's records. His computer has got a number of horses listed under each trainer with an explanatory note about either their running or their forthcoming engagements. When I got to Mr Jessop's name there was a complete list of all his horses, and this in itself was unique to this list. On top of that a number of horses had symbols against them, such as an asterisk or letters or numbers, but no key to what these meant. However, a few of the horses were underlined in red.' The policeman looked at Jay.

'Can you think why that might be?'

'Not a clue. Can I have a look at that list?'

'Of course,' said the young man. 'I'll get it now.'

He returned with a couple of printed sheets of paper from the dead journalist's computer. Jay scanned the list with a puzzled expression that quickly turned to one of shock.

'Do you know what the underlined ones are?' he asked. The other occupants of the room shook their heads. 'They are our horses that Jed spotted had won when the form horse had been withdrawn at the last moment.'

The long silence that followed was broken by Jackson.

'That would indicate that there is a possible connection between his death and your horses, but does this mean that there's a connection between his murder and the other two?' Blank looks all round.

'I think we'd better interview all the contacts of the

68

jockey and the trainer again,' said the policeman. Jay and Giles nodded, serious expressions on their faces. They shook hands and were on their way. From the car, Jay phoned Eva and filled her in on the whole conversation, including the Harry Clough development.

'I wonder if you would like to phone Fiona?' suggested Jay. 'After all, she trained for him for a long while. Also with all her contacts in South Africa she may like to dig around there. I know she'll be tactful, and with her past connections with Clough and her many friends in South African racing, you never know what she might find.'

Jay rang Benny and filled him in on the meeting with the police.

'I'll tell you what,' suggested Benny. 'I'll get one of my friends in Singapore to see if he can find out anything about this gentleman both there and in Hong Kong. After all, the gambling that takes place there is huge, and if he has been up to anything there's a chance that Sammy Wong will be able to find out what it is.'

When he got back to County View Eva told him that she had phoned her mother who was out, but she had left a message on the answerphone for her to ring back before 7.30 if possible.

'Why before 7.30?' asked Jay.

'Because I am going to take you out for a really good dinner. You have been under so much pressure over the last few weeks I thought it would do you good to get away from County View, and for us to have a quiet evening together. What's more, I'll do the driving so you can drink as much champagne as you like, and we will forget all about skulduggery, County View, and all the races that are coming up.

69

There's another ulterior motive, but that can wait until dinner.' With an enigmatic smile she left the room.

The evening arrived. Eva and Jay had both dressed up for the excursion and Eva drove them to the Lygon Arms in the village of Broadway, one of the most famous hotels and restaurants in the Cotswolds.

After a superb dinner and lots of non-racing chat, with a cigar in one hand and a brandy balloon in the other, Jay looked at his gorgeous wife.

'Well, what's the big subject?'

Never one to beat about the bush Eva looked him straight in the eye and announced, 'I want to have a baby.'

Jay gulped and then smiled. 'What a great idea. I assume you think that we are going to make it long term.'

'I've never had any doubt that you're the man for me.' With that she called for the bill and Jay knew her too well to argue. Arriving back at County View Jay had a quick look around the yard and was soon upstairs joining Eva in bed.

'Why don't we start now?' he suggested with a smile.

'It's not going to be quite that quick,' said Eva, 'but I think I will stop taking the pill. However, there's no reason why we shouldn't start practising,' she giggled.

Within minutes they were making the tender and passionate love that had always been a delight to both of them.

Chapter Twelve

Jay and Jed were deep in conversation. They had already agreed some days earlier that it was time to give Splendid Warrior a run which, after his Chepstow racecourse gallop, would put him spot on for the King George race at Kempton on Boxing Day.

They were trying to work out which would be the most suitable track. Kempton is right-handed and almost flat and the fences, although not huge, are still big enough to need good jumping. Splendid Warrior was a magnificent athlete, and his jumping was not a cause of concern. However, they were cautious about running him over a track with small fences in case he fell into the trap of being a bit too casual when he got to Kempton. After a lot of deliberation they settled for Huntingdon. This is also a right hand track, is fairly flat and has fences that demand respect. As a back up they pencilled in Sandown in case the going at Huntingdon was not suitable. However, Sandown is a very testing track and the two men felt that it would be more physically demanding, and the calibre of horses that Splendid Warrior would be up against would probably be higher than at Huntingdon. They wanted a good test but not one that would be really gruelling.

The days before the race passed peacefully and,

with the going good at Huntingdon, Splendid Warrior was routed in that direction.

To Jay's dismay when the entries came out the field would not be very testing for Splendid Warrior, but at least on paper he would have fourteen opponents. When the declarations were confirmed, however, the picture had changed dramatically. It was clear that their champion had scared off a number of potential opponents and there were only four left plus Splendid Warrior himself. Of these, three would undoubtedly be disputing minor place money, and only The Friendly Jackal would be likely to give Splendid Warrior a run for his money. He had already won three two and a half to three mile races this season, and was a confirmed front runner which gave Jay a degree of comfort. So, all being well, Splendid Warrior would have a really worthwhile workout.

Talking about the substantial reduction in the field they felt it impossible that this could be connected with previous events. Too many horses were involved, and there was no serious threat to Splendid Warrior, even in the field of fifteen runners.

The day came, and they all set off for Huntingdon in good time. There they were to meet Barry Davies, Splendid Warrior's owner who was an enthusiastic supporter of Jay. With him was Jack Symes, Splendid Warrior's trainer before he retired. Jack had been very influential in the horse moving to Jay's yard, and was very friendly with Jay.

When they got to the racecourse Jay checked on the horse and the declaration, then went off to the owners' and trainers' bar, which was already heaving. Finding the two connections, Jay suggested that they went and had a quick lunch in the restaurant in comfort rather than a snack in the bar. When they were seated and talking generalities Jack Symes suddenly asked, 'What's all this about you paying trainers not to run horses against you? I've never heard such nonsense in my life.'

Jay explained the situation in some detail, and his two friends shook their heads in disbelief.

'What I can't understand,' exclaimed the older man, 'is why there's no betting pattern if somebody really is fixing races.'

'That's puzzling all of us and we are just hoping that it will die down.'

The time came for the race and Splendid Warrior, who more than lived up to his name, was striding around the parade ring in the manner of a true champion.

The crowd at Huntingdon was huge, mainly attracted by his presence, and the racing press were there in force.

Freddie was talking to Benny, Jack and Jay before jumping onto Britain's most highly regarded steeplechaser. The conversation had been friendly but cursory. All four of them knew exactly how Splendid Warrior ran so there was no need for last minute instructions.

The first circuit of the track was without incident and, as expected, The Friendly Jackal made the going at a good pace. Splendid Warrior dropped in three or four lengths behind him, with one of the outsiders alongside, and the other two bringing up the rear.

Passing the stands with a circuit to go, the positions were unchanged. As the field rounded the bend and entered the back straight the first fence brought a casualty. The outsider alongside Splendid Warrior was now struggling and, as a result, met the fence completely wrong. He struggled to clamber over but landed so steeply that his jockey had no chance but shot straight over his head. Fortunately the horse ran sideways as they approached the next fence and ran round it, not interfering with Splendid Warrior or the other two horses that were behind him and desperately trying to remain in contact.

By the time that they had left the back straight for the final time, it had turned into two separate races. The outsiders were fighting for third place, but were now some twenty lengths behind Splendid Warrior, who had closed to a length behind The Friendly Jackal. As they entered the home straight, Freddie brought Splendid Warrior upside the leader and they took the second last side by side. At this stage Freddie gave the horse a slap and he showed the amazing acceleration he was famed for. A roar of approval rose from the crowd as he flew towards the last fence. He was now gaining the affection of the racing public in much the same way as Arkle and Desert Orchid had in their racing days.

Three strides before the fence he appeared to slip. Freddie steadied him, but some of the momentum had gone. Freddie sat quietly and let the horse take the fence in his own time. Unfortunately, in so doing, he took off a stride too soon, clearing the fence with his front legs, but dragging his back legs through the birch. He stumbled on landing, and a murmur of anxiety rose from the huge crowd of watching fans. All was well, however, and the horse sweetly passed the winning post five lengths clear.

Jay went down to meet the horse, whilst the other two waited by the winners' enclosure. Walking alongside the famous horse he asked Freddie how the race had gone.

'The horse is in fantastic form,' replied Freddie, 'but he really hit that last fence and I thought he was going to go down.'

'He is sound, isn't he?' asked Jay.

'Oh, he seems fine,' Freddie replied.

At that moment Jay looked down and was horrified to see blood pouring down one of the horse's back legs. He alerted Freddie who jumped off and led the horse into the winners' enclosure.

Blood was still welling from the horse's leg, but the vet who is always on hand in case a placed horse needs his help, quickly bandaged the wound and told Jay, 'I'll do it properly when he's been dope tested – but from a quick look, I'm sure he's going to need a couple of stitches. Don't worry – it's not as bad as the blood makes it look.'

There was obviously some anxiety, and Jay was asked a lot of concerned questions by members of the media. He repeated what the vet had said, that the horse would probably need stitches, but that the gash should heal quickly and so it should not interfere with his preparations for the King George. Jay promised to keep them informed. He had complete faith in this vet so went off to join Jed, Barry and Jack in the owners' and trainers' bar and they shared a bottle of champagne. Jay had only one glass as he was driving. The conversation revolved round Splendid Warrior's well being and their hopes for the King George. Shortly after this pleasant interlude Jed and Jay were on their way back to County View. Once there they waited anxiously for the horsebox to arrive. The horse had travelled well and seemed unaffected by his mishap. With a joint sigh of relief they went indoors to join their wives, share a simple supper and settle for an early right.

The next morning a shade before seven o'clock a stunning-looking young woman arrived at the yard. At five foot nine, slender but with all the curves in the right places, she was a welcome addition to the usual staff. She strolled athletically up to Jay and shook his hand.

'Good morning. I'm Amanda Lambert,' she announced.

'Where did you learn to ride?' Jay asked.

'Well, my father worked in Argentina for a long time. In fact that's where he met my mother who is Argentinian.' Jay thought that would account for her dark complexion and raven hair.

'Almost as soon as I could walk I was on the back of a pony. We returned to England when I was fourteen and I have been involved with horses ever since. I have had some success point-to-pointing – something that I enjoy enormously – hence my telephone call to you.'

'Sounds good,' said Jay, 'but let's see what you're made of.' He turned to Danny who had been listening to the conversation. 'Let's give Amanda Pegasus.' Pegasus was an eight year old who had come from Jed's previous yard. He was as safe as houses but could take a bit of a pull, so would test her ability without taking any risks.

However, Jay felt that this was a young lady who was confident, but not cocky, and he would be surprised if she did not handle the horse well.

Usually Jay rode out but this time he decided to watch from the sidelines to get a better view of the stunning young lady's ability. All went well and Jay was suitably impressed. Everyone, including Amanda, then went back to Jay's kitchen where Cathy served tea and coffee.

'Well, what did you think?' asked Amanda, looking him frankly in the face.

'You did well. I'd like to see you jump. Have you got time to do that this morning?'

'Certainly, I'd love to,' replied Amanda. Twenty minutes later she was sitting on Fast Cruiser, one of Jay's less successful handicap chasers, but a horse who had still managed to win a race around Worcester and another around Hereford. Danny was riding Paddy's Pal, and they were soon approaching the first of the four medium size fences. Everything went so smoothly that Jay told them to go on and jump the fences that were almost full size. Once again it went without a hitch and the girl came back beaming with pleasure.

Soon they were back in the yard and she handed her horse over to one of the grooms.

'Could I have a quiet word with you, Jay?' she asked.

'Of course,' he replied and led her into his office.

'My father thought that, if you felt I was competent enough, he would like to buy me a decent horse to ride in hunter chases. He would obviously like you to train it, as you are so conveniently placed near the agricultural college.'

Jay thought for a moment and then said, 'I don't see why not. Can I be rude and ask how much your father is willing to spend?' Amanda looked rather uncomfortable before replying.

'Daddy is very rich, and I don't think money will be a problem. What he wants is for me to have a really decent horse that I can enjoy, and at the same time is as safe as any steeplechaser will ever be.' Jay nodded his understanding, and taking out his pad he wrote down Mr Lambert's telephone number, and promised Amanda that he would contact him that evening. At that moment Jed came in looking very worried.

'Warrior has got some swelling in the other back leg,' he announced.

'Hell,' said Jay. 'I'll talk to you this evening, Amanda, after I've spoken to your father.' With that he was on his way across to Warrior's box at a fast trot. As he entered the box Jay was relieved to find Warrior happily munching his hay. He examined the other leg. The previous day they had noticed a very small cut, but had just cleaned it out and treated it with an antiseptic spray plus a small bandage to prevent any infection getting in. Jed had taken the bandage off that morning and it was a little later that he saw the swelling and inflammation.

Jay was on his way back to the office to phone the vet when he saw Amanda again.

'Do you mind me looking around, and what news of Splendid Warrior?' she asked.

'Stay as long as you like,' replied Jay. 'I'm just phoning the vet.'

Within twenty minutes Chris Langridge had arrived. He knelt down and felt the leg carefully before saying, 'I think he may have a touch of birch poisoning. Poultice it now and I'll come back this evening. If nothing has happened by then we will scan him tomorrow morning. Any chance of a coffee?' he asked.

'Sure,' said Jay.

'Could I have one too?' asked Amanda, who had been watching the proceedings over the door.

'Of course.'

When they were sitting at the kitchen table Amanda asked Chris what birch poisoning was.

'Well, essentially it is just like a splinter. A little bit of the birch from the fence gets into the leg and acts like a splinter. It results in an infection and usually leads to a certain amount of pus coming out, depending on how deep and how big the splinter is. We normally treat it with a poultice and antibiotics and this usually results in a rapid recovery. However, sometimes after a few days or even a week the cycle will repeat itself. This inevitably means that there is another piece of foreign matter further into the tissue which has not been drawn out by the poultice. That's when we do a scan.'

'Let's do the scan anyway,' suggested Jay. 'We've not got that long until Boxing Day and I don't want his work schedule interrupted more than is absolutely necessary.'

'That's fine,' said Chris, 'and I will have a look at those stitches when I come back this evening. I didn't want to disturb the bandages this morning. Let's keep our fingers crossed.' With a cheery smile he was on his way followed by Amanda. Chris had parked his car next to Amanda's soft top Mini Cooper, and they were happily chatting away before getting into their respective vehicles and driving off.

That evening Chris came back and checked the stitches.

'Those look fine,' he assured Jay. 'He'll be healed up in a few days. Don't swim him, but there's no reason why he shouldn't be led out, or even walked gently for a day or two. We don't want to do anything that is going to stretch the skin around the stitches and make them burst.' He removed the poultice on the other leg and showed it to Jay and Jed. There was a yellow stain on it where the pus had been drawn out but no sign of a splinter.

'Poultice it again tonight,' said Chris. 'Get him over to the yard as early as you can tomorrow morning.'

On the way back to his office, Jay remembered his promise to call Mr Lambert. He did so and was put through to the business man who was still at his desk at half past six. He sounded extremely pleasant and, when they had gone through the preliminaries, the inevitable question of cost came up.

'Well, from the way Amanda was talking, I would say around £40,000 for the horse. You will then have the weekly training fees on top of that, transport to the races, entry fees, vets' fees – hopefully not too much – but one way or another you're probably looking at £60,000 for the season.'

'Fine. How do we get the horse?'

'I've got a lot of contacts both here and in Ireland and I will put out some feelers and come back to you when I have got some news,' suggested Jay.

'Thank you. May I call you Jay?' asked Mr Lambert.

'Of course, and what shall I call you?' There was a chuckle at the other end.

'Unfortunately, my name is Albert, but my friends are nice enough to call me Al.'

'Done, I will get back to you as soon as possible,' promised Jay.

Feeling that the day had been very long, Jay still felt that it was important to phone Splendid Warrior's owner and, as a matter of courtesy, Jack Symes. This done, and with everything explained in detail, there was no need to go into any unnecessary patter. They were both fully aware of the implications and would wait patiently for the results of the scan.

The next morning at 8.30 Splendid Warrior was on

his way to the vet driven by Harry Pearce, the horsebox driver. Jay made a couple of phone calls then followed ten minutes or so behind. When he arrived, the horse was already in one of the examination rooms and the scanner had been set up. Harry was one of the key members of the County View team. He was an ex-National Hunt jockey who had suffered a number of injuries. Although none was serious, he was eventually advised by his doctor to stop riding. He became a groom for a Lambourn yard and drove their horsebox part-time. He found that this suited his lifestyle. He was married to a much younger woman and, although he was sometimes away overnight, he did not work the constantly long hours of a groom.

He said little about his wife but rumour had it that she was attractive and worked in an up-market casino in Swindon. When he did speak of her it was with some considerable pride. He appeared to be a gentle man, and the fact that he was familiar with horses and the racing environment and routines was a huge advantage. He had come to Jay with good references, had proved reliable and got on well with the rest of the stable staff, though in a rather reserved sort of way. He never came to stable functions even when big wins were celebrated at the Shepherds Rest. He also politely refused all invitations for an after work drink.

After a while the staff just stopped inviting him, knowing what the answer would be. A little over five foot six, he was nevertheless well built and rumour had it that he had been a successful amateur boxer in his youth. His rather bent nose could be a testament to that, or perhaps it could have been caused by a head first fall from a horse. All in all he looked like a man one would not cross without first thinking about it. He was well liked and respected by all the grooms who found him more than helpful whenever they went racing.

Both of them were watching the image on the screen when almost immediately Chris exclaimed, 'Look.' There was a small mark, which indicated a foreign body.

'Fortunately it doesn't look too deep,' said Chris. 'I'm going to see if I can locate it – I'll give him a local anaesthetic first.' With the injection done, Chris very gently inserted a very fine pair of tweezers. Suddenly he grunted. 'I think I've got it.' He removed the tweezers which came out covered in blood and a certain amount of pus, but there firmly gripped between the ends was a splinter of wood about half a centimetre long.

'Not very big, but enough to cause problems. The antibiotics he's having for the other leg should be sufficient for this too but keep the poultice on. We'll keep an eye on it, but there is no reason why he shouldn't still have gentle exercise of the sort we discussed this morning. I think we can safely say that there shouldn't be any recurrence of this particular problem.'

Jay grinned with relief, shook the vet's hand, and was soon on his way back to his yard. He wasn't really surprised to see the Mini Cooper there, but no sign of Amanda. He spotted Jed who told him that Amanda had asked to ride again and Jed had found her another suitable mount. A few minutes later the first lot walked into the yard, including Amanda looking both stunning and extremely cheerful.

'I hear you spoke to Daddy last night and I am absolutely thrilled,' she said.

'When do we start?' was her next question.

'Start what?' asked Jay.

'Looking for the horse.'

'Hold on,' said Jay. 'Telephone calls today, get a short list, and after that you and I can go and look at them. In the meantime you are always welcome to ride out here, but don't forget you have got work to do at college.'

'Wow, you sound just like Daddy!' she chuckled. 'Was that a slapped wrist?'

'Not at all,' smiled Jay. 'Go on, off with you and do some work. I look forward to seeing you in the morning.'

At that moment the horsebox came into the yard, and she stopped.

'How is he?' she asked.

'Fine, now off you go.' Jay turned on his heel, went into his office, and rang Barry Davies and Jack Symes to keep them informed of his early morning trip to the vet.

Chapter Thirteen

Later that day Eva and Jay were sitting relaxed in the early evening having just watched the news on Channel Four. The telephone rang and Jay got up to answer it.

'Hi!' he said with great enthusiasm and chatted for a minute before turning to Eva.

'It's your mother.'

Soon Eva and Fiona were deep in conversation, with Eva looking coyly at Jay while she told her mother of the decision to try and start a family. Jay could hear the chortle of pleasure coming down the line from South Africa. They went on to discuss Fiona's forthcoming visit to the UK and a fairly heated conversation took place between mother and daughter.

'Mother wants to talk to you now,' Eva said to Jay.

'What was the argument about?' he whispered.

'Tell you later,' she whispered back.

'Hello again, Fiona,' said Jay. 'I hear that we are going to see you in the not too distant future.'

'Yes, but I am not staying with you all the time whatever my daughter tries to do. I want to spend some time in Lambourn looking up my old friends, and some time in London – which I have to admit to missing quite a lot. I suspect Harrods and Bond Street are going to see a lot of me.'

Jay chuckled. 'Will you need a horsebox to bring your trophies back?'

'Probably,' she replied. 'Anyway Jay, what I wanted to tell you is that I have done some digging about Harry Clough, and it does not sound too great. He has got about twenty horses here in training, and also about a dozen brood mares at a stud he bought two or three years ago. The gossip is that none of them are doing well and it must be costing him a fortune. What's more, it is interesting to know that he has been over here two or three times and has made no effort to contact me either by phone, or a visit.

'I know that you don't like him, but he did have horses with me for a long while, paid his bills on time and his wife was always charming. It just seems a bit odd. If I hear any more I'll let you know.'

'Thanks a lot. Anything else you want to say to Eva?'

'No thanks. Just give her my love and tell her not to be silly. I will see a great deal of you both, but you know how independent I am.'

'Bye, and look forward to seeing you soon.' Jay hung up and turned to Eva.

'What was that all about?' he asked.

'I thought Mother would like to stay with us but she is insistent that she wants to spend part of her time in Lambourn and part of her time in London.'

'That seems reasonable to me, and I am sure that we are going to see a lot of her. Now, let's have some food,' her husband suggested.

The next day Jay phoned Giles and gave him the news from South Africa.

'Strangely enough, I got more or less the same story from the Jockey Club there. It didn't come through to my home until late last night, so I was going to let you know this morning. Also, I understand that Mr Clough does have horses in the Far East and I have been promised details within the next few days. However, let's not jump to conclusions. The fact that he doesn't like you and is spreading nasty rumours about you, doesn't mean that he's trying to fix races for you to win. It doesn't really make a lot of sense, does it?'

'No,' mused Jay. 'From where I am sitting, none of this makes any sense.'

'I don't suppose it does,' countered Giles. 'But if you sat behind my office desk you would be amazed at how many things appear to be equally unlikely.'

That night Jay received a call from Jonathan Teal, the head of the National Trainers Federation. He and Jay had already discussed the rumours, and both agreed that it was better to let sleeping dogs lie. They had followed the party line when he received a number of media calls.

'I went abroad visiting a number of my colleagues in other major racing countries a couple of days after Matt Jenkinson was murdered. Since I have been back and have heard all these rumours something came back to me. A few days before he was killed, Matt rang me and told me that he'd had an approach from someone wanting him to withdraw a horse from a race. When he refused an offer of money, the caller got quite threatening. Matt thought he was just a nutcase, and took no more notice, but he let me know just for the record. I know it's a long shot, but I thought that you also should know about it.'

'That's really interesting,' replied Jay. 'Did he say any more?'

'Only that the caller was a man, well spoken with a

slight foreign accent. He wasn't sure where the accent was from.'

Jay paused. 'Have you spoken to Harvey Jackson, the policeman in charge of this case?' he enquired.

'No.'

'Well, I think you should. You never know when something is going to strike a chord with someone, or fill in one of the many missing pieces of the puzzle.'

'It's as good as done. Keep in touch and I'll see you at the races soon,' promised Jonathan.

Jay sat deep in thought for a moment or two after putting the phone down. He left a message on Giles's phone to call him the next day, and then he rang Benny.

By now it was December and Jay was giving his main attention to Boxing Day at Kempton and the New Year meeting at Cheltenham. Splendid Warrior and Pewter Queen had both recovered from their minor setbacks and, in Danny's words, were both really 'on song'. There was no doubt that Splendid Warrior would go to Kempton for the King George, but there were valuable hurdle races both there and at Cheltenham. After a long chat with Danny and Jed, plus a telephone call to Freddie Kelly, it was decided that Pewter Queen would go to Cheltenham. She had already proved herself there and had handled the really stiff course with its particularly tough finishing straight. It was agreed to stick with a proven formula. As he was going in to lunch he got a telephone call from Pat O'Hara, an Irish trainer he had ridden for at Cheltenham a couple of years earlier, when he had won a valuable amateur race on Oaktree Mile. Jay had asked him to look out for a possible horse for Amanda, and Pat had rung to tell him that he had got three candidates, any one of which he felt would be suitable. He told Jay that one was Bounty Hunter, a point-to-pointer, that had won two races. The second was The Agitator, a decent seven year old handicap chaser with one win, three places and not many miles on the clock. The third was Elegant Queen, a six year old mare who had won a bumper plus two point-to-points. They would all be expensive but still fell within Jay's price range of £40,000 to £60,000.

He waited until the end of the evening then rang Amanda's father to tell him the news and to ask him if would be all right to take Amanda over to Ireland. Al Lambert agreed and said that he would love to come too but his business commitments would probably prevent it.

'One other thing,' Jay went on, 'I would like to take Chris, our vet, with us. He is brilliant at spotting any weaknesses, and if we do buy a horse then he is the one who will be looking after it from a medical point of view.'

'No problem at all. Two expert heads are always better than one in my view.'

Jay then telephoned Amanda. She was ecstatic and said that she could take a day off college without a problem.

'It's more likely to be two,' said Jay.

'Even better, I could do with a break.'

Next on the list was Chris who gave him two or three dates and said that it would suit him well as he wanted to discuss a professional matter with a certain vet in Ireland. Jay phoned Amanda back and it was agreed they would go in two days' time. Eva said she would book the flights, Pat arranged for them to be met at the airport, and he would fix accommodation at a nearby country hotel off the beaten track.

'A bit of peace and quiet will do me good,' Jay told Pat, 'but I am not sure that the two young people will have the same view.'

'That's up to them, but there's not a lot of nightlife anywhere within twenty-five miles which helps me get the staff to start on time in the mornings.'

Chris and Amanda were told the score and Jay went back to planning the races for the next few weeks. He had horses running the following day, but conveniently only one when he would be in Ireland and Jed would be well able to look after that.

A thought occurred to him and he was back on the phone, this time talking to Howard.

'You know that I'm going to run Splendid Warrior and possibly Pewter Queen at Kempton on Boxing Day. Well, as you also well know the traffic is always a nightmare, and I wondered if we might have use of the helicopter again?' He had used it once or twice, when they had two runners at different meetings on the same day. Once when he was tied up he had sent Jed in it to Wetherby to look after two runners and it had saved him the long, tiring journey. Jed had a stubborn streak in him and it was difficult to get him to be driven by anyone other than Jay.

'There is one other thing, Howard.' Jay paused. 'I would like to run The Conker at Huntingdon on the same day. There is a new and valuable race there and I think the course would suit him down to the ground.' There was silence at the other end of the line.

'Well, you're the boss,' came the reply. 'But heaven knows where I'll go!'

There was no problem with using the helicopter so

he told Eva and Jed that they would be travelling in style, although somewhat noisily.

Because of the importance of the race and the excellent chance for Splendid Warrior, they decided to send him up the night before with Danny and his stable lass. This of course meant that their Christmas Day would be seriously interfered with, but racing yards were used to that. With many meetings on Boxing Day there was also the chance for moderate horses to pick up some worthwhile prize money.

Jay had almost made up his mind not to run horses anywhere else as it would mean Jed missing Kempton, when Jed returned to the office to announce:

'I am going to Huntingdon on Boxing Day. It is very kind of you to offer to take me to Kempton, but you know very well that The Conker could win at Huntingdon, and the King George will be shown on television at every course in the country. I didn't join County View to be a passenger and, as far as I am concerned, Boxing Day is no different from any other. What's more, remember that The Conker has been with me longer than with you.'

Jay knew that there was no point in arguing with Jed when he was in this mood, so he smiled his agreement before walking over and putting his arm around his old friend.

'You really are a brick. What would I do without you and Cathy?'

'Bloody well,' was the reply.

With that they went to the schooling ground where a number of horses, including Pewter Queen, The Conker and Splendid Warrior, were being schooled over hurdles or fences. Whilst he was watching them, Jay's mobile rang. It was Eva.

'Come back to the house as quickly as possible and come alone.'

Excusing himself, he told them that an urgent overseas telephone call had come through.

'What is it?' asked Jay when he got back to the house.

'Giles Sinclair has just rung to say that he needs to speak to you and that you need to be alone.'

Jay went into his office, closed the door and rang Sinclair's direct line.

'There has been a very, very serious new development,' he told Jay.

'Shoot.'

'We have just had a telephone call from Brian Joyce. He is a very good young trainer and was seriously upset. Just after morning exercise, he received a telephone call and was told that he was not to run Sunshine Express against you at Fontwell Park in two days' time. He laughed at them, and told them that it was his best chance of winning a serious prize for a long while. They must have been just outside using a mobile phone, because moments later a car roared into the yard, two men jumped out and threatened him with a gun. They then pushed him into a chair, tied him up, put a plastic bag over his head, grabbed his wife, and told him that if he went to the police and ran the horse, he would never see his wife alive again. With that they dragged her out.' Giles continued. 'Thank God he's a sensible man who knows that kidnappers need dealing with professionally. As soon as one of Brian's stable staff came in to see what all the commotion was about, he was on the phone to us. Nobody got a good look at the car, but he says it was a large dark blue saloon that looked fairly new. We are obviously going to keep this as quiet as we can and we have told the trainer to carry on as normally as possible. If people ask where Mrs Joyce is they are to be told that she has gone to visit her sister before the Christmas season really gets busy. I have phoned Jackson who has had Brian's telephone tapped and he should be able to trace any mobile calls made too. The only problem is that if these thugs are professional they will probably make any demands or contacts through a pay-phone. Jackson is putting a top team on the case and wants to meet a.s.a.p.

'The main reason I have phoned you is obvious, as this again involves your horses. Also, I thought your friend Benny might be useful. We have our under-cover sources, but he seems to have his ear really close to the ground.'

'No sooner said than done,' promised Jay, and he was straight on the phone to Benny.

'Oh God, I'm going to be in trouble. I was going to take the old girl up the West End for a slap-up meal and a film, but I guess that will have to wait. Me and the boys will start moving now. Kidnapping is a bit of a specialist field, you know. Nine out of ten times the people involved stay hush about it as they are too terrified not to.'

Jay then phoned one of his old friends. Percy Cartwright had been at university with Jay and had always taken an interest in his racing activities. He had even recently been discussing moving his two horses to Jay's yard. However, Jay had dis-suaded him as his current trainer was in his last season before retiring, and as a friend Jay didn't want to poach. It was agreed they would come to Jay when the retirement took place.

After Cambridge, Percy had entered Lloyds of

London, where, thanks to an extremely agile brain and his father's excellent connections, he had rapidly risen to be head of one of the largest underwriting firms in the City. Jay happened to know that one of their specialist areas was kidnapping. He rang Percy and asked him if there was a possibility of them having dinner together that night. Percy was free and they settled for the Mirabelle where Jay knew he could get a very quiet table.

At eight o'clock Percy walked into the bar and gave Jay a piercing look.

'What's all this about?' he demanded.

'Let's have a drink and go in,' said Jay. As Jay was staying at his Hays Mews London base, they split a bottle of champagne, which saw them through dinner. Both of them missed a starter and went straight into grilled Dover sole.

'Let's go back to my place,' said Jay when they had finished. 'I have got some decent brandy, some excellent coffee, and a humidor almost full of Montecristo No. 3.'

'Sounds irresistible.'

Walking down Curzon Street into Berkeley Square, they avoided the temptation of popping into Annabel's, and were soon sitting in Jay's London home where they had spent many an evening together before he married Eva and moved to County View. Jay outlined the whole situation before coming to the point.

'I know that you have a very substantial business in kidnapping insurance, and it seems to me likely that you have a few specialists in tracking these people down. I wondered whether or not you could ask any of your contacts if they have heard anything about this, or could be helpful in any other way.'

'It's as good as done,' promised Percy. 'You ought to let Jackson and Sinclair know I am involved. We don't want any crossed wires.'

It was then that Jay filled Percy in on Benny and his friends.

'They seem like extremely useful people,' commented Percy. 'Tell them that they may be getting a telephone call from someone called Marvin Jones who will mention my name and it would be useful if they co-operated.'

With that they turned their attention to the brandy, the cigars and the prospects for Splendid Warrior, Pewter Queen, The Conker and some of Jay's other leading lights who would be racing in the next few weeks. Like Jay, Percy was an early riser and, making a call to his chauffeur, he shook hands just before eleven, and promised Jay that he would be in touch as soon as he had something concrete to report.

Passing Lambourn the next morning Jay's thoughts turned back to their racing plans for the next few weeks. For this time of year the weather had been very mild and, although heavy rain had resulted in some meetings being abandoned, these were very few compared with the normal losses through frost and snow.

As a result of this County View had been able to send out a number of runners, and it had been encouraging for all of them that their young horses had acquitted themselves well in their initial races.

Jay's policy of buying young store horses from Ireland, and a few useful horses off the flat from France, was beginning to pay dividends.

He had also been to Poland and had made some useful contacts there. Although he had bought nothing, he had seen one or two of the more entrepreneurial young trainers exploit this source with some considerable success. He was also interested in the New Zealand bloodstock industry, but had not yet been able to find the time to get over there for long enough to do justice to the work that would be needed. He and Eva had a quiet lunch together and she looked particularly thoughtful.

'Which do you think are our best young horses?' she asked.

'Well,' said Jay, 'as far as bumper runners are concerned, I think that we have got real potential with Try Again and True Resolution. When it comes to hurdles, Headswim, Mythical King and Keep Rocking and, although I think Dancing on Sand has got a huge amount of talent, I am sure that another year on his back will be a great advantage. The Novice Chasers are an entirely different matter. Here I've no doubt that Friendly Persuasion and Opening Bid will probably win some good races. But I think the most exciting one is The Real Thing. His point-to-point form in Ireland was exceptional, he has been jumping our schooling fences like the proverbial stag and he can keep up with anything on our home gallops. As you know, his sire was a very useful flat horse and I've no doubt that he has inherited his speed. My hope is that in two or three years' time he could be a real Champion Chase hope.'

The Champion Chase at Cheltenham is a two mile race and has the reputation of being run at breakneck speed and producing some of the most exciting horses and thrilling finishes of Cheltenham. 'They're all going to run fairly soon,' Jay continued, 'but The Real Thing is the first, and he's running in a two mile Novice Chase at Uttoxeter the day after tomorrow.'

'Well, you are certainly throwing him in at the deep end,' commented Eva. Uttoxeter is an undulating and stiff course with big fences that take a lot of jumping. The Midlands Grand National is run there, one of the most testing and competitive of all the really long distance steeplechases, with the exception of the world famous Grand National.

'I realize that, but he has had a lot of experience from his point-to-point days in Ireland, and remember, when he came second in his bumper at Leopardstown, the winner went on to take the Champion Bumper races at both Cheltenham and Aintree. I know he's fit because, if you remember, I took him with Try Again and Headswim to the VWH point-to-point course and gave them a really hard piece of work over two miles,' said Jay.

Eva smiled at him. 'I think I'll make a special effort to come to that one.'

'You know you're always welcome, as long as you don't get in the way,' Jay said with a grin.

'I know, but somebody has got to stay behind and do the office work.'

Jay thought for a moment and then said, 'That's raised a question I've been thinking about for some time. Don't you think we ought to get a full time secretary? You are not getting to the races nearly as much as you used to. You really enjoy it, and I miss your company. Let's face facts, we don't see that much of each other, and when I do get home after a long day involved with the horses, the entries, then going racing, I am wiped out. I can't be very good company in the evenings.'

'Rubbish,' was her quick response. 'I love hearing what's been going on in the afternoon and we knew what we were letting ourselves in for when we took on County View. However, I do think that you have a good point. Let's put it to Howard and Victor, but check out what it will cost in advance.'

'I will leave that ball in your court.'

'What a surprise!' Eva chuckled, as she leant over and kissed him lightly on the cheek.

They were both silent for a while. 'I have had another idea,' volunteered Jay. 'You know we've been talking about the possibility of buying some overseas horses? Why don't you speak to Fiona? You know that she is every bit as good a judge of horses as I am, and there just might be something running on the flat over there that we could make into a good class hurdler. What's more, it would give you a chance to go over to South Africa, spend a bit of time with your mother, and enjoy some decent weather too.'

'That's a great idea,' agreed Eva, 'but it would have to wait until after the New Year, and remember that she is due over here in a couple of weeks' time to spend Christmas with us. Anyway, I will give her a call. She might as well start keeping her eyes open.'

'Excellent,' agreed Jay.

Chapter Fourteen

The following day Benny rang. 'I have got to see you urgently,' he said to Jay. 'You may want to bring Giles Sinclair along.'

'What's it about?'

'I need to show you as much as tell you.' Jay rang Giles straight away and said he'd had this urgent request for a meeting from Benny. With a certain amount of reluctance, Giles agreed to meet them at the East End gym. By now Jay was getting to know it pretty well. Just as a precaution they arranged to travel there separately. When Jay arrived he found Giles and Benny already sitting in the back office, with Benny giving Giles a guided tour of a number of the many photographs adorning the wall. As soon as Jay entered Benny stopped talking and they all sat down. Benny produced a sheet of paper from his pocket and laid it on the table.

'Somebody is backing your horses in a big way. Individually they are not huge stakes but when you add them up they become very significant indeed. For example, Splendid Warrior has been backed down from two to one to odds on for the King George, Pewter Queen from seven to two to even money, but the interesting one is The Conker. He is completely out of favour. He has gone from being favourite at nine to two for his race at Huntingdon, to seven to one, with great lumps of money on Avon Ruler, now the three to one favourite.'

Benny continued, 'When you take into account that these are all anti post bets, the bookmakers I've spoken to are intrigued. What's more all the wagers are cash bets, no credit, and apparently three unknown men have placed everything.'

Giles scratched his head. 'Are there any more unusual bets like this on horses in different yards?'

'None that we've been able to trace. That was one of the first questions we asked, and we have even been to other bookmakers who haven't laid these bets.'

'Any ideas?' This question was directed to Jay but he just shook his head.

'I've no notion what's going on. Is it just my horses, and why are two being backed and the other one not? The Conker has got just as much chance as the other two, and in one sense his odds were more attractive even before they started to lengthen.'

'Perhaps someone is going to come in at the last minute and lump it on him,' suggested Giles.

'If that happened the odds would drop like a stone. It would just look as if somebody was trying to manipulate his price,' countered Jay.

'If it wasn't for all the other things going on I would be tempted to think that this is somebody trying a real coup,' said Giles. 'But the coincidence with your horses is just too strong for it to be that simple.'

Benny had been thoughtful. Now he spoke up. 'Suppose this is just a smoke screen – I mean the betting on the other two horses. What if there is a really genuine big bet going down on the second favourite On the Up. Perhaps the intention is to make sure that The Conker does not run, or if he does, he runs badly. Personally, my money would be on ensuring he doesn't run.'

'That makes sense,' agreed Giles. 'You're going to have to step up security in a big way. We'll give you all the help we can in advance but I don't have spare manpower – particularly at Christmas.'

'We can look after that,' volunteered Benny, 'but I strongly suggest you increase the security on your entrance as well.'

This had to be the sensible course of action. The group split and Benny went away to work out the schedule, and to generally review the situation with Jed. Clearly everything must be kept as low key as possible, but the regular stable staff were bound to notice strange men suddenly appearing in the yard, particularly as they would be staying overnight. Additional cameras must be installed at locations in the yard at sites suggested by the Jockey Club's expert. 'Just keep an eye open for anything unusual,' Giles told Jay, 'and in particular if any strangers appear to be taking an interest in the yard.' As an afterthought he went on, 'Have you taken on anyone new recently?'

'Yes,' Jay answered, 'we've recently hired Billy Dean, a very good experienced work rider from Ireland, but he came with excellent references.'

'I'll have him checked out carefully. Is there any-one else?'

'No, he's the only one and I only took him on because one of the girls broke her arm.'

'I'll check her out too,' said Giles.

As soon as he was in his car Jay rang the incident room at Newbury and asked for Harvey Jackson who was out but expected back at any moment. Jay asked that Harvey call him urgently and left his mobile number.

He had barely got past Heathrow when his mobile rang.

'Jackson here,' said a gruff voice.

'Could you spare me ten minutes in about half an hour?' asked Jay.

'Of course. I'll see you shortly.'

In a little over half an hour Jay was shown into Jackson's small but highly efficient-looking temporary office. After a brief greeting they got down to business. Jay quickly told Jackson about his conversation with Benny and his concern about The Conker. Jackson approved of the precautions.

'I just have an instinct that there is a connection between the three murders and what's going on in relation to your horses. If we are right about an attempt to interfere with your horse it is still a criminal offence. Once you've got your plans finalized and schedules set up, let me have them and I will make sure that there's back up all the way from your yard to Huntingdon. I assume that once you get to Huntingdon the Jockey Club security will be watertight.'

'That's absolutely guaranteed,' promised Jay, 'but my East End friends will be there too.' With a warm handshake they parted, and Jay returned to County View.

The next day Jackson phoned both Giles Sinclair and Jay to give them some disturbing news. It turned out that Billy Dean had a criminal record in Ireland, and had been involved in petty robbery and the burglary of a big private house. He had played a minor role in both crimes, so had only spent a short time in jail.

He did have considerable riding experience, but the reference had come from his father-in-law who had apparently let family ties sway his judgement in the hope that a new country would give him the chance of a new start.

'What do you think we should do?' asked Jay.

'My advice is to keep him but to keep a very close eye on him. If you know he is there and that he might be involved in something dodgy, at least you will have the upper hand.'

Jay rang this news through to Giles Sinclair who thought that Jackson's advice made good sense. Jed and Danny shared the intelligence and Benny was also brought up to speed.

Chapter Fifteen

Two days later Eva and Jay drove to Uttoxeter. The Real Thing had left early for the long journey as the traffic around Birmingham could be horrendous. Jay's mobile rang and Eva answered it for him.

'That's great, we'll see you soon.' She turned to Jay. 'They've arrived safely and The Real Thing travelled well and is completely settled in the stable yard.'

'I am not surprised,' Jay replied. 'He'll have experienced some pretty big crowds at his point-to-points, plus his bumper run at Leopardstown should have got him used to the big stage.'

Although they crawled around Birmingham they eventually left it in their wake, and then turned off the motorway to do the last few winding miles to the attractive country racecourse. As was his custom, Jay went to see his charge in the stables and to the weighing room to check that the declaration was in order.

Because this was the horse's first run in England there was a note against his name on the declaration list saying that he and his passport would need to be seen by the vet. This was a precaution to check that the passport was up to date for the mandatory injections, and just as importantly that the horse in the stable was indeed the horse on the passport.

Mistakes had been made in the past. As he was confident on both scores, Jay went off with Eva to have a light lunch before the first race. He thought so highly of The Real Thing that he had asked Freddie Kelly to ride him. The jockey was delighted to do so, particularly as he had three other rides that afternoon. He had been offered another ride in the Novice Chase, but had turned it down in favour of Jay's runner.

Just before the bell went for the jockeys to mount, Howard and Victor jogged into the parade ring, both of them puffing like steam engines.

'I didn't expect to see you here!' exclaimed Jay.

'We didn't know if we could make it,' came the breathless reply. 'Victor and I were talking on the phone this morning, and both of us mentioned how good it would be to see this young horse run. Then we discovered we could get a train directly to the racecourse, so here we are. There was a bit of a delay so we didn't have many minutes to spare – hence our breathless state,' explained Howard. At this stage Freddie joined them and after a brief chat, was legged up on The Real Thing and was being led out on to the racecourse itself. Freddie had schooled the horse at County View and, knowing his speed from Ireland, there was no need for any instructions.

With his point-to-point and bumper experience the horse took everything in his stride. He cantered smoothly down to the start and joined the runners already there. Soon the full complement of ten Novice Chasers were circling behind the tapes having their girths checked before being asked to make a line and then called in by the starter. At this moment one of the more excitable horses charged forward straight through the tape. He went thirty or forty yards down the track before his jockey anchored him, turned him around, and got him back with the others. The tape was repaired and at the second attempt the field was off and running.

On the first circuit all these relatively inexperienced horses jumped well with only minor errors. The field was still intact as it left the home straight and ran round the bend before facing the back straight for the second time. This had a strange right hand kink towards the end of it as the horses climbed the hill. At the first of the back straight fences one of the two leaders went straight through the top of the birch and, although he remained on his feet, the stuffing had been knocked out of him. He dropped to last. Obviously out of the race, and not sure how much damage, if any, had been caused, his jockey quickly pulled him up. Meanwhile the remainder, still fairly tightly bunched with only seven or eight lengths between first and last, turned into the uphill finishing straight. The two leaders injected more pace and it was at this moment that Freddie pulled his horse to the outside and started to mount his challenge.

Knowing that The Real Thing could accelerate, Freddie bided his time a length and a half behind the two battling leaders. He challenged them as they covered the ground leading to the last fence. The horse's speed and rate of acceleration were soon evident as he came upsides the now second horse that had struggled but failed to match the leader's pace. Coming up to the final fence Freddie sat quietly on his mount and steadied him a few strides before the fence. He took off and cleared the obstacle with such ease and fluidity that he landed upsides and was soon a length in the lead.

At this moment the horse went desperately lame and virtually stopped. Freddie leapt off, fearing the worst – a seriously damaged tendon. To his relief, when he looked down, he saw that the front nearside hoof had half its shoe sticking out at almost right-angles. This would certainly have been more than enough to be extremely uncomfortable, but would also act as a sort of brake.

He led the horse towards the exit from the track, and was met by a breathless and very worried stable lad. 'He's fine,' reassured Freddie, pointing to the offending shoe. By the time they had passed the winning post a deeply concerned Jay was already on the course. Eva, Howard and Victor were standing by the exit. As soon as Jay saw the situation, his disappointment turned to relief. The Real Thing would be fine to run again in a few days' time once he had a new shoe and had recovered from the exertions of the race.

In the owners' and trainers' bar Jay filled Howard and Victor in on the kidnapping. Of course they knew nothing about this development as it had been deliberately withheld from the newspapers. He promised to keep them informed. He also told them that the next day he would be going to Ireland for a couple of days to try and find a hunter chaser for Amanda. Victor and Howard stayed behind in the bar for another drink, whilst they waited for their train back to London, and Jay and Eva returned to their car. He phoned Jed, who had watched the race on television, to let him know what had happened. Then Eva waited in the warm car whilst Jay returned to the stable. He discovered that the black-smith had already taken the damaged shoe off, that the racecourse vet had had a precautionary look at the horse, and had confirmed that no damage had been done.

Jay and Eva drove home, disappointed but relieved.

Chapter Sixteen

Jay was due to leave for Heathrow at 8.30 the following morning to catch an Aer Lingus flight to Ireland. Just after six, Amanda arrived in a state of great excitement. Jay sat her down and made her a cup of coffee. She drank down this boiling brew but refused the offer of food. 'I am just too excited,' she explained. Chris was making his own way to the airport. He planned to stay on an extra day as he wanted to discuss some veterinary problem with an Irish colleague.

On the way to the airport Amanda chattered non-stop. The normally sophisticated young woman had reverted to an extremely excited little girl behaving as if she was just about to open all of her Christmas presents.

She bombarded Jay with questions about the horses they were going to see, and he patiently explained that he couldn't answer any of them as he hadn't yet seen a hair of their hides. All he knew was their breeding and racing history to date. He reminded Amanda that he had not only told her all this but e-mailed it to her as well.

Arriving at Heathrow Jay parked in the long term car park and they made their way to the departure lounge. Even at this time in the morning there were huge queues for security checks, but eventually they were through and made their way to Garfunkel's café, where they had arranged to meet Chris. They spotted him engrossed in the *Horse and Hound*. Jay went off to get himself and Amanda a coffee plus a refill for Chris. That done, they sat cheerfully chatting waiting for their flight to be called. On the way to the aircraft Jay checked Chris's seat number and found he was sitting in a different row. 'When we get on the aircraft, let's change places,' Jay suggested. 'You two can chat and I have brought quite a pile of paperwork with me to do.' Amanda looked far from displeased at this arrangement, and before long they were settled in their places, with seatbelts buckled, ready for take off.

During the flight Chris suffered the same barrage of questions that Jay had endured with good grace all the way up the M4 motorway. Amanda's first question to Chris was 'What will you be looking for?' His reply was 'Signs of previous tendon injuries, any irregularities in heartbeat or breathing, and the general conformation of the horse.'

He explained that so far as the last point was concerned, Jay was equally as expert as him, and probably not far behind on most other issues as well. However, a vet's professional opinion was normally needed for insurance purposes.

Amanda then turned the subject to the prospects of a number of the horses in Jay's yard, but Chris, on Jay's instructions, carefully avoided the subject of the runners that had been strangely withdrawn.

Arriving in Dublin they were met at the airport and whisked off to the countryside just outside Clonmel that boasted one of the best known racecourses in Ireland. They were driven to their hotel where Pat O'Hara was waiting for them. He suggested that they checked in and got unpacked, and then went straight to the local racecourse where there was a good afternoon's sport in the offing. On the way there he gave each of them a piece of paper with the potential horses' names on it, together with as much information as he had been able to glean. He explained that none of them were trained close to his yard, and for that reason he had suggested a trip to the races that afternoon. They would look at two candidates the next day and the third on the way to the airport the following day. They all enjoyed a splendid afternoon's racing with the normal good humour that is synonymous with Irish racing, fuelled in a number of cases by hot Irish whiskey and a plentiful supply of draught Guinness. Pat O'Hara had one runner which came a respectable third in the feature race of the afternoon.

They had been invited to Pat's home for dinner and were promised an early night. The evening flew past as Irish racing stories were recounted, some of them true and some, to say the least, embellished. At ten thirty they started to make their farewells and Pat asked if any of them would like to ride out in the morning. Jay and Chris politely declined, but Amanda said that she would love to. She had brought her riding gear with her to try out the horses they would be seeing. Pat said that they should be ready to be collected at seven the next morning.

Back at their hotel Jay said he was off to bed, but Amanda asked Chris if he would like a nightcap. He nodded an enthusiastic agreement. Smiling to himself, Jay retired.

Soon the two young people were chatting away about their private lives, and Amanda discovered that Chris had no regular current girlfriend. By the time they were on their second brandy, the atmosphere was definitely on the border line of intimate, and slowly they made their way upstairs. Pausing outside Amanda's door, Chris bent forward to give her a gentle goodnight peck and found himself in a passionate embrace with a long and sensuous kiss. Opening her door Amanda drew him into her room before closing it firmly.

'Are you sure this is a good idea?' the slightly concerned but definitely excited young vet asked.

'No, it's a brilliant one!'

Before Chris could move, she had his jacket and tie off and was unbuttoning his shirt. 'I think I can finish the rest,' he assured her, and with that she pulled her sweater over her head, kicked off her shoes, undid the button holding up her skirt, and stood before him in just her bra and tights. Inwardly Chris gave a gasp. When fully clothed she was attractive, but like this she was sensational.

Within seconds the tights were off and the bra unhooked. He drank in her slim but highly curvaceous body. Her breasts were surprisingly big with large dark nipples, already erect. Tumbling on top of the bed they were soon in the throes of uncontrolled lust, before panting away from each other in delirious exhaustion.

Chris was no novice when it came to action between the sheets but he had never known anyone with the appetite of Amanda. At two thirty in the morning, he suggested that he really did need some sleep, and reluctantly Amanda let him go. Putting just a towel around his waist, and bundling his clothes and shoes under one arm, he crept back to his room and fell into a deep and thoroughly exhausted sleep.

Before he realized it the alarm on his watch was beeping and somewhat befuddled he dragged himself out of bed. On his way to the bathroom he had a thought and rang reception and asked to be put through to Amanda's room. To his amazement a cheery voice asked him how long he would be and, when he said ten minutes, she replied that in that case she would wait for him in the restaurant downstairs.

She waltzed into the restaurant and greeted Jay with a breezy good morning. They both glanced at the papers which had been ordered the night before and exchanged a few comments before Chris arrived. Jay was amused to see that Chris did not appear to be at his sparkling best and looked exactly what he was, a man who had had a very energetic night, with not much sleep. Putting two and two together, Jay was impressed with how vivacious and sparkly Amanda was at this time of the morning. Whatever Chris had been up to with her was clearly good for her, mused Jay to himself. They were soon on their way to the yard, and Amanda put the night before out of her mind as the excitement of riding a racehorse in somebody else's yard began to envelop her.

When they arrived the horses were already walking around the loose sand school, and she was soon legged up on a small but very elegant grey mare.

'Don't let her size put you off, she has got a really good engine,' Pat assured her.

Soon, led by the head lad, they were on their way to the gallops, and were using the grass as the going was absolutely perfect. Chris and Jay sat in the Land Rover along with the trainer three quarters of the way up a gently sloping gallop. Jay had brought his own binoculars, but Chris was using a pair of borrowed ones as they watched the horses come past in single file at a real swinging gallop. Now at the top Pat asked Amanda how she felt, and would she like to go up again, this time upside at racing speed. Looking at Jay, she asked if they had time, and when the nod was affirmative she beamed. A few minutes later five pairs of horses were on their way. Amanda, beginning to look like a really polished rider after her few weeks at County View, went flashing past them.

'She'll do,' grunted the Irishman. 'Let's get back and have a coffee before we start on our journey.'

Sitting at the kitchen table they were soon joined by an exuberant Amanda. Her thanks to the Irishman could not have been more effusive, or more genuine.

Ten minutes later they were on their way to see The Bounty Hunter, trained by Noel Malpas, one of Ireland's top point-to-point trainers.

Pat O'Hara made the introductions and a fine athletic horse was led out. Chris quickly ran his hands over the horse's legs, and had him trotting in a circle, then towards him and then away from him. This allowed him to see if there was any unevenness in the horse's movements, but he was quickly satisfied that all was well. The trainer's head lad then legged up Amanda and along with a companion they made their way to the gallops.

Noel's horses were using the all weather gallop and, after a steady warm up canter, they returned to the start and did a seven furlong gallop at three quarters racing speed. Jay was perfectly happy with what he had seen. Chris then listened to the horse's lungs and heart to check for any abnormalities.

Keeping a poker face Jay told the trainer that they had seen all they needed and forty-five minutes after arriving they were on their way.

Amanda couldn't contain herself once they were in the car.

'Well, what do you think?'

'Can't find anything wrong with him,' said Chris.

'Looks all right to me,' agreed Jay. 'What did you think of him?'

'I liked him a lot. He was a bit strong the first time, but settled well when we were travelling a stride faster.'

'You could be happy with him?' asked Jay.

'Yes.' There was a pause. 'Well, what are we going to do?'

'We're going to cool down and see the other two horses before we make our minds up about anything. We may then want to see one of them again.'

'Well, at least we seem to have got a possibility,' Amanda observed, and the other two, with wry smiles, nodded.

It was just over an hour's drive to the next yard which was owned by an old friend of Jay's called Lanky Murphy, so named because he was one of the tallest and certainly the thinnest jockeys in Ireland during his riding days.

Jay was greeted with the enthusiasm for the proverbial long lost son, and after the smiles and handshakes, he was given the opportunity of introducing Chris and Amanda. Lanky could not have been more helpful, and soon his candidate was being led around the yard.

Running Wild was a big bay horse, not particularly good-looking but clearly powerful. Jay sensed that Amanda was not as keen as she was on the previous one, but felt they couldn't leave too quickly and offend Lanky. Subsequently they went through the same routine of Chris carefully checking the horse, before Amanda was legged up.

Lanky turned to Jay. 'I am sending an unraced young gelding to work with Running Wild. He's a three year old that I picked up from a breeder's widow who's selling off her stud and all its stock. I just really like the look of him and thought you might like to cast your eye over him too.'

Soon the two horses were at the start of the gallop hacking past them at a steady pace. Turning they went back to the starting point again and this time went up at near racing pace. Amanda's horse had a big strong stride but carried his head rather high. The three year old was poetry in motion. Jay turned to Chris.

'Run your ruler over him when this is over, would you please.'

Soon Amanda and Lanky's work rider were with them and were told to trot back to the yard. Once there Chris finished his examination of the older horse, and then turned to the three year old and gave him the same thorough vetting.

'Nothing wrong with either of them,' he assured Jay.

They all went into the kitchen and had a cup of coffee whilst Jay discussed prices of both horses. Amanda's Running Wild was £35,000 and the untried three year old was £18,000.

'I still work in pounds,' explained Lanky. 'Euros confuse me.'

Jay promised Lanky that he would be in touch with him by the end of the following day, and with warm farewells he returned to the car with Amanda and Chris, where Pat was talking to Lanky's head lad. This time it was Jay who started the questioning, asking Amanda what she thought of the horse.

'I just didn't feel as comfortable on him as I did on the first horse. He moved nicely but he carried his head rather high for me. If it comes to a choice then there's no doubt I would choose the first.'

'Actually, I agree with you,' replied Jay. 'Right, let's go and have a snack lunch.' Turning to Pat in the car he asked him and his wife to join them later that evening.

'We would love to' was the instant response.

Both Jay and Chris needed to make some telephone calls and Amanda said she would try to do some studying if she could keep her mind on it.

When they got back to the hotel Jay had a long phone conversation with Jed and learned that all was well. He then phoned Benny who said that nothing had happened yet, but that he was due to talk to Percy's contact the next day.

Shortly after seven Pat and his wife arrived. After a couple of drinks in the bar they retired to the restaurant, where they enjoyed a large, simple but extremely good dinner. Chris and Pat stuck to draught Guinness, whilst Jay, Amanda and Mrs O'Hara split a bottle of decent red wine between them.

The conversation was almost entirely centred round racing. Pat wanted to know all about the prospects of Jay's leading and better known horses, and if he had anything in the pipeline as good as Pewter Queen, The Conker and Splendid Warrior. Jay described two or three of the younger horses, and Pat made a note so that he could watch them with care when they next ran.

Jay then gently steered the conversation to Pat's yard, and was told that he was having a reasonable season. He had got one really good horse that he planned to run in the top amateur race at the Cheltenham Festival the following March. 'I only wish you were still riding, Jay,' said Pat.

'Sorry, but I'm not,' was the cheerful reply. 'Once I hung the boots up, that was it for good.'

They returned to the bar for coffee and, with the exception of Mrs O'Hara who was driving, and Amanda who settled for another glass of wine, they all had brandies. Jay's trademark Montecristo No. 3 was produced, but he was the only one smoking. The conversation turned to more general racing topics, and Pat raised the thorny subject of betting exchanges. Giving Chris a meaningful look Jay was non-committal. He said that as his was an almost non-betting yard, it was not a subject that he felt qualified to discuss.

Soon they decided to call it a day, and Jay escorted the O'Haras to the car park. He thanked Pat and agreed to be at his yard at about ten o'clock the following morning so that Pat could supervise his first lot before he led the way to see the third horse. They would then continue from that yard to the airport.

Returning to the bar, Jay saw that the two youngsters were deep in conversation and had got another drink each. Discreetly he bade them goodnight and went up to his room, smiling knowingly to himself.

It wasn't long before Chris, slightly shyly, suggested that it might be time to retire. Amanda immediately agreed. As soon as they were in her room, after a long and passionate kiss, they discarded their clothes as quickly as possible. Having learnt a bit

117

about each other's love making the night before, there was the same enthusiasm but in a slightly more controlled manner. This time Chris was persuaded to stay the night with Amanda. He did, however, set the alarm on his watch for seven, just in case Jay rang or came knocking on his door early in the morning.

Little did he realize that Jay had already cottoned on to their nocturnal activities, and was far too discreet to cause any embarrassment.

Chris joined Jay for breakfast just before eight thirty. Amanda arrived a well calculated ten minutes later. They chatted cheerfully about the previous day's activities. When they had all finished their breakfasts, Jay ordered another large pot of coffee and they moved to the comfortable lounge where they scanned the English national newspapers, as well as the local daily.

The *Racing Post* was avidly passed from one to another. There was nothing of any importance but turning to the season's statistics, Jay saw that he was still in third place, but had closed to within less than fifty thousand of the second. This meant that he was within striking distance of the leader if he continued with his current rate.

They went upstairs to pack their bags. Returning to the lobby, Jay paid the bill, Pat arrived and they followed him out to the car park. They took two cars as Pat would be returning to his yard. Chris would then drop Jay and Amanda at the airport, before going off to meet his vet friend. Jay suggested that Chris and Amanda went in the hired car together, a tactic he thought would give the two love birds a chance to talk before they were split up for a time.

It was a two hour drive to Connor O'Brien's yard,

118

where they were to see Elegant Queen, the last of their three candidates. Jay knew Connor from the days when the young trainer had ridden in some amateur races in England, and they were pleased to see each other again. The mare was brought out and Amanda's eyes lit up. Almost black, the horse was truly elegant and looked in the peak of condition. This time not only was she led round Connor's school but he lunged her as well. With little bucks and squeals, she demonstrated how well she was. It was obvious from her attire that Amanda was hoping to ride her. A strong gelding ridden by the stable's head lad led them on to the gallops. Soon they were following the familiar pattern for Amanda. A swinging warm up canter was followed by upsides at not far short of racing speed. Jay had to confess to himself that the mare and Amanda looked made for each other. As soon as the horses joined them Connor asked Jay if he would like Amanda to pop the mare over a couple of small fences. Amanda nodded vigorously and the two horses turned away and cantered over to the far side of the gallops. The three men climbed into a Land Rover and drove over to three fences which Jay felt were somewhat misleadingly described as 'small'. However, he reassured himself with the fact that no one trying to sell a horse would take unnecessary risks, particularly with a lady amateur that he had never seen ride before.

Turning about one hundred yards from the fences the head lad led Amanda into the three obstacles. All were cleared easily and with precision.

Coming back Connor asked Amanda if she would like to go upsides again and again the response was an enthusiastic 'Yes please.'

This time they travelled faster than the first time, and the mare and Amanda sailed over all three obstacles in great style.

They cantered back across the gallops and walked into the yard where Chris quickly finished his examination of the horse. Jay went off into the trainer's little office and had soon negotiated a price of £40,000. He explained that the three of them would have to have a debate on the way to the airport, and then they would need to talk to Amanda's father. As soon as a decision had been made, and Mr Lambert had agreed to fork out the money, Jay would let all three trainers know the choice.

Returning to the car they thanked Pat for his kindness and the trouble that he had taken. Jay wanted to make sure that if they did buy one of these horses Pat would get a good commission. Pat smiled.

'I might be Irish but I'm not that green!' was his smiling response.

Final farewells were made with a promise to keep Pat in the loop, then the three of them set off to the airport. Amanda's enthusiasm knew no bounds. 'I really want her. What do you think?' she asked. The two men looked at each other.

'Well, I'm not so sure,' Chris said slowly, and Jay agreed. There was a stunned silence from the back seat.

'But she's lovely! You said that she was perfectly sound, and jumps wonderfully. What's wrong with her? I can't believe you don't like her.'

The two men roared with laughter. 'I think she would be great,' said Jay, and Chris nodded his head in agreement.

'I'll kill you both!' shouted Amanda. 'Once you stop driving of course.'

When they reached the airport, Amanda asked, 'Can we phone Daddy now?'

'Are you sure he won't mind being interrupted during his day's work?'

'Not by me,' was the rather smug reply. The call was quickly made and sure enough it was accepted by the indulgent father. Amanda babbled on about what they had done and all three horses, and raved about the mare.

'Let me speak to Jay,' interrupted her father. Slightly reluctantly Amanda handed the phone to Jay.

'What do you think?'

'Of course we can't be certain until we have raced her with Amanda on her. We have also got to get her qualified for hunter chasers, although I might be able to do that with the experience she has had hunting in Ireland.' Jay then told him the price. Without hesitation Al Lambert said that it seemed he had just purchased his daughter's Christmas present. 'You'd better put her back on the phone.' A brief conversation was interrupted by a squeal of delight from the young lady, who poured effusive thanks down the telephone.

'All right,' said her father, 'I have got some work to do. You and Jay can make the arrangements. As soon as she's at County View, your mother and I would love to come and see this creature that has captured your heart. Thank Jay and Chris for all the work they've done for me, and don't you forget to thank them too. Talk to you soon.'

'Well,' Amanda announced, 'I think it's my turn to buy us all a glass of champagne. If you two have to be a bit cautious because of your driving, then I really don't mind drinking more than my fair share!'

That said she led them over to the bar, insisting on buying the whole bottle, whilst continuing with her bubbling conversation – in every sense of the word – until it was time to board the aircraft.

Chris made his farewells, and before long Jay and Amanda were on board. Jay had already phoned Lanky to tell him of their decision about Running Wild, but confirmed he would buy the three year old. He then phoned Connor to make the arrangements. Connor was pretty convinced that he could have the mare and Lanky's youngster on their way to England in two days at the most, and Jay promised that the money would be transferred to his bank account the next morning. He had already agreed this with Lanky.

Sitting on the aircraft Jay expected a further bombardment of questions, but the combination of the excitement of the previous two days, riding the horses, her strenuous nocturnal activities and the champagne had eventually caught up with Amanda. Jay had a peaceful flight with the opportunity to read some of the papers and to look at the entry forms he had failed to make any inroads into during the previous few days. Approaching Heathrow Jay gently woke Amanda and, as they only had hand luggage, they were soon sitting in Jay's car and on their way down the M4. When they arrived at the Agricultural College on the outskirts of Cirencester, Amanda leant over and gave Jay a big kiss. 'I have had a really great time, I am so excited, and you have been fantastic, Jay. Thank you, thank you, thank you.'

'All part of the service.'

'And I really enjoyed Chris being there,' added Amanda.

'So I noticed.' Jay raised one eyebrow. Amanda had the grace to blush but said nothing as she jumped out of the car. Grabbing her bag from the back seat she then said, 'See you at the gallops tomorrow' and fled in a state of semi confusion.

He and Eva were having a simple cold lunch, and Jay filled her in on the outcome of the trip. She was really pleased that Amanda had found what she was looking for, but raised an eyebrow when Jay told her about the three year old.

'I know I shouldn't have let you loose in Ireland by yourself,' she quipped. Jay went into an enthusiastic defence of his actions, and pointed out that he hadn't bought many bad horses in Ireland.

'What's more,' he reminded her, 'Lanky is as good a judge of horse flesh as I have ever met, and I am glad that he thought of me first.' He went on to fill Eva in on what appeared to be a burgeoning romance between Chris and Amanda.

'I told you he was a dish,' she reminded him. 'It will be interesting to see what happens, but be discreet, Jay. We don't want to lose Chris and Amanda is a jolly addition to the yard.'

'I agree,' said Jay. 'I'll go out now and see what's happening in the yard, have a chat with Jed and Danny, and then go round evening stables with them. I thought you and I might go out and have an early dinner, and when we get back perhaps we could have an early night.'

'Followed by more practice?' was Eva's mischievous response. 'Who knows?' replied her husband, with a smile. 'We can't let those youngsters have all the fun!' With that he was through the door, and enjoying the sensation of being back in familiar surroundings.

Chapter Seventeen

Benny was sitting in his kitchen eating his normal hearty breakfast of two fried eggs, two rashers with a slice of fried bread, when his mobile rang.

'Is that Benny?' questioned a rather cultured voice.

'Who wants to know?' was the response.

'My name is Marvin Jones. Percy Cartwright suggested that we should meet.'

Benny's tone went from being guarded to enthusiastic. 'Of course, when and where?'

'I have two personas,' Marvin informed him. 'One rough and one smooth. As I may have to use my rough appearance if we wind up working on this project together, perhaps I will put on my Sunday best. How about we meet in the American Bar at the Savoy at eleven o'clock? I can't imagine that anyone we don't want to see us will be there at that time.'

'Right. I'll see you there. How do I recognize you?'

'I am over six foot tall, wearing a dark grey suit, white shirt, and I am black. Very black.'

Benny nearly said that he wouldn't have known, but thought better of it.

'Well, I will be in a brown leather jacket with coffee coloured slacks, and a pale blue shirt. I am medium height, hair that was once ginger, but is now mainly grey.'

'We should make an interesting couple!' laughed Marvin. Marvin had read languages at Cambridge, and was fluent in French, German and Russian. He could also get by in Arabic, and even a little Chinese. The minute Benny saw this extremely strong-looking guy, who exuded confidence, he was sure that he would be a much better ally than enemy. They rapidly filled each other in on their backgrounds, and Benny was amused and slightly disbelieving when he learnt that Marvin had been born and brought up in the East End.

As if sensing Benny's scepticism, he quickly continued the conversation in an accent that was peculiarly distinctive Cockney with an undertone of Caribbean.

He explained to Benny that he had a network of informers, and that the sort of people who were usually responsible for kidnappings were either members of a very well orchestrated group of some sort, or first time individuals. These usually did it for strictly personal reasons – such as a parent snatching a child who is in the custody of the other parent. He explained that experienced kidnappers took a professional interest in other kidnappers' activities, and that true professionals kept their ears to the ground. He further volunteered that he had a number of well paid informers who had close contacts with or had been involved in kidnaps. Some were from the East End. From time to time in his East End persona Marvin would have meetings with them and real villains who had perpetrated some of the most audacious and vicious kidnappings.

Having heard the way in which Mrs Joyce had been snatched he was pretty sure that this was a professional job, and reasonably confident that in a few days' time he would have a clue who was behind it. In the meantime he asked Benny if he knew of two or three people. 'Right villains all of them,' came the response. 'If I don't know them myself, I know people who do, but I have heard of them all.'

'Put out some subtle feelers for me,' asked Marvin, 'and let's keep in touch by mobile if there's anything interesting. I'll keep Percy informed of what we are doing and you do the same for Jay. By the way, things might get a bit rough later on, so perhaps we will keep the Jockey Club and the police out of this for the time being.'

Benny was soon on the phone and visiting one or two pubs which he knew were frequented by some of the people he wanted to talk to. He also contacted Kipper Fish, a famous character in the East End, who was well known to Howard as well as to Benny.

Sitting at a quiet table, without explaining the kidnapping situation, Benny said he would be very interested if Kipper heard of anyone who appeared to have become suddenly flush with money in the last few days, or if he heard anything else that was unusual enough to excite his interest. Finishing the last of his pint of bitter Kipper agreed and was soon on his way. By the time Benny had visited another five pubs, and had a convivial pint with a number of dodgy characters, he was pleased that he had taken the precaution of getting Angel to drive him around – leaving him in the car to remain abstinent. When he got home he phoned Jay to bring him up to date.

Jay rang Percy and thanked him for his prompt action, and let it be known how impressed Benny was with Marvin Jones.

'I can assure you it's very mutual,' Percy told Jay. 'I've had Marvin on the phone. He says that he is certain that the two of them will work really well together.'

That evening after having an early supper with his wife, Benny was watching East Enders, when the phone rang. It was Kipper. 'Are you alone?' he asked.

'To all intents and purposes,' replied Benny. 'You can say what you want.'

'Would your enquiries have anything to do with a lady being kidnapped?'

'Could be,' was the cagey reply.

'Well, in that case I've got a name for you – Mickey Lane appears to be flush, and he and his girlfriend, Julie, were having a few drinks. It seems that Julie asked him how long he was going to keep "the girl" and she got a smack across the face for her troubles. I know that he's been involved in that sort of caper before, but he has been lucky. He wouldn't be the brains behind it but it might be worth your while having a quiet word with him in a very private place.'

'As good as done – I owe you one. I'll be in touch.' Benny rang off and immediately phoned Marvin. 'We need to meet quickly and I suggest you drop the suit this time.'

'OK, any suggestions?'

'How about the Reef Bar upstairs at Paddington Station?' suggested Benny. 'It's on both our tracks and the tables are a reasonable distance apart.'

Forty-five minutes later they were sitting opposite each other, Benny in his normal leather jacket and jeans, and Marvin in a baseball cap, a shabby grey polo neck sweater underneath an equally old-looking denim jacket, and a pair of stonewashed jeans that had certainly seen better days.

Benny quickly filled Marvin in on his information from Kipper.

'Do you know how to get hold of this guy?' Marvin asked.

'Almost certainly. I know where he lives and I know the pubs he normally uses. He's also a bit of a snooker fanatic, and spends a lot of his spare time in the snooker club if he is not in the betting shop.'

'Let's move,' said Marvin.

'Right, but wait here,' continued Benny. 'We need some soldiers. I'll get my boys to join us.'

'Not yet,' Marvin said. 'Let's keep you out of it as much as possible. He doesn't know me, and you might be an additional unpleasant surprise we can keep for later on.'

Marvin made two quick telephone calls and turning to Benny he said, 'I'll call you in ten or fifteen minutes. Meet me outside the Burger King in London Street just across the way from here.' Benny nodded.

True to his promise, Benny's phone rang fifteen minutes later, and two minutes after that he was sitting in the back of an old pick-up van that had been fitted with surprisingly comfortable benches along each side. Benny's quick eyes also noticed a number of rings securely fixed to the sides and floor which would certainly provide a basis for securing any fragile goods, whether living or inanimate he thought. There were three other men in the back with Benny and two others sitting in the front with Marvin. No introductions were made but cheery smiles passed between all of them.

'OK, let's have the directions,' said Marvin.

Three pubs yielded no results, but the snooker club did. Having spotted his quarry leaning against the bar, Benny went back outside and told Marvin. A moment later the three guys in the back jumped out, leaving the doors open. Minutes after that they hurled an ashen faced Mickey Lane into the back of the van. He was then tied up and a sack pulled over his head. The back doors were slammed shut and the van sped off. Again there were no comments, but broad grins and thumbs up signs were exchanged. Benny was intrigued to know what would happen next but refrained from asking anything as the rest were keeping silent. He realized that this in itself would unnerve the undoubtedly terrified man on the floor between them. Twenty minutes later the van slowed to a halt, and Benny heard metal gates being opened. The van drove through them and he heard the gates clang shut behind them. Marvin then turned the van around and reversed towards a large up-and-over door. This was then pulled down and one of the men in the front of the van jumped out. He turned on a powerful torch and walked over to the wall, where he found the light switches. Light immediately flooded the cavernous area, and to Benny's amazement he found himself in a workshop. There was a ramp, pulleys and all the equipment necessary to maintain the assorted varieties of vans and cars which filled half of the floor space. All four men donned black balaclava masks and, with a sign from Marvin, the human bundle was pulled out of the van and securely tied on the top of a large metal trolley with his feet protruding from one end. He was then wheeled over to an area where a set of welding equipment was neatly arranged. With a nod from Marvin, one of his colleagues turned on the welding torch. With a whoosh the flame was adjusted. At that stage the sack was removed from Mickey's head, but not before Benny moved into the shadows out of view of the trussed figure. The sight of Marvin walking towards him with the flame shooting out the end of the torch resulted in a piercing scream from the now frantically struggling figure.

'Take his shoes off,' commanded Marvin. This was done and his rather unsavoury off white socks were exposed to view.

'I am going to ask you a simple question and I want an immediate answer or I'll use this on one foot,' said Marvin. 'If you still refuse to answer then I'll use it on the other. If you don't answer then, I will use it on one of your hands. By then you will probably be unconscious with pain and be of no further use to us, so we will kill you.'

Benny had seen terrified men before, but the bulging eyes and the dark stain that suddenly appeared down the front of his trousers showed that here was a man truly beside himself with fear.

'Have you got that?' snarled Marvin in a menacing voice. Mickey nodded his head as vigorously as he could, tied up as he was.

'Where is the woman being kept?' The words came out very slowly and very deliberately. The man said nothing, and Marvin moved down towards his feet holding the torch high enough for the thug to see it very clearly. Immediately there was a scream. 'I'll tell you, I'll tell you!' Marvin walked back towards his head, but did not put the hissing torch down.

'Well? I'm waiting,' he said.

'She is in a store room in a disused factory near Vauxhall Bridge.'

'What's the address?' demanded Marvin.

130

'I don't know, I really don't know.'

Marvin moved towards his feet.

'But I can show you!'

'Right, get him back in the van,' said Marvin. This time Benny sat in the front of the van and only the back of his head was visible. Their prisoner was sitting looking towards the back windows. As they approached Vauxhall, Marvin demanded, 'Right, where do we go?'

'Go past Vauxhall Bridge station on your left and keep going until I tell you.'

In a few minutes they were past the station, and half a mile later they were told to turn left. They were now in a very run down street with a few small industrial units at the end of it.

'Which one is it?' snarled Marvin as he turned the van lights off.

'The second on the left.'

'How many guards?'

'Normally two plus an alsatian,' was the rapid response. The prisoner was then secured to the floor, his legs tied up again. This time he was gagged, and the sack put back over his head.

Two heavy bags were removed from the van, and torches, coshes, two realistic replica revolvers and cans of mace were distributed between the men. Benny was again told to keep behind them, but he had been armed with a baseball bat and a can of mace. Whispering for them all to stay where they were, Marvin went off to reconnoitre and was gone barely five minutes.

'There are only two ways in,' he told the waiting group. 'The main door, and a fire exit at the side. The windows are high and probably too difficult to use as an entry. There are no signs of life inside, but there

131

is a car. I could see this guy when I was climbing the fire escape which gave me a partial view of the inside. I think the trick is for two of us to guard the main door, two the fire exit, and the rest of us make our way up the fire escape and hopefully get in that way.'

He looked around the group and picked two who were wearing trainers.

'The quieter the better,' he explained pointing to their footwear.

'You come with us, Benny.' Benny always wore Nike trainers unless going somewhere smart. He frequently also wore them on those occasions, much to his wife's dismay.

Marvin led them silently up the fire escape ladder until they reached a small platform outside a door. Reaching into his pocket he produced a small jemmy and a thin narrow strip of flexible steel. After a few minutes of prodding and lifting, there was a click and the door opened. The hinges had clearly not been oiled for some time, and it creaked as it swung open. They paused motionless trying to hear any noise inside the building. There was nothing. Opposite them was a small door which proved to be unlocked. Again Marvin led the way along a gangway with a rail on one side and doors into rooms on the outside wall side. These clearly provided access to either store rooms or offices.

Gently opening each door at a time Marvin found that they all led into one large room which was entirely empty apart from two very ancient and dusty chairs. Continuing along the walkway they came to more metal steps which led down to the concrete floor of the building. Descending they looked around. Again there were doors leading into rooms similar to those directly above them. The car that Marvin had caught a glimpse of through the window turned out to be a not very new people carrier, with blacked out windows.

Motioning them to stay where they were, Marvin crept over to the vehicle and gently opened the driver's door, before turning his torch on to briefly examine the interior. There were a couple of holdalls in the back, but nothing of any particular significance. Interestingly enough, the keys had been left in the ignition, so Marvin quickly removed them, found the one that operated the central locking system, and put them in his jeans pocket. There would be no quick getaway in this vehicle.

He beckoned to the others to follow him and led the way along the side with the doors, pausing at each one and listening carefully. At the third he could hear mumbling. Working on the principle that anyone inside might see the door handle turn, he motioned to one of his colleagues to join him four or five paces from the door. At his signal they turned and hurled themselves at it, shoulders first. It was not very substantial and gave way under their assault. Followed by the others, Marvin rushed in. Two of them had got guns out, and completely shocked the two men who were sitting in ancient armchairs watching a rather battered portable television. One of them reached for his pocket, but Marvin growled in a menacing voice, 'Move and you're dead.'

Two of Marvin's men grabbed the two sitting targets, frisked them and found a gun on one and a knife on the other. Each had a mobile telephone. All of these were removed. Then Marvin demanded, 'Where is she?' At first it looked as if there might be some resistance, but one of them thought it wasn't worthwhile. Pointing to a door in the side wall he nodded. Benny and Marvin opened the door and found a young woman tied and gagged lying on a camp bed with a few grubby-looking blankets for company.

Her eyes started from her head when she saw the masks and guns. Benny quickly went over and said, 'It's OK, Mrs Joyce, we have come to rescue you.' He removed the duct tape from her face as gently as he could, and all the while he and Marvin kept reassuring her that all was now well. Marvin produced a knife from his pocket, and Mrs Joyce's bonds were sliced through. Clearly in a state of shock, the young woman was still not convinced that she had truly been freed. At this stage Benny reassured her that in a few minutes she would be on her way home.

'I think it's best that I leave you to deal with the police,' he said to Marvin who nodded his agreement. Benny then phoned Angel, who arrived in ten minutes. The next call was to Giles Sinclair. Marvin was contacting Jackson, whilst his colleague bound the two men. Mickey Lane was brought in to join them.

Thinking about it, he thought it best not to mention Jay's involvement in front of the still shocked woman.

By the time they reached her husband's yard on the edge of the Marlborough Downs Mrs Joyce had started to relax, realizing that she really was going home. A telephone conversation with her husband had done a lot to boost her morale.

When they drove into the yard they found two police cars waiting for them, each with a driver sitting behind the wheel. Mrs Joyce walked into her kitchen, rushed into her husband's arms and promptly burst into tears. After a few moments she settled down and was introduced to Jackson. He was extremely solicitous as he explained that it was important to ask a few questions. Sitting next to her husband and holding his hand, she answered what were routine questions, but she was unable to be really helpful. The two kidnappers had hardly spoken in front of her. They had brought her food and drink three times a day, and had escorted her to the rather primitive toilet when she needed it.

Otherwise she had been locked in the other room, and did not hear their conversations which in any case were usually drowned out by the television. Turning to the trainer Jackson asked, 'What are you going to do about running that horse?'

'It's too late,' he replied, 'the race was today, and frankly I felt I dare not risk it.'

Nodding understandingly, Jackson said, 'We will obviously come back later on. I am so pleased that it has turned out well.' Turning to Benny with a firm look he announced, 'I would like to have a word with you outside.'

When they were out of earshot, he asked rather briskly what had happened. Benny looked all innocence. 'Mr Marvin Jones contacted me to see if I could help at all. I put out some feelers in my manor, and got a name – Mickey Lane. Mr Jones persuaded him that it would be sensible to volunteer the information, which then happily led to Mr Jones rescuing the young lady. I have merely been a messenger, and now a chauffeur.'

A wry smile settled on the policeman's face. 'If I believe that I will start to duck the flying pigs up

135

there,' he said with a sigh. 'Anyway, thanks for your help. I may need to talk to you again after I have spoken to Marvin Jones, and interviewed the three villains who are now safely in separate cells.'

Benny got into his car and rang Jay. He thought that it would be a good idea if they met with Percy and possibly Marvin within the next day or two. Jay said that he would make the arrangements.

Chapter Eighteen

With the excitement of the kidnapping over Jay was relieved to get back to concentrating on training horses and preparing for the forthcoming meetings. The three year old and Amanda's Elegant Queen arrived from Ireland. Amanda's car must have been waiting with its engine running because in just a few minutes the Mini Cooper came to a screeching stop in the yard to be met by a rather stern-faced Jay.

'I can understand you being excited, but don't ever drive in here at that speed again,' he admonished her. She looked genuinely crestfallen and stammered her apology.

'I am so sorry. I was just not thinking.'

'Well, don't let it happen again.' Then softening his demeanour a trifle he said, 'Come on, let's go and have a look at her.'

Danny was nearby and promptly found a head collar and leading rope, and then brought the mare out. The light was fading fast, but it was still good enough for Amanda to walk round and round the mare pausing every now and then to give her a pat. She had brought a tube of Polos which the mare sniffed suspiciously and refused to eat.

'She's probably never seen those in Ireland,' suggested Danny. 'She'll get used to them here. Try her

137

with that.' He brought a carrot out of his side pocket and the mare munched away happily.

'What next?' asked Amanda of Jay.

'Well, we will give her a quiet couple of days to get over the journey, and she'll be led out or put on the horse walker. She can go for a walk with any of our older and sensible horses after that. I'll get Danny to ride her just to make sure that she doesn't explode, then afterwards you can jump on her for a very steady canter.'

'Will it be all right for Daddy to come down on Sunday?' she enquired.

'Of course. I look forward to meeting him.'

'Can I have a look at the other one?' was her next question.

By this time the light had faded, so she had a look at him in his box. He seemed to be none the worse for his journey and was happily munching his hay when the three of them joined her. Jay was still as pleased with him as he had been in Ireland.

'What are you going to call him?' asked Amanda.

'I think I am going to give him to Eva, so we had better let her make the decision. It will be interesting to see what she comes up with.'

They all trooped into the kitchen for a leisurely cup of tea, whilst Jay gave Eva the news that the new horse was hers, and she had the job of naming him.

All sorts of suggestions were tossed about, when Eva held up her hand.

'We had such a great time on our first holiday together, so I am going to call him Tobago Song.'

Everyone agreed that had a nice ring about it, so Jay got out a naming form, handed it to Eva to complete and send off to the naming department at Weatherby's.

'Well, I think you'd better phone your father now,' Jay suggested to Amanda, as he handed her his phone.

'I'll use mine. He will recognize my number – particularly if I phone him on his mobile.' She was soon enthusing again about her premature Christmas present. It was arranged that both her parents would come down the following Sunday allowing themselves enough time to have a proper look at the mare, see Amanda ride and have lunch with Jay and Eva. Shortly after Amanda had left, Jackson rang to have a word with Jay. He explained that at first the three thugs had refused to answer any questions. Eventually one had agreed to, on the understanding that there would be a degree of leniency in how he was treated; needless to say it was Mickey Lane. It was, however, made quite clear that kidnapping was a serious crime, and that he could expect a pretty lengthy stay enjoying Her Majesty's hospitality.

'We haven't got a lot further,' he explained. 'It was all set up via a telephone call, which was inevitably made from a public phone box. However, he is almost certain that it was made from an airport as he could hear what sounded like flight departure times being announced in the background. The first thing we did when we knew this was to check on Harry Clough's location but he has been in Singapore, and is still there, so that's a bit of a long shot. However, the fee paid to the kidnappers is a great deal more than a dinner at your local Indian.'

'Damn and blast,' swore Jay. 'Anything else?'

'No. I was hoping you might have some news.'

'Not at the moment,' replied Jay. 'In fact, it has all been pleasantly quiet on our front.'

'Long may it last,' was the terse response, 'but I've a feeling it won't!'

Later that evening Fiona rang from South Africa to confirm that she would be arriving in England on the 20th December, and hoped that she could stay with Eva and Jay at least until Boxing Day. Assuming that they were going to Kempton on Boxing Day, she thought that it would make sense for her to continue her journey to central London, where she was booked to stay at the Dorchester Hotel for a few days, seeing friends and going on her shopping blitz. The fact that it was sale time had not escaped her. She would then return to County View for a few more days before travelling on to Switzerland to see a couple of friends and have a few days on the ski slopes before returning to South Africa.

Both Jay and Eva thought this was a fine plan and both told Fiona how much they were looking forward to seeing her.

Chapter Nineteen

The following Sunday, just before ten o'clock a gleaming black Bentley came to a smooth stop in the yard. Out stepped an extremely distinguished-looking man. He was dressed in elegant casual clothes topped with a superb brown suede jacket. With a quick wave to the waiting group he opened the other door. Out of the passenger side stepped a truly gorgeous-looking woman in her late forties or early fifties. One look at her figure, her raven hair and flashing eyes left no one in doubt that this was Amanda's mother.

Their daughter rushed across to them hugging and kissing both of them in turn. She led them across to where Jay, Eva and Jed were standing, and introduced them all. Amanda's parents were as friendly and charming as they were elegant, and were clearly anxious to see their daughter's new acquisition.

'Do we need wellies or are we OK as we are?' asked her mother.

'No, you will be fine as you are, Mrs Lambert,' answered Jay. 'We'll go up in the Land Rover and the grass is perfectly dry.' She gave him a stern look.

'My name is Maria, not Mrs Lambert,' she scolded him. 'How would you like it if I called you Mr and Mrs Jessop?'

'Not a lot,' acknowledged Jay with a broad smile. They walked across the stable yard to where Elegant Queen was waiting, having been groomed to within an inch of her life. Jed led her out and it was clear from the Lamberts' reaction that they were thoroughly impressed by the mare. She and Dancing on Sand was quickly saddled and with Amanda and Danny on board they made their way to the start of one of the grass gallops. On the way, Al tapped Jay on the shoulder.

'I obviously don't want to ask you this question in front of Amanda, but how competent is she?'

'She is actually very good, and getting better with every week she spends with us. She works really hard, and listens to advice. In fact I was going to discuss with you the possibility of Amanda taking out an amateur licence to ride under rules. Frankly, if this mare is as good as we think she is she will certainly be up to amateur races, and I am confident that Amanda would do just as well in those as she would in hunter chases. Although the horses on the whole may be better, so are the jockeys, and there are more opportunities. What's more, there are a growing number of mares only races and amateur races, so we should be able to pick and choose with relative ease.'

'Well, that is encouraging,' said Maria. 'We will certainly take your advice. Don't let her enthusiasm run away with her. She has always been a bit of a bull in a china shop.'

'I have noticed!' chuckled Jay, and Amanda's parents joined in the laughter.

Soon they were a little more than halfway up the gallops, and Jay brought the Land Rover to a halt. They all climbed out and Jay was interested to note

142

that both the Lamberts had brought their own binoculars. This showed a degree of familiarity with racing which was encouraging. Turning to look down the gallops they saw that Danny and Dancing on Sand were at the start, and had already broken into a sedate canter.

Elegant Queen was a few lengths behind. Going past the group of onlookers Jay felt genuine satisfaction with both the horse and her glamorous young rider. When they reached the top they turned and trotted back to the waiting group. 'How did she feel?' Jay asked Amanda.

'Absolutely great! After a couple of little bucks before we started, she has been as good as gold.'

'Would you like to do it just a little bit faster this time?' asked Jay.

'I'd love to,' she enthused.

'Well, stay behind Danny, and he'll make sure you don't go too fast. Remember, she has had a long journey and two or three quiet days.'

With an understanding nod, Amanda turned the horse and followed Danny at a sensible trot to the bottom of the gallop. As they turned around, the onlookers could see Elegant Queen give a couple of bucks and a fly leap. Amanda stayed rock still in the saddle.

'I think that she's going to be one of those mares that always have a bit of fun at the start. As long as she doesn't play up when it comes to the real work we are none of us going to be upset about that,' commented Jay.

As they went past it was clear that Amanda was rapidly building up an understanding and excellent relationship with what was undoubtedly her pride and joy.

After a further chat with the two riders, the four spectators climbed back into the Land Rover for the return journey to the house. 'Let's go in and have a drink while the other two walk back,' Jay suggested. 'If you want to have another look at her, then you can do that after they have been washed down. I mean the horses!' he added with a grin.

'I am glad to hear it!' chuckled Al.

'A dose of cold water might do her good,' commented her mother.

At that moment the door opened, and in walked Chris. Addressing the Lamberts he said, 'Hello, I'm Chris.'

'I thought you might be. We have heard so much about you. I am so glad that you are able to join us for lunch,' Maria welcomed him. Jay and Eva exchanged meaningful glances.

'I hope you don't mind,' said Al. 'Amanda has insisted that this should be our treat and she has booked us into somewhere called the Shepherds Rest. It seems to feature quite heavily in County View's activities,' he added. 'She also said that Chris had been so helpful in Ireland, she very much wanted us to have the opportunity to meet him and thank him personally.'

'I was only doing my job,' Chris replied modestly.

Jay had to turn his back and pretend to concentrate on opening a bottle of champagne in case anyone saw the look on his face. With great difficulty he suppressed a huge laugh, and Eva came up beside him with the glasses and gave him a knowing nudge in the ribs. Within minutes a flushed Amanda joined them.

'Well, what do you think?' she demanded of her parents.

'Do you mean Chris or the horse?' asked her mother.

'The horse of course!' a blushing Amanda replied. 'Oh I'm so sorry, that was rude,' she added to Chris.

Both the Lamberts were serious and then enthusiastic about Elegant Queen. For a while they sat and talked generally about racing and County View before Al looked at his watch.

'Come on, let's be going. I don't want to leave it too late as we have got a long drive after lunch.' With that they piled into their respective cars and pulled up outside the Shepherds Rest. Amanda had already ensured that a table was reserved and Al tactfully made sure she was sitting next to Chris. He was next to Eva and Jay was next to Maria. Once the first course had been served Jay turned to Al and asked him how he had been involved with horses, and had obviously learnt a fair amount about them.

Al explained that he had ridden as a boy and as a young man and hunted in England, but had a break when he started working. He eventually went to Argentina where he formed a close friendship with a business contact who had a very successful polo pony stud on the side. Al rode nearly every weekend and learnt much about horse husbandry in the process. It was there he met and married Maria before returning to England when Amanda was a baby. He concentrated on building his business, but he and Maria went to local point-to-points and to local race meetings whenever they could. They soon came to the joint view that National Hunt racing was much more fun than the Flat. By the time she was twelve, Amanda was riding enthusiastically and frequently, and went hunting for the first time at fourteen. As soon as she was old enough Al bought her a point-to-point horse. That brought them up to date.

The lunch continued in a convivial and relaxed manner until the time came for the Lamberts to be on their way. Jay excused himself to go to the Gents and was promptly followed by Al.

'I thought this was an opportunity for us to have a quick word in private,' said Al. 'Maria and I talked on the way and if you think Amanda really can ride in amateur races then we are certainly not going to stop you. All I would say is don't let her rush you. I know what she is like.'

'I won't even tell her yet,' replied Jay. 'Let's see how the next few weeks go. We have got plenty of time before the end of the season.'

Outside the pub they all shook hands and waved as the Bentley left the car park. It was clear that Amanda and Chris had joint plans. Jay and Eva excused themselves with the pretext of an urgent telephone call to make.

On the way back to County View Eva turned to Jay. 'What delightful people. You can see how they have produced such a stunning daughter and such a nice person. I've got a feeling that Maria has a shrewd suspicion that there's more to the Amanda and Chris relationship than meets the eye.'

'I think you could be right, but let's see what happens,' agreed Jay.

Chapter Twenty

On the run up to Christmas Jay's horses continued to perform well, giving him three winners, one second and two thirds. He was closing rapidly on the two trainers above him in the prize money table.

Having looked at the available races it had been decided that Splendid Warrior, Pewter Queen and The Real Thing would all go to Kempton. The Conker would go to Huntingdon again for a recent addition to the calendar, a three and three quarter mile race sponsored by one of the new breed of internet bookmakers. With winning prize money of over £30,000 it was worth missing Kempton. What was more, with his win earlier in the season, the horse had proved he could cope with the course.

The three Kempton horses were travelling the night before their races and after some debate Jay decided that The Conker would also leave the night before. This would avoid the inevitable Boxing Day traffic jam around Oxford, and the potential delays nearing both racecourses. Although, to aid television coverage, the Huntingdon race did not clash with the King George it was impossible for Jay to see all his runners even with the use of the helicopter.

Jed was to travel in the horsebox with Archie, the part time but very regular reserve box driver. The Conker's normal lass, Janet, was going to lead the horse up but, after a lot of begging, Billy Dean went with them to give The Conker a gentle canter on the morning of the race. Janet was not happy with this arrangement.

Billy explained that he had a sister who lived near Huntingdon and it would give him the chance to visit her. He would make sure, however, he was back in time for the race.

Jay agreed to this but felt it was worth conferring with Giles, Jackson and, of course, Benny about the whole security situation. Benny came down but they met in a pub not used by the staff. He was adamant that some serious precautions should be put in place. Two of Benny's brothers would travel in the back of the box with The Conker, but Jed would make certain that Billy was not about when the horse was loaded, and Janet would be sworn to secrecy. Both of Benny's men were armed with baseball bats, cans of mace and replica guns.

Benny would travel in a car with three other cohorts. They would stay well behind the horsebox while keeping it in their sights. Harvey Jackson told Jay that a police car would not be far away for the whole journey.

'Tell as few people as possible about your time of departure or any other details of the journey,' he instructed Jay. 'That does not include me!' he added with a bit of a chuckle.

Christmas morning came and although there were lots of 'Happy Christmas's' and cheerful smiles around the place, essentially it was a work day just like any other. The horses running the next day were given a walk around the perimeter of County View, and then a gentle canter. Those that were running in the next few days, in particular the New Year Meeting, were given more strenuous exercise. Most of the staff would work more or less a full day, although one or two with special commitments had been given the day off. This meant that those left behind had to do a bit extra, particularly with horses going to two different meetings later that day.

To help inject a bit of Christmas spirit for the working staff Jay had arranged a slap up Christmas lunch at the Shepherds Rest. The non-drinkers ferried people back and forth. The landlord had promised that the alcohol intake would be kept under close scrutiny as Jay certainly didn't want drunken stable staff turning up at his yard for evening stables on the eve of such an important day. There was an extra surprise when the local paper and radio stations turned up to interview Jay and some of the staff. It seemed that they felt their activities were of special interest in the locality.

Jay had already had long conversations with Victor and Howard and one or two of his owners. However, as his mother-in-law and Eva were settling down to a proper Christmas dinner the phone rang. It was Hal from America wishing them the compliments of the season, and wanting to know if there were any significant developments. Jay filled him in on what was happening, which left Hal somewhat bemused. 'I'll be back over in a couple of days so you can give me all the news then.'

By mid-afternoon on Christmas Day the horses had been fed, loaded and were soon off to their respective destinations. Although no trouble had been anticipated with the three Kempton-bound horses, one of Benny's gang nevertheless sat in front with Harry the driver. He was also armed with a baseball bat. Again, a car with four other burly, well

149

armed East Enders travelled a good distance behind, but kept the box in their sights.

Jackson had given Jed, Danny and Jay a special telephone number to call if anything suspicious appeared to be happening, and both drivers had this with them. Because the trip to Huntingdon was longer and less direct, The Conker left an hour before the Kempton trio set off.

Driving round Cirencester they were quickly on to the A40 which they had joined at Burford, then continuing along there to the Witney bypass. A short while after this Billy turned to Jed and said that he was bursting for a pee, and could they stop at the next lay-by. Somewhat reluctantly Jed agreed, and a little further on they pulled into a large lay-by that had some shrubs and trees screening the dual carriageway. Billy was out of the cab as fast as he could, and within seconds two men with stockings over their faces appeared, one each side of the cabin. Sawn-off shotguns were being pointed at Jed and Archie and they were told to stay where they were. Neither had a chance to use a mobile phone. Meanwhile two more men had gone to the back of the box and were undoing the tailgate. Billy had run over to a nearby parked car which had a driver sitting behind the wheel with the engine running. He jumped in the back. Behind this another horsebox pulled up.

As the tailgate was lowered and the two half doors opened, the two men were completely surprised when Benny's two colleagues rushed down at them waving their baseball bats. At that moment Benny's car pulled into the lay-by and all four jumped out, brandishing an assortment of replica firearms. Realising they were outnumbered, the two men at the front of the horsebox turned and ran back towards their car. However, their escape route was barred, and they reluctantly dropped their weapons.

Two of Benny's men had the horsebox open in a flash and brought out the beautiful and confused creature.

All four of the thugs were quickly handcuffed with plastic restraints and now Jed phoned the special number while Benny and his colleagues hid their firearms, leaving the attackers' sawn-off shotguns as evidence for the police. Two police cars with blue lights flashing and sirens wailing were there within minutes. They had already been briefed over the telephone regarding the likely scenario. The four thugs were then rehandcuffed with police cuffs. A police van arrived within minutes and the four of them were bundled into it with two more policemen to ensure they did not have the chance of escape.

The car with the driver and Billy in it had sped off the moment it was obvious there was trouble, but a rapidly erected road block at the end of the Witney bypass resulted in the two occupants also being put under arrest. The other horsebox driver was arrested and taken off to Witney police station.

Jed now told the police he had a really valuable racehorse to get to Huntingdon.

'Is it all right for us to go on?' he asked.

The senior policeman made a call, and after a brief conversation was told that the second police car would escort them all the way to Huntingdon. He also asked for Benny and his friends to stay behind and explain what had happened. After a few moments the policeman's phone rang, and after a fairly long conversation he turned to Benny. 'That was Mr Jackson who said you are free to go on, but he will want to talk to you tomorrow. I understand he knows where he can contact you?'

'Absolutely,' Benny agreed cheerfully.

The Conker was re-loaded and was soon back on his way. As had been previously agreed Benny's men in the back of the horsebox stayed there for the rest of the journey. It had been cleared with Giles Sinclair that they would remain outside The Conker's box all night. Benny and his colleagues now resumed their journey to Kempton where permission had been granted for them to provide extra security overnight for Jay's three runners.

Jed rang Jay from the horsebox to bring him up to speed.

'Well,' said Jay. 'We can now see why the odds were being changed so dramatically.'

'Agreed,' replied Jed. 'By the way, The Conker didn't seem at all concerned with all the commotion going on. I will call you again when he's settled at Huntingdon.'

Not long after that Danny rang from Kempton to confirm that all was well at that end, and that the three horses were settled down for the night contentedly munching their hay. Benny's three guards were already in position outside each stable.

At Kempton one box had been left empty next to Jay's three runners, and was being used by the back-up team. They were working a two hours on two hours off shift pattern for the whole of the night.

Jay went around his yard checking all the horses before returning to the kitchen. Eva greeted him with a cheery smile and the information that Jed had rung from the course, and all was well there. Fiona gave a chuckle.

'Well, training racehorses was never quite like this

in my day!' she joked. Jay did not reply but walking over to the pine dresser he opened the cupboard underneath and produced a whisky bottle and three glasses.

'I think we all deserve this. In fact, I think we desperately need it after the last few hours,' he announced. Eva nodded agreement and quickly produced a jug of water to slightly dilute the Black Label Whisky that had been a present from the ever generous Victor. Again she refused any alcohol. Settling for an early night, they ate a very light supper before retiring. They were emotionally and physically tired after an extremely adventurous and rather stressful day. Fiona, who was still tired from her long journey, was first up to bed.

As always Jay was up at his usual time in the morning, and supervised the first lot. These were the horses that would race within the next week, and the rest would go for good walks or be put on the horse walker. Jed and Danny had phoned respectively from Huntingdon and Kempton to say that their charges had eaten up well and all of them were being led out. Janet was delighted that she would now give The Conker a gentle canter and Danny was going to do the same at Kempton with Splendid Warrior. Pewter Queen and The Real Thing were just being ridden around the racecourse at a brisk walk followed by a half-mile trot.

Jay organized the first lot of horses doing serious work and supervised it himself before returning home to have a light breakfast and to get ready for Kempton.

By ten o'clock on Boxing Day they were all changed and ready to go to Kempton. Eva and Fiona both looked smart without being overdressed and Jay was proud to be seen with them. After a few minutes they heard the sound of a helicopter hovering overhead. It settled on a prearranged spot far enough away from the yard so as not to spook any horses.

One of the lads drove Eva, Jay and Fiona across the grass, and they were soon airborne gazing down at the stunning countryside below, on a crisp and glorious winter's day.

They landed by prior arrangement at Kempton, and crossed to the front of the grandstand. Eva and Fiona strolled to the owners' and trainers' restaurant where they had arranged to meet Howard, Bubbles and Victor. Howard had had a mighty internal battle – should he go to Huntingdon to watch The Conker, or to Kempton to watch Pewter Queen?

Pewter Queen won narrowly, mainly because his home was close to Kempton Park, but he felt very guilty at abandoning The Conker. This would be his first run without Harold being present.

Jay had gone to the stable block, cleared the security, and had found his three charges still being guarded by Benny's men and Danny. The stable staff who were leading the horses up were having lunch in the stable lads' canteen. Danny told him that the early morning exercise had gone well. Then Jay walked briskly back to the grandstand and joined his two partners. Very quietly he brought them up to date with the events of the previous evening. He had phoned Howard the night before with a brief run down of events in view of the fact that The Conker was Howard's horse. Victor seemed stunned at the speed and seriousness of what had happened.

'Now what?' he asked.

'God knows,' came the reply. 'Let's hope we can get through the afternoon with some success and four sound runners at the end of the day.'

There were vigorous nods of agreement from everyone around the table.

Chapter Twenty-One

Half an hour before the first race, a Novice Chase, Jay got up and left to go and saddle The Real Thing. Splendid Warrior was running in the third race, and conveniently enough, Pewter Queen in the fifth. This meant there was a reasonable space between each of his runners. Freddie Kelly, who was riding all of them, would be busy, although for safety's sake he had opted not to ride for any other trainer that day. He was taking his chance on The Real Thing in the Novice Chase but Jay's runner had been so fluent, both at home and at Uttoxeter, he felt the chances of disaster were fairly remote.

Arriving at the saddling boxes Jay put Freddie's saddle on The Real Thing. The horse was completely relaxed, interested in his surroundings, totally calm and not fretting at all. Soon he was on his way to the parade ring with Emma, his lass, as proud as punch and very excited at leading a horse up at Kempton for the first time – particularly on such a big day. Her horse looked absolutely magnificent, and shortly before the jockeys were asked to mount it was announced that she had won the 'Best Turned Out' prize. The £100 involved was a really good extra Christmas present for her, and a well deserved one, Jay told her, as he legged-up Freddie.

Victor, Eva and Fiona had all joined him in the

parade ring, but Howard had gone off to have a bet. He loved walking up and down the on-course book-makers' pitches to get the best odds. He was not a huge gambler but was an enthusiastic one when County View horses had a real chance. Victor always seemed more interested in the race itself, rather than the betting.

Fiona complimented Jay on the appearance of his horse, and asked about his background which Jay was pleased to provide. The going was good, but probably a little on the fast side of good. This would suit his first two runners rather than Pewter Queen. It would certainly be the sort of ground that Splen-did Warrior loved.

Soon the nine horses for the Novice Chase were at the start. Girths were checked and the starter called them on the track. Approaching the first fence a grey horse had taken a real grip and was bowling along in front at a very generous pace indeed. The other horses let him steal fifteen lengths, but resisted the temptation of chasing too hard too soon in the race. Passing the stands with a circuit to go they were almost in single file. Freddie was seventh of the nine runners and hugging the rails in his customary manner, to make sure he went the shortest way. Going down the back straight the second horse increased his pace and gradually cut down the dis-tance between himself and the leader. The pack, with the exception of the last two who were struggling, moved with him.

By now there were only seven or eight lengths covering first to seventh, with the original leader back-pedalling as the second horse took over at the front. All the fences were jumped cleanly by all the runners. The Real Thing was particularly fluent,

157

passing a horse at each of the next two obstacles, and was soon sitting in a very handy fourth position behind the original leader who was now struggling.

Freddie moved out to pass this horse and stalked the two leaders who were now upsides and turning for home. They were racing flat out and jumped the second last still upsides, but one hit the top of the fence so hard that he sent the brush flying and staggered to one side. As the horse came down Freddie's mount was caught a glancing blow, and not surprisingly swerved away from it. The jockey was almost out of the saddle, but fortunately the horse straightened up and he was soon back in control on an even keel. The manoeuvre had only lost Freddie half a length but a careless jump had cost the joint leader five or six lengths and he was now struggling. Freddie moved up behind the new leader as he came to the last. He was half a length down but well on the stand side. Both the horses effortlessly cleared the remaining fence but now Freddie, with a slap down the shoulder, asked his horse for a final effort.

As he expected, The Real Thing immediately responded and shot past the one remaining challenger with ease. Eva and Fiona were jumping up and down with excitement as he passed the winning post with two lengths to spare. Hearty congratulations were the order of the day from Howard, Victor and Bubbles. Jay rushed from his position on the stand to greet Freddie and Emma on their way in. Emma looked like the proverbial cat who had swallowed a bowl of cream. Freddie was grinning and bending down to pat the horse as he said to Jay, 'I knew at Uttoxeter that you had got a good horse. We've got a real star in the making.' He dismounted and trotted off to weigh in. The press gathered around Jay asking his future plans for the horse. He explained that it was still too soon, but this run had been extremely encouraging and good class Novice Chases were likely to be the main objective. He also pointed out that the ground was very important. Too much rain would see him having an easy time until the going became good again. Jay insisted that photographs were taken of Eva and Fiona with the horse, plus one of Emma with the horse on her own. Emma was absolutely thrilled and congratulations were being showered on them from all sides as they left the ring. There were also good wishes for Splendid Warrior. There was no doubt that he had gained a huge following and enjoyed the affection of the real enthusiasts for National Hunt racing.

The next race was run and Jay was then walking across to the saddling boxes with Freddie's saddle over his arm. There was an excited crowd of spectators already gathered around the pre-parade ring looking at the joint Gold Cup and King George hero. Jay politely pushed his way through to stand by the box where Splendid Warrior was going to be saddled. By this time Barry the owner had also arrived.

'Where's Jack Symes?' Jay asked.

'Oh, he thought that on a day like this it would be better if he left you and me alone until after the race. He said to me, "It's your show today."'

'No it's not,' replied Jay, pointing at the horse. 'It's his. He made the horse. I'm just enjoying the fruits of his labours.'

'Tell him that after the race,' Barry suggested.

Minutes later a saddled Splendid Warrior was led

into the parade ring and a spontaneous ripple of applause greeted his appearance, along with shouts of 'Good Luck!' This time Howard and the girls joined the party in the middle of the ring. There was no sign of Victor. It was obvious that everyone was nervous including Jay. The one completely cool head was that of Freddie, who was oozing confidence and chattering to everyone, Fiona in particular. The mounting bell rang and Jay legged the champion jockey up on to his champion horse. With a pat and a final 'Good luck' Jay went to join the others.

As a group they made their way over to the stands. Jay, Barry, Eva and Fiona took up their position in the part of the stand reserved for owners and trainers. The other three had found a good vantage point fairly high up on the grandstand. A cheer of expectation arose from the crowd as the horses were paraded in front of the stand before being released by their grooms and cantering down to the start.

This was a field of highly experienced top class chasers who took the proceedings in their stride. None of them showed any signs of being difficult. Circling behind the tape, girths were checked, the starter studied his watch, the tape was up and the field was on its way.

As always Freddie had Splendid Warrior settled more or less in the middle of the fourteen horse field and they were streaming past the winning post fairly tightly bunched. The pace was as brisk as could be expected from such a high class field, and certainly suited Splendid Warrior with his economic, high cruising speed. The first mishap occurred as the horses jumped the first fence after the bend. There was an 'ooh!' from the crowd as one of the jockeys fell sideways out of the saddle. Later it turned out that the saddle had slipped which probably meant it hadn't been put on properly. The unfortunate jockey was lying third when this happened and he received some very nasty kicks and remained motionless as the field galloped past him.

Within seconds the ambulance was with him, and to the crowd's concern, he was seen being carried off the track on a stretcher. For a moment or two most of the crowd's attention was focused on the incident but Jay remained riveted to his runner. Fortunately, although the mishap had affected two of the horses in front of Splendid Warrior, Freddie had seen a gap, gone easily through it and was now lying in fifth position.

There were no further problems and the eight remaining runners stayed fairly closely bunched with the loose horse running alongside outside the fences. As they turned for home for the last time the loose horse swerved and ran right across the bunched up field. The two leading horses had no alternative but for the jockeys to take a hard pull. One of them was carried right across the fence almost into the wings. He scrambled over the fence, but had lost so much ground and momentum that he was well out of contention.

The injection of pace which was now put into the race by the leader soon had the field strung out. Splendid Warrior moved easily into third place, and with his normal fluency moved up to second as they jumped the penultimate fence. The leader was showing a great deal of resolution and Freddie had to give Splendid Warrior plenty of encouragement to cut down the gap between them as they approached the

161

last. By now Freddie realized that he had a serious battle on his hands and he elected to ask Splendid Warrior for a real commitment to the jump. Four or five strides from the fence Freddie knew he either had to go for an extravagantly long jump, or take an extra stride and fiddle over it. Knowing the horse as well as he did he decided on the riskier of the two options. Without a moment's hesitation Splendid Warrior showed the class act that he was and flew over the last obstacle with ease and authority. He landed full of running and one slap on the shoulder and a hiss from Freddie, demonstrated his famous acceleration. The crowd roared as he forged into the lead and tumultuous cheers rang out as he went past the post to retain his crown, and further enhance his reputation as a truly great steeplechaser.

Jay ran down to the chute where the horses came off the course before going to the winners' enclosure behind the stands. Patting the horse and Freddie's leg alternately he beamed from ear to ear. They met an ecstatic group in the winners' enclosure and huge cheers from the crowds. Again the press and photographers swarmed around them and this time Jay was a little more forthcoming.

'He will probably have one race between now and Cheltenham. Of course the Gold Cup is our main objective,' he announced.

Photographs were taken, more questions answered, and a steaming Splendid Warrior was led out to the dope box, which would be followed by a wash down before being returned to his stable.

Jay joined his party in the owners' and trainers' bar, but declined a drink other than glass of sparkling mineral water. However, he promised this would change when the afternoon was over. Now all eyes turned to the TV screen where the big race from Huntingdon was about to be shown. Howard was as nervous as a kitten.

'Do you think young Paul Jenkins is up to it?' he asked Jay for the twentieth time since the decision had been made to let the young man ride the horse.

'He wouldn't be on him if I didn't think so,' Jay assured him. 'He rides him for nearly all his work at home, he schools him every time except when Freddie's been up, he's watched video tape after video tape. I've got total confidence in his ability, not just to look after The Conker but to give him a thundering good ride. Do remember though that this is a handicap, and he's carrying plenty of weight.'

All eyes were glued to the television screen. They saw that the horses were already at the start and The Conker's gleaming dark chestnut coat was soon evident. The crowd who were watching the race on the big screen on the race track murmured as the race started, and a few of Jay's trainer colleagues in the bar wished him good luck.

The race was a very competitive one and The Conker was carrying top weight. However, Paul was able to knock a few pounds off his back as he still qualified as a conditional jockey. With a circuit to go The Conker was lying third, and much to Jay's relief the pace had been a strong one from start to finish. At this stage Jay took a long and nervous pull on his cigar as he watched what Paul did.

As if he was receiving a telepathic message from Jay, the young jockey pulled The Conker to the outside of the two in front of him and made his way towards the first fence down the back straight, taking up a position in the middle of the fence. The Conker put in one of his famous leaps and was in the lead. At this stage, instead of sitting quietly, Paul decided to use his horse's stamina and with a slap on the shoulder he upped the tempo leaving all but two of his rivals in his wake.

One of them set off in pursuit but The Conker kept up a relentless gallop and jumped the next two fences fluently. Turning for home he had now built up a commanding lead of four or five lengths with only two obstacles in his way. Paul sat quietly on the horse as he approached the penultimate fence. Knowing how well the horse jumped at home he went steadily into the fence and the chestnut cleared it majestically. Galloping on to the last fence Paul had a quick look over his shoulder. He saw that he was a good ten lengths in the lead from My Special Rascal. This time he steadied The Conker as he went into the last jump and again the chestnut popped over it with no trouble at all. Cheers greeted him from the enthusiastic crowd as he passed the winning post. The same was true of the crowd watching the TV in the centre of the course, and the small ones in the Kempton bars.

Although he hadn't started as favourite he was always a popular horse. This was due to his front running tactics and the fact that as one commentator had said: 'This little horse never gives up.'

Back at Kempton Howard was jumping up and down, hugging Bubbles and shaking everyone's hand.

'Well, that was easy!' he exclaimed.

'Very,' agreed Jay. 'We were lucky to get him there, you know.' Howard looked serious for a moment and nodded.

'It doesn't matter now,' he grinned. 'I'm a very happy man because I had a bet on him as well as the prize money.'

'Somebody won't be happy,' said a thoughtful Victor. Howard looked puzzled. 'I mean the person who put lumps of money on The Rascal and clearly expected The Conker not to get to the race course.'

There was a moment's silence and a touch of gloom was evident as the unpleasant incidents of the past few months came back to them. It was nearly time for them to attend to Pewter Queen and the conversation quickly turned to her chances.

'Are you going to make it four in an afternoon?' Victor asked Jay rather anxiously.

'It's a very tough race, and the ground is not ideal for her but really she should win it. However, we have to recognize that Blackthorn Bank and Martha's Joy are extremely good horses and will probably prefer this fast ground. Let's keep our fingers crossed.'

A few minutes later they were all clustered in the parade ring waiting for the beautiful grey mare to appear. Ears pricked and totally relaxed she strode around looking every bit the queen as Freddie joined them.

'What do you think?' demanded Howard.

'It's a hot race,' replied the Irishman. 'I would be happier if we were at Sandown or somewhere with a stiffer finish. We know that she is a class animal and she always runs her guts out. By the way, I suppose there won't be any more rides on The Conker for me, will there, Howard?'

'Perhaps if Paul gets injured,' was the mischievous response.

A few minutes later the horses were cantering past the stands and, although it was a valuable race, there was no parade this time.

The tape was released and the race was run at a

scorching pace. Freddie very sensibly played his normal waiting game staying as close to the rails as possible to go the shortest distance. Halfway down the back straight for the final time he had gently coaxed Pewter Queen up to fourth position as the race started in earnest. Daylight appeared very quickly between five horses and the remaining nine. Jay peered intently through his binoculars.

'Freddie's having to work on her already. This doesn't look too good,' Jay remarked to Eva. Jumping the next hurdle Pewter Queen was relegated to fifth place, and she cleared the obstacle with nothing like her normal fluency. A hundred yards later there was a gasp from the crowd as the race course commentator announced that Pewter Queen had been pulled up.

To Jay's relief Freddie did not jump off the horse. This is normally a sign of real concern about lameness. Instead he gently walked her back to the stand where he jumped off and where Jay and the stable lass met him.

'There is something just not right, Jay. She was never going like the Pewter Queen we know of old, and there was just nothing there when the pace increased.'

Jay looked carefully at the horse's head. There were no tell-tale signs of blood in her nostrils which could indicate a burst blood vessel.

'I don't think it's that,' said Freddie. 'Obviously a scope will show. She didn't stop as quickly as they normally do with a burst vessel. It was just that she never seemed to be going that well after the first circuit.'

Whilst they were standing talking about Pewter Queen's performance an official came over and said that the stewards had ordered that she should have a dope test. This was in view of the fact that she had been a heavily backed and extremely disappointing favourite. Jay was not in the least surprised. Accompanying the mare to the dope box he asked the vet if he would give her the once over at the same time, which was agreed.

'Nothing wrong with her legs,' he assured Jay. 'Her heart seems fine. Tomorrow you should do a separate blood test and have an examination with an endoscope. Clearly that run was just not up to her normal performance.'

Although disappointed, the fact that nothing desperate seemed wrong with their star grey mare left them able to celebrate the three earlier wins.

'You will be nudging for the top place in the trainers' table depending on how your two rivals have done at the other meetings,' pointed out Victor who seemed to be preoccupied with this aspect of the season.

Jay gave him an old fashioned look. 'We won't get too excited yet. There is a long way to the end of the season. There is big money at a number of courses as well as New Year's Day at Cheltenham, the Cheltenham Festival, and then there's Aintree. I'm not saying that we can't do it, but let's not count our chickens,' he warned them.

For once Howard, Hal and Victor did not come back to County View to join in the celebrations. Howard had got his grandchildren coming over, and Bubbles had laid down a three line whip that he would be there. Victor had some social engagement which Jay suspected probably included playing some serious poker. He seemed preoccupied and not his normal self.

Jay and Eva put Fiona in the chauffeur-driven car they had arranged for her. They wished her a happy time for the next few days in London, and told her how much they looked forward to seeing her upon her return to County View.

'Let's go and have a glass of champagne,' said Jay. 'I've not had a drink all afternoon and I think we deserve a little celebration. After all, we have got the helicopter waiting for us.'

On their way into the bar more congratulations were showered on Jay, but eventually he and Eva found a corner where they were able to open a bottle of champagne with a degree of privacy.

They had barely sat down when an extremely sun-tanned and well dressed young man approached them accompanied by a stunning-looking oriental lady.

'Good afternoon, Mr Jessop, my name is Roddy Clinton-Bowes and this is my wife Jerline. I know now is not an appropriate moment to talk to you but I would very much like the opportunity to have half an hour of your time – either in London, or I would be happy to drive down to your training establishment. I understand it is somewhere in Gloucestershire.'

'You're right,' nodded Jay. 'Can I ask you what it is about?'

'I have one or two friends who would be interested in forming a syndicate owning two or three good National Hunt horses and you are one of the trainers we would most like to discuss this with.'

'I would be very happy to meet you and have a chat,' said Jay. 'I have to warn you though that we have a number of inflexible criteria when it comes to taking on new owners.'

168

'I understand. When would be convenient?' asked Roddy.

'If you give me your card I will give you a call when I get back to Gloucestershire, probably tomorrow,' Jay told him. 'I need to look at our racing plans over the next few days. I am very happy to meet you in London, but perhaps it would be more sensible if you came and saw what we have to offer, in case we do come to some sort of agreement. If you don't mind I suggest we leave it until after New Year's Day.'

So far Jerline had stood dutifully and silently next to her husband. She suddenly smiled and her whole face lit up.

'I love racing, and I think that thoroughbred horses are the most beautiful creatures in the world,' she announced. 'Would it be a great inconvenience if I joined Roddy?'

'Of course not,' answered Jay.

'You would be more than welcome,' added Eva. 'Make sure that you have some old flat shoes with you. It's the only comfortable way of getting around at home, and it also saves you throwing away really nice footwear,' she smiled.

'Thank you,' she replied with a repeat of her dazzling smile.

With that they shook hands with Jay and Eva, and with little bows they disappeared into the throng. Eva looked at Jay.

'What do you think?' queried Eva. Before replying Jay read out the business card.

'Roddy Clinton-Bowes, RCB Ltd. Venture Capital and Financial Advice.' Underneath was an address in Canary Wharf, land line, mobile phone and fax numbers plus an e-mail address.

'Judging from the address and their appearance they are not short of a penny or two,' commented Eva. Jay thought for a few moments as he sipped his champagne.

'Appearances can be deceptive, but that name rings a bell with me. I'll get on to Percy and see what he knows about our new friend Roddy. There's not much that goes on in the City without him knowing about it.'

With that they changed the subject and relived the excitement and the one disappointment of the afternoon. When they had finished their champagne they then made their way back to the helicopter and almost before they realized it they were descending on County View.

Evening stables had been completed and the staff had set up trestle tables in one of the empty hay barns and were all set for a big dinner and a night of merriment. Nearly all of them had put bets on the stable's hopefuls that afternoon, hence they were all feeling particularly cheerful. Danny told Jay and Eva that they would be most welcome, and Jay promised that he would call in for a short while to show his appreciation of their efforts over the holiday and how much he valued the teamwork they demonstrated time and time again.

Jed was back and in high spirits. He gave the two of them and Cathy a graphic description of everything that had happened since he and The Conker had left County View.

Shortly after this the telephone rang and Jackson told Jay that questioning of those arrested had already begun, and he would come back to Jay in the morning. It appeared that the driver of the unmarked horsebox was innocent, and had been told

that it was a normal switch of horses as the ownership was being changed. He could see no suspicious
circumstances until they went into the lay-by.

'I don't think he would have got to the intended
destination,' Jackson suggested. 'I fear the horse may
not have lived to tell the tale, or alternatively the
driver would have been dumped and one of the
crooks would have driven the box to wherever they
had in mind. The significance of all this underlines
the fact there is some considerable organization and
money behind events. On the other hand we should
get some information from this little bunch we have
got under lock and key.'

Jay and Eva returned to their comfortable sitting
room where Jay opened another bottle of champagne, and invited Jed and Cathy to join them.
Although almost teetotal Cathy did enjoy half a
glass as they celebrated an eventful and highly
successful day. This left Jed and Jay with the lion's
share as Eva drank water on the excuse that she had
already had enough, and too much gave her a head-
ache. Whilst they were chatting the horsebox from
Huntingdon arrived. Jed met the horse with a huge
grin on his face. Having had total responsibility that
day, it took him back to the time when he trained
himself. The Conker had been his stable 'star' before
he joined forces with Jay. Once the chestnut had been
settled he wanted to hear all the news from Kempton. He knew the results, of course, and was clearly
concerned that Pewter Queen had not figured.

'We'll have a good look at her when she gets back,'
he said. Two glasses of champagne later, the horsebox arrived from Kempton. The three horses were
unloaded and taken to their boxes, where Jay and Jed
gave them a thorough check. The two winners were

in fine form so they made their way to Pewter Queen's box.

'I don't know if it is anything to do with a bad run, but she has come heavily into season since the end of the race,' said the stable lass.

'That could do it,' said Jed. 'I still think we should have her checked out in the morning.'

'I'll phone Chris tonight,' said Jay. 'Let's hope he's not in the north of England.'

Jed looked puzzled, but Eva jumped in and, to Jay's amusement, announced, 'He has family up there somewhere. I think they are also spending time with his sister.'

Jed and Cathy excused themselves, but said they would put in an appearance at the party a little later. Jay and Eva changed into casual clothes and rang Fiona before walking over to the barn where the party was in full swing. The two of them split up and wandered about, as did Jed and Cathy, chatting to little groups individually and making sure that everyone knew how much they were appreciated. The atmosphere, after such a successful afternoon, was buoyant although the lass who looked after Pewter Queen was clearly concerned at the mare's poor form that afternoon.

'There is nothing we can do about it tonight,' Jay assured her. 'Enjoy yourself and let's see what the vet says in the morning. It doesn't look very serious.' After about forty-five minutes Jay stood on a bale of hay and clapped his hands.

'This isn't going to be a speech. All I want to do is thank you all very much. I can't believe there is a team in any racing yard in Britain that is as good as this one. Enjoy yourselves but remember we all have to start at the crack of dawn tomorrow.'

One of the lads called for 'three cheers' and with these ringing in their ears, Jay and Eva gave their happy band a wave and left them to enjoy themselves without being restrained by the guv'nor's presence. A few moments later Jed and Cathy did the same and the party was soon in full swing with music pumping out across the yard from an imported disco.

Chapter Twenty-Two

First thing the next morning Jay checked his voice mail to find a number of messages, most of them congratulations on the previous day. The most important one was from Chris who promised Jay that he would be with him by half past ten at the latest.

Joining Jed in the yard Jay said that he would like to ride first lot himself, so would Jed take on the role of watching the whole string. Jed agreed. The gallop went without incident and Jed had only positive remarks to make when they returned to the yard.

While the second lot were being prepared, Jay arranged for yesterday's runners, with the exception of Pewter Queen, to be turned out in three small adjoining paddocks. The opportunity for some freedom and a quiet pick would do their minds a lot of good, even if there was not much nourishment in the grass at that time of year. The three grooms were instructed to keep an eye on them and then bring them in. Jay returned to his house and invited Jed to join him for a cup of coffee and their usual slice of toast. Eva was already busy in the office ploughing through the paperwork and getting the entry forms for the next few days in order so that Jay and Jed could go through them later. She had already determined that there were no declaration deadlines for that morning.

Before they had finished their break and modest intake, the door opened and in walked Chris followed by Amanda.

'I hope you don't mind me coming along but I wanted to hear everything about yesterday. Although I did watch the races on the television, I am very interested in Pewter Queen,' she said.

'No problem,' replied Jay. 'I'm afraid your horse has already been exercised, so there is nothing for you to canter as we're having a light day. You could always go with the walkers if you want to.'

'That's OK, I have been riding my old point-to-pointer every day whilst I have been at home so I shouldn't have lost too much fitness.'

'Let's go then,' said Jay, and the four of them went over to the yard. He quietly but fully told Chris of the events of the day before, and repeated both Freddie's and the racecourse vet's comments. Taking the horse's temperature and checking her heartbeat Chris could find nothing obviously wrong. Her tendons were fine and there was no sign of soreness in any of her feet.

'I would like to get her over to my place,' said Chris.

'Fine,' replied Jay. 'It will be a little while as I have got to ring Harry who is having a day off, and arrange for him to take the box over. I would normally do it myself but I really have got too much to do this morning.'

'I'll do it,' volunteered Jed.

'No you won't – doctor's orders as you know full well,' said Jay.

'Let me do it,' said Amanda. 'I've driven my horsebox all over the country to point-to-points, and it's certainly no smaller than your two-horse vehicle.'

175

'Are you quite sure?' asked Jay.

'Absolutely. I'll follow Chris over at a sensible pace, and bring her back when he's finished. The more experience I get of seeing vets at work, the better it is for my studies at Cirencester.'

'OK,' agreed Jay. 'I'll get over in about half an hour. Is that too soon?'

'Make it an hour to be on the safe side,' suggested Chris. 'I have got to do the tests, and we won't know the results of some of them until tomorrow. On second thoughts why bother? It's going to be very easy for me to come back here and I can let you know what I think at that stage.'

With the various pressures on him, the heavy workload and the strain of the past few days, Jay agreed. Within fifteen minutes the box was on its way out of the yard and the two men returned to the house to review the workload and racing commitments up to and including New Year's Day. The morning flew by. Before they realized it the horse-box was turning back into the yard. Hurrying out to meet Chris, Amanda and the Queen, Jay was obviously concerned about the outcome. Chris said to Jay, 'The one thing I can tell you is that she has certainly got some muck in her lungs. It's not a huge amount, but it is certainly enough to affect her racing, and we will know more when we get her blood test results. I don't think you need be unduly concerned, but I would suggest that she is only walked around for the next few days until we get the final analysis.'

'So you don't think it's anything to do with her coming into season?' asked Jay.

'It might be, but she's never been affected before, has she?'

176

'Not that I can think of.'

'Well then, let's see the test results. My bet is she is not quite one hundred per cent,' the young vet said.

The relief on Jay's and Jed's faces was obvious and as it was now past 12.30 he invited the two young people to stay for lunch. There was some hesitation before they turned and looked at each other then Chris grinned and said, 'That would be great.'

They all went in and cold food, including left-over turkey, was served along with hot bread, a cheese board and a large bowl of salad. Everyone tucked in while chatting about the three successes of the previous day. After finishing his coffee, Chris got up and, turning to Amanda, said, 'I need a quiet word with Jay before we leave.' He walked into the office and closed the door. 'I have found out a bit about the vets. I am assured that two of them are above reproach although I don't know them personally. Another has got a reputation for not keeping his clients and there is a rumour that he is having some financial difficulties. The interesting thing is that all four of the remaining yards are served by the same vet. His name is Derek Franks and he has a less than good reputation. As far as his professional skills are concerned, there is no question that he is competent. He is, however, known to be a serious gambler who is always looking to make a fast buck.'

'Thanks a lot,' said Jay. 'By the way, you and Amanda seem to be getting on well.'

'We are, and to be perfectly honest I spent Christmas with her at her parents'.' Jay didn't look unduly surprised. Chris continued, 'A few days before Christmas, her mother, Maria, phoned me and said that it was probably a bit of a surprise but she wondered if I would like to come up and spend

177

Christmas with them. She hadn't mentioned the invitation to Amanda who had spent a full week alone with her parents since college broke up. Maria thought that she had done her parental duty, but she thought that Amanda was too shy to ask me, but would love me to come. I was going to spend Christmas with my sister, her husband and their kids, and frankly it would not be much of a rest from my point of view. The kids drive me mad with their bad behaviour. So I said that I would be delighted to come. The next day I got a call from a rather hesitant Amanda, asking me if I would like to go there for Christmas, not knowing that her mother and I had already had a conversation. I said that nothing would please me more. There you have it in a nutshell.'

'That sounds great! I hope you were a good boy.'

'It's really none of your business,' said a grinning Chris, 'but the answer is no.' Jay roared with laughter and putting his arm around Chris's shoulder they walked back into the kitchen. The girls had obviously heard the laughter.

'What was that all about?' enquired Eva.

'Just a dirty joke and much too vulgar to repeat in front of either of you,' said Jay.

'OK, we have taken up enough of these nice people's time. Let's get going,' Chris said to Amanda. They said their goodbyes and left. Eva shot Jay an enquiring look and he relayed the conversation to her.

'It looks as if we have got a budding romance on our hands.'

'I told you so,' she reminded him.

They were sitting relaxing before evening stables when once more the telephone rang. This time it was

Harvey Jackson. 'I've got some news for you,' he said. 'We have had some co-operation from the four crooks we caught yesterday. Two things have emerged. Separately they have all said that the man who contacted them spoke good English with a slight foreign accent. Only two spoke to the caller more than once. One of them tried 1471 but it was, of course, a public call box. One of them spoke to the caller several times and he thought the accent was South African. He worked there for a while helping train security guards after he came out of the army. The other information is, not surprisingly, that they say they had nothing to do with the three murders. They all really did not seem to know anything about Mrs Joyce, and are all adamant that they had no idea their horse kidnapping job had anything to do with either the murders or Mrs Joyce. In view of the fact that we have already got the people responsible for Mrs Joyce, I think it's probably fair to say that there is no direct connection. However, I will e-mail to you all their names and addresses and perhaps you could get your friend Benny to check out if there is anything he can dig out about their background, or if there is any connection between the two gangs. I'll do our normal background search.

'That's all for the moment, but I do feel that we are making some progress. By the way, well done for yesterday. I must say that ever since I have become involved with Giles and you,' he added, 'I've taken an entirely new interest in horse racing, your runners in particular. Talk to you soon, keep in touch.' With that he hung up.

Jay told Eva of the latest developments then rang Benny who listened and then thought for a moment. 'I'll find out as much as I can about these four men,

179

though I have told you most of what I know about Mickey Lane and his crew but the others are bound to be pretty well known by some of my contacts. The South African voice is interesting and may well give me another avenue to follow.'

Jay rang Giles who had already been informed by Harvey Jackson. Jay then added the information that Chris had given him about the vets.

'Have you told Harvey this?' asked Giles.

'No, I completely forgot.'

'OK, I'll do that,' promised the Jockey Club man. 'I have to talk to him anyway about something completely different. I will also ask our head vet to enquire about the two suspect vets.'

'Thanks a lot,' replied Jay.

'By the way,' said Giles. 'What are your running plans between now and Cheltenham?'

'Between now and New Year's Day I've got entries at Chepstow, Newbury, Taunton and Haydock, but haven't finalized my plans. On New Year's Day I'll have two or three at Cheltenham, one at Leicester and probably one at Fontwell. I'll let you know when the plan is finalized.'

'I see from the *Racing Post* that you are now second in the Trainers' Championship and only a few thousand pounds behind Harry Solomons. Depending on how the two of you do over the next few days you could probably go into the lead.'

'I know, it's all very exciting,' replied Jay.

A little later Howard rang to ask how his horses were and was reassured that The Conker was bursting with vim and vigour and that Pewter Queen didn't look too bad.

'I will try to get down to Cheltenham,' he told Jay. 'I am not quite sure what Bubbles has arranged with the family, and she's been really good about my increasing time spent at the racecourse.'

'I know, but it's lovely to have you there when we do race, and Bubbles too of course.' Barely had he finished talking to Howard when Victor telephoned. He immediately launched into the season's statistics and wanted to know not only who Jay was running and where, but also the sort of prize money involved, and what Jay thought about each horse's chances. He was always enthusiastic about County View's runners, but he seemed to be particularly excited about the possibility of Jay winning the Championship.

He then asked if there were any developments on the attempted kidnapping of The Conker, and Jay just said that the four crooks were still being questioned. In view of the fact that the information had been passed to him by the police, he thought it might be incorrect to spread it around, even to such close associates as Victor and Howard.

By noon the next day Jed and Jay had mapped out the plans up to and including New Year's Day at Cheltenham, Leicester and Fontwell. With a total of eight horses running it was going to be a very busy time. Not only would Jay's two horseboxes be fully occupied, he had also made provisional arrangements with one of the horse transport companies to take some runners to certain of the courses he had provisionally mapped out.

Jay had a strict rule when he used public transport. Only his own horses travelled by this method in any one box. This helped minimize the risk of infection from another yard. He had to pay a premium price for this privilege, particularly at such a busy time as New Year's Day.

They had barely finished their conversation when Jenny, Matt Jenkinson's widow, rang. After exchanging a few pleasantries with Eva, who had answered the phone, she spoke to Jay. 'Jay, I know this is a tremendous nerve and I am asking you for something you don't normally do, but I am stuck in getting one of my runners to Leicester and I know that you are planning to run one of yours there. I have tried all around Lambourn, and the only public transport available going to that course is the one you have already pre-booked. I just wondered if you could do me an enormous favour and let me share it?

'I am quite happy for your vet to come over and blood test the horse, but touch wood, we seem to be clear of any viruses since before poor Matt was murdered.'

Jay sucked his teeth for a moment and then replied, 'OK, but don't let it be known.'

'Of course,' she replied. 'By the way,' she added, 'I was having a drink in our local pub last night when one of the regulars came over and had a quiet word with me. He has a bit of a reputation with the police so didn't want to go to them. Something had happened early on the morning that Matt was murdered which he thought just might be of interest.

'A guy on a motorbike in full gear stopped him and asked him the way to our gallops. Obviously he was unrecognizable under his helmet, but having thought about it since my husband's murder, he thought I ought to know. As far as he could tell the man was a bit above medium height, well built with a South African accent. He is quite certain of the accent because his sister is married to a South African. He visits them from time to time whenever he can afford it, and they come over here too.' Jay paused to let all this sink in.

'Bless you,' he said. 'I am going to let Harvey Jackson, the senior policeman in charge of this investigation, know this. He will probably want to talk to you, and he will certainly want to talk to your contact. Don't say anything to him at the moment, but I know that Harvey is discreet and won't make any waves unless your guy is hiding something.

'Jed or I will ring you to let you know what time we will pick your horse up, and I hope it runs well for you. I certainly won't be there, but if Jed or Danny are not there you can be sure that I will send a very experienced person to be on hand, as well as the groom looking after our horse.'

'Many, many thanks,' she said. 'I have only one other runner that day and it's likely that I will go with this horse anyway. He probably stands a better chance of at least being placed than the other one. If that happens then Terry will go with the one we fancy the least. Thank you again and let me know what the police say.'

'Of course, and good luck with your two runners.'

The period between Boxing and New Year's Day proved to be profitable for County View. Soulful Sound won the bumper at Newbury, Mythical King was second at Taunton where Pegasus won a very uncompetitive steeplechase and Keep Rocking was third in a novice hurdle at Chepstow. The one disappointment was at Haydock where Opening Bid fell at the second and came back very bruised. The other runners were perfectly satisfactory and added a helpful total to Jay's winning prize money. The trainer who was third drew a complete blank, but Harry Solomons did have one £10,000 winner from the only horse he ran. The gap between them was now down to less than £55,000. With all the racing coming up the margin was not particularly significant.

New Year's Day arrived with a great deal of excitement at the yard. Jay was sending My Final Fling to run in the handicap hurdle at Cheltenham, and Mrs Harty was coming over from Ireland. See You Sometime was running in the handicap stee-plechase, and Wot A B in the new bumper at the end of the afternoon. All three were in with really good chances, and the yard was particularly excited about Wot A B's opportunity in a seriously competitive race. Peter's Pall was running at Leicester with Jenny Jenkinson's horse and Friendly Persuasion was going to Fontwell with Jed.

As he had trained in Sussex Jed knew he would meet a lot of old friends, so Cathy insisted that she did the driving. Jay quietly favoured both horses' chances.

Mid-morning Chris rang to say that all the tests had come back and indicated that Pewter Queen had a mild infection. He thought it would be best to isolate her, and Jay advised him that he had done this the minute Chris had left the yard. He had told people that there was something slightly amiss with her, and he was just hoping he had isolated her in time and that nothing had passed on to the other horses that had gone to Kempton with her.

'Let's keep a close eye on them and I will blood test them later today on my way back from Cheltenham,' said Chris. As an afterthought he added, 'Amanda and I are going to lend moral support though I doubt very much that you will need it.'

'You always need luck,' responded Jay with feeling.

184

Arriving at Cheltenham with Eva, Jay went through his customary routine of checking the horses before going and checking that the declarations were in order. The pair of them then went to Barry Cope's Fish Bar, where they found Victor and Fiona. They were quickly joined by Mrs Harty and her sister-in-law. The ladies joined them in a glass of wine, but had had a late breakfast, so passed on the food. Howard had rung to say he would not be able to make it for family reasons, but would be watching it on television. It was a complete scrum in there as Jay guessed it would be. He had rung Barry in advance and ordered all of them a cold lobster salad with a bottle of dry white wine. He had also taken the precaution of having two bottles of sparkling mineral water put in an ice bucket as well.

Managing to get one of the small round stand-up tables, they tucked into their lobsters while chatting about the prospects of the day. Eva and Fiona were full of their normal enthusiastic optimism, but Victor was asking even more searching questions than he normally did.

'Have you got a big bet on today?' Jay asked him.

'Not at all. You know how seldom I bet, but I'm really interested in County View doing well and for you to become the Champion Trainer. That to be honest is my main interest in this afternoon. A good afternoon here and at the other two meetings could put you in the lead as long as neither of your two main rivals have bonanzas.'

'All we can do is wait and see,' was Jay's reply. 'It's in the lap of the gods now.'

After another glass of mineral water he left the three of them, promising to see them in the parade ring in a few moments once he had saddled See You Sometime, his runner in the first race.

There was a field of nine in See You Sometime's Handicap Chase and, with the winner's prize money of £16,000, it was sure to be a competitive race. Paul had gone off to ride at Leicester, so Freddie had all three of Jay's rides at Cheltenham. He was very familiar with See You Sometime so there was no need for any instructions.

The first mile was run at a snail's pace and Jay was beginning to worry that it would turn into a sprint at the end, which would not necessarily be to See You Sometime's advantage. He was near the bottom of the weights, and a searching gallop would be to the disadvantage of those carrying a stone or more than him. As if sensing Jay's worry, Freddie smoothly took See You Sometime into the lead as they went down the back straight and turned for home. This encouraged two of the other runners to go with him and gave Freddie the chance to slot into third place on the rails.

They were all seasoned handicappers and there were no falls as the field streamed past the stand and on to the last circuit. One horse made an error at the open ditch and lost so much ground that the jockey pulled him up. By the time they got to the top of the hill the two leaders had put a good twenty lengths between themselves and the pack.

However, at this stage, the favourite, a big grey horse, emerged from the chasing group and made steady and impressive headway to join the leading three as they went down the hill. Turning for home Freddie decided to use See You Sometime's weight advantage, and injected further pace into the race as they started the climb up the hill. His two previous companions at the head of affairs faltered, but the grey came strongly upsides as, neck-and-neck, they approached the second last.

Both cleared it with ease and landed full of running. Freddie got down to seriously pushing See You Sometime with hands and heels. Approaching the last there was still nothing between the two horses and both jockeys were now furiously at work. They flashed past the post neck-and-neck and from the stands Jay had no idea what the outcome would be.

By the time he had got to the chute the announcement came that See You Sometime had been beaten by a short head. He walked with the horse into the winners' enclosure where he was met by Joan and Don Dalling who had owned the horse since he was a youngster, when he had been trained by Fiona and ridden by Jay.

'Bad luck,' sympathized Jay. 'It was touch and go.'

'Don't worry at all,' said Joan. 'This horse just gets better and better. This is definitely the hottest race he has run in.'

'As long as he comes back in one piece, you know we are always happy,' her husband added.

'Well, he certainly seems to have done that,' agreed Jay.

After a quick word with Freddie, Joan and Don excused themselves.

'We have got a long drive home, you know, and we would like to beat the worst of the Bank Holiday traffic,' they commented. 'I'll call you in the morning and let you know how the old fella is,' said Jay. After a peck on the cheek from Joan and a firm handshake from Don, Jay turned his attention to the next race. This was My Final Fling, Kate Harty's pride and joy, named by her late husband before he had died. The horse had turned out to be a top class handicap hurdler and one of the characters of the yard, of whom Jay was particularly fond. My Final Fling was running in the most valuable hurdle race of the afternoon which was worth £20,000 to the winner and had attracted eighteen runners. Having previously been placed at the Cheltenham Festival, and won races at a number of the major tracks in the UK, it was not surprising that he was one of the three most heavily backed horses. He was normally ridden by young Paul Jenkins, but this afternoon it was going to be Freddie's responsibility. Kate Harty was almost as excited about having the champion jockey riding for her, particularly as he was Irish, as she was at having her horse run at Cheltenham. She and her sister-in-law bubbled with enthusiasm in the parade ring before the bell sounded for the jockeys to mount. She couldn't resist asking Freddie how he thought the horse would run.

'Oh, I think we will win by at least a hurdle,' he said with a big grin. 'Seriously though, I think we have got a good chance, and I'll be disappointed if we are not in the prize money.'

Unlike See You Sometime's race, the hurdlers went off at a good gallop from the start. Freddie hugged the rail but kept much further behind the leaders than he often did, knowing that the best way to ride the horse was to come with a late run. He also felt the pace was too extravagant for a number of them to last out – particularly up the hill at Cheltenham on the run in. It turned out this was just as well. Approaching the first hurdle down the back straight, one of the horses went desperately lame. Horses had to swerve in both directions to avoid the stricken animal, and a number of heavy bumps resulted. This

188

also led to five of them being put off their stride and hitting the hurdles. Two fell and the three others slowed right down. It was amazing that there wasn't total mayhem, but the whole complexion of the race had now changed.

Freddie, hugging the inside of the track, had managed to avoid nearly all of the confusion and suddenly found himself in third place. This had all happened without him asking for any effort from My Final Fling, but he kept a firm grip of the horse's head and made sure he didn't start his effort too soon. Cruising down the hill and turning for home he was still in third place. By now the two leaders were showing signs of fatigue and Freddie was worried that he would pass them more quickly than he really wanted to. He was saved from his dilemma as an almost completely black horse moved up alongside him and started overhauling the horses in front. Sitting a length and a half behind him and slightly on the outside, Freddie let the horse act as a pacemaker as they steadily overhauled the two long time leaders.

By the time they had cleared the second last they had moved up into first and second places and Freddie was still a little over a length behind the new leader. Remembering the time that Paul had gone too early at the Cheltenham Festival and been pipped on the line, Freddie sat quietly and got up to within half a length of the now strenuously ridden leader. With fifty yards to go, Freddie gave the horse one crack behind the saddle, and immediately got a surge of extra power which took him past the other horse before its jockey had time to respond. Mrs Harty and her companion who were standing in front of Jay were screaming and hugging each other.

189

Off they went to the winners' enclosure where they could greet their hero. Kate Harty was now shedding tears of joy and gave Freddie a huge kiss when he jumped off her horse.

'This is the most exciting day of my life!' she cried. 'I only wish my husband had been here to see him.'

'He's a grand horse,' replied Freddie. 'Thank you so much for giving me such a great ride.' Kate was all for buying a magnum of champagne on the spot until Jay reminded her that he had still got another horse to saddle. He suggested that the two ladies went off to enjoy the celebration and that he would be more than happy to take Eva along after the last race.

By the time Jay had run the gauntlet of the racing press and accepted congratulations of trainers, officials and people that he didn't even know, the time for Wot A B's race was fast approaching. Seizing the opportunity of a couple of moments alone, he walked into the Tote Credit office to have a look at the results from Leicester and Fontwell. Peter's Pal had come second at Leicester, but he noted that Jenny Jenkinson's horse had won. At Fontwell Friendly Persuasion had won by an easy four lengths according to the information on the board. Now satisfied with the afternoon's activities he walked back into the weighing room to get the saddle for Wot A B.

As at Stratford, although on her toes, she behaved perfectly well whilst the equipment was put into place and she was led into the parade ring. She was clearly interested in the world about her but she behaved just as well as she had on the previous occasion.

Suddenly the horse immediately behind her shot

190

forward and attempted to bite her. With a squeal of displeasure Wot A B lashed out, catching the unfortunate stable lad a cracking blow on his shoulder. He was hurled backwards and let go of the leading rein. His horse, sensing freedom, charged across the parade ring, scattering owners and trainers in all directions.

For a few moments pandemonium broke loose as other horses started bucking and kicking, before an official grabbed the loose horse. The young lad had been helped to his feet, and although he was clearly in pain, he did not appear to be badly injured. He was led into the weighing room to be examined by the course doctor in the medical room. Meanwhile the errant horse's trainer had grabbed him and was leading the horse around the ring himself until the jockeys came in. He legged his jockey up and was given permission to take the horse immediately on to the racecourse.

By this time Wot A B had settled down again, but just to be on the safe side Jay walked alongside her groom until she in turn was released on the racecourse to make her way down to the start.

Following her impressive win at Stratford she was joint second favourite out of the field of seventeen. As he watched her going down to the start, standing next to Victor, with Fiona and Eva on the other side, Jay let them know about the results from the other two courses. Victor positively bloomed. 'What about Harry Solomons' horses?'

'Well, he's done nothing here,' came the reply, 'but I didn't look at the other courses.'

'I'll check that out after this race,' promised Victor.

They then turned their attention to the start where fortunately all these young horses were behaving well. After the incident in the paddock the other jockeys were keeping well clear of the rear end of Wot A B. Within minutes they were on their way and, as was normal at Cheltenham in National Hunt flat races, the pace was a generous one. Once again Freddie kept his mount on the rails, and whilst they were all bunched up on the first circuit, he kept her in the middle of the pack. Streaming down the back straight the field started to spread out, and the hill resulted in a number of horses being unable to stay with the leaders.

This time, however, there were still seven horses tightly grouped as they swung down the hill and round the bend into the finishing straight. With a furlong to go there were only a couple of lengths between the first and Wot A B who was now lying in fifth place. Freddie sat quietly on her and moved to the outside of the other four horses. Given a slap on her shoulder she exhibited the same acceleration she had shown at Stratford and she shot into the lead to win by a comfortable three lengths.

The County View team were ecstatic and were soon in the winners' enclosure congratulating Freddie.

'This is a seriously good horse, Jay,' said the Irishman as he jumped off. 'One of the very best mares that I've ever sat on.'

'Let's hope we keep her sound,' said Jay. 'It would be good to go to the Festival or Aintree with her.'

'She won't be much of a price those days that's for sure,' was the reply. Holding firmly on to his saddle, Freddie made his way into the weighing room.

Jay and his two ladies made their way through a small crowd of well wishers but were soon in the owners' and trainers' bar. Moments later Victor panted up to them with the news that Harry Solomons had only had one winner that afternoon, and Jay had now moved into the lead by something in the region of £40,000. They were all very excited and were joined by Chris and Amanda who added to the general sense of euphoria. Kate Harty and her sister-in-law were soon on the scene, with not one, but two magnums of champagne!

If all of them were pleased then Victor seemed overjoyed and was alternately either shaking Jay's hand or patting him on the back.

'You're going to do it, my boy. I always knew you could,' said Victor.

'The season is far from over yet, and just remember that Cheltenham and Aintree are still to come. Harry Solomons could even tie it up if he won the National in which he will probably have two runners and I haven't even got an entry,' cautioned Jay.

'I still don't understand why you didn't enter The Conker,' said Victor.

'I'm not at all sure that he's an Aintree horse,' replied Jay. 'He has had a hard season and I want to have a go at the Midlands Grand National. If we decide to go for Aintree next year, I'll plan his campaign with that specifically in mind. We will also need to know what weight he's going to carry. With his record the handicap is not going to let him off lightly, and he's too small a horse to hump huge quantities of lead around four and a half miles at Liverpool.'

Victor nodded in an understanding if rueful way. 'Well, we have plenty of other irons in the fire,' he replied with his normal enthusiasm. They sat and chatted a bit longer allowing the crowds to dwindle before all of them made their ways home. Fiona was staying at County View for a few days before travelling to Switzerland and then returning to South Africa. Chris and Amanda were also going to County View where Chris was due to take blood samples, and Victor had got a driver waiting to take him back to London. After the hectic period of Christmas and the New Year Jay, Eva and Fiona agreed that they would stay in. Chris took his samples whilst Jay made a belated round of the stables as Danny and Jed were at Leicester and Fontwell.

All was well and it wasn't long before the Cheltenham runners returned in good heart and health. Chris promised that Jay would have the blood sample results as quickly as he could get them processed, and he would telephone the minute he had them. He and Amanda then wished them a cheery good evening and walked off together hand in hand.

'They seem to be going from strength to strength,' commented Eva watching them.

'What's all this about?' asked Fiona. Eva gave her an update on the budding romance.

The next horsebox soon arrived decanting Friendly Persuasion who had won, and Jed who was in high spirits having seen the Cheltenham results. The other horse and Jenny's were staying overnight as it was a fairly long journey, especially as it was likely to be very heavy Bank Holiday traffic. At that moment Jed turned to Jay and asked, 'Hell, how did Jenny Jenkinson's horse run?'

'It won,' replied Jay, 'and it won easily. I am so pleased for her.' Realizing he had not spoken to her, he immediately phoned to offer his congratulations.

'I hear congratulations are in order!' Jay announced.

'I am so thrilled,' she said. 'This was one of Matt's favourite horses and it would have meant so much to him to win a decent race. Of course it will be marvellous for the morale of the yard. You've been a wonderful friend to us, Jay, and I really appreciate everything you have done.'

'That's my pleasure. By the way, with everything else that's been going on, I forgot to ask you how my two youngsters are coming along.'

'They are fine. Both of them have been as good as gold, eat everything we put in front of them, and there is no one in the yard who doesn't look forward to riding them.'

'Have a good time tonight,' said Jay. 'Danny will be good company.'

'So I have found out!' she said with a laugh. 'I'll have to remember to lock both my doors!'

'Good thinking,' chuckled Jay. 'See you soon.'

'Hang on a moment. Any news from the police?'

'Not yet,' he replied, 'but Harvey was absolutely delighted to have the information, and you can be sure he will leave no stone unturned until he is satisfied that he knows whatever was behind the encounter.'

'OK, and I guess from the results I have heard that you must be top of the trainers' tree by now.'

'Probably a seven day wonder,' was Jay's self-effacing reply.

'I doubt it but anyway well done and thanks again. Love to Eva.'

Chapter Twenty-Three

The next day Eva had a call from Roddy Clinton-Bowes asking if it was convenient for him and his wife to come down to County View either that evening or the following day. Eva asked him to hold on. She quickly told Jay of the request and handed him the phone.

'Hi,' he greeted the City man. 'It's entirely up to you when you come. If you come early in the morning you can watch the horses work, or if you come this evening you can have a look around and watch evening stables with me. Whichever suits you better. I'm not sure what time I will be back from Ludlow.'

'I would love to come in the morning, but it would probably make sense if we came down this evening. Would it be all right if my wife came with me?'

'Naturally. What I suggest is that we book you in to stay at the Shepherds Rest, which is nearby. If you arrive by, say, nine thirty, Eva and I will come over and have a drink with you. Then we can meet up again at the yard at seven thirty tomorrow morning.'

'That sounds ideal. Where is this Shepherds Rest?'

'It's very simple. You take the road from Cirencester towards Stroud, and you will see it on your right-hand side. County View is only a mile or two beyond that.'

'That's great. Look forward to seeing you around nine thirty tonight then.'

He put the phone down and said to Eva, 'This might be interesting. At least we may get to the bottom of what it's all about.'

'I'm not so sure I took to that young man, though he was charming,' said Eva. 'His wife seemed rather different.'

'I agree, let's just play it by ear.'

'They seem an interesting couple – I'll be fascinated to know what transpires.'

Both of them settled down to do some office work, whilst Fiona took the opportunity to catch up on her correspondence to South Africa and made one or two calls. They had a quick lunch and then the two girls went off to Cirencester for a shopping spree.

Fiona invited herself to join Jay for evening stables. She excused herself by saying that after twenty-seven years of training horses, she couldn't resist the chance to go round a yard if given the opportunity. 'Even when I was five or six years old my father used to take me round the hunters with him in the evening. Then there were the point-to-pointers, and you know the rest. It's just so deeply in my system that in some ways it's like a drug.'

'I know I'm still a novice compared to you, but I am already totally hooked. I sometimes surprise myself with the way I've taken to training without really missing the race riding. I don't think I lost my nerve, but there was an element of relief when the spartan regime came to an end,' confessed Jay.

As they wandered round from horse to horse, Fiona gave each one an appraising look and an affectionate pat. She reserved her comments for only a handful, but when she spoke it was always relevant and informed. Eventually they reached the box where Pewter Queen was waiting patiently for her evening feed. She had been placed well away from the main yard for obvious reasons. Her girl groom led her out, and the horse had a little snort and jig jogged.

'Well, she certainly looks full of herself,' remarked Fiona. 'She's not going to take long to get back into racing shape.' Jay agreed, adding that he should have all the blood sample reports back by the next morning. He was hoping that not only Queen but all the Kempton runners would receive a clean bill of health.

When they got back to the house Jay dealt with a few routine calls before he joined mother and daughter for a glass of wine. They sat down to eat huge bowls of pasta and salad, which was both an easy dish for Eva to rustle up, and a meal that all three of them enjoyed enormously. Jay treated himself to a brandy and cigar as he watched the recording of the afternoon's racing on television.

As arranged, later that evening Eva, Jay and Fiona drove to the Shepherds Rest and joined Roddy and Jerline who were sitting comfortably in a quiet corner of the bar. Roddy had a cigar and a whisky and water in front of him, whilst Jerline was apparently drinking sparkling mineral water. Greetings and handshakes were exchanged, and everyone sat down. Roddy was excited about the performance of Jay's horses over the previous few days and had certainly done his homework. His wife said less, but it was clear that she was also well informed, and certainly not stupid.

'I suppose we ought to at least touch on business tonight. I am not sure what you are looking for?' Jay pointedly questioned Roddy.

'My father-in-law is extremely well connected, and indeed quite influential in the Far East,' explained Roddy. 'Frankly it's a business opportunity rather than a small syndicate, that really interests us.'

Jay gave no sign of being well aware of the depths of Mr Tang's involvement in the bloodstock industry.

'The Tang Group was founded as a limited company by his grandfather but is now a huge and diversified collection of companies. It also owns some thoroughbred studs,' Roddy continued. 'He would like some sort of interest in both France and the UK and has asked me to do some research for him, and start negotiations where appropriate. We are well on our way to doing a deal with a major flat yard in France, but he felt it would be more interesting to go for a jumping yard in this country.' Jay nodded his understanding but still kept his counsel. Jerline then entered the conversation.

'You see, my father has growing UK business interests, and he is gradually turning his Asian activities over to my two brothers. This will have the advantage, from his point of view, of working them in gently. At the same time it will give him the opportunity to build up what are, in his terms, still fledgling business activities in the UK and the rest of Europe. By having an interest in horse racing on both sides of the Channel it would give him an opportunity to relax a little when he is over here. He is certainly not an old man, but he feels that the time has come to enjoy himself a bit more, and pass some of the pressure on to the next generation.'

'That seems eminently sensible,' agreed Jay. 'To be honest, we are really not looking for a capital injection into County View. We are a very small group of share holders. You have probably discovered that already. I would be surprised if any of the share holders would want to surrender a significant part of their equity, and I am not sure what's in it for them. There's no doubt that Eva and I would be very reluctant to hand over our shares, and we would not be prepared to work in a situation where we didn't have overall control of everything that goes on at County View – which is, after all, our home.'

Roddy thought for a while before he answered. He was obviously a man who was used to money buying him almost anything when it came to business deals.

'You know, I more or less expected that to be your point of view,' was his surprising comment. 'Nevertheless, I can't help feeling that there ought to be some sort of compromise. It seems to us that the critical issue is what we can bring to the table. You don't need money, you have got fantastic facilities and you and your partners own most of the horses yourselves. Those outside owners that you do have are the crème de la crème and their horses, without exception, have outstanding ability or tremendous potential.'

Jay nodded his agreement. Roddy continued, 'The one thing we could add is young bloodstock. We already have excellent studs in Malaysia, New Zealand, South Africa and we will soon be adding France to this list. With the exception of New Zealand, all these are almost totally dedicated to producing flat horses, but it would be very easy for us to select robust and successful staying mares from our paddocks and have them covered by the sort of stallion which would hopefully produce first rate jumping stock. Not only would you have first choice of each year's crop but County View, or your current syndicate, would be given shares in each of the studs that you have interests in. I am sure that the New Zealand one would fit this bill because, as you are aware, New Zealand stock has already proved to be successful in the UK in a number of major jump races as well as in the more run of the mill contests.' Jay had to agree without divulging that he had already shown a significant interest in New Zealand, but had not been able to follow this up simply because of the pressure of work.

'Let me give it some thought. I will have to talk to my partners, and clearly we are not going to rush into anything as major as this. I will be honest and say that I am not turning it down out of hand.'

'We can't ask for more than that at this stage,' said Roddy with a grin. 'I won't shake hands with you tonight because we've not got a deal and I don't expect us to have one tomorrow. If you do show interest, however, we would want you to have a look at the studs, meet my father-in-law who will be here in a few days, and talk it over in detail with your other partners.'

'That sounds more than sensible,' said Jay, and looking at his watch he drained his glass. 'I hope you don't mind if we leave now,' he said. 'We have had some long days and we have got an early start tomorrow as usual.'

'Not at all,' replied Roddy. 'We will both be with you at seven thirty sharp.'

'That won't be a problem,' Eva assured him. 'The landlord is used to having guests who want to be at the yard early in the morning. He will make sure that you don't stay in bed too long, even if you want to!'

'It sounds like being back at school!' Jerline said with a broad smile.

After saying their goodnights, the three of them were soon on their way back to County View. Nobody said anything on the short run back to the house, but once there and sitting around the kitchen table, they looked hard at each other.

'Well, that's certainly not what I expected,' admitted Jay.

'It's not without appeal,' commented Fiona. 'You are not going to be able to get everything you want from Ireland. Anyway, the prices are likely to sky rocket as those you select prove their worth. Your competitors are not going to be slow to knock on some of the doors where you have been most successful.'

'It will be interesting to see what Howard, Hal and Victor have got to say,' said Eva. 'Hal will go along with anything. From his point of view he is only an enthusiastic amateur, but I am not too sure how the other two will feel.'

'Well, there's only one way to find out,' said Jay. 'We will talk to them as soon as tomorrow's over and we have a better idea of how the deal might be set up, and most importantly, whether we trust this young man and his gorgeous wife.'

With that he suggested that they all go to bed, and it was not long before all of them were fast asleep.

The next day dawned clear and dry but with a cutting north wind. Jay was already in the yard when Roddy and Jerline walked in, having parked their car opposite the house and been given directions by Eva. They were sensibly dressed in jeans, polo necked sweaters, sheepskin jackets and what looked like Timberland boots.

As each horse was led out and mounted, Jay gave its name, breeding and racing record to date. He was surprised at Roddy's knowledge, not so much of Jay's horses, although it was quite clear that he knew about most of them, but of their breeding. It was quite clear that he was well informed on many aspects of the bloodstock industry in the UK. It was also interesting to note that he was by no means showing off. In fact, to Jay's further surprise, he seemed almost modest.

As soon as the horses were on the way to the gallops, Jay loaded Roddy and Jerline into the back of the Land Rover, and he and Jed clambered into the front. When they arrived at the gallops he explained that the group were being split into two lots. They would all have a swinging canter to warm up and then, at the start of the second time, eight of them would go off first at a really fast working pace while the rest would come up again at a swinging canter.

'Why is that?' asked Jerline.

'The eight are all due to run in the next few days and need to be sharpened up. All our horses are now thoroughly fit, so it's a matter of keeping them ticking over or honing them for that extra edge before they compete again. They also go for long walks over the adjoining countryside, and there is a farmer nearby who lets me hack them through his woods. All of this helps to keep them fresh and interested, and not become staled by the same routine day after day,' explained Jay.

'One of my cousins was a champion track athlete when he was at college in the States and I can remember him explaining to me the importance of keeping fit but varying his schedule from time to time. I guess it's the same with horses,' said Jerline.

'There are many similarities,' Jay agreed. 'In both, sports science is helping us to learn important ways of improving performance. It is not just training techniques, but also knowledge of correct nutrition and the prevention, as well as the cure, of the inevitable injuries that occur in these highly competitive sports.'

With the work finished they returned to the yard. Jay politely turned down an invitation to join their visitors for lunch.

'I'll talk to my partners and come back to you in a day or two,' he promised Roddy.

'Do you ever come to London?' Jerline asked Eva.

'Quite often,' she replied. 'He occasionally lets me off my chain to go and see friends and do a bit of shopping! I also look after the PR for County View, so sometimes I go up to see a journalist, but more often I meet and talk to them at race meetings, or they want to come here.'

'Any plans in the near future?'

'Strangely enough, I am going up on Friday.'

'I wonder if you would like to meet me for lunch? I don't know many people in London and Roddy is so busy I spend a lot of time alone in the hotel. Either that, or visiting art galleries or going on my own to matinees at the cinema or theatre.'

'I would love to. What sort of food do you like?'

'Anything but Chinese!' was the smiling response. 'It's not that you can't get good Chinese food here, but as you can imagine, we see plenty of it when we are visiting my father.'

'How about fish?'

'I love your English fish,' Jerline enthused.

'Right,' said Eva. 'There's a Wheeler's Fish Restaurant just off St James's Square, and I will meet you there on Friday at quarter past one if that's OK.'

'I really look forward to it,' replied Jerline with a smile.

Eva grabbed a piece of paper and wrote down the address of the restaurant and her mobile telephone number.

'Just in case anything goes wrong at your end,' she explained, handing the paper to the young oriental woman. Jerline tore the piece of paper in half and borrowed the pen to write down her mobile number.

'Just in case you get held up, but I'll assume that we'll meet at one fifteen unless I hear from you.'

'Agreed,' said Eva and shook Jerline's hand.

As the two visitors left Jay gave Eva a slightly searching look.

'You seem to be getting on OK with her,' he commented.

'Actually, I rather like her,' replied Eva. 'You never know, I might find out something useful at lunch from the business point of view.'

'Ah, women's wiles,' sighed Jay, giving her a warm hug and kiss.

They were joined by Fiona, and Eva explained her new arrangements for Friday.

'Don't forget that we are going to the theatre,' Fiona reminded her.

'Of course not, Mother,' said her daughter in a feigned exasperated tone. 'Why do you think I told her I was going to be in London then? Do you want the two of us to go up the night before or are you all right for an early start?'

'I have got a ten thirty meeting with my bank manager. I still haven't got out of my routine of

205

being a trainer. Let's spend the evening with Jay and leave here early in the morning.'

Eva went back to the office leaving her mother to make a few calls and read the paper. She found that there were more comments on Jay's performance over the New Year in the *Racing Post* and, in particular, that the odds on him winning the Championship had shortened, and those on Harry Solomons had lengthened. It seemed that there had been no heavy bets on Jay. However, his high profile on television and in the papers over the holiday period had attracted a small number of punters to cash in on his odds before they shortened further. If he followed up his holiday performances with a string of successes, even at relatively small races, he could widen the gap to a really significant amount.

Hal rang to announce his return from the States. Jay suggested he should come down to catch up with events and the next evening Hal arrived around seven o'clock. In spite of his protests, Jay and Eva insisted he had dinner with them, rather than him taking them out to the Shepherds Rest. After Hal had been given with his customary vodka martini the two men settled down, whilst Eva prepared a simple but tasty supper of avocado vinaigrette followed by rump steak. She remembered that Hal liked his steak almost raw.

'So what the hell's been happening?' asked Hal. Jay proceeded to fill him in right from the initial stages of the murders. As he proceeded through the strange withdrawals of horses, the involvement of the Jockey Club and the police, the kidnapping of Mrs Joyce, and the attempt to snatch The Conker, Hal's expression went from one of amazement to one of concern.

'You're into something pretty damn deep, my friend,' he said. 'From where I am sitting it looks bloody dangerous.'

'I agree,' responded Jay. 'But I don't see what else we can do. Apart from complete support from Giles Sinclair and Harvey Jackson, I've also got my own support team of Benny, and to a lesser extent, Percy Cartwright and his colleague Marvin.'

'Let me think about it for a bit,' said Hal. 'Now tell me about this Roddy Clinton-Bowes.' Jay went on to outline the proposed deal whilst Hal nodded his agreement or understanding as each point was made.

'What do you want to do?' he questioned.

'I'm not at all sure,' Jay replied, 'but it does have a lot of advantages.'

'I can see that,' said Hal. 'From my point of view, I would have no objection to it at all. If you wanted me to surrender my shares I would, but it would be with some considerable sadness and regret.'

'That's the last thing I want you to do. Not only do I respect your friendship, but it's really good to have an experienced outsider like you looking at it from a strictly business point of view.'

'Let me throw another thought into the ring,' said Hal. 'How about if I used some of my contacts in the States, and we add a stud over there to the venture. That would really make us international, although I appreciate that from the United States' point of view, it would be largely flat.' Jay paused for a moment.

'I can't see anything wrong with that. It would give us the opportunity to work in another huge market, and it would also spread our risks to a degree.'

'I think you should have a chat to Howard and Victor about it, and if they see any merit in it, why don't we all meet Roddy Clinton-Bowes. With a double-barrelled name like that he would certainly go down well in the States!' joked Hal as they went in for dinner. As they ate they chatted about County View's successes to date, some of their future plans, and the prospect of Jay winning the Champion Trainers title.

'What's on the menu for tomorrow?' asked Hal.

'I've just got one horse running at Ludlow. It's a nice young horse called Soaring Buzzard. It ran well in a bumper but I have decided to put it straight over hurdles. The good bumpers are getting very competitive and unless there is something extraordinarily talented like Wot A B, they are after all only intended as a preliminary to jumping. Buzzard has been schooled and schooled, and I think would have a very good chance tomorrow, particularly as it's not a very competitive race.'

After more general chat, Hal returned to the pub and Eva and Jay opted for an early night.

The next morning Hal was there bright and early. Jay elected to ride first lot and, allowing Danny to lead the string, came up last. Jed, accompanied by Hal, was sitting in the Land Rover three quarters of the way up the gallops watching what was going on. When he reached the top Jay trotted over to Danny and said, 'Come on, let's you and I have a bit of fun.' First he had a word with Jed to enquire if there was anything worthy of a comment. 'No, all the horses look as good as we could hope and I couldn't see anything unusual. Even the last rider looked reasonably competent,' he joked.

'The last rider, along with his friend Danny here, is

going to have a well earned bit of fun. You supervise this lot and get them back to the yard. Danny and I are going to jump a few hurdles and fences.' Danny looked as surprised as Jed.

'I thought you'd given up that side of the business,' he exclaimed in what was almost an accusing tone of voice.

'Well, you know, I more or less have, ever since I had that leg broken, but I just feel like letting off a bit of steam this morning.'

'OK, you're the boss,' came the reply. 'Don't go mad though. I'm not as young as I used to be either,' Danny reminded him with a grin. 'It's two old crocks upside, isn't it?'

'Dead right,' agreed Jay.

They trotted across to the far side of County View and were just about to line up for the schooling area when the Land Rover came roaring across the gallops. Jay's heart skipped a beat. Oh God, what's wrong now? he wondered as he and Danny waited for Jed to join them. 'What's the problem?' asked Jay.

'Nothing at all. I just couldn't miss the opportunity of seeing you two risk breaking your necks again!'

'That goes for me too!' added Hal. 'I've not seen you on a horse since your glory days.'

'That was yonks ago!' Jay reminded him. 'Let's hope I don't fall off.'

With a cheeky wave Jed put the Land Rover into gear, and parked where he and Hal could see all the flights of hurdles and the schooling fences. For the next twenty minutes the two men had enormous fun. They were both riding highly experienced horses who enjoyed the break in their normal routine. After jumping four flights of hurdles three times they went over and showed the horses the fences. This time Jay decided that discretion was the better part of valour, so he and Danny agreed that they would settle for the middle range. These were still worthwhile obstacles, but were well short of racecourse jumps they had faced when they were both jockeys. At the end of another three runs they trotted over to the Land Rover where Jed and Hal were grinning from ear to ear.

'I suppose I have seen worse,' Jed admitted. 'Did you enjoy it?'

'Enormously. You can see why I still use Danny when I need a real professional to school our horses.'

Jed nodded his agreement. 'I'll get back to the yard and see you two later.'

'I'll chat up your lovely wife and enjoy a cup of coffee,' Hal added.

Jay and Danny trotted their horses halfway home before slowing to a walk to let their two mounts cool off.

Jay walked into the office and was sitting down glancing at the papers when Hal entered the room.

'I've had a telephone call whilst we were up on the gallops. I am going to have to go back to London this morning. However, I think that we have covered everything. Keep me informed, and if there is anything I can do to help you know I will.'

'Thanks, I appreciate it,' said Jay.

Chapter Twenty-Four

Having discussed the morning's activities with both Eva and Fiona, Jay was just about to ring Victor and Howard when his phone rang. It was Benny.

'I've learnt something very interesting,' Benny told him. 'It seems that shortly before the murders, a tanned foreigner bought a revolver and a rifle from a well known guy called Jake in the East End. He's sold weapons illegally for years, but has always managed to avoid the law. The chap said his name was Kruger, and he paid for the weapons and ammunition in cash. However, when he paid Jake he took the money out of an envelope addressed to a man called Jan Strauss. I'll keep checking but I thought you might want to pass that on to Harvey Jackson.'

'Thanks a lot,' replied Jay. 'I'm going to be in London later this week to talk to Howard and Victor, so we can meet up if anything seems relevant.'

'OK, boss. Any information from the kidnappers?'

'Nothing more that I've heard, though I am sure that I will know the minute there is.'

When he put the receiver down he rang Howard and Victor and explained that there had been a development as far as County View was concerned. He felt it important enough for the three of them to get together. They would meet for breakfast at

Simpson's the next morning, a favourite meeting place for business discussions since the early days of County View. Peter, the head waiter, always made sure that they had a completely discreet table in one of the boxes where conversations could not be overheard.

'What's it all about?' queried Victor on the telephone.

'Nothing to do with the kidnappings etc,' Jay told him.' It's all rather complicated but nothing to worry about at all. Let's wait until the three of us meet.'

'All right,' said Victor reluctantly. Howard had taken it all in his stride as usual.

As soon as these calls were over Jay rang Harvey Jackson and gave him Benny's information.

'That sounds extremely interesting,' said the policeman. 'I'll get on to my contacts in South Africa and see if that name means anything to them. I'll also see if immigration has any record of where this man arrived from, and when.

'This Jake sounds interesting. I've not heard of him myself, but I'll have him checked out, and perhaps pay him a visit.'

Later that afternoon, back in County View, they were sitting down having a drink before watching a film on the television when Fiona followed Eva out to the kitchen and said, 'If it's not a delicate question, as a prospective grandmother, is there any news on that front?'

'Not yet,' Eva replied, 'but we are still trying enthusiastically,' she added with a shy smile.

'Hope you don't mind me asking but, as I am sure you can appreciate, I am somewhat interested.'

'Of course, Mum!' Her daughter gave her a big hug and a kiss on the cheek. 'Come on, let's go and join Jay now or he will think we are gossiping about something we don't want him to know about.'

For once they had an almost completely uninterrupted evening as far as the telephone was concerned. At ten o'clock Jay put the land lines on answerphone and his and Eva's mobiles on to voice mail. They had a final cup of coffee and discussed future arrangements for Eva to join her mother in South Africa for two or three weeks as soon as the Aintree meeting was over. Jay promised that once the dust had settled after Liverpool, he would join them too, depending on how the Trainers' Championship was going. If it was clearly lost by then Jed was more than capable of holding the fort in his absence, but if Jay was still in the reckoning, it would be unfair to saddle Jed with that responsibility.

The next morning Jay decided to go to London with the two women leaving County View in the capable hands of Jed and Danny.

He promised not to interfere with their arrangements as there were a few people he wanted to see including touching base with Benny, Giles Sinclair and Percy. This he planned to do after his breakfast meeting with Victor and Howard. Shortly after six o'clock they set off for London, dropped Fiona off at her hotel, and Eva plus their bags at Hays Mews. Eva gave him an affectionate kiss and read the paper for an hour before leaving for her morning meeting with her bank manager. She would then be joining Jerline for a lunch which she viewed with both pleasure and some intrigued anticipation.

Jay parked the car in the garage under his flat and took a taxi to meet Howard and Victor at Simpson's.

When the three of them were sitting at their discreet table, and had ordered their food, the two older men looked at Jay with a degree of expectancy. He quickly filled them in on the proposition that Roddy had put to him. They both paused and Jay was intrigued to see which would be the first to respond. After what seemed like ages, Howard broke the silence.

'Clearly it has a number of plus points, but to a large degree it must be your decision, Jay. You and Eva have put your whole lives into this whereas Victor and I are just enthusiastic and indeed involved partners. As a matter of courtesy we also have to consider Hal's position.' Jay nodded and waited for Howard to continue.

'Personally, I would not want to surrender any of my shares. The venture has worked beyond any of our wildest dreams – at least I think that's right,' he said looking at each of them, and both nodded agreement. 'Being rather conservative, I don't relish changing a winning formula. However, we have to look to the future, and in this sense it's very much your call. The one thing that I am insistent on is that you, Jay, have to retain overall control.' He turned to Victor awaiting his response. Probably to both of their surprise it was totally different.

'Let's face facts. Although it is an enormous amount of fun and provides us all with excitement, it is after all, a business. If we were a public company with a large board of directors and outside shareholders, I have a feeling it would be our duty to recommend that this goes ahead. After all the checks have taken place. To a degree we have to take Jay's assessment of Roddy on trust, though I am sure we would all want to have the young man checked out very carefully. Of equal if not more importance, is to check out Mr Tang and his empire.' The other two nodded agreement. 'How do we do that?'

Jay responded. 'My understanding is that he is in London now, and is anxious to meet all of us. In addition to that my friend Percy at Lloyds has influential contacts all around the world and I know for a fact this includes the Far East. I'm having dinner with him tonight, but I've already phoned him and asked him to put out some feelers.'

'We might have guessed that you wouldn't be slow in safeguarding our interests,' Howard commented with a broad grin.

'When can we meet Mr Clinton-Bowes?' asked Victor. 'I presume it would be sensible to have his son-in-law there as well when we meet Mr Tang?'

'I think that's his call,' said Jay. 'There's no doubt that I want the two of you to meet him as soon as possible. What about the shares?'

Howard looked slightly uncomfortable but Victor showed no such reluctance.

'I would be very happy to surrender a number of my shares,' he volunteered, 'but I would want at least two and a half times my investment for however many that was, plus my minor share in the studs at no cost. After all, we all took the big gamble and are now looking at a proven success.'

'Well, I suppose I would be prepared to lob in a few of mine if it made the difference between the deal going through or not,' Howard conceded, though he did so with less enthusiasm than Victor. 'I repeat, control must continue to rest in Jay and Eva's hands.'

Jay thought for a moment. 'At least it seems that we've got a basis for talking to Mr Clinton-Bowes and his father-in-law before we have to make up our minds. We should also get the response to our enquiries within the next few days at the latest.'

'What about the murders, kidnappings and threats?' asked Victor, changing the subject.

'Nothing new on that front,' replied Jay, feeling slightly dishonest, but sticking by the arrangement he had with Giles and Harvey. After all, neither of them could really add anything to the current enquiries, and it was silly to raise what might be false expectation.

'No new information or theories at all?' queried Victor pursuing the subject.

'None that I am aware of,' Jay replied, feeling even more uncomfortable.

'How are things looking on the Champion Trainer front?' Howard asked.

'I'm not going to change any of the existing plans,' Jay explained, 'but one or two horses I had thought of roughing off until next season I am keeping in training, just in case we could pick up a couple of the lesser races with them. They could still add £50,000 to £100,000 total prize money if it looks as if this sum could be a significant factor.'

'I am delighted to hear it!' said Victor, once more exhibiting his enthusiasm for the idea of Jay becoming Champion Trainer in only his second full season.

'After all,' he added, 'it won't do us any harm when it comes to negotiating the price of any shares we decide to release.'

'That's true,' agreed Howard. 'As Victor said earlier, County View is still a business, although one that means more to us than that by itself.'

They turned to a more general conversation, although Victor somewhat gleefully could not help himself from pointing out that Harry Solomons

216

hadn't had a winner for a couple of days, so Jay's lead remained unchanged.

'It's still only a very slight lead in relation to the potential rewards at Cheltenham and Aintree,' he reminded them.

At this point he left them to continue their chat as Victor was adamant that he would pick up the bill. Knowing full well it would come out of Victor's expenses for one of his several companies, Jay felt no compunction in accepting this.

Jay grabbed a black cab in the Strand and returned to Hays Mews where he had arranged to meet Benny.

The East Ender was waiting outside in his car with Angel but had nothing significant to add to his report. As they entered the flat the phone rang. It was Harvey Jackson. 'Can you talk?' the policeman asked.

'I'm in my flat reviewing the situation with Benny,' Jay told him.

'That might be just as well as I have got some information that your friend might be able to add to. The South African is indeed Jan Strauss, although he has a number of aliases which include the name Kruger. He is well known to the South African police as a one man band who has worked for a number of shady businessmen. He has almost certainly been involved with making threats and is under strong suspicion of being involved in at least four murders. He has also worked as a mercenary in the past on at least two occasions, and is generally considered a very dangerous individual. An interesting new aspect of his character has come to light. He has never been known to be involved in drugs, gambling or too much alcohol. He does, however, apparently have one weakness. Women. He has never been married

217

but frequently employs a high class call girl to be his companion for a few weeks at a time. He never uses the same one twice, and never picks up street whores. After a few weeks he either tires of them or moves on to another destination – presumably for a new job – and never sees that particular young lady again. He is apparently always very generous to them. Also, interestingly enough for someone in his profession, he is not averse to going to high profile restaurants and clubs with these young ladies. Though we have yet to track him down, we have no reason to believe he has left our shores. It seems to me that a few discreet enquiries by your friend Benny might determine whether or not he has indulged in this particular hobby whilst in London.'

'Hang on a moment,' Jay interrupted, 'I'll bring Benny up to date whilst you are still on the phone.' Jay quickly filled his East End friend in on the details so far and waited for the response.

'If he's gone to one of the top class escort agencies it shouldn't be difficult to find out,' Benny promised. Jay told this to Jackson.

'Why am I not surprised at that reply?' chuckled the law man. 'Tell him I have the utmost faith in his ability to deliver.' Jay relayed the message again and Benny roared with laughter.

'Compliments will get him everywhere!'

'I heard that!' exclaimed Jackson. 'Keep me informed and I'll do likewise.'

'Does Giles know all this?' asked Jay.

'Not yet, but I am talking to him later on this morning, and I will tell him then. I'm also interested to know if he's dug anything up on the suspect vet.'

'You're not the only one,' was Jay's reaction – said with some feeling.

'I'll be in touch,' promised Jackson and rang off.

Benny looked at Jay. 'Well, I better get moving,' he said. 'I think that there's a very fair chance that we'll find something. If this guy came to London and is the loner we understand he is, it's unlikely he will have contacts who could put him in touch with the sort of woman he's looking for. My guess is that he will look up the escort agencies in some of the more dubious magazines, or he might even have contacted the hall porter wherever he has been staying. A lot of these guys provide this service as part of their personal perks.'

'OK,' said Jay. 'Get cracking.'

'Sure, boss!' mocked Benny. 'Anything you say, boss!'

'Be off, you cheeky sod!' Jay replied. He got up and opened the door for Benny, giving him an affectionate pat on the back as he went out to his waiting BMW, driven by the faithful Angel. With a last wave Benny disappeared into the car, and with a screech of tyres he was gone.

Jay then telephoned Roddy, and said that he'd met with the other two main partners and that they would like to meet with his father, as well as with Roddy of course. The response was enthusiastic and the young man promised to get back as soon as possible. 'I hear our wives are getting together over lunch,' commented Roddy.

'So I gather, we can both expect our ears to be burning!' Jay replied.

'I bet!' was the response. 'I'll get back to you as soon as I've spoken to my father-in-law.'

'Make sure you give me two or three dates,' Jay cautioned him. 'They are both very busy men.'

'Understood. I'll be in touch.'

By this time Eva and Jerline were sitting at a favoured table in Wheeler's with a bottle of dry white wine in front of them, having ordered dressed crab, followed by grilled sea bass with a side salad. Eva said she had been to see her bank manager on personal matters, and Jerline volunteered she had been to the hairdressers and also had a manicure. It was evident that her immaculate grooming was not entirely self administered. She took a sip of wine and started to talk.

'You're probably wondering why I wanted to have a chat with you, apart from the fact that I don't know many people in London. I think you ought to know one of the reasons why my father is so anxious for this deal to go through. My two brothers have been brought up in the business, even before they left school. They have both had considerable success and are highly regarded in Far Eastern business circles.

'My father is concerned that, although Roddy has been successful in what he has done in London, he is not really a big player in the way that my brothers are. To offer him a role in the family business would mean that he would constantly be compared with my brothers, and to a lesser extent, my father. My father therefore had the idea of finding an entirely new avenue which was interesting from his point of view, while at the same time utilising Roddy's skills both as a business man, an administrator and a negotiator. It would give him a chance to stand on his own two feet. If he makes a success of this he is going to be high profile in his own right.

'Believe me, this is not charity on my father's part. It is a genuine concern that my husband should have a sense of independence and a worthwhile job which he will enjoy. He also knows that it will make me happy if I see Roddy make a real name for himself in international circles rather than in the small circle in which he operates in London.'

Eva thought this over for a moment before replying.

'Your father seems a very wise man and I can see exactly where he is coming from. I must say that Jay and I were impressed by Roddy's knowledge of breeding and bloodstock, and he seems much less aggressive than was our first impression at Kempton.'

'He was very nervous on that occasion,' Jerline informed her. 'If he had been turned down flat, it would have been difficult for him to face my father, though I am sure there would have been other avenues open to us to develop the same concept. He has, however, over the last two years, become an enormous fan of Jay and of County View. This is why he has set so much store by trying to persuade you all to accept this proposition.'

'Well, that's fine, but he is going to have to realize that Jay is the ultimate boss. All the other partners never question that, and whenever there has been one of the very few disagreements, Jay has always won his way. That's not to say that he hasn't been persuaded to change his views from time to time. After all, the other three shareholders are all highly successful men who have backed him unstintingly.'

'Results have proved them right,' concluded Jerline with a broad and charming smile. 'Now let's talk about girlie things.'

'Let's,' said Eva. 'Before we do that, let's concentrate on this delicious-looking sea bass that has just appeared before us.'

221

Jerline agreed, giving Eva another of her dazzling smiles. Whilst this conversation was taking place, not very far away Jay was sitting in Giles's office, bringing him up to date on his conversations with Harvey and Benny. Harvey had already passed most of it on to the Jockey Club security man, but Jay was able to add one or two things about the South African, and their proposed course of action. He did this with the prior agreement of the policeman.

'We've not got anything solid yet on the vet,' volunteered Giles, 'but the feedback is every bit as disturbing as we thought it might be. I am going to invite trainer Flintlock to come and see me, and I am hoping that away from his domain and in the headquarters of the Jockey Club, he might be nervous enough to be a bit more forthcoming than he has been to date. I think that Harvey will put a little gentle pressure on him before that meeting takes place, and he may be worried about losing his licence.'

Changing the subject he then turned to Jay's position in the Trainers' Championship, and also on the betting.

'As you know we keep a close eye on this,' he remarked to Jay, who nodded understandingly. 'So far nothing odd has surfaced, but there's no doubt that it has become a much bigger betting issue than any of us can ever remember before.'

'We could hardly have missed that,' Jay volunteered. 'The trusty Benny is also having a dig around there.'

'What would we do without him?'

'Heaven knows,' was Jay's shrugged reply. 'One last favour,' he added. 'Could you check out a Far East business man called Tang? He has a big group of companies and also some studs.'

'No problem,' promised Giles.

With little else to discuss, Jay was soon on his way to Hays Mews. He found Eva there, recently showered and wrapped in a bath robe, devouring *The Times* and the *Racing Post* which she had not had time to look at earlier in the day.

They exchanged news, and just as Jay was about to enter their little bathroom, Eva called. 'By the way, I have discovered why Mr Tang has the unusual Christian name of Hamish.' Jay stopped and gave her an enquiring look. 'It seems that his father was helped in the early days of building his business by a very influential Scotsman called Hamish. Both his parents were so indebted and grateful to him for his help, that as a matter of respect and gratitude they called their son Hamish.' Jay smiled at the news.

'Also,' Eva added, 'both father and friend lived to a ripe old age, and saw Jerline's father already making enormous headway towards the outstanding position he and his companies command today.'

A few minutes later, feeling totally refreshed, Jay joined his wife on the sofa and they talked about their evening. Eva was very excited about seeing the revival of *The History Boys*, a tremendous box office success of a few years ago. Although Jay was meeting Percy with a business agenda, they were such longstanding friends and had enough in common to ensure that he would have an entertaining, as well as a very useful business conversation.

Eva left first to join her mother for a light supper at her hotel, before going off to the theatre together.

Jay glanced through the papers but found nothing of relevance to any of his current activities, so switched on the Channel Four News. After half an hour of this he briskly walked to Claridge's to meet Percy in the Gordon Ramsay Restaurant.

Percy was well known there and they were given a discreet table in the corner. The Lloyds man was already seated and enjoying a vodka martini which Jay declined in favour of a Tio Pepe on the rocks.

Having both ordered a starter of scallops followed by fillet steak, they got down to the business that was the primary reason for their meeting.

'I've made a degree of progress,' Percy announced. 'Your friend Hamish Tang has an impeccable reputation not only as an extremely shrewd business man but also as a person of impeccable integrity. This was underlined a few years ago when one of his companies undertook a joint venture project with another very powerful Chinese business man. One of Tang's young accountants became suspicious about some of the accounting practices and alerted Tang's financial director.

'He in turn alerted Tang. Although not actually illegal, it was sailing so close to the wind that Tang pulled out lock, stock and barrel even though it cost his company a considerable forfeit at the time. It seemed for a couple of years that for once he had made an error of judgement, but suddenly the stock market authorities became concerned. After an exhaustive enquiry the company was de-listed, the outside shareholders lost a significant sum of money, and Tang's ex-partner was not only discredited but was very lucky not to end up behind bars.

'I have had information from three different sources in the Far East and all of them come back not just with clean sheets but with glowing reports on this man as a businessman and as a human being.'

224

'I look forward to meeting him,' said Jay. He went on to explain what the possible deal might be. This included the role that Roddy would play.

'Don't be put off by Roddy's reputation of being a little on the sharp side,' said Percy. 'He was a little over exuberant when he first started his operation, but he seems to have settled down. There is no doubt it has made steady, if unspectacular, progress. What's more, I imagine that your Hamish will have done some pretty thorough research himself before allowing his daughter to marry him. Remember how important "face" is to the Orientals. Family or not, he would be reluctant to damage his standing or reputation in the Asian business circles in which he is so influential. Including his sons, the family is now in the third generation of building what is now a truly multinational business.'

Jay thanked him for his efforts and felt distinctly reassured. Percy then changed the subject to enquire how the kidnapping, and the other strange and worrying happenings around Jay's yard were developing. Jay felt able to be completely frank in view of the fact that Percy's colleague had been so influential in bringing the kidnapping to a satisfactory conclusion.

'Why don't you contact Marvin again?' Percy suggested. 'He and your Benny seemed to have struck up a very good relationship, and Marvin has his own extensive network, with some of the more dubious members of the less than savoury twilight business involved in extortion, violence and of course drugs and prostitution.'

'I will suggest that to Benny,' promised Jay. 'You have been enormously helpful.'

They finished their cigars and coffee and went

their separate ways. The next morning on their way back to County View Jay and Eva turned to the subject of Amanda's first race. As had been discussed with her father, Jay had supported her application for an amateur licence which had been quickly issued, and the race was only ten days away. Amanda was riding out two lots per day and schooling Elegant Queen twice a week. The two of them really looked like a team, and Jay was quietly confident they would acquit themselves well.

The next few days passed without any major event apart from Fiona coming down to spend a couple of days with them before leaving for Switzerland on her way back to South Africa. She promised Jay she would start looking out for potential National Hunt horses for him, and would also keep her ears open to see if there was any news on the Harry Clough front.

As far as the Trainers' Championship was concerned there was little change in the rankings of Jay and Harry Solomons. Both of them were pulling clear of the now diminishing threat of the trainer placed third, who seemed to be in one of those frequent, but unexplained, losses of form amongst virtually the whole of his stable. Early the following morning, Benny was on the telephone in a state of considerable excitement. Both the time of the call and the tone of his voice were unusual for the East Ender, who was very much in the habit of waiting until after the first lot before calling Jay.

'We've hit the jackpot!' he shouted down the phone. 'We've found a bird who has been with our South African friend for over four weeks. Her real name is Vanessa Green but she works under the name of Vanda Blue.

'We just struck dead lucky. As you know I met up

with Marvin and told him everything. By chance he had been to school with a woman who runs one of the most discreet and most expensive high class escort services. As soon as he had the details he rang the lady and described our South African friend in detail. She keeps a record of the days her girls work, but is very discreet about the names. However, for one client to use one of her birds for that long is, to say the least, unusual. Benny was given an introduction and went to see her. He was given some very interesting information.

'Her client was a South African who called himself Henry Kruger. Still the same surname but a change of first name. He was extremely reticent about what he did, but she got the impression that he had been mainly in the southern part of England. She did, however, overhear one part of a telephone conversation when she was in the bathroom. He apparently got quite angry and said, "I'm still waiting for the second half of my money and I don't like being kept waiting." Evidently the person on the other end of the phone placated him to some degree, because by the time she came out of the bathroom the bad mood seemed to have evaporated.'

'That is interesting,' said Jay. 'I'll let Harvey Jackson know and see what he thinks should be done next.'

'I'm quite happy to go round and see her again,' Benny volunteered, 'but I am not sure if a policeman, and a particularly senior one, would not get more out of her. After all, these escorts are very cautious about releasing details of any sort regarding their punters.'

Jay told him that he understood and promised to get back to Benny as soon as he had spoken to Harvey Jackson.

227

As soon as he put the phone down on Benny, he rang Jackson on the police mobile reserved for special situations. He felt that this was one of them.

Harvey thought for a moment before responding. 'Get her address and I'll send one of my most tactful but persuasive officers to go and have a chat. My experience with these ladies is that threats seldom do anything other than drive them into a state of defiance, but if you take them at least half into your confidence about why their client is being investigated, they are normally co-operative. The fact that a woman has been kidnapped and three men murdered all of whom have a positive connection to this man may well persuade her to be co-operative. I'll keep in touch,' he said, bringing their conversation to its normal abrupt end.

Jay phoned Percy to bring him up to date as Marvin had been a factor, but once again decided not to involve Howard, Victor or Hal. An hour later Harvey phoned Jay.

'Have I got news for you! She is a paid political informer, and will help my man any way she can. This might be just the break we need.'

'Let's hope so. We could do with a change of fortune.'

'I know,' the policeman agreed. 'I'll keep in touch. Talk to you soon.'

228

Chapter Twenty-Five

As the day for Amanda's race approached she became more and more excited. Jay became slightly concerned that she wasn't paying the sort of attention that she should to her studies. She was riding out at least two lots a day and had confessed to Chris that she was going to the gym and running as well. On the other hand Jay had to admire her dedication and was convinced that when the time came she would undoubtedly do herself and the horse justice. Nevertheless, he did display some qualms, and it was the experienced Jed who reminded him that Jay himself had not been that different from Amanda when he had set out on the arduous and challenging business of riding as an amateur under rules – which was a far cry from point-to-pointing.

Leicester had been chosen as the race meeting as there were four hunter chases, an amateur hurdle and an amateur novice chase. This was to be Amanda's, and indeed her horse's, first experience of what she viewed (not unreasonably) as 'the big time'. Her enthusiasm and lack of snobbishness had made her a real favourite in the yard. They were all hoping for the best of possible luck and gave her a stack of encouragement as she watched her horse being loaded at seven o'clock on the morning of the race.

Chris was driving her to the meeting and would

walk the course with her. Jed had quietly asked him to keep her as occupied as he could in an attempt to keep her mind off the race until it was time for her to get changed, weigh out and get involved in the frantic activity that precedes any race but in particular one that involves amateurs.

At half past ten Jed, Jay and Eva got into the car. Eva was driving to give Jed and Jay a chance to talk about plans for forthcoming runners. They were meeting the Lamberts well before the first race to give them time for a drink or a cup of coffee before Amanda rode in the second race. After that, in the words of her father, 'we can either celebrate or commiserate over a proper meal'.

When they arrived at Leicester racecourse Jed went to check the declarations were in order and found that Danny was already there chatting to some of his erstwhile jockey friends. Like him they had now all retired for a number of reasons, in the main revolving round old age or injuries. However, they were still deeply involved in the game they loved.

Jay had gone down to check on the horse, who looked both magnificent and totally relaxed. He then found the Lamberts who were trying to calm their over-excited daughter. Chris was standing by as a bemused but totally committed member of her supporters' club. For once Amanda seemed to be almost unaware of his presence. Chris gave Jay and Eva a grin and a shrug of his shoulders as if to say – I am certainly not the centre of attraction today – and Jay nodded in agreement. From Amanda's point of view time seemed to hang heavy until Jay gave her a friendly word of advice.

'Are you going to get ready to ride today or just

stand there talking too much?' Her instant reaction was to wonder if he was serious or not, but then she realised that he was at least half pulling her leg before saying, 'Perhaps I had better go and start getting ready.' With that she rushed off. As soon as she was out of earshot Maria Lambert looked Jay straight in the eye and asked, 'What do you think?'

'Well,' he replied, 'she's worked like hell, the horse is as fit as is possible and the two of them get on really well together. They couldn't be more ready for the race. She is up against a couple of very experienced jockeys on very good horses, but if everything goes her way I can't see why she won't be in the first three. We mustn't get over excited though. Nerves and luck could still play an enormous part, but I promise you that she and the horse could not be more ready. Let's hope they both enjoy it – after all that's what it's all about.'

'I couldn't agree more,' said Al. 'I'm just as nervous as my wife is. She is my daughter as well, I'm led to believe!' he added with a very naughty chuckle. His wife gave him a pretend slap.

'You are such a rascal!' she admonished him.

'Come on,' said Jed. 'Let's go and check the horse and give Amanda some moral support from the moment she leaves the weighing room.'

A few minutes later Jed had got the horse saddled and Danny was walking alongside as the regular groom led the mare out into the parade ring.

Al turned to Jay and Chris. 'You two couldn't have done a better job of choosing a horse for its looks and style. Let's hope my daughter is up to giving her the best possible chance.'

Chris leapt to her defence. 'She's done so much work they are already a real team,' he enthused.

'OK, OK, I'm sure you're right,' responded her father, holding his hands up in surrender.

Moments later his daughter, looking wonderful in her racing colours, was standing next to him. The conversation was meaningless as all the instructions and plans had been made well in advance, but it was a sort of ritual dance that always preceded any race, particularly an amateur rider's first race under rules. The mounting bell rang out and Jay legged up his glamorous amateur jockey into the saddle.

Returning to his small party of supporters he looked at Maria.

'If it's any consolation,' he told her, 'I am probably nearly as nervous as you are.' She gave him a grin.

'Will you stand next to me during the race? I don't think I can bear only having Al close by. He's probably going to have a heart attack of anxiety.'

'Rubbish!' her husband chided her. 'It's you who is getting over excited.' They left the ring at the same time as the horses and made their way to the area of the grandstand reserved for owners and trainers. Watching the animals canter past the stands Jay couldn't help but feel a touch of nostalgia for the early days when he had been in the same position, and his loyal and loving aunt had gone all over the country to give him her moral support and knowledgeable understanding. Sometimes amateur races are a little chaotic at the start, but both horses and jockeys seemed to be under control, and it was only moments before they were on their way around the essentially right-handed Leicester course. There were no mishaps or incidents in the early stages of the race. Amanda, looking both relaxed and controlled, was hugging the rails, as she had been repeatedly instructed. Passing the stands with a

232

circuit to go she was seventh of the fifteen runners and they were beginning to get strung out. It would be touch and go if a number of them finished as additional pace was injected into the race.

Entering the back straight two of the jockeys pushed their horses into a faster pace and it was clear that this came from their experience rather than over enthusiasm. They were currently lying third and fifth in the Amateur Jockeys' Championship, and one had previously won the point-to-pointers championship, the other being second the same year.

Amanda allowed her horse to creep past three tiring horses and was soon lying fourth and rapidly closing in on the third. A splendid jump by Elegant Queen took her into third place and she seemed to be travelling more easily than the two horses in front.

Jay turned to the Lamberts and said, 'She is doing fantastically well, looks sure to be placed, and I think she might even win!'

They didn't take their binoculars off their daughter as they watched every stride. Turning the bend she had moved up to within a length of the two leaders. Unlike them, she was sitting quietly while they were riding hard with their hands and heels and the leading jockey had already resorted to a couple of firm slaps behind the saddle.

Entering the home straight she sensibly and quietly pulled Elegant Queen out beside the two other horses, and quickly strode past the second horse. Jumping the second last it looked as if it was all over bar the shouting. As they approached the last there was a collective gasp from the crowd and one of horror from Amanda's mother. Her daughter had suddenly shot out sideways from the saddle and hit the turf with a resounding bump.

The horse continued on its way, running past the final fence, whilst all eyes rested on the prostrate figure of Amanda. Before the ambulance got to her she was sitting up and pulling herself groggily to her feet.

'What the hell happened?' asked Al.

'I've no idea,' replied Jay, 'but we'll soon find out.'

They rushed down to the chute that led from the racecourse to the unsaddling enclosure to be met by Danny who was now leading in the riderless horse. Immediately it was apparent what had happened. There was only one stirrup still attached to the saddle.

A few moments later Amanda stepped out of the ambulance and was immediately surrounded by her parents, a very concerned Chris, Jay, Jed and Danny.

'I lost an iron!' she told them. 'I think the leather broke.'

A few moments later one of the ground staff arrived with the iron and the leather, and Jay could see the problem at once. The buckle had broken and with all Amanda's weight on it and no support, she had gone out of the side door.

'Somebody will pay for this!' exclaimed an angry Jay. 'Who the hell checked her saddle?'

'Not me,' replied Danny.

'Why the hell not?' Jay demanded.

'Because it wasn't one of your saddles,' Amanda explained. 'It's all my fault. I brought my saddle down and obviously hadn't checked it carefully enough.' Her father gave her a hug.

'Well, sweetheart,' he said. 'You rode the horse beautifully and it's clear to me that the two of you are going to make a team, so let's just put it down to experience . . . and check your bloody saddle next time!'

To everybody's surprise, Maria exclaimed with a broad smile, 'The real apology you owe is not just to the County team, but above all to Elegant Queen who did her best for you. It's not her fault you fell off her.' Amanda gave her mother a hard look before realizing she was having her leg pulled. Chris put a comforting arm around her shoulders.

'At least I'm proud of you if no one else is,' he said.

'Too bloody right!' said her father. 'Come on, it's not the end of the world, they both live to fight another day.'

He then invited them all to join him in a glass of champagne. When all their glasses were full he looked around and said that he would like to make a toast.

'I would like to thank the County View team for everything they have done. If this is not exactly a celebratory glass of champagne, at least we can drink to survival and I am sure many victories in the future.'

There was a pause before Jed spoke. 'I may get fired for saying this, but if any of you would like to know, Jay fell off at the third fence in his first race under rules, so you did a bloody sight better than him, Amanda.' There was a loud hoot of laughter.

'You're right. I'll give you your cards in the morning,' promised Jay with a broad smile.

Chapter Twenty-Six

The meeting with Hamish Tang took place in his suite at Claridge's. He turned out to be taller than they had expected and immaculately dressed. His charcoal grey suit was set off by a sparkling white shirt, an understated black and white spotted tie, and green cufflinks which Jay took to be jade.

The handshakes were warm but formal. Jay, Howard and Victor were asked to sit in comfortable chairs around a glass-topped coffee table. They all declined a hot beverage but accepted the offer of sparkling water. Hamish opened the conversation with a surprisingly cultured English voice, with just a hint of an Edinburgh accent.

'Let me tell you a little bit about me,' he suggested. Very quickly he went through the background of his father and Hamish Campbell, which they already knew about. He added to this information by telling them that as a result of his father's friendship with the Scotsman, he had spent four years at Fettes College in Edinburgh before reading economics at the London School of Economics followed by a year at the Harvard Business School.

'You can see that I am well steeped in western education, although I remain deeply committed to the cultural roots of my Chinese background. As you can see, Roddy is not yet with us and I believe that

Jerline has explained to Jay's wife my hopes for him.'
He looked at Jay.

'Yes, very understandable. I have relayed this to
Howard and Victor,' said Jay.

'Well,' continued Hamish Tang, 'it seemed to me
that it would be a good idea if we met for half an
hour or so before Roddy joins us. Let me state quite
categorically that I do not see this venture as some
glorified hobby.

'I never enter any business proposition in a half-
hearted manner, and this would be no exception.
Roddy would have to run it with the same financial
constraints and objectives that are applied to all my
group ventures. If he does not perform, we will find
somebody who can. On the other hand I must say
that what I have seen of him has impressed me. He
has initiative, is extremely enthusiastic, has a good
business brain, seems able to get on with people, and
certainly seems to have done his homework in terms
of thoroughbred bloodstock.'

Jay nodded his agreement as Hamish Tang continued. 'I assume that the basic proposition that has
been outlined is at least of some interest to you,
otherwise you wouldn't be sitting here with me
today.'

'That's true,' said Howard, 'but you need to understand we were not looking for an injection of
capital or a dilution of our shareholding. The company has done better than our wildest dreams and
we are reluctant to lose control of something we have
built up. All of us have put in a great deal of time,
effort and money to get the achievements already
posted.'

Victor nodded vigorously before adding, 'I am
sure you understand that if we did decide to part

with any of our equity we would expect a very commercial price for it. That's not to say that we would be unrealistic.'

'I understand,' replied Hamish Tang. 'Frankly I would be surprised if money was a problem. It's much more about how you gentlemen feel you can work with me, and in particular, about how Mr Jessop feels he can work with Roddy – assuming he wants to do so at all.' He looked questioningly at Jay.

'To be honest I wasn't very impressed with Roddy when I first met him,' Jay said. 'I thought his timing at Kempton was less than perfect, and he did seem rather full of himself. I have, however, modified my view since then. I agree with you that he certainly seems to have worked hard to understand the blood-stock market – not only in this country but also in Europe.

'I am not familiar with it in the Far East and Australia. The big question is if he understands and accepts that I will have total control. Although I listen to Howard and Victor, when the chips are down it is always my final decision as far as running the horses is concerned. This also applies to anything to do with their welfare. The financial and business side have a greater degree of input from my partners, and here I often bow to their greater experience,' Jay continued. 'As far as the stud situation is concerned I think that the proposition Roddy outlined is extremely fair. In the same way I would expect to have tight control and autonomy of the racing activities, I would understand that he would be in the same situation when it came to the blood-stock side.'

'That seems more than fair,' commented Mr Tang. 'How do you think we should proceed?'

'It seems that we have a fair degree of agreement,' said Victor. 'Now it seems that we need to get something on paper that we can all look at.' Howard thought for a moment and then spoke.

'Why doesn't Roddy put down his basic thoughts, and we will use that as a working document. My suggestion is that Victor works with him in the initial stages, and then Jay and I will add our comments once this stage has been reached. I assume that you would do the same from your side?'

Hamish Tang nodded. 'Would it be convenient to have Roddy join us now?' he asked.

The other three all agreed in the affirmative. Hamish picked up the telephone and dialled a number which was clearly somewhere else in the hotel, and invited Roddy to join them. A few minutes later there was a knock on the door and in he walked.

He bowed to his father-in-law and shook hands with the three Englishmen. His father-in-law quickly outlined the conversation so far, and it was clear from the expression on his face that Roddy was delighted that the next stage had been reached. It was agreed that he would work on the document over the next few days and then phone Victor to arrange a meeting once he had drafted the outline. He would ensure that Victor had at least a day to look at it before the meeting.

'I think it would be useful if Howard, Hal and I also had copies,' suggested Jay. 'Although we might not come to the first meeting, we might very well see areas where we can be positive or indeed have concerns about the way in which it has been drafted.'

Roddy agreed and changing the subject he gave Jay a smile and said, 'It looks like you are going to be Champion Trainer.'

'I'm not at all sure about that,' responded Jay. 'There is still a fair way to go in the season and there's big money available at Aintree and Cheltenham, which could swing the outcome one way or the other very quickly.'

As they were about to leave Hamish Tang stopped them.

'You have shown Roddy and Jerline your facilities, and your success and background are common knowledge. You have not seen our studs. I would be happy for two or three of you to visit them – all at our expense naturally,' he said. The other three partners looked surprised.

'Let's think about that,' said Jay, 'but we do appreciate the offer.'

Polite but warm farewells were made and the three County View principals took the lift to the ground floor.

Pausing outside the hotel Victor suggested they all went somewhere to have a brief talk about the meeting. As Jay's flat at Hays Mews was close by they decided to walk there. Eva was sitting reading the newspaper, and they quickly brought her up to date on the conversation. At that moment Jay's telephone rang and he listened intently to the information being given to him.

'That's great. Thank you so much,' he said. 'I owe you a drink.' Whatever it was, the response caused Jay to chuckle, and after another 'Thanks again' he terminated the call and turned to the other three.

'That's interesting,' he said. 'Giles Sinclair from the Jockey Club has just come back with the same glowing reports about the character and business acumen of our new friend Hamish Tang.'

Howard looked at Jay.

'It seems sensible for at least one of us to look at the studs. Victor and I are not really expert enough on the horse front to make a sensible judgement. Could you be free?' he asked.

'Not for some time,' replied Jay. 'What about Jed and Cathy? It would give them a wonderful break. Fiona could do South Africa and Jed and Cathy New Zealand and Malaysia.'

'What about his health?' asked Howard.

'Good point. We should have to get his doctor's view, but if they travel first class and go in easy stages, it might do them the world of good. Cathy would stop him being silly.' There was immediate agreement, and Eva was given the task of sounding out Cathy before Jed was approached.

'Cathy can check with his doctor too,' pointed out Howard.

Eva looked at the three of them with a very serious expression on her face. 'I think it's really important that we do not let word of this possible deal break. It will be all over the newspapers, and that's all we need with all the other problems we've got at the moment.' Howard nodded vigorously, and Victor suggested that Jay ring both Hamish and Roddy to stress this. Jay agreed and within seconds he was dialling the number of Claridge's and was put through to Hamish Tang. Roddy was still with him, and Jay explained their strong desire to keep this under wraps until a decision to go ahead or not had been made. He added that they would like to see the studs but needed to work out who and when.

'That shouldn't be difficult,' said Mr Tang. 'As far as I know, only my daughter, son-in-law, myself and the four of you have any knowledge of our discussion so far.'

'That's true,' agreed Jay, 'but we have another shareholder. An American who has been with us since the beginning. He is only a small equity holder, but he has been a great friend and supporter. As a matter of courtesy I would want to tell him. I can assure you that he is a man of immense discretion. He is the man that I sold my business to, so I know him well.'

'That's fine by me,' replied Hamish Tang. 'I look forward to seeing what Victor and Roddy come up with on paper, and also to seeing you all again soon and having a chance to talk about it.'

'Me too,' said Jay, and finished the conversation.

Howard and Victor left shortly afterwards, leaving Jay and Eva to mull over the day's events. They settled for omelettes for supper then watched an hour's television before having on an early night. At six o'clock the following morning they were on their way back to County View.

Chapter Twenty-Seven

By the time they got back to their home the stable yard was buzzing with activity and the first lot was almost ready to go on the gallops. Jay quickly changed and trotted across the yard to join Jed in the Land Rover to jointly watch the morning's work. Everything went like clockwork. By the end of the morning Jay felt completely relaxed as he normally did when he'd been working with or around his horses.

The next few days passed uneventfully. His runner came third at Uttoxeter on Saturday. On Sunday morning, as usual, he watched the week's weather forecast on Country File. Having seen it he walked into the kitchen with a serious expression on his face.

'What's the problem?' asked his wife.

'I've just seen the weather forecast. It seems that we are going to get a very heavy frost tonight and they expect the cold snap to last until the end of this week. The temperature forecast says "low" but I doubt if we'll get any racing.'

'That's a bore,' Eva commented sympathetically. 'I know you were hopeful of getting good results at Sandown and Plumpton.'

'I just hope it clears up by next weekend. I've got runners planned at both Hereford and Worcester and I was going to give Amanda a ride in the bumper. I thought the experience would be useful for her, even though there are no jumps.'

'Let's keep our fingers crossed. Does Amanda know about your plan?'

'No, I haven't told her yet,' admitted Jay. 'I wanted to make sure that I had a suitable mount.'

'Well, I wouldn't tell her,' said his wife. 'Let's not build her hopes up then dash them.'

The weather forecast turned out to be discouragingly accurate. Racing was abandoned all over the country and by Friday it was clear there would be no racing at the weekend.

County View's horses were being kept on the go with the use of the all weather gallops, but loads of salt was being spread in the yard every day and on the asphalt path to the edge of the gallops. The frost gave no sign of relenting.

On the Sunday Jay once more tuned into Country File to learn that the Arctic conditions showed no signs of relenting before Thursday at the earliest.

This led Jay and Jed to sit down and re-plan the whole of their entry strategy, as they now had a backlog of runners as indeed did nearly every other trainer in the country.

When racing did resume the fields would be enormous.

At last the temperature started to rise and the following weekend Jay sent runners to Fontwell, Warwick and Newton Abbot. Jed once more opted for Fontwell, so Danny went to Newton Abbot and Jay to Warwick. They were three runners at both Fontwell and Newton Abbot, plus four at Warwick. They were all in for a busy afternoon, Jay in particular.

There was a bumper at Warwick so Jay stuck to his original plan and gave Amanda the ride. Needless to say she was thrilled, and her personal fan club of Al and Maria Lambert plus Chris were all there to cheer her on. Jay was in a particularly good mood on hearing that both Jed and Danny had had a winner, and Jed's other charges had come second and third. Danny's other two had run creditably, but were unplaced. Jay had two winners and one unplaced by the time it came to the bumper.

Amanda was as excited as she had been at Leicester. Her parents were considerably more relaxed, partly because it wasn't her first race, and partly, Jay thought, because it was a flat race and not a steeplechase. The preliminaries went smoothly, and soon Amanda was on Hyde Hero and on her way to the start. The horse had one previous run and had come a creditable fourth in the hands of young Paul. It was clear that two miles was on the short side for him. However, Jay had decided to give him the extra chance of gaining racecourse experience before sending him an extra half mile or so over hurdles.

Amanda was the only female rider in the race and was subjected to some good-natured leg pulling as the horses circled at the start. Freddie was also riding in the race. He kept alongside Amanda, encouraging her and fending off some of the quips aimed at her. There were twenty-two runners in the race so there was bound to be a mad scramble at the start.

'You keep next to me,' Freddie advised Amanda. 'We'll keep out of trouble at the back for the first half. With this going, and a lot of totally inexperienced horses in the race, you can be sure there will be the chance to make up ground in the last half mile of the race.'

Sure enough the start resembled the Charge of the Light Brigade. There was a fair amount of bumping going on at the front. Freddie had let Amanda stay on his inside against the rails so she would be well protected in the early stages of the race.

Going down the hill at the beginning of the back straight Freddie started to thread his way through the horses in front of them. He yelled at Amanda to stay with him if she could. Dropping in a length behind him she followed the champion jockey as they made their way into seventh and eighth place respectively. Freddie stayed in this position as he left the back straight and rounded the final bend. As soon as he got to the finishing straight he kicked his horse on and left Amanda to sort herself out. She immediately urged her horse to follow Freddie which he attempted to do but he didn't have the same acceleration as the champion's mount. With half a furlong to go Freddie was in dispute for second place and Amanda was now lying fifth.

She began to make up ground but could see there was no way she was going to reach the leading two who were locked in battle. However, to her amazement and delight Hyde Hero passed the two horses in front of him and took off in pursuit of the leaders. He lacked their acceleration, but Amanda was still thrilled to pass the winning post in third place.

Pulling up she turned the horse around as Freddie trotted over to her.

'How did you do?' he asked.

'Third,' was her breathless reply. A huge smile spread over his face.

'Well done, well done. We'll make a jockey of you yet!' he chuckled.

'What about you?' she asked.

'Just managed to get my nose in front. Come on,

let's hack back and you can join me in the winners' enclosure.'

Leaving the course Amanda was immediately mobbed by Jay, Chris and her parents. All of them clapped her enthusiastically. Jay asked how she felt.

'Thrilled but completely knackered!'

'I'm not surprised,' he replied. 'You rode a good finish, young lady. I'm proud of you.'

Jumping off Hyde Hero in the spot reserved for the third placed horse, she got a big hug from both parents and a slightly shy kiss on the cheek from Chris.

'I hope you can do better than that later,' she whispered in his ear, before going off to weigh in.

Jay had a celebratory drink with the Lamberts before driving home. He rang Howard and Victor to tell them the news, but both of them had caught up with the results on the racing channel. Victor told Jay that Harry Solomons had got two, compared with Jay's three winners, so the gap had widened a little further.

'Oh well, let's see what happens at Cheltenham,' said Jay. 'It's only a little over four weeks away now.'

Jay, Jed and Danny concentrated even harder on preparing the horses for the Festival. Freddie came over most days to work or school them, along with Paul and Danny.

The other horses were also being given plenty of attention, and the minor meetings which still provided good prize winning opportunities were far from ignored.

Amanda rode first lot every day, and was now becoming so competent that Jay let her school some of the more experienced horses. Those who were still learning their game were left in the more experienced hands of the other three.

All had been quiet on the police and Jockey Club front.

No sooner had he sunk into a state of relative calm than Harvey Jackson rang.

'We've had some more information from South Africa. It seems that our friend Strauss alias Kruger is on the "Wanted" list in Zimbabwe. The government there believes he has been involved in an attempt at a coup, and they have requested his extradition, not realizing he's no longer there.

'I don't know if Benny's told you, but he and I have had a brief chat. I've set up a countrywide search for our suspect, and Benny has done the same.'

Moments after he had put the phone down Benny rang to bring Jay up to date with this development and to confirm that in this instance he was working alongside Jackson.

The normal routine of the yard continued until a few days later when Jackson rang with some positive news.

'Our quarry is still in the UK and has evidently been shooting in Scotland before spending a few days in Gleneagles. He was friendly with the bar and restaurant staff, did not over indulge, and gave nothing away to anyone about his future movements. However, the head porter knew the taxi driver who took him to the station, and we've had him traced. It seems he drove him all the way to Edinburgh and it appears he was then travelling to London by train. We are intensifying the search in the London area. Perhaps you can let your friend Benny know this?'

'As good as done,' Jay assured him.

'By the way,' added Jackson, 'give Benny my

mobile number, and if he hears anything he's to phone me straight away and not come through you. Time may be critical.'

'I understand,' Jay assured him before relaying the message to Benny. This done, he turned his concentration back to the business of training horses. He was in his office ploughing through the paperwork when Eva came in and closed the door behind her.

'I've got some news for you,' she announced. Jay looked up questioningly.

'I'm over three weeks late with my period, so I took a pregnancy test this morning which I got from the chemist. It looks as if we are on our way to becoming parents!'

Jay gave a whoop, then got up and gave her a big hug. 'You must phone Fiona at once!' he cried.

'Hang on, it's early days yet,' she cautioned. 'Let's keep our fingers crossed. I'll wait another couple of weeks, and then I'll go and see the doctor.'

'I think this calls for a glass of champagne!' said Jay.

'No,' came the firm reply. 'First of all we are not sure yet, and secondly I am not going to drink alcohol at all if I am pregnant. What's more, apart from my mother, let's keep this strictly to ourselves for at least a couple of months.'

'All right,' Jay reluctantly agreed. 'I can't tell you how thrilled I am!'

He then filled her in on his telephone calls with Jackson and Benny, which in turn gave Eva something to be enthusiastic about.

'I can't believe it!' she exclaimed. 'Perhaps we are at last somewhere near to finding out what's been going on and coming to the end of this nightmare.'

'Maybe,' said Jay, 'but, as you said a few moments ago, let's not start counting our chickens.'

249

During the next few days Jay ran one or two of his younger horses, and they all performed incredibly well on their first racecourse outings. None of them added to his prize money however. On the Saturday Jay had chosen Hereford as the course for Tobago Song to make his debut. Although he had been schooled and shown great ability over hurdles, Jay still decided to run him in at least one National Hunt flat race.

The weather had been dry with some light rain, so the going was good, and there were none of the softer heavy patches which can sometimes occur there. Needless to say Eva was extremely excited, and Jay quietly shared her enthusiasm.

As he had done so much of the work at home, it had been agreed that Paul had the ride. Chris and Amanda were determined to be there, having been with Jay the day he had first seen the horse in Ireland.

In spite of Jay's strongest persuasion, Jed insisted on staying behind to keep his eye on County View as the Cheltenham Festival was only a few days away.

Arriving at Hereford on a cold but sunny day at the end of February they immediately ran into Danny who assured them that all was well. He had checked the horse and the declarations, and there were two overnight withdrawals cutting the field to fifteen. As Paul had no other rides that afternoon it was agreed that Danny would collect the saddle early so as to avoid unnecessary hurry in preparing him for the race. This would give him plenty of time in the paddock before going through what is normally an enthusiastic crowd, each side of the chute, on the way to the racecourse. The horses then made their way to the start on the inside thus reducing the amount of wear on the course itself.

By the time Tobago Song was being led around the ring Eva was getting seriously excited.

'I'm not sure it was a good idea to bring you,' Jay whispered to her.

'I would have been in a worse state waiting at home I can assure you,' she replied. A few moments later the jockeys were in the ring. When the bell rang Jay legged Paul up and walked with him down the chute and onto the track. Tobago Song was alert and interested but showed no sign of nerves.

Soon the fifteen runners were circling at the start having their girths checked. They were called into line but at the last moment two whipped round causing the whole procedure to be repeated. The starter instructed the jockeys to take a turn and somewhat reluctantly some of them wheeled their horses round before walking back. The majority of the runners were an inexperienced bunch and the sooner they were on their way the happier everyone would be. This time all seemed to be well until at the last moment one of the two previously errant horses planted itself and refused to run.

It was too late and the rest of the field were on their way. Tobago Song was pulling very hard which slightly surprised Jay as he was a very settled horse at home. Obviously the excitement of the occasion had got to him to some extent. Paul sensibly settled him towards the rear of the field. The two leading horses had bolted away from the twelve remaining runners, and were twenty lengths clear of the field leaving the back straight. At this stage one of the two leaders started to fade, but the other was still full of running. With a little encouragement from his jockey, he had opened the gap to about thirty lengths. By this time the pursuing pack had started to realize the danger and were gradually urging their horses to cut down the margin. Five of them, including Tobago Song, moved steadily up. Paul was now lying fourth of these five. The others were fading rapidly.

Turning into the home straight three of the pursuing pack passed the now struggling original joint leader. At this stage Paul gave Tobago Song a slap on his shoulder and he responded by increasing his pace. This increase was not in the dramatic way that Wot A B had demonstrated in her races, but it was effective enough to take him into second place. He began to steadily cut down the lead of the long time pace setter, and with a hundred yards to go, Eva was beginning to think that he would make it. However, frantic urgings by the leader's jockey saw a brave response from his horse, who passed the winning post with a length and a half to spare over the rapidly closing Tobago Song.

In spite of Jay's efforts to restrain her, Eva was dashing from the grandstand across to the chute from the course in time to meet Paul before he reached the unsaddling enclosure. 'Well, what's the verdict?' she panted, looking at Paul.

'I probably left it too late,' admitted the young jockey. 'None of us thought the leader would keep going at that pace. He is a lovely young thing, and he'll certainly win races, but I think to be honest he would be better with another half mile.' Jay put his arm around Eva's shoulders.

'There's nothing to be disappointed about with that run, and frankly I agree with Paul. The next decision, and it's got to be yours, is whether we go for another bumper, or go straight over hurdles with him.' Eva thought for a moment.

'I think if we can find a bumper on a stiff course, as long as it's not too hot a contest I would be happy to do that. Otherwise let's go for a hurdle race.'

'No problems with that,' Jay replied. 'After all, you're the owner.' They walked into the space reserved for the second horse and Eva had her photograph taken with both Tobago and young Paul.

Almost immediately Amanda and Chris joined them, congratulating Eva in particular, and full of enthusiasm for the horse's future.

'I've got an idea,' said Chris. 'Amanda and I have found a really nice pub just outside Malmesbury. Why don't you two join us for an early dinner?'

'We'd love to,' said Eva before Jay had a chance to reply.

'Of course,' he agreed. On the way back to County View he asked, 'Are you sure this is a good idea after all your excitement today?'

'I would just like to savour the evening with our two young friends.'

'You're the boss, but take it easy tomorrow,' insisted her husband.

Later that evening they were sitting at a round table in front of a blazing log fire. They had all ordered different starters, but settled for the restaurant's special of the evening for the main course. This was roast pheasant. To Jay's surprise, Chris had ordered a bottle of champagne. When it arrived Eva politely declined with the excuse that she was driving, and resisted Chris's valiant attempts to get her to change her mind, to the extent of just one glass. Having failed but filled up the other three glasses, he announced, 'Amanda and I have got some news for you. She has just agreed to marry me.'

Eva leapt up and flung her arms around Amanda giving her big kiss, followed by a repeat performance with Chris. Jay followed suit with Amanda, but grinning at Chris he said, 'I think I will just settle with shaking your hand!'

'So what's happening about your aspirations to become a vet?' Jay asked Amanda.

'Well, I have given up the idea of going on to university – I had already come to that conclusion before Chris asked me to marry him. As soon as I have finished at Cirencester, Chris has got me a job at Bristol Veterinary Hospital, which of course means I will still be able to live with him and commute each day. When I am experienced enough, I will join him in running the practice, and as a veterinary nurse.'

'That's wonderful,' said Eva. 'So we won't be losing touch with either of you.'

'Not on your life!' responded Chris. 'That's unless you decide to fire me!'

'I don't think that's too likely,' promised Eva. An hour late, after a magnificent meal, they said goodbye to the young couple and were soon on their twenty-minute drive back to County View.

'I am absolutely thrilled for them,' said Eva. 'I'm sure she'll make him an excellent wife.'

'I just hope she doesn't kill him in bed,' joked Jay.

'What on earth do you mean?'

'Well, I gather she has a very healthy appetite when it comes to the amorous side of life.'

'Where did you learn that from?' demanded Eva in a mock accusing tone.

'Never you mind, that's my secret!' joked Jay, and

254

within minutes they were driving past the security gate at County View.

After checking that there were no urgent messages, Jay joined a very contented Eva in bed and they were soon sleeping the sleep of the just.

When Jay got up the next morning there was just one message, from Benny, that had been left at just after one in the morning. He sounded very excited.

'We've had a real breakthrough, and I got hold of Jackson about half an hour ago. Vanda spotted Strauss going into one of the apartment blocks in Mayfair that are let out on short leases. She immediately phoned me, her point of contact, and I got some of my boys to go round and camp outside, just in case the police got held up. Jackson rang to say "back off". He will be in touch with you as soon as there is any news.'

Before Jay had time to make some coffee his mobile rang and it was Jackson.

'We've got him,' said a very contented sounding policeman. 'Your friend Benny hit the jackpot for us. We arrested him just before three o'clock this morning – it took us a little while to find out which apartment he was in – and although he was armed he gave up very quickly when he saw the strength of our team who were all armed to the teeth. He protested he had diplomatic immunity and he produced a diplomatic passport in the name of Hanson. We have got him in Paddington Green station and we are waiting for the South African Embassy to check the situation for us. As soon as there is any more news I will be back to you.'

Jay tossed up as to whether to wake Eva with the news, but then decided that an extra hour's sleep would do her more good. At this time Danny and Jed arrived to finalize the morning's activities. Jay explained to them that he had something very pressing, and would they supervise all the work. A round table discussion quickly agreed what each of the horses would do, and the two of them were on their way, still full of enthusiasm for Tobago Song's run on the previous afternoon.

With great difficulty Jay settled down to do what seemed to him a never ending pile of paperwork, whilst impatiently awaiting the next call from Jackson. Eventually Eva came down and he gave her the exciting news.

Completely out of his normal calm character Jay could control himself no longer. He rang. The policeman was very sympathetic but explained that the South African Embassy had got to do a number of checks with both their own diplomatic corps and their police. He promised Jay that he would come back to him the minute he had any information.

'Why don't you go off, work with your horses, or do something else to take your mind off it,' he suggested. 'I promise I'll call you on your mobile the minute I can,' and with a chuckle he added, 'and don't forget to keep it switched on!'

'Thanks for reminding me,' Jay replied, his voice dripping with sarcasm.

'Well, I know how absent-minded you young characters can be,' retorted Jackson. 'I mean it – I'll call you the minute I have some news. By the way, keep this to yourself. Don't even tell any of your shareholders. It's strictly under wraps for the time being.'

'Of course, and thanks for letting me know what's going on.'

'It's a pleasure,' was the reply. 'The sooner we can

wrap the whole thing up the better it will be for all of us, and in particular, you.'

'Agreed,' Jay replied with feeling and put the phone down.

Bringing Eva up to date and taking Jackson's advice, Jay went off in time to watch the second lot, which included a schooling session for Jay's runners at the forthcoming Cheltenham Festival. It had been kept for the second lot so that Freddie could ride out at Lambourn first before coming over to share most of the work with Paul and Danny.

After the session had been successfully completed the two jockeys joined Jed and Jay, whilst Eva plied them all with coffee.

'Have you finalized your plans yet?' asked the champion jockey.

'Not really,' replied Jay. 'I'm still planning to run all of them, but obviously the weather will affect us. It's unlikely to get too firm for any of them, but heavy rain could see at least Pewter Queen and Splendid Warrior missing their races. It would be a hell of a shame for the Warrior to miss the chance of defending his crown.'

'I agree,' was Freddie's response. 'I think that Pewter Queen would probably handle good to soft as she is getting stronger all the time, but the Warrior certainly prefers good or even a touch faster ground. After all, it would be no disgrace if you sidetracked him to either Aintree or, of course, the big race at Sandown, which I still think of as the Whitbread.' Jay nodded and turning to Paul he said,

'You can be sure that you're going to get some rides there, Paul, but I know you understand that Splendid Warrior and Pewter Queen will go to Freddie, unless he goes and does something stupid like getting himself a ban.' Freddie gave a rueful grin. He had just served two days' suspension for careless riding, and in view of the fact that it was a selling race at Kempton, he had had his leg pulled unmercifully by his weighing room colleagues and had been subjected to a number of acerbic comments from some of the racing press.

'I hope he gets banned for all four days,' grinned Paul, 'and you can be sure that if there is anything I can do to make it happen I'll jump at the chance!' He just ducked the cork table mat that Freddie had hurled at him, and all of them burst into the good humoured laughter that was the hallmark of the happy atmosphere at County View.

When they were all on their way to their different work and destinations, Jay phoned his owners to bring them up to date, and to reassure them that at the moment all was well. Howard was particularly keen to learn that Pewter Queen was still on course for Cheltenham, but that Jay had more or less made up his mind to route The Conker to Uttoxeter for the Midlands Grand National a few days later.

As soon as he spoke to Victor it was quite clear from his questions that the Trainers' Championship was still at the top of his mind.

'When will you be making up your mind?' he questioned Jay.

'I'll let the press know my basic plans next week. The going will be all important. Ideally we want it to be mainly dry between now and the fifteenth of March, and then rain like hell at Uttoxeter to ensure soft or heavy going for The Conker.'

'I see,' said Victor. 'Any news from the police?'

'None at all at the moment,' lied Jay, feeling more

258

uncomfortable each time he evaded the truth with his two now long-standing partners.

Once the activity of the morning had subsided Jay's impatience to know of any developments on the Strauss/Kruger front resurfaced.

'Come on,' he said to Eva. 'The suspense is killing me. Let's go and have a snack at the Shepherds Rest. Maybe that will take our minds off things for half an hour or so.'

They had just ordered their food and got a glass of wine for Jay and a sparkling mineral water for Eva, when his mobile rang. Grabbing it out of his pocket, Jay pressed the receive button. It was Jackson.

'Well, the passport is an extremely good forgery,' he announced. 'There was a Hanson with a diplomatic passport, but he died six months ago. We are therefore holding him as an illegal entrant and being in possession of an illegal firearm. This will give us a chance to get to work on the more serious potential charges. The one thing we know is that while he is under lock and key, he can't get up to any more tricks. The other thing I have done is to record all the interviews I have had with him. I have taken sections of tape to let people who have spoken to him on the phone listen to them. I will mix them up with a couple of foreign accents, one New Zealand and one Australian, and see if they manage to pick him out. It's unlikely to prove conclusive, but it could be an extra lever when we are talking to him. The other thing, Jay, is that we have not let him know what our true suspicions are, and we have just told him that we recently arrested Jake the gun dealer, who had tipped us off that he had bought some weapons. It was just bad luck that Vanda spotted him going into the flats. I lied and told him that she'd been a police

259

informer for some time and she had some suspicions about him when he had employed her. She had earned her customary fee by letting us know he was in the UK. We told him that we knew he'd used the name Kruger, but we didn't let on about our additional knowledge regarding South Africa, or indeed, his Strauss identity. That's all I can tell you at the moment, Jay, but I'll keep you informed as things develop. I am going to have to go now.' Jay thanked him warmly and wished him good luck with his future enquiries.

He had barely returned to County View when Roddy rang him to tell him that all the preliminary work had been done and that the draft document would be circulated to those concerned the following day. Thinking that he had enough on his plate at the moment without having to pay attention to such a potential major development as the future of County View in general and in his and Eva's life in particular, Jay felt that he might as well strike while the iron was hot and have a meeting with his three partners as soon as possible. This would leave him free to concentrate on the final preparations for Cheltenham. He rang Howard and Victor and a meeting was fixed for the following evening. They were happy for Hal to join them and a phone call confirmed that he was available. Jay then rang Roddy back who said he would courier the document to each of the partners the following morning to give everyone a chance to study it in some detail before the evening meeting. Victor, who had been heavily involved in the initial stages, was already pretty well in the picture.

Feeling emotionally and physically drained, Jay and Eva settled for a quiet evening in with supper on their knees in front of the television.

Earlier on Eva had telephoned her mother, and they were laughing at the fact that the wildly excited grandmother-to-be was already asking about possible names, and whether they had thought about godparents. The answer to both of these questions was a firm no.

Chapter Twenty-Eight

Next morning Jay woke up even earlier than usual and tried to concentrate on finalizing the work list for that day, based on a tentative plan devised by Jed and Danny the previous evening.

The morning was uneventful with all his potential runners over the next few weeks giving a good account of themselves both on the gallops and being schooled.

Just as Jay began to feel that he had got a window of normality, his tranquility was shattered by a telephone call from Giles Sinclair.

'I thought you ought to know that there has been an extraordinary development in the betting on the Trainers' Championship,' he said. 'Lumps of money have been placed on Harry Solomons' winning, and even more against you. Have you any idea why this should be?' Jay was completely dumbfounded. He had a useful, though not commanding, lead over Solomons, but potentially he could win more money at Cheltenham than his main rival, and there was no doubt that The Conker would be the favourite for the Midlands Grand National. Aintree was still a little too far in the distance for anyone to be able to take account of that, except for the obvious fact that Harry had entries in the Grand National and Jay didn't. Relaying these thoughts to the Jockey Club man Jay promised that he would give it some thought and call back if anything occurred to him.

'There's one other thing,' added Sinclair. 'It seems there have been some significant bets laid in the Far East, and a couple of substantial wagers in South Africa. I've got my team looking into it, but the bookies who have taken these bets say they have all been placed through two or three intermediaries, all of whom swear they have no idea who the sources are. What is more, the money has been deposited with a very well known firm of solicitors in London who, needless to say, are claiming client confidentiality. As you can imagine, Jackson is looking into that.'

Thanking Giles for his information, Jay phoned Benny and Percy to let them know of the betting situation and to ask them to keep their ears open.

'I'll put Marvin onto this,' promised Percy. 'As you know he has the most amazing contacts, but this could be outside his sphere of activity.'

Thanking Percy for his promise of help, Jay sat down and tried to puzzle out the meaning behind this very strange turn of events.

He gave Jed a quick call and asked him and Danny to come over as soon as they had finished checking round the yard. Ten minutes later the three of them were sitting in Jay's office discussing the horses' work for the following day because, as he explained, he had to go to London at very short notice. He told them that he would probably be back in time, but he would call at six thirty in the morning to say whether or not they should press on without him if he was not back. They nodded understanding without enquiring why he was off at short notice and left him to a bit of peace and quiet. He made himself a sandwich and, after a few more routine calls, he rang Eva to let her know that he would be leaving soon.

His drive to London was without incident and he was soon at his Hays Mews base, parking his Jaguar in the garage underneath the little house. As soon as he was indoors Jay rang both Giles and Harvey Jackson to tell them of his movements. He took these few moments of quiet respite to relax while watching the racing channel and was soon engrossed in the afternoon's cards even though they were all relatively minor meetings. In between races there were comments from time to time on the prospects for the forthcoming Cheltenham Festival. Jay was interested to learn that there was a growing feeling that the French trained horse, Duc D'Avignon, was the prime rival for Splendid Warrior. Duc D'Avignon was now down as second favourite at five to one behind the Warrior's current price of three and a half.

Although reasonably familiar with the horse's standing in France, Jay made a mental note to check up on his form in more detail when he returned to County View. After a refreshing shower he put on a clean shirt and v-necked sweater. He then slipped on his suede jacket before dumping his grubby jeans and woollen polo shirt in the little washing machine.

As he was confident that he would have more than a couple of glasses of wine he called for a taxi to take him to Simpson's where the meeting was to be held. Victor was already sitting at Jay's normal table, and they had a chat about the County View horses for a few minutes. To Jay's surprise, Victor had not raised the subject of the Trainers' Championship by the time Howard joined them. They continued their conversation and Howard asked about the well-being of the horses in general but Pewter Queen and The Conker in particular. He also took the opportunity to say that he thought Tobago Song's run was very encouraging and, almost as an afterthought, Victor agreed with him.

At that moment a slightly breathless Hal arrived. He apologized for being ten minutes late, explaining that he had got a call from the States as he was on the point of leaving. A waiter took their order. They all missed out on starters. Howard and Victor went for the roast beef, and Hal opted for the lamb saying it was much more difficult to get decent lamb in the States than beef. Jay decided to join Hal in the lamb.

The documents were soon spread on the table. All three fellow directors looked enquiringly at Jay.

'I have given this a lot of thought,' said Jay. 'I have also talked it over with Fiona whose judgement I value greatly, but with nobody else. It seems to me that in principle it's an extremely good deal. My main concern is that I retain overall control of County View, and I don't want to spend too much time trotting from stud to stud. However, since the idea was first mooted, and I have met and spoken to Roddy on a number of occasions, I feel that he is perfectly capable of doing most of that work. It would also give him a high degree of autonomy. I am sure that Hamish would be more than happy with that situation, and Roddy, I imagine, would be delighted.'

Howard was the next to voice his views. 'I too have warmed to it since it was first mooted and, looking at this document, it represents virtually no financial drain on our main activities. The proposition is that the Tang Group finance the great majority of it, and we just sit and pick up our five per cent. I guess that would be a consolidated five per cent and if any of the studs lost money those losses would go into the overall pool, in the same way that the profits would.'

'That seems eminently fair,' agreed Jay.

'I have to say that I am very much in favour of it,' announced Hal. 'It would give us a huge and valuable pool of young bloodstock. I can see no reason why it shouldn't be profitable, after all it's only the New Zealand stud that is not making a profit at the moment, and that's only in its third year. As I understand it the first year's crop are going to hit the market this year. Looking at the appendix, Roddy seems to be confident that there would be very little capital investment needed in any of them, other than, of course, additional stallions and mares or stud fees. As you know my two friends and I have only got a small holding but if it became vital to get the deal through, we would surrender that.'

'I have already said that I would be happy to toss in some of my shares,' said Howard, 'just as long as I retain a worthwhile interest and, as has already been said, Jay retains overall control.'

The three of them turned and looked questioningly at Victor.

'I am prepared to hand in half my equity,' he informed the other three, all of whom were genuinely surprised. 'With ten per cent from me and five per cent from Howard, I would have thought that fifteen per cent was a more than worthwhile holding as far as Tang is concerned. I don't think that Jay or Eva should give up any of their shares, and frankly I don't think that in this situation Hal's five per cent is going to make the difference between swinging the deal or not. If it does, I suggest we drop it and carry on as we are for the time being. After all, the way things are going at the moment, the value of the operation should go up rather than down and, if Jay did win the Championship, that in turn would give it a huge boost. My own view is that we should do the deal before that is decided to show the Tangs our genuine desire to co-operate with them, and that we are forgoing an opportunity to increase the price of our shares, should Jay be successful.'

There were nods all around the table. This time Jay spoke.

'I'd like to hand over the next and hopefully final stage of negotiations to Victor and Howard. I'm not going to be able to give it the sort of concentration it needs, with both Cheltenham and Aintree coming up so quickly. Both of you have got far more experience in doing this sort of deal than I ever have,' he said, looking at each in turn.

'Well, I don't know about that!' laughed Hal. 'You didn't do a bad job in selling your company to me.' The other two smiled their agreement.

'Has anyone got any objection to that?' asked Jay. All three shook their heads. Howard looked at Jay.

'How does Eva feel about this?' he asked.

'She's actually very enthusiastic about it,' Jay told them. 'This is partly because she has come to like and respect Roddy and his charming wife, but also because Fiona has been very positive about the proposition.'

'OK,' said Hal. 'I think you two boys have got a job on your hands, and a fairly urgent one at that.' They all agreed on this course of action before Howard raised the question of the betting.

As there had been no mention of the heavy gambles against Jay winning he decided to keep his counsel and shook his head, again feeling uncomfortable and not a little disloyal. With that they drank their coffee and agreed to break up the meeting. On the way out Hal put his arm on Jay's arm.

'I'd like to have a nightcap with you if that's convenient,' he said. 'Just you and me,' he added.

'What about my place?' asked Jay.

'Certainly,' was the reply. Saying good night to Howard and Victor, who were making arrangements for their next meeting, Jay and Hal walked onto the Strand, grabbed themselves a black cab and were soon sitting comfortably in Hays Mews with cigars.

'You are most welcome to a brandy,' said Jay. 'Frankly though I feel more like a glass of champagne.'

'Good idea.'

Conversation paused while Jay extracted a bottle from the fridge, passed Hal a cigar and cutter, poured two glasses of champagne and sat down opposite his colleague and friend. Hal gave him a searching look.

'Jay, you and I have been friends for a long while. We have done business together, we have argued over deals, we have enjoyed dinner alone or being at large social gatherings, and I have certainly enjoyed going racing with you. I have got to know you very well. Frankly I am worried about you. I know you have got problems. You explained some of them to me at County View, but tonight when you were discussing one of the most important potential developments in your and Eva's life you were not really with us. I have no arguments with the decisions you made, or the points of view that you expressed, but you were not the one hundred per cent focused, switched on man that I have come to

268

know. Come on, tell me what the problem is.' Jay paused, thought for a moment and then started.

'Well, Hal, you know there has been some talk of me paying other trainers to stop their horses, or more accurately, not to run them. You know there have been three murders in the racing industry which somehow seemed to be possibly connected to this. You know there was the kidnapping of a trainer's wife, apparently to stop him running a horse against one of mine. You also know there was a very serious and well organized attempt to kidnap The Conker on his way to a really important race.

'Whilst all this has been going on somebody has been steadily backing me to win the Trainers' Championship. This has resulted in the odds on me doing that shortening dramatically and, at the same time, the odds on Harry Solomons, the current champion, have lengthened just as substantially. Today I learnt that in the last two days huge sums of money have been laid against me winning the championship, and on Harry winning it. All this money has apparently come from an anonymous source, placed through agents, but the stake money has been lodged with a major and extremely well respected firm of London lawyers. Each of these developments on its own is worrying, but added together they are truly alarming. What makes the situation worse, a great deal worse, is that neither the Jockey Club, the police, nor I know if there really is a connection, and if there is, what the real objectives behind these incidents are. Frankly I am worried sick.

'Thank heavens I drew the Jockey Club's attention to the fact that horses were being mysteriously withdrawn at the last moment before competing with mine. Otherwise I might already be under serious investigation by them. We have been very lucky so far that the media have not connected these incidents. Although there has been some implied criticism of my actions, so far the main incidents have been seen as news items in themselves and not some convoluted plot.' He stopped and looked at Hal who took a long draw on his cigar before commenting.

'As an outsider, Jay, it looks to me as if most of them must be connected. Let's look at some of the relevant facts. Firstly you appear to be directly or indirectly involved with all of them. Secondly, it's highly unlikely these are individual and unrelated incidents, it's just too much of a coincidence. Thirdly, they could all potentially discredit you or lead to you in some way being discredited. At the very least they are likely to raise very big questions in the media about your integrity or your way of operating, and indeed in the minds of the racing fraternity and general public, who do not know you as well as your owners, colleagues and close friends.

'Therefore it seems to me that this is a carefully orchestrated plan to discredit you. The big question is why, with what objective, and by whom? Normally this would have the mark of a vendetta from somebody who dislikes you. It seems to me though that it would take a significant amount of organization and money to achieve that for spite only. We have to consider if there is potentially a substantial monetary gain that someone or some organization can achieve by these actions. Have you any ideas?'

'We know of two people who do not like me. The Irish drug dealer, who is probably also a murderer, but he is languishing in jail. The other is an owner with substantial business interests, who developed an antipathy to me when I was still a jockey. Frankly

270

I doubt that he has the resources to set up such a complicated and costly operation.'

'You can think of nobody else?' Hal insisted.

'No, and it's not for want of trying,' Jay vigorously replied.

'You tell me that the police appear to have made a breakthrough in that they have arrested a number of people connected with both the kidnapping and the attempt to snatch The Conker, and it would seem that this character alias Strauss, Hanson or Kruger is deeply involved. A South African accent has been associated with a number of these incidents, and at least one of the murders. Surely this should be the breakthrough you have been waiting for?'

'I bloody well hope so!' countered Jay. 'Though he has been firmly under lock and key whilst these massive bets have been taking place. Anyway, he certainly does not have the resources or organization to carry out this scale of operation, even though he may be associated or employed by an organization that does.'

'All you can do is to sit back and give it as much thought as you can, said Hal. 'Essentially you should leave it to the authorities, and hope that they get another breakthrough as a result of these arrests. In the meantime, my advice to you is to concentrate solely on winning more money than any other trainer at Cheltenham, and go on to make sure of that title at Aintree. As we agreed at dinner this evening, Howard and Victor are more than capable of progressing the Tang deal, until it's a simple situation of you and Hamish Tang signing on the dotted line, shaking hands and walking away.'

'You're a good friend, Hal,' Jay said with a smile. 'I know what you say makes sense. I promise you that I'll do my best, but it won't be easy on either count.'

'I bloody well realize that,' responded Hal, 'but it's the only sensible thing for you to do.'

'You're right, and I promise I'll try,' said Jay.

'Excellent,' said Hal. 'I'll finish my cigar, drink another glass of your splendid champagne, and then I suggest that we call it a day. I'm sure that you have to be up at the crack of dawn tomorrow to get back to County View, and I'm not going to be staring out of the window wondering what to do all day.' Jay smiled and obediently filled up the two glasses.

The following morning Jay was on his way back to County View just after five thirty. It was a clear cold morning as he waved at the security guard as he entered the yard. A white frost was glistening on the grass, but his earlier phone call to Jed had reassured him that the grass gallops were perfectly safe to use.

He parked his car and walked into the stable yard in time to see the first string being mounted. The plan was to give all the runners for Cheltenham a serious piece of work that morning. The Festival was only ten days away, and it was planned to run Keep Rocking and Bucks Fizz at Stratford on the Monday. This was the traditional curtain raiser to the most important National Hunt week of the year. It was always a competitive meeting, and very often Irish trainers who had horses running at Cheltenham took the opportunity to fill up their horseboxes with some of their lesser lights, and to compete for the not huge, but certainly worthwhile, prize money at Stratford. These two were accompanied up to the grass gallops by Splendid Warrior, Pewter Queen, Tobago Song and Wot A B, all of whom were still on course to run at the Festival.

Once more Freddie had come down to County View to be involved and he was going to ride Splendid Warrior for the first lot of work, and Wot A B for the second. Paul was going to ride Pewter Queen upside Splendid Warrior and Tobago Song alongside Wot A B.

With all the work being completed on a more than satisfactory note, Jay invited Paul and Freddie to join him and Jed in their normally frugal, but convivial breakfast, in Jay's kitchen. Eva was up and looking radiant, and welcomed them in with a broad smile.

'I've had a chance to glance at the *Racing Post*,' she announced. Looking at Jay she said, 'You and Harry are now joint favourites to be top trainer at Cheltenham, and Freddie is favourite to be the leading jockey.'

'What price am I?' was the cheeky question from Paul, and they all laughed.

'You may well laugh,' he said, 'but the bookies don't know that I am going to have all of Freddie's rides. I have arranged for him to be nobbled before the race.'

'I'm terrified!' exclaimed Freddie, throwing his hands up in mock horror, which made them all laugh again. Eva quietly gave Jay a thumbs up sign, pointing to the *Racing Post* which was a signal to say there was nothing in it of a negative nature as far as County View was concerned. Her husband breathed an inward sigh of relief.

The rest of the morning was taken up with the normal routine, and Jay as usual went indoors to have a light lunch with Eva. He was just about to sit down when his mobile rang. Hal was on the line.

'I've been thinking of our conversation last night. Would you mind if I made some discreet enquiries of

273

my own? Frankly at this stage it probably would be better if you were not involved. Apart from the fact that you have got enough on your plate, the chances are that I will turn up nothing, or just wild rumours. I would sooner not complicate your life any more than it is at the moment,' said Hal.

Jay thought for a moment before responding. 'Hal, anything you can do would be more than appreciated, and I know that I can rely on your discretion. In particular I don't want Victor or Howard to think I am doing anything behind their backs. As you know I already feel guilty enough.'

'That's fine,' said Hal. 'Remember I am a director and shareholder of the company, and if I decide to take any action which I feel might be protecting my interests and those of my two friends, they can hardly complain.'

'That's absolutely OK by me,' Jay assured his friend.

'Probably nothing will come of it,' said the American. 'Let's hope it's a question of the more the merrier, rather than too many cooks,' he concluded. 'I'll be in touch.'

'Thanks a million, and if I hear anything I'll keep you in the loop.'

'Great,' said Hal and rang off.

Shortly afterwards Giles Sinclair was on the phone.

'We've had a minor breakthrough,' he said. 'One of the trainers has got cold feet and came to see me this morning. He has admitted that he was paid a substantial sum of money to withdraw his horse. He never met the telephone caller, and the first half was paid when he agreed, and the second half on the day of the race in which his horse should have run. The

274

money on both occasions was deposited in a locker at Waterloo Station and the key sent to him via registered post. I have told Harvey Jackson who is going to interview the man, but he is pretty confident that the safe deposit box will have been paid for by cash, and needless to say, the two envelopes have long since gone up in flames. The one additional factor is that on both occasions it was a foreign accent on the phone that he thought was Australian – I think we can guess who it really was.'

'Thanks a lot,' said Jay. 'What are you going to do next?'

'I have spoken to Harvey Jackson, and he feels now is the time for his men to revisit the other trainers concerned and tell them without naming the trainer what has happened and to say that he has a suspect under arrest. He can also say that, strictly speaking, they've not broken the law (or indeed Jockey Club regulations) by just withdrawing the horses. If they insist on not divulging what happened he might be able to charge them with obstructing justice. If we also promise to keep them out of the press that might help matters, although one can never be certain that will happen. Although they may not have broken the law or our regulations, I can't imagine their owners would be too thrilled if they got to hear about the situation.'

'I think you might be right!' laughed Jay at what was obviously a huge understatement.

'Either Harvey or I will let you know what happens next,' promised the security man. Feeling that perhaps a few things were beginning to break his way Jay took the opportunity to phone Hal to add this little bit of information to the still huge and complex puzzle. The next four days passed without any more information concerning the arrests. Jay was left in relative peace and quiet to concentrate on putting the finishing touches to his runners for the following week. He was grateful for the normality of following a well trodden routine. His team were on their tiptoes ensuring that not a single corner was cut, and Howard, and even more unusually Victor, left him in peace. No further major betting activity was reported; if there was any it was below the radar of the Jockey Club and the major bookmaker who had provided most of the information to date.

There had been no contact from Hal, and Jay breathed another sigh of relief on what he hoped was the justifiable feeling of no news was probably good news. The *Racing Post* commented on the change of odds on the Trainers' Championship, but put it down to the fact that a number of industry pundits had suggested that Jay's incredible run couldn't continue, and that Harry Solomons was due for a change of luck. They also pointed out that it looked as if Harry would have a stronger hand at the forthcoming Aintree than Jay. The continuing support for the French horse was also leading to the opinion that Jay might well fail to capture the really big prize money of the Gold Cup itself. Jay let this all wash over him and determinedly concentrated on his runners for the next week.

Fiona rang from South Africa to say that she couldn't possibly let the Cheltenham excitement go without being a part of it, so would it be all right for her to join them. Eva was delighted that her mother was going to be around but made her promise not to fuss over her, nor behave in anything other than the way she normally did with her much loved only child.

On Sunday night Jay and Jed were talking about final arrangements for the coming week. Stratford was perfectly straightforward, and it was agreed that Paul would ride both horses. Secretly Jay felt the fewer rides Freddie had before the four golden days, the more chance he had of escaping injury or, worse still, an unfortunate suspension. He refrained from letting either of the jockeys know this.

The horsebox set off early on Monday morning with Keep Rocking, who was to run in the Novice Hurdle, and Bucks Fizz who was competing in the Handicap Steeplechase. The Handicap Steeplechase was first and was run at the breakneck pace so often associated with races at Stratford-upon-Avon. Paul kept Bucks Fizz in the middle of the field, and by the time they were leaving the back straight for the second time the twelve runners were well strung out with Paul lying fourth. Turning for home he quickly produced the horse on the inside rail seeing a good gap. He jumped the last in second place and, as hard as he tried, he could make no impression on one of the Irish raiders. It was a satisfactory performance and Danny who was standing in for Jay on the day before the Cheltenham Festival was quick to congratulate him.

Keep Rocking's Novice Hurdle had a field of twenty-two. Again this was run at a fast pace. It was so bunched up that it was difficult for Paul to make any progress towards the prominent position preferred by the horse. There were still seven horses in contention as they swung off the final bend and straightened up for the winning post. Paul was still seventh and the traffic in front of him refused to open up. Keeping his nerve, not losing any ground on the leaders, he waited until the last hurdle. Seeing half a gap he urged his horse into it, and with an excellent leap he came out in fourth position. The run to the winning post was short, but getting down to work as hard as he could, he urged his horse on and once more came second. This time only by a neck.

He was disappointed but Danny was once again very enthusiastic about the ride Paul had given the young horse. Back at County View Jay, who had watched the racing on television, was also quick to praise his young jockey. A buzz of excitement surrounded evening stables as everyone got ready for the first day of the Festival.

Chapter Twenty-Nine

It was the first day of the Festival. Jay tried to concentrate on the paperwork necessary to make the declarations for Wednesday. Moments later he saw the headlights of motorbikes and a motley collection of cars belonging to those stable staff who did not live on the premises as they made their way in to work. There was a knock at the door and to his surprise there was Simon Bailey, who ran the local newsagents with good humour and efficiency.

'I thought you might like the papers, and in particular the *Racing Post*, a bit earlier today,' he said with a smile. 'I'll make sure that you get them at this time for the rest of the week too.'

'Thanks so much, I really appreciate it.'

'I expect there will be a fair amount about you and your horses in it, and I'll be watching on television this afternoon. Good luck,' he added.

'Thanks. We all need that in National Hunt racing, and particularly this week. Again, I really appreciate this.' Turning away he went back into the kitchen with the papers under his arm. Clearly there would be mention of him and his horses, but to his relief he could find nothing to cause alarm. Finishing his coffee he walked out into the yard which was already a hive of activity under the careful scrutiny of both Jed and Danny. He was surprised to see Cathy, Jed's wife, walking up to him with what appeared to be a plate in her hand. On it was what turned out to be a toasted bacon and egg sandwich.

'Here, get this down you,' she said. 'I know what you're normally like as far as breakfast is concerned at the best of times. You are going to need a bit of fuel for the long day ahead.' Reaching into the pocket of her voluminous apron she produced a bottle of tomato ketchup. 'Want some of this on it?'

'No,' laughed Jay. 'You really are a brick.' Giving her a peck on the cheek he took the plate and sat down on a nearby mounting block, and dug into the sandwich with relish. Cathy stood over him like a mother hen until he had finished the last mouthful. She took the plate and asked if he would like another one. With a vigorous shake of the head and a broad grin he admonished her.

'Get thee behind me, temptress!' he said as he walked back across the yard.

All the horses were happily munching away on their breakfast apart from today's two runners, who would be fed after their light work. They were already tacked up and groomed to within an inch of their lives.

With perfect timing Freddie walked into the yard with his stick in one hand and riding helmet in the other. Within seconds he and Paul were legged up and walking up to the gallops. Jay was keeping a watching brief on these whilst Jed supervised the yard. Danny was following Freddie and Paul on the gallops and he trotted out of the yard to catch them up. Freddie turned to Paul.

'I hear congratulations are in order for yesterday,' he said.

280

'They both ran well,' was Paul's modest reply.

'I know that,' said Freddie,' but I'm told you gave them both a cracking ride. Keep Rocking would probably have been fourth if it wasn't for the way you rode her.'

'Ah well, you know what it is,' countered Paul. 'I'm after your title!'

'In your dreams!' replied the Irishman as they arrived at the start of the gallops.

The short sharp pipe openers went well, and Jay drove the Land Rover back to the yard, leaving the three jockeys to walk their horses back and allow them to cool off.

He noticed that Harry Pearce the box driver was putting the final touches to the gleaming horsebox which he always kept in immaculate condition. Walking over Jay gave him a pat on the back.

'It looks a picture here,' he told the driver.

'I always feel that the state of the transport says a lot about the yard. It's an important advertisement for us as it travels around the country.'

'Too true,' answered Jay. He wandered into the kitchen. Eva was already up and busy.

'Are you going to eat something today?' she enquired.

'I already have,' Jay surprised her, as he told her about Cathy's sandwich.

'She's an absolute treasure. I don't know what we would do without the two of them.'

'Work a great deal harder, and have a lot less peace of mind,' her husband countered. They were joined by Fiona, looking as fresh as a daisy and wrapped in a white towelling bathrobe.

'I have already had a shower and used the bathroom. I thought it might be a bit frantic there later on.'

281

'Could be, how about some coffee?' asked her daughter.

'I'd love some. Anything in the papers?'

'I've not had a chance to look properly yet,' said Jay. 'Why don't you do the reading for me and tell me if there is anything I ought to know.'

Seconds later the door opened and in walked the three jockeys followed by Jed. It was unusual for all of them to have breakfast together, but Jay had felt that this week it probably would make sense, as well as a sign of real team work. The eight people made the kitchen very cosy, but nobody seemed to mind. The other national papers were grabbed and turned to the racing pages. Looking at the betting on Jay's runners, it was clear there had been no significant change from the previous day. Mythical King was in the first race, and Headswim in the last. Harry Solomons' runner in the Champion Hurdle was joint favourite with an Irish trained horse, and Jay was without a representative. Jay remembered to switch on his mobile and check the going. The overnight rain had turned the going to good, which was greeted with a mixture of 'Great!' 'Brill!' and other exclamations of delight from the assembled crowd. After a short break and more idle chatter they all got up and went into the yard.

Jay and Jed checked that the two runners for that day had all eaten their food, and Harry was told to get the horse ramp down ready to load them. Travelling boots and all the other necessary equipment were put on them or packed into the box, along with the solitary feed for Headswim, as had been agreed the night before. Good luck pats and wishes were administered to the three runners as they were led out to be loaded, and the sense of excitement and anticipation rippled through the yard. At this moment Jed walked up to Harry giving him two buckets and a plastic bag.

'Here's the feed for Headswim,' he said. 'Add the garlic to the nuts with that small amount of sugar beet in the other bucket. Phone Danny when you are on your way up at about twelve, and he'll meet you at the stable yard security gate.' Harry nodded and placed the buckets behind him in the cab. A few minutes later the ramps were closed, the two grooms were sitting in the horsebox, and Harry was driving it out of the yard on its way to Cheltenham. Jed had insisted that this day he would stay at home and supervise the exercise for all horses who were running later on in the week. Danny was going to travel with Paul who was riding in the first race.

By the time Jay returned to the house Fiona had changed, and reassured Jay that there was nothing of particular note in the newspapers. She kindly offered to drive the car to Cheltenham so that Jay could read the *Racing Post* and other racing papers on the way. Meanwhile Eva was upstairs putting on one of her favourite racing outfits, and was almost ready by the time Jay had finished his shower and shave. He put on one of his several smart, but slightly country, suits which were reserved exclusively for his attendance at major meetings. Having finished dressing, he went for a final check on the yard, knowing full well that all would be under control with Jed's more than capable supervision.

Going back to the kitchen he shepherded the girls into the car, tucking the *Racing Post* and a couple of tabloids, *The Times* and the *Telegraph* under his arm.

'I don't think you will get through all of those by the time we get to Cheltenham,' Fiona said, smiling at him.

'Don't worry, it's only the racing pages I'll bother with today,' replied Jay.

Accompanied by shouts of 'Good luck!' and lots of enthusiastic waving, his Jaguar was soon on the way to Cheltenham with Fiona behind the wheel. Fiona felt that the clock had been turned back to the days when she had runners there, and had driven herself from Lambourn, sometimes with Jay as her passenger if he was riding for her.

Arriving at Cheltenham they gradually made their way into the racecourse through the already heavy traffic. They parked in the area reserved for trainers and threaded their way into the racecourse via the very careful security checks which were now part of every major race meeting in the country. The two women went straight up to the box which Hal and his friends rented each year. Jay went through his customary pre-race routine of visiting his horses and then checking the declarations in the weighing room. As always, everything was in order, and whilst making his way through the crowd he met a number of well wishers, racing friends and colleagues before eventually reaching the sanctuary of Hal's box.

His friend greeted him with enthusiasm and introduced him to the other guests whom Jay had not met before. Hal's two friends who made up the other members of his Big Apple Syndicate were already there. Bart Eastington and Len Lavinger greeted him warmly and refrained from asking him any silly questions. Hal took him to one side.

'No real news for you, but I'm working on it as promised. I really think you ought to make an effort to be at this meeting with Hamish Tang on Saturday night.'

'I hear you,' was Jay's response. 'Let's see how the week goes.'

Hal nodded his understanding and went back to his other guests. He made a big effort to ensure that both Eva and Fiona were introduced to everyone. The time before racing passed so quickly that Jay, having grabbed a first course of the lunch laid on by Hal, found it was time for him to go down and supervise the saddling of Mythical King. On his way he smiled to himself as he thought about how much he now appreciated Cathy's egg and bacon sandwich.

County View's first runner of the Cheltenham Festival was in the very first race. The two mile Novice Handicap Hurdle was worth £58,000 and, like all the races that week, would be highly competitive. Jay was quietly confident that Mythical King would perform extremely well. Not over exposed, having only run seven times, the horse had come on from strength to strength as the season had progressed, and Jay had always had Cheltenham at the back of his mind. The good going was in the horse's favour, and although far from favourite the eight to one price with the bookmakers showed that his performance to date had not gone unnoticed.

This was one of the rides promised to Paul, and the young man was very excited when Jay went to collect the saddle.

'It's just another race,' Jay assured him. 'It happens to be in front of a huge crowd and for more prize money than we normally compete for. I have every confidence you will give the horse a good ride, otherwise you wouldn't be here now,' he concluded with an encouraging pat on his jockey's back. Jay then left to go to the pre-parade ring to saddle the horse.

In the parade ring Jay was joined by Victor and Howard, as well as Fiona and Eva. As this was a County View-owned horse, there were no outside owners. Hal had stayed in his box to entertain his other guests. The conversation before Paul arrived was about the horse's chances. Jay for once was enthusiastic.

'I think we've got away well with the weights,' he said. 'I'm not saying we'll win, but I'll be very disappointed if we're not in the first four.'

'What's the prize money?' asked Victor with his eye on the financial aspects.

'Fifty-eight thousand to the winner,' said Jay. 'Not too bad is it?'

'Is this one I should back?' asked Howard.

'Up to you, but it's as good an each way chance as we are probably going to have over the four days. But do remember that this is some of the most competitive racing in the world,' replied the trainer.

A few moments later Paul joined them, and he and the horse were on their way down the chute to the racecourse itself. Jay and his companions returned to Hal's box, where they were introduced to those of Hal's guests not met on previous occasions.

'Before you ask,' Jay announced, 'I think he's got a very good chance, but you never know with National Hunt racing, and particularly here.' Two of Hal's guests went off to have an each way bet on the Tote, and by the time they returned the race was almost under way.

As is always the case at Cheltenham, the first race was greeted with a huge roar from the crowd as the field started. This is usually instigated by the massive Irish contingent, who come not only to back their own horses, but to have a good 'craic' during the four days. Paul had eighteen competitors to contend with. Following his strict instructions from Jay and Freddie, he was hugging the rail and keeping out of trouble over the headlong dash of the first two hurdles. Turning away from the stands, the field started to sort itself out, but was headed at a strong gallop by an Irish and a French horse.

Going down the back straight there was little change in the order, though five of the runners were beginning to find the searching pace a little too strong for them. Paul, still on the rails, had moved up to seventh and was holding that position as they turned to climb the hill.

More or less freewheeling as they took the descent towards the home straight, he was pleasantly surprised to find that Mythical King moved comfortably into fourth place without any urging. Remembering only too well his mistake of the previous year, when he hit the front too soon on My Final Fling, he slowly but surely edged his way into second place with one hurdle to jump.

The leader was still four lengths ahead of him but was carrying nine pounds more weight than Paul's horse. Both of them flew over the last hurdle, and Paul gave his horse two stiff whacks behind the saddle. The result was instantaneous. First of all the horse dived away from the whip, but then straightened up and, as Paul waved the whip at him without touching him, he sped past the other horse to win by a comfortable two lengths.

Hal's box was euphoric. Virtually everyone amongst his guests had backed the horse, which paid out just over ten to one on the Tote. Jay, Victor, Howard and Eva could hardly have hoped for a better start to the Festival. Jay excused himself, and this time accompanied by Howard, Victor, Hal and the two women, he rushed down to welcome Paul back into the winners' enclosure. The young man was beaming from ear to ear.

'That was absolutely brill, guv'nor!' he exclaimed. 'I can't believe I've won the first race at the Festival!'

'Well you did, and you did it bloody well!' countered Jay. 'I'm proud of you, Paul, I really am.' As the young lad jumped off, Eva gave him a hug and a big kiss.

'I hope that didn't embarrass you,' she said, 'but we are all thrilled for you and the horse.' Blushing he stammered his thanks, and rushed up the steps into the weighing room. Jay went after him, grabbed him as soon as the formalities were over, and dragged him back to make sure he featured prominently in the photographs.

Jay was being subjected to the normal barrage of questions, when one particularly interesting one came up.

'You obviously think a lot of this young man, or you wouldn't be putting him up on important races. How far do think he will go?' Jay paused before replying.

'You have seen today how well he rides. He's got a brain as well as being strong, he listens to advice, and is blessed with not having a problem with his weight. My own view is that if he keeps working as hard as he does now, I can see no reason why he shouldn't get to the top. To win the opening race at Cheltenham at nineteen years old can't be bad, can it?' The journalist nodded his agreement.

Going back to the box they were all thoroughly enjoying themselves when inevitably the conversation turned to Jay's hopes for Headswim. He was in the Juvenile Novice Handicap Hurdle at the end of the afternoon.

'It's a bit of a lottery,' he confessed. 'The horse has only had three runs over hurdles, but has got better each time. The bookies seem to think we have got a good chance judging by the morning papers. The starting price forecast is only five and a half to one.'

'I see that you have switched jockeys to Freddie Kelly,' noted one guest.

'True. He is our number one jockey. The young man in the first race is extremely good, and needs encouragement and experience at the highest level if he is to have the success I believe he will, but Headswim will benefit from more experience on his back.'

Sitting on the balcony enjoying a coffee and a cigar Jay was suddenly alerted to an announcement on the loudspeaker.

'Will Mr Jason Jessop please go to the stable block as soon as possible.' The announcement was repeated, and everyone in the party had heard it.

'What do you think that's about?' asked Victor.

'No idea,' answered Jay.

Not waiting for the lift, he sprinted down the stairs and hurried as best he could through the heaving throng behind the grandstand and down to the stable yard. He was met by a worried Danny who said that Headswim was definitely under the weather. Jay asked him to be more specific as they hurried to the horse's stable.

'Come and take a look for yourself,' said Jed. They went into the stable and sure enough the usually bright, slightly highly strung horse was looking far from his normal self.

'What do you think it is?' asked Jay.

'I'd say he was sickening for something. Whatever it is, I can't see him running this afternoon.'

'I agree,' said Jay. 'Let's call for the vet.' Going out to the security office he asked for the vet to be called to box ninety-seven.

When he arrived the vet took one look at the horse and agreed there was definitely something wrong with him. He checked the heart beat, then asked for the horse to be walked, and then trotted outside the box. There was nothing wrong in the movement, and no heat in the legs or feet.

'It seems to me that the horse is either allergic to something it has eaten, or it has been drugged,' announced the vet. Jay was aghast.

'I just don't understand that,' he said. 'He's got the same food as every other horse in the yard. He's not been out of our sight or attention since we arrived here. That's right isn't it, Danny?'

'Absolutely. Either Jackie who looks after him, or I have been here the whole time. You know what Jackie is like. She sits outside his box like a body-guard, and the only time she went to have a break I took over from her.'

'What do you suggest?' Jay asked the vet.

'I don't think you can run the horse for sure. Would you like me to take a blood sample?'

'I think that's a very sensible precaution.' Turning to Danny he went on, 'I suggest you take the two horses home as soon as the vet has finished. I'll ring you to see if the authorities want to be involved in any way.'

Going across to the weighing room Jay sought out

the stewards' secretary, and explained the circumstances.

'I'm very sorry,' the secretary told him. 'It must be a big disappointment after your success in the first. I'll let the stewards know, and if they want to see you I'll give you a call,' he concluded whilst jotting down Jay's mobile number.

Jay walked slowly back to Hal's box, pondering on this sudden development. As soon as he was in the box, he was surrounded by people asking him what had happened. He explained it to them and Howard looked worried.

'Do you think somebody's got at him?' he asked Jay.

'I really don't know. With the security here, I just cannot believe it. Perhaps it's as the vet says, and he's allergic to something here. Whatever it is, it has certainly knocked the stuffing out of him.'

A few moments later his phone rang. The stewards' secretary told him that the stewards understood the situation. As the horse had been withdrawn more than forty-five minutes before the final declaration time, there would be no further action as far as they were concerned – particularly as the racecourse vet had agreed the horse should not run.

Jay made his apologies and explained that he really did want to get back to his yard. Hal and his guests were all very understanding.

Taking the two ladies with him they were soon threading their way out of Cheltenham, and on the way back to County View, passing the horsebox en route.

When they got back to the yard, the two women went into the house whilst Jay waited for the box to arrive and the horses to be unloaded. To Jay's amazement Headswim looked in the best of health. By this time Jed had joined him and was as puzzled as Danny and Jay.

'Let's wait for the blood test,' Jed suggested. 'There's no point in us speculating all night.'

Jay agreed and returned to the house. They settled in for a quiet evening, knowing that Wednesday would be another frantic day at Cheltenham.

Bright sunshine bathed the Cotswolds as Jay and his team got their two runners ready for the second day of the Festival. Pewter Queen was competing in the valuable two mile five furlong Handicap Hurdle, and Wot A B was running in the Champion National Hunt Flat Race at the end of the afternoon. After a lengthy discussion it was generally agreed that Wot A B would be given a light meal shortly after arriving at the racecourse. The mystery deepened when Headswim still looked as bright as a button, showing no sign of the malaise that had affected him at the racecourse the previous day.

Once more the two runners were given very light exercise before being boxed up and on their way to the racecourse. After supervising the early morning work, Jay returned to the house to change and collect the ladies for another day of high expectation. Because of his long association with his horse, Jed was going to the racecourse today, and Danny was staying behind to supervise the running of the yard.

They arrived at Cheltenham and Jay arranged to meet his wife and mother-in-law in Hal's box once he had gone through the pre-race checks. All was in order so he went up to the box. Once there he found Victor and Howard already comfortably seated with their American host, having travelled down by helicopter. An animated conversation circled round the mysterious happenings of the previous day. Jay explained that he was still awaiting the results of the blood test. The topic of conversation moved on to the chances of Pewter Queen and Wot A B.

Jay was enthusiastic about both horses' chances. Pewter Queen had already proved she handled the Cheltenham course extremely well, and although high in the weights, he still thought she had a good chance of landing the £45,000 prize money. Wot A B was a different proposition. He had no doubt about her outstanding ability, but there were a number of runners from Ireland and France, and there was no real yardstick to compare their relative merits. He was convinced, however, that she would acquit herself well, and would go on to become a top class hurdler. Len and Bart joined the party along with one or two of Hal's other business friends. Jay's phone rang just as he was finishing his main course and was starting to think about going to saddle his talented grey mare. It was Jed.

'Can you come up to the stables as soon as possible. I need you to look at Wot A B.' Jay behaved as it was just a routine matter and left the box. Eva threw him a worried look as he was leaving and he returned it with a reassuring smile. He got to the stable block as quickly as he could through the huge crowd and found a very worried Jed at the gate.

'Wot A B looks just like Headswim did yesterday. I don't think we can run her.' Jay went into the box and saw the telltale listless look about the horse. He went back to the security office to ring the vet, who arrived in minutes.

'I don't understand it,' said the vet. 'This horse looks just like the one yesterday and there isn't anything obviously wrong with her. Would you like me to take a blood sample again?'

'Yes please,' said Jay. After giving the mare an affectionate pat, he left and went to Pewter Queen's box, to find that she appeared to be her normal bright self.

Once more he went across to the weighing room to report to the secretary that lightning seemed to have struck twice in the same place. Sympathetically the secretary told Jay he would inform the stewards, and would call him if it was necessary. As on the previous occasion, the horse had been withdrawn before the deadline, and the course vet had confirmed that the horse was not fit to run.

He returned to Hal's box, and announced to a stunned group what had happened to his horse. Sympathetic groans greeted his news. There was obvious concern in the eyes of Eva, Fiona and Victor, and Howard just looked at him with one eyebrow raised.

Trying to put the worrying event behind him he watched the first two races before going off to saddle Pewter Queen whilst the Queen Mother Champion Chase was taking place. Pewter Queen looked wonderful and did a great deal to lift Jay's dampened spirits.

It was not long before he joined Eva, Fiona, Victor and Howard in the ring. They were joined by Hal who had excused himself from his guests explaining to them that he had always had a special affection for this horse. The party was enlarged by the presence of Jed who greeted his old friend Howard warmly but made no comment regarding Wot A B's withdrawal.

No sooner was Freddie on the mare and on his way to the racecourse than Jay was surrounded by a number of media representatives from both the press and television. The announcement had been made that Wot A B had been withdrawn, and it hadn't taken long to register that this was virtually a repeat performance of the day before. A somewhat irritated Jay commented that he had no idea what the problem was, and that he wanted to go and watch his horse run.

By the time he got to Hal's box and positioned himself on the balcony the horses were at the start. The racecourse announcer went through the betting, and Pewter Queen was joint favourite at four to one.

Jay's grey mare was one of those horses blessed with considerable stamina, but was also able to quicken at the end of a race. She didn't have the same awesome acceleration as Splendid Warrior, but could always find an extra gear at the end of a contest. She had also shown that she could handle the stiff uphill climb at Cheltenham with relative ease.

The big field of twenty-one included a lot of experienced horses, and not surprisingly, a number of Irish entries. It was an Irish horse that was joint favourite with Pewter Queen. Although it had contested a few of the more valuable races in the UK, the two had never met on the racecourse before. The only concern that Jay had was that Pewter Queen's preparation had been interrupted to a degree as a result of the mild infection following Boxing Day. He did feel, however, that he had got her tuned up well enough to give a very good account of herself.

The first circuit passed without incident, and the field was still intact as they went down the back straight for the last time. Freddie was in his usual position on the rails, in fifth or sixth place. The Irish joint favourite was tracking him.

As they turned to the ascent up the first half of the final bend the field became strung out, Freddie moving easily into third place with the mare racing well within herself. Turning for home the champion jockey started to exploit her stamina, and her renowned ability to cope with a fast finish.

Pulling the mare slightly wide, Freddie brought her upside the two leaders, as they jumped the penultimate hurdle. At this moment the Irish challenger joined him on the outside. Four of them raced neck and neck for the final hurdle, and the whips were up and the jockeys urging their mounts to even greater efforts.

Surprisingly it was the Irish horse that cracked first. This was quickly followed by one of the two long time leaders. Now it was down to a two horse race, and bit by bit, Freddie felt his mount edge ahead of her game rival. There was a sudden roar from the crowd, and as Freddie went into the lead, he assumed it was in anticipation of the popular grey mare's victory. To his amazement, up the inside came another grey horse, who sped past Freddie in the last few strides before the winning post. There was a stunned disbelief in Hal's box, as they realised that their stable star had been beaten by a fifty to one outsider. Sympathetic murmurs and a pat from Eva did little to raise Jay's now very dampened spirits. Joining Freddie in the winners' enclosure Jay was relieved that the jockey was confident there was nothing wrong with the horse.

'It's just one of those days,' Freddie said. 'That other horse ran out of its skin.' Giving him an encouraging pat on the back, Jay said he was looking forward to the next day, and he returned to the box.

Once more there was speculation about the mystery ailment that had now struck Wot A B, and again Jay made his excuses for an early departure. This time he arrived at the yard after the horsebox. He went over to look at both horses. Exactly the same thing had occurred as the previous day. Wot A B appeared to be her normal sparkling self, and had shaken off whatever had affected her as easily as Headswim had. Jay was joined by Chris, who had also left Cheltenham early with Amanda, and had decided to come to County View of his own volition. He was equally perplexed.

'I'm afraid the only thing I can think of is that both horses were given some sort of sedating drug, which has a relatively short effect, but would knock the stuffing out of them at the time. Whatever it is it will show up in the blood tests,' said Chris. With an encouraging pat on Jay's shoulder, he took his fiancée by the hand, and returned to his car, before leaving for whatever their evening activities were going to be. A very subdued Jay returned to the house and watched the replays of the afternoon's racing on the television. A dark cloud of serious concern hung over the three of them as they ate their evening meal. Fiona walked round the stables with Jay after dinner as he did his customary last check of the day. She tried to raise his spirits.

'Come on, Jay,' she said. 'We've still got some very good chances tomorrow and Friday. After all, you have won one big race and come second in another. Go on, go and have an early night, and let's be ready for tomorrow,' she added giving him a kiss on his cheek.

As Jay walked into the yard, there was none of the underlying bubble of excitement that had been so evident on Tuesday and Wednesday. Everybody was getting on with their jobs, but there was a distinctly subdued atmosphere. It was clear that the staff didn't know what to say to their normally exuberant boss. Encouragement would be seen as patronizing, and sympathy a sort of negative response to the situation. They just got on with their work in a business-like manner, avoiding eye contact if possible.

A little later on, looking at the *Racing Post*, Jay noticed that Paddy's Pal was third favourite at eight to one to win the Mildmay of Flete Handicap Steeplechase, worth £50,000 to the winner. Try Again was an outsider at sixteen to one for the two and a half mile steeplechase, which was the second race on the card. 'At least I've got nothing in the last race,' he thought, which had seemed to be the kiss of death as far as the previous two days were concerned. With a touch of nostalgia he looked at the runners and riders in the famous National Hunt Amateur Steeplechase over four miles. In his riding days he had won this race on The Conker. With the advantage of hindsight, he wondered if perhaps he ought to have run the horse in that race today, instead of the Midlands National later in the week. There was no doubt the top amateur jockeys would have been queuing up to ride a horse that had both won the race before, and gone from strength to strength over the last two seasons. Too late for such negative thoughts; much more interesting to savour the exciting prospect of Splendid Warrior's run the following day, and more immediately, his two runners today. Looking at the previous day's results, he reluctantly noticed that Harry Solomons had closed the gap between them to little more than £2,000. He had five runners that day at Cheltenham, whereas

Jay only had two. This difference in entries did not go unnoticed in the racing pages, and there was speculation on the possibility of County View suffering from some sort of virus, which had resulted in the sudden withdrawal of two horses in the first two days.

Sitting in a somewhat sombre mood, Jay became aware of someone coming down the stairs. His mother-in-law came over and put her arms around him.

'It's not the end of the world, darling,' she said. 'You've done fantastically well. Even if you don't win the Championship, you are certain to be number two. That for a trainer in his second full year is extraordinary. I am proud of you and I know Eva is proud of you. Just walking around the yard I can see that all the staff adore you. They understand the sort of pressure you are under. Even if they don't know about the apparent criminal activities in the background, they really care and admire you, and they wouldn't want to work anywhere else in Britain.'

It was a huge boost for Jay, who turned round and gave his long time friend and previous trainer a huge hug.

'As mothers-in-law go, you're not bad,' he said, with a slight smile.

'That's more like the Jay I know,' she replied. Eva walked into the kitchen.

'I always suspected you two were having a secret affair!' she said.

Her mother looked at her over Jay's shoulder.

'I'm beginning to think I've missed out. I don't think you realize what a lucky woman you are.'

'You're bloody right!' Jay grinned as he walked across and gave his wife a hug and kissed her.

Jed appeared in the doorway. 'Am I interrupting something? If not, I'd just like to say that everything is ready for today.' Giving Jay a hard look he said, 'It's OK guv'nor. These things happen in racing.'

Fiona put an arm around Jed. 'That's life,' she said. 'It's not the end of the world is it, Jed?'

'No it bloody well isn't,' he replied. 'If it hadn't been for that young man over there, I would probably have been in a box and six foot under by now, and Cathy would be the first person to agree.'

On a decidedly more cheerful note they all trooped out to watch Paddy's Pal and Try Again being loaded into the box. The driver looked a bit crestfallen, and Jay noticed that he avoided eye contact with him.

Feeling a bit of exercise and fresh air would do him good, Jay asked for a horse to be saddled for him to ride. He told Danny to lead the horses up to the gallops and that he would follow up behind to watch the schooling. His spirits lifted when he heard a cheery Irish voice.

'I'm here and I'm sober!' called an effervescent Freddie, as he walked across the yard with his helmet in one hand, and his stick in the other.

'Let's put the last two days behind us,' said the champion jockey. 'As me dear old mam used to say, "Live for today," and that's what I'm going to do. Can you imagine how I felt lying in that bloody hospital in Cheltenham, and watching you win the Gold Cup on Splendid Warrior? I was thrilled for you, but I thought my last chance of ever winning the most important race had gone. Thanks to you Jay, I won it last year, and I'm quite sure I'm going to win it tomorrow.'

'Come on,' called Jay. 'I'm going to ride this

morning. It'll do my head good as well as my body.'

The trainer and the champion jockey walked out together, and Jed soon had Pegasus ready for Jay to ride. The trainer felt decidedly more cheerful after he enjoyed a swinging canter up the gallops. He trotted over to chat with Danny and Freddie before they all returned to the yard.

An hour later they were off to Cheltenham, where Try Again was running in the first race. This was the Novice Handicap Steeplechase, over two miles five furlongs. The Mildmay of Flete Handicap was the fourth race of the day and Paddy's Pal had an excellent chance. Both races were worth about £50,000 and either would prove important in a neck and neck finish between Jay and Harry Solomons. On the other hand, Solomons had a well fancied runner in the three mile hurdle worth nearly £120,000 and Jay did not have a runner. One way or the other, the afternoon would determine who was going into the lead on the last day.

Arriving at Cheltenham, accompanied by his two ladies, for once Jay did not do his normal pre-race check, as Danny had already done it for him. Jed had decided to stay at the yard on this occasion and supervise the work of the rest of the team. The young Irishman suggested that Jay just enjoyed himself for an hour or so before preparing Try Again.

Jay had complete faith in Danny so he, Eva and Fiona went straight to the grandstand where they took the lift up to Hal's box. Again, Victor and Howard had beaten them to it as they had again arrived by helicopter. Hal had given himself the job of cheering Jay up after the disappointment of the previous day. He studiously avoided raising the matter, including the health problems of the two horses. The only reference he made to the business of the yard was to ask if there had been any developments as far as the deal with Hamish Tang was concerned. Jay explained that he had taken a back seat and had left the ball in Howard and Victor's court.

In the congenial and articulate company of Hal's box the time flew past, and it was soon time to saddle Try Again. Jay excused himself and signalled to Eva and Fiona to stay where they were. He told them he would back as soon as possible.

This time Paul was riding the horse. Jay collected the saddle and went around to the back of the weighing room to the saddling boxes and put the breast girth and saddle on his runner's back.

The last minute routine went smoothly and minutes later Paul was on his way to the start. The experience of winning the first race of the Festival had done a huge amount to boost the young rider's confidence, and you could almost see the increase in stature that had come with it. Try Again had an excellent chance in the race and Jay knew Paul got on well with the horse having done most of the schooling at home. He just wondered if the apparent jinx was going to leave him today.

His horse was in the middle of the weights, but Jay was confident he could cope with the extended two and a half miles and the big fences. This time the instructions were for Paul to stay near the tail of the field, making sure not to lose too much ground, but avoiding using up too much of the horse's known speed too early in the race. For a Novice Handicap Steeplechase the race went extremely smoothly. The first circuit went without a faller, but the last time down the back straight the big open ditch claimed two victims. Unfortunately both horses fell in front of Try Again and nearly brought him down. Showing a cool head Paul refrained from pushing the horse too hard, and gradually got him balanced again going round the long bend before facing Cheltenham's uphill finishing straight.

Sitting in a distant seventh place Paul encouraged his horse to make up ground. This was achieved steadily and they had moved into fourth place by the time they jumped the penultimate fence. At this stage Jay was hopeful that the horse would finish in the top three. However, he rapidly saw the telltale signs of fatigue showing. The effort of making up all that ground finally told. Although the horse ran on gamely, he finished in fifth place a good fifteen lengths behind the winner.

Paul was deeply disappointed but Jay was the first to exonerate him from all blame. Now it was time to see if Paddy's Pal could make up for the disappointment in the Mildmay of Flete Handicap Steeplechase.

Not the most valuable of contests, the Mildmay of Flete is always a highly competitive race. Paddy's Pal, although winning a number of races, had never won a major contest which would result in his handicap rating being high enough to give him an extreme weight to carry.

As he was in the middle of the weights and had shown such good form already that season, Jay's flagging confidence was given a boost. Freddie was equally enthusiastic about the horse, but by no means thinking it was a certainty. After the disappointment of Pewter Queen it was clear that over confidence was not a major factor in the thinking amongst the County View contingents.

Nevertheless, it was a cheerful Freddie who was legged up onto the consistent little horse, and was on his way to the two and a half mile start. The race was run at a competitive but sensible pace, and the experienced handicappers were taking the fences with confidence and fluency. Freddie was hugging the rail as always, but was making sure his mount could see each approaching fence a good number of strides before having to clear it. Turning for home with just the final fences to jump Freddie had moved the horse up into third place. This time Jay was starting to feel confident. The penultimate fence was jumped with ease, and by this time Paddy's Pal moved into second place, a mere half a length down on the leader. Both appeared to be going well within themselves, and had moved a good five lengths ahead of the pursuing five horses.

Jumping the last looked like it was going to be a neck and neck struggle to the finish. Suddenly Paddy's Pal started to drop back at an alarming rate. For one moment Jay feared the horse had broken a leg or damaged a tendon. Training his binoculars on the horse who was now walking, he could see that Freddie was looking down. Even at this distance Jay could see the blood in his horse's nose, and that some of it had flecked Freddie's boots. Jay just could not believe his luck. Broken blood vessels are far from uncommon amongst racehorses, but this horse had never had this problem before.

He walked disconsolately down to meet Freddie who was slowly walking the horse off the race-course.

'I can't believe it, guv'nor,' he said. 'I'm quite sure we would've won that race. He's never done this before has he?'

'No, never,' agreed Jay, and with half a smile he added, 'Well, I guess it's as the old saying goes, it never rains but it bloody pours. At least we've got Splendid Warrior to look forward to tomorrow.'

'Absolutely!' replied the champion jockey as he took off the saddle and went into the weighing room. 'I'll see you at County View in the morning.'

Returning home his wife and mother-in-law had never seen Jay at such a low ebb. They had barely sat down when the phone rang. It was Chris.

'Have you had the blood test results from the Jockey Club yet?' he asked.

'No, not yet.'

'You know I took Wot A B's blood? Well, I've got my results. There were traces of ACP in it. I imagine the same will be true in the first test.' Jay was staggered.

'Thanks, Chris, I'll be in touch.' Sitting down he gave the matter some thought. Eva and Fiona remained discreetly quiet. Fiona broke the silence.

'I think you should get on to Giles Sinclair. This is a criminal act,' she said.

Jay nodded and reached for the telephone. He knew Sinclair was at Cheltenham and hoped he wasn't too busy to talk at this stage.

The Jockey Club man was genuinely taken aback when Jay told him the news.

'At least you're in the clear because you didn't run either of the horses. Our vet was involved in the decision, and I'll see if I can chase him up to get his results. How the hell could anyone have got to the horses?'

'I've no idea,' said Jay. 'I'll give it a lot of hard thought and come back to you.'

It was at this moment that Eva spoke.

'I've got a horrible feeling it could have been Harry Pearce,' she said. 'He was in charge of both feeds, he would have been able to add the drug to the feed in the privacy of the box, before handing it to either Danny or Jed to give to the horse. Perhaps he even thought it wouldn't show up.' The phone rang again. It was Giles Sinclair.

'Our samples show exactly the same. I'm really sorry, Jay. Have you got any idea who could have done this?' Jay repeated Eva's suspicions.

'Get on to Harvey Jackson immediately,' Giles instructed Jay. 'This is too much of a coincidence, and it must be connected to the other activities.'

Jay did as he was told and the policeman responded immediately.

'Behave as if nothing has happened,' he said. 'I'll investigate this man. It's likely we will arrest him, at the very latest, tomorrow morning.'

'OK,' said Jay. 'What I'll do is get hold of my other horsebox driver and have him standing by to take my horses to Cheltenham tomorrow if Harry is not available.'

'I'm pretty confident he won't be. Even if he's innocent, the questioning can be time consuming.'

Jay told Eva and Fiona what was happening and then phoned Archie. After that he went and collected Jed and brought him up to date. His usually genial friend and colleague was fazed by the news. With a shake of his head he went back to preparing for the following day and the Gold Cup.

On Friday morning Jay knew it was essential to put on a brave front. He, Danny and Jed rode round as if no problems had occurred in the previous few days, and Jay supervised those horses that still needed exercising.

When he returned to the house he sat down and toyed with the breakfast prepared by Fiona. His wife and mother-in-law stood over him whilst he ate something. A number of racing journalists telephoned, but all the calls were taken by Eva or Fiona, and Jay opted out of discussing the events of the previous few days. This time Jay drove to Cheltenham, having seen Splendid Warrior boxed up and on his way. Archie, who was driving, had been told that Harry Pearce was not well, and that was why he had the responsibility of getting the Gold Cup Champion to Cheltenham.

Once more Jay went into his old routine of checking everything. Arriving at the stable block Danny assured him that everything was in order. Jed had again decided to stay at home and supervise the work that had got to be done, including making sure that Percy's horses were properly exercised. Amanda had come over to ride Big Breakthru, and Chris had arranged to bring her to Cheltenham later on.

Sitting in Hal's box, Jay tried to appear as confident and pleasant as possible, but he noted the press had commented on the fact that he was now trailing in the Trainers' Championship. Harry Solomons had had a really good few days and was ahead by nearly £80,000. With any luck, Splendid Warrior could put that right. The reigning champion trainer didn't have a runner in the Gold Cup, though he did have runners in a couple of other important, but less valuable, races.

Even Jay was feeling nervous as he collected the saddle from Freddie in the weighing room, and walked around behind the building to the pre-parade ring and saddling boxes. Splendid Warrior looked absolutely magnificent, and Jay congratulated Martha, the groom who looked after him, on his immaculate appearance.

As always, Splendid Warrior was a perfect gentleman, and stood stock still while Jay put on the saddle and breast girth. He was watching the other horses with great interest. As he was led out of the box on the way to the parade ring he gave a tiny squeal and a buck, just to show how well he felt.

They were soon standing in the middle of the ring with Eva, Fiona and Barry Davies, the Warrior's owner. Once more Jack Symes had decided that he didn't want to appear to muscle in on what was Jay's day. Freddie walked across the turf and set about encouraging them.

'I've heard a lot about this French horse,' he said, 'but we are the class act.'

Turning to Jay he continued, 'I'll ride him as I normally do, and keep that wonderful burst of speed he's got until the last few hundred yards. Assuming of course that I've managed to get us up into a close third or fourth position by then.' The jockeys' mounting bell then sounded and Jay legged him up.

As they circled the parade ring before leaving to make their way to the course, an announcement was made that Martha had won the prize for the Best Turned Out Horse. Jay was thrilled for her because it was a very worthwhile additional little bonus and one that she thoroughly deserved. The problem with looking after the stable star was that most of the riding was done either by Danny, Freddie or Paul so in many ways she got the unglamorous end of the stick.

Because of the huge crowd on Gold Cup Day Jay had asked Hal if he could bring The Warrior's owner into the box for the race itself. Hal in his usual generous way not only agreed but invited Barry to spend the whole day there. Side by side Jay's party pushed their way out of the parade ring and made their way as quickly as they could to the grandstand, Jay receiving various pats on the back and good luck wishes, as they made their way into the stand and up to Hal's box.

By the time they got onto the balcony, the horses were already circling at the start. Jay could see that the Warrior was his usual relaxed, composed self, as the various pre-start preliminaries were conducted. With twelve runners in the race, Jay thought there should not be too many traffic problems. It would be interesting to see what tactics the French decided to use.

As always it was an extremely high class field, but there were three or four horses in the race who, although good handicappers, were unlikely to trouble the principal contestants. But as everybody in racing knows, it's surprising how something can come out of the blue to win even the hottest races. The day that Norton's Coin won the Gold Cup at a hundred to one is still one of the best remembered days of this famous race.

The runners were soon on their way. Freddie was in the middle of the pack in his normal rail hugging position. The champion jockey noted that Duc D'Avignon was lying third and was jumping very well. Passing the stands with a circuit to go the field was still closely grouped, but began to stretch out a little as they climbed the hill and rounded the bend to the final straight.

Going down the back straight, the first fence claimed the first casualty as the horse hit it and unseated his rider. The open ditch accounted for another of the rivals in front of Freddie as the horse completely misjudged the situation. Although clearing the fence, he had landed too steeply and had crumpled in a heap. The jockey and horse were soon up and none the worse for their incident.

Leaving the back straight, Freddie was now fifth and moving comfortably. He felt very confident that, barring a major mishap, his horse would retain his crown. The fence at the top of the hill saw no changes, and knowing that Splendid Warrior did not like to go flat out downhill, Freddie kept hold of his head and lost a length in doing so. Turning for home he crept up to equal fourth. He saw that by now the French horse had struck the front, but was still moving very easily. Freddie moved into third place as they jumped the final fence.

There was a huge roar from the crowd as they saw their favourite closing in on his rival. Jumping the fence, Freddie had moved outside the second horse, and was now only half a length down on it, and two lengths from the French leader. At that moment the tiring horse in front of Freddie started to drift to the right.

Because Freddie was virtually upside, there was nothing else he could do except try and get past it as soon as possible. He gave the Warrior a slap, and his mount immediately responded. Unfortunately the horse beside him also responded to his jockey's urgings, and continued to drift towards the stand rail. The French horse was going straight as an arrow on the rails up the other side.

Eventually the other jockey smacked his horse, which straightened him up, and gave Freddie a chance to use Splendid Warrior's speed to go into pursuit of the leader. The Warrior was cutting down the distance between them with every stride, and the crowd was on its toes. They flashed past the winning post with the whole width of the track between them. It was almost impossible to judge which had won.

Jay was rushing down the chute towards the incoming horses when the photo finish result was announced. 'First number three, Duc D'Avignon, second number eight, Splendid Warrior.' Jay for once was seriously disappointed at a result. Looking at Freddie as he rode the ex-Gold Cup champion towards him, he could see the same emotion on the Irishman's face.

'I'm so sorry, boss,' he said. 'I just couldn't get away from that other horse.'

'I know. That's racing. He looks fine and we live to fight another day. When we've got over this week, we can make up our minds as to whether or not we think about going to Aintree or Sandown with him, for one last race this season.'

Returning to the winners' enclosure he found Barry Davies already waiting in the position reserved for the second horse. Splendid Warrior got a huge and sympathetic cheer as he came into the ring. Barry was stoic about the loss.

'We've had two great wins with him,' he reminded Freddie. 'It was just bad luck today. It certainly won't take anything away from his reputation and the affection in which the British racing public hold him.'

Feeling a bit comforted, the Irish jockey ran off to change, weigh in, and get ready for his next race. Although Jay was asked a few polite questions by knowledgeable and sympathetic racing journalists, today it was the turn of the French trainer and owner to be mobbed as they rejoiced with Gallic enthusiasm in the tremendous feat of winning the Gold Cup.

Walking back after the race Jay ran into Victor. Instead of receiving thoughtful condolences, he was amazed to be the subject of a violent verbal attack by Victor.

'What the hell is going on? Are you deliberately trying to throw away the Championship? Harry Solomons wins the Champion Hurdle and three other races. You win one miserable handicap, you let a bloody French horse beat Splendid Warrior in the Gold Cup, and you withdraw two of your horses before they had even set foot on the racecourse! What the hell do you think this is doing to our reputation? How the hell do you think Hamish Tang is going to feel about it?' Jay's normal equanimity deserted him.

'What the hell are you talking about, Victor? Splendid Warrior was unlucky, and we are all entitled to suffer that once in our lives. I suppose you never bloody well have. This happens to be the most competitive National Hunt racing in the world – or had you forgotten? All our horses that have run have run well. They were just not good enough on the day. It happens, and the two horses I withdrew were not fit enough to run. If you don't bloody well like what's going on at County View, I will be happy to buy you out. It seems to me that you have forgotten why we all went into this partnership!' Turning on his heel he strode off.

By the time he met Fiona and Eva he had calmed down a bit. It was clear to the two of them who knew him so well that something had really riled him.

'What's happened?' asked Fiona.

'I'll tell you in the car,' he said. 'I'll just say goodbye to Hal.'

He went up to Hal and said goodbye to his guests, subduing his pent up fury which fooled everyone apart from his American friend. As he left the box Hal accompanied him. 'What's happened, Jay?' His conversation with Victor was quickly and accurately recounted.

'Come on, Jay, we all lose our cool from time to time. You know how he has set his heart on you winning the Championship, and County View enjoying all the associated limelight. We've always known this was a big ego trip for him. In every other way he has been a good director, and he's worked bloody hard on the aspects you have asked him to, not least on this deal with the Tangs. Just sleep on it, it will look better in the morning,' he added soothingly.

Jay graced him with a wry smile. 'You are probably right, I'll see you at Claridge's tomorrow evening.'

'I'm delighted,' replied Hal.

Getting into the car it was obvious that Eva and Fiona were on tenterhooks, so once more he recounted his extraordinary conversation with Victor that had got right up his nose. Eva sprang to his defence immediately, whereas Fiona took a rather more impartial view.

'Come on, Jay, we all knew what Victor was like,' she said echoing Hal's earlier comment. 'It's the first time you two have had a serious disagreement for years, so don't get it out of proportion. I know you are really worried about what's going on and you have every right to be. You are still in with a chance of winning the Championship, and even if you don't, coming second is hardly a disgrace after the short time you have been at it.' Jay slowed the car and looked around.

'You're talking to me just like you used to after I had lost a race I ought to have won when I rode for you,' he said with a wry smile.

'Well, that comes with old age,' his mother-in-law replied with a chuckle.

'I won't be as forgiving as you two seem to be prepared to be,' Eva positively growled.

'All right, let's forget about it,' said Jay. 'Let's try and have a nice evening.'

Feeling that a normal routine was the best way to soothe his frayed nerves, Jay went into the yard in time to walk round the latter part of evening stables. Meanwhile in the kitchen Fiona was soothing her daughter.

'Don't stir him up more than he needs to be,' she advised. 'He says he's not disappointed and he kept on saying that anything could happen. But in his heart of hearts I'm sure he thought it was all over bar the shouting. All the events of this week must have been a huge blow to him, the Gold Cup in particular. You are married to a remarkable young man. He's not a god and he's not infallible. Now is the time for a lot of TLC and I'll do all I can to help him.' With a wicked smile she added, 'I know you're pregnant, but you ought to be able to take his mind off his worries later tonight!'

'God you're impossible!' laughed her daughter.

'I know and I'm not going to change,' Fiona promised her.

'I'll tell you what really worries me,' said Eva. 'I think the press will have a field day with this.'

'I'm afraid I agree,' said her mother. 'But don't

worry – it will all settle down in a few days' time and, if The Conker wins the Midlands Grand National, a lot of this will be forgotten.'

'You're probably right,' was the slightly rueful response. 'Anyway, let's change the subject. He'll be in shortly.' On cue the kitchen door opened and in walked the subject of their conversation.

'They're back from Cheltenham and they're all in one piece, so let's bloody well forget about problems tonight. I'm going to join Fiona in a large scotch, and you can have a few slices of lemon in your sparkling mineral water,' he informed his wife.

'The last of the big spenders! I'll do the honours.'

True to form the press were full of Jay's misfortunes the next day. 'Has The Bubble Burst?' 'Championship Dreams Dashed.' 'Solomons Grabs A Commanding Lead.' These were just some of the headlines that greeted them as they scanned the Saturday morning papers.

'They're no worse than I expected,' the young trainer announced.

At that moment in walked Jed. 'You know, Guv'nor,' he said, addressing Jay in a way that he seldom used, 'I spent some time last night looking at the programme between now and the end of the season. As long as Harry doesn't win the Grand National, we're still in with a very good chance. The Conker should pick up £58,000 at Uttoxeter and we should have three runners at Aintree as long as the ground doesn't get too fast. I think it will all be down to Sandown. Splendid Warrior should be ready for that, and we know that barring an accident or a mistake he is still the best steeplechaser in the country.'

'You may well be right,' said Jay. 'You carry on looking at the programme, and when I get back from

London tomorrow night let's you and I have a really hard look and see if we can find some other races where we have got a cracking chance. I'm glad we kept a few of those youngsters in training just in case we needed their contribution.'

'I'll do that with pleasure,' said Jed and with a broad grin he left the room.

'Well, that's a bit more like the Jay Jessop of old,' commented his mother-in-law. 'Now you get out and work with the horses, and why don't you have a decent ride for a change. We can make our way up to London after an early lunch.'

Accepting this wise advice, Jay finished the rest of his coffee and walked out into the familiar surroundings. He looked around the yard with pride and pleasure in what they had all achieved in such a sort time and his blues of the previous day rapidly dissolved like early mist in morning sun.

Chapter Thirty

Having digested the events of the previous four days and the newspaper coverage, Jay had a quiet lunch with his wife and mother-in-law.

'I think you ought to go to this meeting with Hamish Tang tonight,' Eva said. 'It will take your mind off things. Anyway, it's really important from all our points of view.' Fiona vigorously agreed and made a suggestion.

'Why don't the three of us go up together? This meeting can't last that long. We can all stay in London tonight and I was going up to London tomorrow anyway. Let me treat you both to a slap up dinner. I'll book us into the Oxo Tower for nine o'clock. Eva and I will go on, and if you are held up a bit you can join us later.' Her son-in-law took very little persuasion and he rang Jed to tell him his plans.

'It will do you good,' agreed the older man. 'I'll look after everything in the morning, and you can give me a call when you know what time you will be back.'

'Thanks a lot, you really are a brick, Jed.'

'Not at all, that's what you pay me for. See you sometime tomorrow.'

It didn't take them very long to get ready for London, and Jay was soon driving his beloved Jaguar up the M4. Depositing his mother-in-law at the Dorchester he went on to Hays Mews with Eva.

They watched an hour of television in a half hearted manner before Jay kissed his wife and walked round to the Connaught where he was meeting his three co-directors, Hamish Tang and Roddy.

By the time he got there, everyone but Howard was already seated in Hamish's suite with the draft document in front of them. He was warmly greeted by both Roddy and Hamish who discreetly avoided reference to events at Cheltenham. Moments later Howard came bustling in with apologies and complaints about the horrendous traffic at this end of the M4, as he opened his briefcase and removed his copy of the papers.

They went through it clause by clause, with the odd comment and minor alteration proposed from time to time.

'Essentially I am more than happy with it,' said Hamish. 'You are too, aren't you, Roddy?'

'Absolutely,' Roddy replied.

'There is, however, one suggestion I have which you might like to consider. It seems to me that in the event of any of the shareholders wanting to liquidate their holdings it should be offered to other shareholders before being made available to any outsiders. Likewise I would expect us to be given the first option to buy back your shares in the stud business, if any of you decided to pull out of that.'

'That seems eminently sensible,' commented Hal. 'Has anyone got any disagreements with it?' It seemed that nobody had.

'If more than one of the other shareholders was interested, I assume we would agree that they could go to the highest bidder,' commented Victor. Jay smiled to himself. Victor was always one to extract the best out of any situation, he thought wryly. He could hardly complain though as this was only par for the course for Victor, and he knew about this trait long before he approached him to join the County View syndicate.

'Right,' said Hamish. 'That seems to be all agreed. Let's shake hands on it and get young Roddy here to sit down with the lawyers and get the final agreement prepared.'

There was a general consensus that this would be acceptable, and that all of them would have a chance to have a look at the final format before they were asked to sign it.

'I'll get it done as quickly as possible, but you know what lawyers are like. I guess it's probably going to be two to three weeks before we are in a position to sign anything,' remarked Roddy.

'Let's try and expedite it,' said Victor. 'I always feel that once a deal's been done, the sooner it's signed and sealed the better.' There was no disagreement. They all had a glass of champagne, with two exceptions – Victor, who kept to his customary preference for Black Label scotch and water, and Hamish who was indulging in a twenty-five-year-old malt whisky.

'A taste my family learnt from the original Hamish,' he explained.

As they left Hal took Jay to one side.

'Let's go round the corner to your flat if you have time. I've got a bit of information for you.'

Sitting down but this time declining a drink, Hal gave his young friend a hard look.

'When I said I would dig around I called up the head of one of America's leading private investigation services which we have used many times. He is a personal friend of mine, and I know he has a strong operation over here. I asked him to look into anyone who was remotely connected with County View including your co-directors. So far he's not come back to me as far as Victor is concerned. He has dug up some interesting information on Howard though.'

Jay looked startled. 'You didn't explain to me that was what you had in mind.'

'I thought you might object,' was the response. 'This is too serious an operation to leave any stone unturned. Anyway, we did find something interesting about Howard. A couple of weeks ago he handed over forty-nine per cent of the equity in his major companies to both his son and his son-in-law, leaving himself with two per cent. Evidently the thinking behind this was that if there was a major disagreement between the two of them over a fundamental policy issue, he would have the casting vote. Part of this deal is that he has an extremely generous pension for life which would pass on to Bubbles in the event of him pre-deceasing her. The other thing I found out was that he has a couple of properties in Barbados which he rents out, but both of these are in Bubbles' name. More interesting is that he has shares in a number of activities with Kipper Fish who, as you know, has been a long standing friend. These include a fairly substantial independent bookmakers in the name of one of Kipper's friends, a lap dancing club near Canary Wharf, a gym and fitness centre in the City, and another in Hampstead. All of these are completely above board, and there is no question of them being anything other than legal. Interestingly enough it appears that Kipper is known to place large bets on commission from time to time. Bets which are too large for his own company to stand by itself.' He paused to let the information sink in. Jay looked genuinely amazed.

'I can't believe he could do any of this without telling me.'

'Why not? None of the companies, with the possible exception of the bookmakers he shares with Kipper, have anything to do with you or anything you are involved in. He may well have been going to tell you about reducing his overall business commitment so that he could spend more time on racing. That could be one of the reasons for his reluctance to sacrifice any of his shares in County View. He has told us for some time that he would like to ease off and spend more time with his grandchildren and at the races.' Jay nodded his understanding.

'I'm still surprised,' he said. 'I thought we were really close, and the fact that he has got a bookmaking connection surprises me. This has never come out in the past.'

'Well, I don't know why that would be, but that's all the information I've got. I would suggest that you don't do anything about it for the time being. Mull it over and talk to Eva and Fiona. If you decide to do anything then have a chat with me first.'

'All right,' said Jay. 'I'm really surprised you followed this course of action.'

'I hope you are not annoyed,' said Hal. 'If I had talked to you about it, I think you might have tried to dissuade me. After all, I'm only trying to do what little I can to cast some light on what might be happening behind the scenes.'

'I know that,' said Jay, with a friendly grin. 'It will be interesting to see what else you come up with. I'm sure nothing can surprise me more than this.'

'Let's hope not. I know you've got dinner with your two ladies, and I've got a busy evening ahead of me too,' said Hal as he got up and walked towards the door. Jay let him out with a friendly pat on the shoulder.

A few moments after Hal had left, Jay walked into Berkeley Square, and grabbed a black cab.

Reaching the Oxo Tower he saw Eva and Fiona already seated at a table overlooking the river. The lights of London were sparkling, and the outline of the London Eye was visible. It was an exciting and beautiful panorama.

'Let's order dinner before you tell us what has happened,' his mother-in-law suggested.

Looking at the menu Jay suddenly realized just how hungry he was, and he asked for an extra large portion of Parma ham, followed by a steak with béarnaise sauce, salad and French fries.

'Well, that should keep the wolf from the door,' commented Eva. 'Right, tell us all.'

Jay quickly filled them in on the meeting with Hamish and Roddy, then paused to get their comments. Both had few questions and were in overall agreement with what was being put together. Jay noticed that Eva was less enthusiastic than her mother.

'You seem a little dubious,' he commented.

'Oh, it's not that,' she replied. 'It's such a huge change in our lives, I suppose I am feeling rather more cautious than I normally am. I still think we should go ahead and do it.'

'Are you sure?' he said. 'I can still pull out.'

'Yes I am.'

He then mentioned that Victor had behaved as if nothing had happened the day before, and then he went on to relate Hal's news about Howard. Both of them were genuinely surprised.

'Are you going to talk to him about it?' asked Eva.

'I don't know,' replied Jay.

'You can't,' insisted Fiona. 'The only way you can raise it is by telling him he is being investigated. How the hell do you think he is going to react to that? You are going to have to be much more subtle than that. I think your best way is via Benny. If he can let you and Howard know that he's discovered that Kipper is a commission agent, it will give you a chance to raise the subject with Howard. Remember though that Benny is going to be loyal to Howard. After all, it was Howard who first brought him on to the scene to help with the Irish situation.'

Jay accepted this wise advice with a nod of the head. 'Let's all think about it, I'm not going to do anything rash. Howard has been too good a friend for too long to jeopardize something that may have little or no relevance in the current situation. If he did keep his plans quiet because he didn't want to louse up the Tang proposition, it would be terrible for me to imply he was being less than straightforward and honest.'

The two women nodded agreement and soon they were all enjoying the excellent food in their spectacular surroundings. After dinner they were all ready for an early night. Getting the cab to stop at the Dorchester to drop Fiona, Jay and Eva decided to stroll the short distance to their little house in Hays Mews. The emotional and physical strain of the last week had taken its toll, and they were soon in bed and fast asleep.

Jay awoke to the sounds of Eva moving around the kitchen. Glancing at his watch he could hardly believe it was already twenty past eight.

'I couldn't bear to disturb you,' Eva said. 'I rang Jed and he knows we are coming home this morning. I thought the lie in would do you good.'

'Bless you!' he said giving her a big hug. He went to sit at the already laid table and had a glass of orange juice. Poached eggs on toast were soon in front of him, along with more toast and some of Cathy's home made marmalade, a jar of which was always kept at Hays Mews.

Jay rang Jed to tell him they would be down in the afternoon as they thought a gentle stroll in Hyde Park would be a restful way to spend Sunday morning. They were passing Heathrow Airport on their way home when Jay's mobile rang. It was Jackson.

'I've got some dramatic news,' he said. 'Mr Pearce has confessed. Evidently his wife has got them into serious financial trouble through gambling. He was approached two or three months ago by telephone, and told there was an opportunity for him to make some money. He was given a mobile number. I don't think there's any doubt that it was our friend Mr Strauss. Harry was given £5,000, with another £15,000 if he did what he was told. These instructions would be relayed to him in due course. He was sent the tablets and told to grind them up and to get them into at least two of the horses' feeds during the Cheltenham Festival. When he learnt he was going to be providing the feeds at the racecourse, the opportunity was just golden. All he had to do was to powder them, and add them to the garlic, which would disguise any taste and appearance. The rest is history. He is now under arrest, and we will see if we can get any other useful information from him.'

Chapter Thirty-One

Jay had barely got in from the first lot when the phone rang. It was Percy.

'I've got some news for you which is sad in one way, but may help you in another. Ben Clarksor has had a minor heart attack. Nothing serious, but on doctor's advice he is going to give up training immediately. I have spoken to him and he knows that I always wanted to send them to you when he retired. He suggested that I send them to you today, if that's all right with you?'

'Of course it is,' said Jay. 'What's their situation with entries?'

'I had planned to run Canada Square in the Three Mile Novice Steeplechase on Thursday and My Little Gamble in the Two Mile Novice Hurdle on the same day. I had also been thinking about running Big Breakthru in the Fox Hunters. Having thought about it I wondered if you would be interested in doing that, and letting that girl of yours, Amanda, ride him. I saw her ride her horse at Huntingdon and thought she was more than adequate. She also did well in that bumper. Is there a race she could ride him in before Aintree, just to get used to him?'

'You organize for the horses to be on their way to me, and I'll look up the various entries. I know all your horses and I'll check back through their recent form. I agree that if we could possibly get Amanda to ride Big Breakthru before Aintree that would be excellent. She has got a lot of point-to-point experience, and she rode her horse extremely well, as you said. She's working like a maniac here, and I don't think she would let you down. Obviously she doesn't have the experience of some of the top amateurs who will be up against her.'

'That's all right with me,' said Percy. 'It will be great fun to have a runner in the race anyway.'

Jay immediately told Eva about his conversation with Percy.

'That's wonderful! They are all decent horses, and you might get two or three wins from them before the end of the season, which could be very helpful as far as the championship is concerned. However, before you get too carried away about the Fox Hunters, don't you think you better have a word with Al Lambert and see how he feels about his daughter riding at Aintree so quickly?'

'I hadn't thought about that,' confessed Jay. 'I'll do that straight away.'

He called Al on his mobile, explained the situation and waited for the response.

'As far as I am concerned, it's up to you. If you think she is good enough, I'll certainly go by your judgement. You've done everything right for her so far, and I don't see any reason why that should stop now.'

'I'll try very hard to find a race for her before Aintree,' Jay promised. 'We can take stock then. I think I'd better tell Amanda, if you don't mind, as she is going to have to start riding the horse at home and concentrate even more on getting fit for the big race.'

'I've no problem with that,' Al responded. 'Let's hope nothing goes wrong and disappoints her.'

'Of course,' Jay assured him, and with a cheery 'I'll be in touch' ended the call. He went into the yard to alert Jed to the situation, so that the three boxes could be made up for the new arrivals. Just to be on the safe side they were put next to each other in the same stable block, as a quarantine insurance. He also phoned Chris and asked him to take blood samples the next morning when the horses had settled down. They would only go for a long walk the next day after their journey, so the blood tests should be straightforward.

He went back to his office to look at entry forms. To his delight there was a suitable amateur race at Uttoxeter the same day as the Midland Grand National, which still left a couple of weeks before Aintree. He also noted that Percy's two horses could run in the two races they had discussed. When he told Jed of the plan the older man was very pleased.

'This will give us a real shot in the arm as far as the championship is concerned,' he enthused. Jay's affirmative nod was slightly tempered as a result of the various problems which had confronted the yard only too recently. He held up his hand with crossed fingers, and went back into the office to ring Percy with the results of his research. His Cambridge friend greeted the news enthusiastically. He told Jay that when the horses had been there a day or two he would like to come down and see them. He would particularly like to see Amanda school Big Breakthru over some fences.

With warm thanks, Jay said he would let him know his assessment of the horse's fitness as soon as he could.

Early that evening he phoned Hal, Howard and Victor to give them the news. Hal and Howard were most enthusiastic. Rather to Jay's surprise Victor was slightly more cautious to start with.

'It will be interesting to see if they are as good as your friend Percy thinks they are,' he said.

'Their form is pretty solid,' Jay informed him.

'Good,' replied Victor, who certainly didn't seem to be holding any grudge as a result of their altercation at Cheltenham.

The next week was full of frantic activity at County View. Uttoxeter was to be followed by Aintree, but in between a number of Jay's young horses would have their last run of the season. The results were mixed with no disasters, but only two winners and three places.

On the morning of the Uttoxeter race Amanda arrived early at the yard to exercise Elegant Queen in the first lot before setting off to the racecourse and her ride on Big Breakthru.

Jay noticed that she seemed more withdrawn and nervous than on the previous occasion. Taking her to one side after she had finished her exercise, he put his arm around her.

'Hi, are you OK?' he asked.

'Frankly I'm terrified,' she answered with a small smile. 'It's just that I know that Percy is a good friend of yours, and I'm so nervous about letting you and the horse down. At the same time, to possibly ride in the Fox Hunters was beyond my wildest dreams when I first came here. I guess it's a combination of all those things.'

'Well, you know that you're going to get plenty of support,' Jay assured her. 'I think Percy made it quite clear to you when he was down here that he had every confidence in your ability to acquit yourself and Big Breakthru well.'

Visibly cheered, Amanda reached up and gave Jay a kiss on his cheek. At that moment Eva appeared.

'I thought Chris would have been enough for you without trying to pinch my husband as well!' she said with a naughty smile. Poor Amanda blushed, before Eva took her by the arm.

'Come on, young woman, you are going to eat some breakfast,' she told her.

'Oh, I don't think I could today, not today,' stammered Amanda.

'I don't care what you think, you're going to need your strength this afternoon.' Arm in arm they marched into the kitchen.

Shortly afterwards Chris arrived at the yard and was soon eating the enormous cooked breakfast that Eva habitually put in front of him when he arrived at County View early in the morning. Chris read the preview of the race at Uttoxeter which was fairly small, with so much attention on the Midlands Grand National. However, it gave a good mention of Big Breakthru although commenting that this was the first time it had been ridden by a lady jockey.

'Chauvinist pig!' commented Eva. 'We'll show 'em, won't we, Amanda?'

'Absolutely,' Amanda agreed.

After a bit more gentle banter, Jay looked at his watch.

'Come on,' he said. 'Let's get the horses off to Uttoxeter. You know how bad the traffic is round Birmingham.'

The Conker and Big Breakthru were quickly loaded and on their way. This time Jed went in the horsebox to look after his long term friend The

329

Conker. Jay phoned Howard, who confirmed he would be going by helicopter and would take Percy with him. Evidently Victor was not feeling wonderful, and had elected to watch the races on television.

The Conker was second favourite to win the Midlands Grand National, and had seldom, if ever, been fitter in his life. Jay's only reservation was that the ground was genuinely good ground, and there was little doubt that it would have suited his little chestnut if it had been a bit softer.

Turning on the television to watch 'Morning Line', he could hardly believe his eyes when they cut to Uttoxeter to preview the afternoon's racing. The rain was coming down in sheets there, and the commentator was saying that the Clerk of the Course had said it would almost certainly be good to soft.

'Perhaps the gods are smiling on us after all,' Jay suggested to Eva, with a rueful grin.

'How do you think it's going to suit the other horse?' she asked.

'I think it will suit him very well. He's big and strong, and has won on soft already,' replied Jay.

Later that morning, arriving at Uttoxeter they were met by Jed who had done all the preliminary checks, normally part of Jay's routine. Shortly after they heard the clatter of a helicopter arriving. It was not the only one due at Uttoxeter that day, but Jay recognised the livery as that of the one they used from time to time. Soon Howard and Percy had joined them and, to Jay's delight, Bubbles.

'How are the horses?' asked Howard.

'They're fine,' replied Jay. 'But Percy's jockey seems to have got a touch of stage fright!' he added. 'She'll be fine once she's on the horse and the adrenalin kicks in. By the way, I am going to walk the course with her. Would you like to come with us?'

'I'd love to,' affirmed Percy. Howard declined the offer. They arranged to meet twenty minutes later.

Meeting Amanda outside the weighing room Jay found that Chris had also elected to have a look at the course with them. The rain had now eased to a gentle drizzle, but as soon as they got on to the course they could tell it had eased the going. This delighted everybody, particularly Jay, when he learnt that the overnight favourite to win the Midlands Grand National had been withdrawn because of the change of the going. The Conker was now firmly installed as the favourite to pick up the £60,000 prize money.

As they walked the course Jay explained to Amanda that, going down the back straight, the steeplechase course took a strange right turn. She could lose a lot of ground if she failed to take the correct line. As Amanda could see, the fences were stiff, but wouldn't be quite as challenging as Aintree. It would, however, give her an excellent opportunity to get to know her horse before what was undoubtedly going to be her greatest challenge to date. Jay quietly told Percy that he had every confidence that his horse should be in the first four, but wasn't going to put the additional pressure on Amanda by building up her expectations too strongly.

Returning to the weighing room they were greeted by Freddie, who was riding The Conker in the Midlands Grand National. This was no reflection on Paul. The Uttoxeter race was always highly competitive, but usually had a large number of entries. Jay had felt that Freddie's greater experience could possibly play a major role.

Not long after this Jay's mobile rang. It was Al and Maria. They had arrived at the racecourse and wanted to know where to rendezvous. Jay suggested the owners' and trainers' bar which, although not very big, was conveniently placed at one of the focal points on the racecourse.

They met as arranged but left almost immediately to join up with the rest of the County View group.

Eva had already booked a lunch table for the whole party in the main restaurant. Amanda would be joining them though not eating very much if anything at all. When they eventually sat down for lunch there was an air of barely subdued tension. Howard and Bubbles were voicing their normal enthusiastic support for The Conker's chances. It was obvious that the Lamberts were putting a brave face on the fact that their daughter was riding in the most competitive race of her life. Percy did sterling work in keeping up everyone's spirits, and before long it was time for Jay to go and saddle The Conker.

The Midlands Grand National was ridden over a little more than four miles. As always, it had a significant Irish entry. The decision had been made that The Conker would be kept out of trouble for the first circuit without losing too much ground. He would then use his well known stamina to try to burn off the competition.

The race went exactly to plan. A few horses made errors on the first circuit, but on the whole the jumping was as fluent as you would expect from a field of seasoned handicappers with many miles of steeplechasing under their girths. Going past the stands for the last time, Freddie moved into third place, and stayed there until reaching the back straight. He then urged the gallant little horse into moving up a gear, and they were soon taking the right hand kink and climbing up the hill at the end of the back straight. By this time the field was well and truly strung out. Freddie had stolen a couple of lengths' lead from the three horses that were still tracking Howard's pride and joy.

Standing next to them on the grandstand Jay was well aware that Howard and Bubbles were getting more and more excited, as they watched their horse turn for home still in the lead, with four fences to jump.

By now the racecourse commentator was concentrating on the four leading horses, and announced that The Conker was in the lead, and still apparently moving very easily. He still enjoyed a two length lead jumping the last, but the three in pursuit were bunched together. The horse on the inside was getting tired. Approaching the fence, instead of jumping straight, it swerved from left to right, in a movement known as 'running down his fence'. The other two jockeys had no chance to do anything other than steady their horses. One of them was so put off by this change of pace that he hit the top of the fence, catapulting his unfortunate rider onto the ground.

By this time it was a bloodless victory. The Conker now had an eight length advantage, and it would have taken a horse with the finishing speed of Splendid Warrior to catch him.

The whole of Jay's party was ecstatic. Leaving the stands to greet their winner they were delighted to see a beaming Jed accompanying this wonderful little horse into the winners' enclosure. Congratulations were heaped on Jay as he made his way to the enclosure, and within minutes TV cameras and journalists were making him the centre of attention.

'That must make you feel a lot better after Cheltenham,' commented one sympathetic journalist,
who had always got on very well with Jay and
his County View team.

'Well, it certainly hasn't made me feel any worse!'
replied the beaming young trainer. At this stage he
whispered to Eva to handle any more questions,
while he concentrated his attentions on Amanda
and Big Breakthru.

There was one more race between The Conker's
triumph and her big moment, and Jay also explained
to his long time friend that for once he was going to
concentrate more on the jockey than the owner.

'With a body like that who can blame you!'
quipped the Lloyds man, deftly avoiding the playful
punch Jay threw in the vague direction of his head.

At this stage he found Chris and asked him to look
after the Lamberts and to try and cool them down.

'They're absolutely great, but they must be worried and excited, so let's try and keep things as cool
as possible for Amanda,' he suggested. The reply
was a knowing smile and a nod, and Chris went off
in search of his future in-laws.

The three and a quarter mile Amateur Steeplechase was run over the identical course to the Midlands Grand National with the exception of it being
approximately a circuit less. It was a competitive
field with fourteen runners of highly experienced
horses. Jay was hopeful there would not be many
incidents.

Having looked up Big Breakthru's previous runs
and spoken in some detail to the very knowledgeable Percy the plan was for Amanda to drop in
towards the rear of the field and steadily make up
ground on the last circuit. Her horse had shown the

ability to quicken towards the end of the race, so her instructions were to try to move up to challenge whoever the leaders were between the last two fences.

The race went entirely to plan, and to Jay's delight Amanda had taken on board the importance of not losing too much ground as the course changed direction going down the back straight.

There were now only two horses in front of Amanda, and Jay was gaining confidence in the belief that she had every chance of winning, but was certainly going to be in the first three.

At this stage her excitement started to get the better of her, as her horse made steady progress towards the two leaders. Jumping the second last, she moved into the lead, and started to urge Big Breakthru on towards the final fence. Instead of letting him do it in his own time, she pushed him into it. The horse took an extra stride to try and put himself right, and crashed through the top of the fence. It was a miracle that Amanda didn't fall off but the momentum had gone, and the other two horses flashed by her. Although Percy's horse tried bravely to make up the lost distance, it was too late, and he finished third. Percy was the first person to join Jay.

'No criticism, Jay, she rode the horse really well until that last fence. She will have learnt a lot from today,' he quickly told him.

Moments later he was saying exactly the same to the two excited but disappointed parents. All of them, along with the ever faithful Chris, were there to congratulate her. It was clear she knew that she had made a mistake, and she was very apologetic.

'Just relax,' insisted Jay. 'You've never ridden in

such a competitive race before, and I'm proud of you.'

Percy gave her a reassuring pat, 'I'll look forward to you going two better at Aintree,' he said.

'You're still happy for me to ride him?' she asked.

'More than happy,' he said. 'In fact I insist.'

Their spirits were high as the County View party sat down and shared a magnum of champagne which Percy had provided. To Jay's surprise and delight, the Lamberts announced they had booked themselves into the Shepherds Rest, and that they were all going to have a pleasant evening together.

Percy, Howard and Bubbles excused themselves from joining them later, as Percy had an important dinner in London that evening. Much as Bubbles had enjoyed the afternoon, and their success, she was equally looking forward to attending one of her grandchildren's birthday parties.

Three hours later they were back at County View sitting in the kitchen waiting for the horses to return. Jed had insisted on travelling with his pride and joy. They soon heard the box coming into the yard, and Jed was supervising the horses being unloaded. As soon as he walked into the yard Jay could see that Jed's previously cheerful demeanour had disappeared.

'What's the problem?' demanded Jay.

'I think he's broken down,' the older man replied. 'In fact I'm sure he has.'

Jay quickly returned to the house to get Chris. Both of them joined Jed in The Conker's box. One look at the hugely swollen front off leg confirmed their worst fears. After gently feeling the horse's legs Chris turned to Jay.

'I'll scan him in the morning, and let's try to get the

swelling down overnight. To be honest I doubt he'll ever run again.'

'Damn and blast!' exclaimed Jay as he made his way back to the house.

One look at his face and Eva knew that all was not well. Jay explained the diagnosis and the fear that the horse would never run again.

'What a race to go out on,' said his wife. 'The one thing we know is that Howard will want us to look after him for the rest of his life. He could make you the most marvellous trainer's hack once we have got him sound again.'

It was some consolation to Jay who was dreading making the telephone call to an owner who, only a few hours before, had been ecstatic about his horse's triumph.

Chapter Thirty-Two

In the few days before the Aintree meeting the racing press was full of speculation about the outcome of the Trainers' Championship. By now it was clearly a two horse race with Jay a mere £4,000 ahead of Harry. On the other hand, Harry had the favourite for the Grand National, and Jay didn't even have a runner. Jay's odds on winning the championship lengthened as money and informed opinion moved increasingly behind Harry Solomons' National runner, the strangely named All Is Not Lost.

The fact that Freddie Kelly was riding it added to the popular following. Jay's friend and stable retained jockey had checked with Jay before accepting the ride.

'Of course you've got to take it,' insisted Jay. 'Remember when you got me the Gold Cup winning ride on Splendid Warrior? You've still not won a Grand National and you'll probably never get a better chance.'

With an obvious sigh of relief Freddie had thanked him down the phone and then rang Harry Solomons to accept the offer.

Harry had got several other runners over the three days at Aintree, and Jay had four. These included Pewter Queen in the Handicap Hurdle on Friday, and Wot A B in the Mares Only National Hunt Flat

Race. After a long discussion with Jed they decided they would probably keep Splendid Warrior for Sandown. The Conker was no longer an option. Much would depend on how much rain the course received before racing took place. Aintree was famous for having fast ground for this meeting, and this would not favour Splendid Warrior's likelihood of participation, but the extra time at Sandown might be better.

Harry Solomons' horses all stood a good chance, and in a number of races he was double handed, with both a soft and fast ground entry. There was no doubt that if Harry won the Grand National, the Championship race was all over. On the other hand, if he didn't, it would all come down to how well his and Jay's horses ran in the other events.

Jed and Jay had a long discussion about the travel arrangements. It was not that difficult a journey from County View to Aintree, most of it being motorway. They spent considerable time in weighing up whether or not the advantage of having the horses at home and in their own environment was outweighed by a crack of dawn start, to make sure they were at the racecourse in plenty of time.

After much debate it was decided that the horses would go up the night before.

Danny insisted on driving the box up and down on the first day, saying that it was far too much to expect Archie to drive up, drive back and then go back up that night. It was probably also illegal. Amanda was going up the night before her ride in the Fox Hunters. Jay readily agreed as this gave himself and Jed more time to make sure the final preparations for the other runners were made under their joint eagle eyes. Jed and Cathy would come up on Thursday morning. Jay would drive up the night before.

On the way up to Aintree Jay and Eva were listening to the sports news and heard that steady rain was falling in Aintree. This was not going to inconvenience any of his other runners, but endorsed their decision to keep Splendid Warrior for Sandown.

When they arrived at the racecourse the rain had stopped, but the puddles showed there had been more than just a sprinkling. A quick telephone call and Danny confirmed to Jay that all was well with his charges.

The day of the race dawned crisp and bright. Jay met Amanda in the hotel lobby and drove her to the racecourse and they walked together to the stable yard. Danny had already got Big Breakthru ready and legged Amanda up. Walking beside her towards the area where horses canter in the morning Jay was joined by a breathless Percy.

'Hey, I don't want to miss out on any of the fun,' he panted. 'What's the plan?'

'Amanda's going to give your horse a gentle canter, and then we're going to walk the course together.'

'I'll come with you,' said Percy. 'The exercise will do me good, and I'd love to see some of these fences close up.'

The canter went smoothly, and the big horse was soon back in Danny's capable hands, who would wash him down and give him his morning feed.

Trainer, owner and jockey then set out to walk round the world famous Aintree course. The Fox Hunters is probably the race that most amateurs would love to win. The thrill of jumping both Bechers and The Chair was enough to set even the most seasoned rider's nerves tingling.

As they walked round Jay explained the idiosyncrasies of the track, and in particular the advantages and disadvantages of jumping the inside or the outside at Bechers. They paused from time to time to make sure that Amanda understood the best line from fence to fence, and also the long run up from the famous 'Elbow' on the finishing straight.

Forty-five minutes later they were on their way back to their hotel. They had hardly sat down to breakfast when they were joined by the Lamberts. Chris was coming up later that morning as he'd had some very important work to do the day before.

It was quite clear that Al and Maria were just as nervous as Amanda about the afternoon. For Amanda the day seemed to last for ever until Jay at long last drove her and her parents to the racecourse.

The crowd was already huge, with that air of excitement that always accompanies big sporting occasions. Giving her a friendly pat on her bottom, Jay said he would see her in plenty of time before she was due to weigh out. Walking over to the stables with Percy they chatted amiably about her chances in this big race today, and that of Percy's other runners.

Jay signed Percy in through the security gate and they were soon outside Big Breakthru's box, where Danny met them and confirmed that all was well, and that the horse had eaten up after the morning's canter.

On the way to the racecourse Jay had reminded Amanda that their strategy was that she should stay near the back of this big field, so that she could avoid any of the early falls, and could use the horse's strength in the latter stages of the race.

Jay was doing his best to soothe the Lamberts' jangling nerves, and thought about suggesting they go and look at some of the fences. Upon reflection he thought that a look at The Chair might make them even more nervous. Eventually they all settled down to watch the first few races. From Jay's point of view it was unfortunate that Harry Solomons won the first, as the situation between them was still neck and neck.

At last the time came for Jay to go and collect Amanda's saddle. Percy had agreed to shepherd the Lamberts into the parade ring. When Jay met his jockey he was pleased to note that excitement was exerting itself over nerves. In the parade ring Big Breakthru was taking everything in his stride, as to the manner born. He was soon saddled and Jay and the County View contingent were quickly joined by Amanda. She chatted excitedly to her parents until the mounting bell rang, when Jay legged her up on Percy's fine thoroughbred. Danny had insisted on leading her down to the racecourse, and in a show of solidarity Jay walked on the other side, chatting to her but not giving any instructions. With a final 'good luck and have fun' he turned away as Danny took off the leading rein, and Percy's horse with its glamorous rider were on their way to the start.

The two and three quarter miles of The Fox Hunters' Chase starts well to the left of the grandstand, and after all of the preliminaries had taken place they were on their way.

There are two plain fences to negotiate before the huge Chair jump in front of the grandstand. Amanda had six horses behind her and the leaders were bunching up as they reached this famous obstacle. One of the leaders fell, bringing down two others.

Chaos followed for a moment or two as horses swerved left and right to avoid the horses and jockeys on the ground who were struggling to regain their feet.

Jay breathed a sigh of relief as he saw that their decision to be near the back of the pack proved extremely lucky from Amanda's point of view. The big horse had plenty of time to jump the fence on the grandstand side to avoid the melee that had taken place in front of him. Clearing the water jump, they then made the sharp left hand turn towards the back straight. Crossing the famous Melling Road and jumping the plain fences, there were two more casualties, neither of them affecting other horses, and they approached the open ditch.

This claimed another faller, but over the next two plain fences, approaching Bechers, there were no more incidents. Amanda had been instructed to jump choosing approximately the middle of the fence to give her enough room to aim at the middle of the next plain fence. Big Breakthru cleared it with ease and took the drop on the landing side in his stride. The plain fence and Valentine's Brook were negotiated safely, as were the following fences. These included the famous Foinavon where carnage had taken place years earlier allowing Johnny Buckingham to win at one hundred to one.

Turning for home they crossed the Melling Road again, and Amanda had moved up into fifth place. Jay was beginning to get quietly confident. Jumping the second last, they had moved up into fourth place, half a length behind the third. The horse in third place was four lengths behind the front two who were racing neck and neck. Big Breakthru jumped

343

the last like the proverbial stag, and moved into third place.

By this time the County View party were beside themselves with excitement. Percy's horse made steady progress under Amanda's frantic urging. With one hundred yards to go the Irish horse on the inside of the two leaders surged ahead, and for a moment Jay thought that Amanda might catch the second. Game as he was, Big Breakthru failed by half a length.

Amanda came third. Hugs and shouts of delight came from her parents and Chris, accompanied by a huge smile from Percy as he vigorously shook Jay's hand.

'Come on,' said Jay, 'let's go and meet her.'

The crowd was too great for them to get into the chute, so they waited for her at the entrance to the famous winners' enclosure. With a beautiful smile, though clearly exhausted, Amanda gave them the thumbs up sign as she caught sight of them all. Danny led the horse into the slot reserved for third place, and Amanda jumped off. Her parents and Chris enveloped her, before Jay gently removed them, told Amanda to undo the saddle, and come and weigh in with him.

As soon as this formality had been completed he led her out to an enthusiastic reception from all of those people connected with her and the horse.

Jay buttonholed one of the course photographers and had a battery of photos taken of her with just about everybody. Eventually Big Breakthru was led away and Amanda went to change. Jay's thoughts then turned to Wot A B and her run in the mares' race at the end of the afternoon.

Having recovered from the excitement of Amanda's

run in The Fox Hunters, it was soon time for Jay to turn his attention to Wot A B's run in the Mares Only Bumper. Jay and his still bubbling party were still in the middle of the ring when to Jay's surprise he was joined by Victor who he hadn't seen all afternoon.

'I decided to come up for the three days,' explained Victor. 'I am staying with a friend over at Southport.'

'By the way,' said Jay, 'we are all booked into a little hotel where I used to stay in my riding days. I took the precaution of booking four rooms about six months ago.'

'Good thinking,' agreed Victor. 'Well, how are we going to do in this race?'

Freddie looked at him with a roguish grin that was one of his trademarks and said, 'Ah Victor, you can bet your boots on it!'

'You know I don't often bet,' replied Victor.

'Well this is the time when you can,' replied the Irishman. 'As far as I can see it's just a steering job for me.'

Jay was slightly surprised at Freddie's enthusiasm but wasn't going to make an issue of it. Having legged his jockey up, the three of them left the parade ring.

'I actually think he's right,' whispered Jed to Jay. 'For once I am going to have a decent bet on the horse,' and with that he went off to walk up and down the bookmakers' stands looking for the best price he could get.

The three of them stood together to watch the preliminaries at the start. Within minutes the horses were on their way and Wot A B was sitting nicely in fourth of fifth position, with Freddie hugging the rails, as was his custom.

As soon as they entered the finishing straight, Freddie gave Wot A B two quick slaps behind the saddle and the horse literally tore into the lead. With only one furlong to go it was all over bar the shouting. With complete ease the mare won by a spectacular ten lengths, easing down.

Jay and Jed were both ecstatic. Jed because he had won several hundred pounds, and Jay because he agreed with Freddie this was a really exciting prospect. Victor dourly pointed out that this put Jay a further £15,000 ahead of Harry Solomons in the Trainers' Championship.

That night they all gathered at the Adelphi with the exception of Victor, who had excused himself explaining that it would be impolite not to dine with his hosts in Southport.

The afternoon's activities were examined from every angle, and Amanda was already asking Jay about her next race, and what was available for Elegant Queen.

'I think perhaps we ought to slow down a bit,' he warned her. 'We've had a fantastic day, and a good start to your amateur career. You have a wonderful prospect in Elegant Queen. We'll see what happens to the going, but I think it would be sensible if you spent the next few weeks concentrating on your studies, and then we can have a hard look at a programme for next year.'

'You can add my horse into that equation,' announced Percy. Amanda's face lit up.

'I think that Jay's suggestion of slowing down for the rest of the season is a good one,' her mother volunteered. Amanda turned to Chris.

'What do you think?' she asked him. Slightly embarrassed he agreed with her mother.

They were all tired after the long day, and they were not late in getting back to their little hotel. Everyone slept that deep sleep that comes with physical and emotional exhaustion.

The next day Jay's two runners were both Percy's horses, one of which was running in the Three Mile Novice Steeplechase and one in the Two Mile Novice Hurdle.

With the successes of the day before at the front of their minds there was a much more positive attitude in the County View team. Freddie was riding both horses. After a substantial breakfast Percy, Eva and Jed made their way to the racecourse. The Lamberts were going home that morning, but Chris and Amanda were staying on and would join them later.

As the Three Mile Novice Steeplechase was the first race, Jay was soon saddling Canada Square and Freddie was joining him and Percy in the parade ring. The horse had already won three chases that season and on one occasion Jay had actually been there and seen him win. He was an efficient jumper but was not carrying any heavy weights as it was not a handicap. In all his wins he had been in the vanguard, and had used his jumping proficiency and his very considerable stamina to see off the opposition. Jay, who had discussed it with Percy, felt that the policy for this race was to make sure he was not overused in the early stages, allowing his stamina to come into play up the long gruelling finish at Aintree.

When they jumped off Freddie took Percy's horse into the lead. Very rapidly three horses passed him at what Jay thought would be an unsustainable pace. Freddie let his horse settle into fourth position, leading the remainder of the field.

Although they were novices, all of them had considerable experience that season, and there was nothing in the field that hadn't won or been placed in some reasonable races. There were only three casualties on the first circuit, but going down the back straight for the last time, the three leaders all began to weaken. Freddie and the pursuing pack started to make headway.

By the time they got to the top of the hill Freddie was joint leader. Turning for home he moved easily into the lead. Two horses emerged from the pack to chase Canada Square, and one of them moved upsides jumping the second last. Freddie urged Percy's horse on to a greater effort, and slowly but surely he inched his way ahead of the challenger as they jumped the last fence.

Canada Square moved on relentlessly and passed the winning post with two lengths to spare. Percy jumped up and down with excitement and Jay was thrilled for him. He made a mental note to add an extra £45,000 of prize money to his season's tally. The Two Mile Novice Hurdle was immediately afterwards. Jay went flat out to meet Freddie, congratulate him, grab his saddle as soon as he'd weighed out, and go back to saddle My Little Gamble. By this time Percy had simmered down, and was speculating on the chances of his other horse.

'This I think is a hotter race,' said Jay. 'The horse has been running well. It seems to have a good finishing turn of speed, so I suggest Freddie holds this one up and waits until he is well in the final straight before he challenges.' Percy agreed and the plan was put to Freddie when he joined them. The Irish jockey nodded his agreement and understanding, was legged up and on his way down the chute to the racecourse itself.

The race started at breakneck speed. By the time they had reached the end of the back straight and were turning for home, the sixteen strong field was strung out over fifty or sixty lengths. Freddie had gradually moved himself up into a middle position, and stayed there until he turned for home. He was then in sixth place. Jumping the second last there were four of them upsides. For a moment Jay thought that My Little Gamble had a very good chance. However, the three other horses all turned out to be a little stronger over the last furlong, and Freddie had to settle for fourth place. Far from being disappointed, Percy was thrilled at how his horses had run at Aintree, and was full of congratulation to Jay on their performances.

'I think we should remember that the real credit goes to their previous trainer. All I did was to put the finishing touches to them.'

'I agree,' said Percy. 'But you also got them spot on for the day, and managed to get me an extremely good jockey,' he added with a grin.

'Well,' said Jay. 'It's been a pretty successful Aintree. If you don't mind Eva and I are going to leave early to get back to County View.

At the end of the afternoon Jay's spirits were really high. He was now significantly ahead of Harry Solomons, but unlike the reigning Champion Trainer, he did not have any more runners, whereas Solomons did, including the Grand National itself.

This time Jay insisted on Jed and Cathy staying overnight, and he and Eva started the long drive back to County View. Exhausted but happy, they fell into bed and were soon fast asleep.

The next two days passed uneventfully at County View. Harry Solomons got a winner but was still behind Jay in the Championship. So much would rest on the Grand National.

Jay and Eva sat glued to the television as the big race started. As always it was a huge field of forty. This is the maximum number of runners allowed. Because of the going, Harry Solomons had only got one representative, but by this time All Is Not Lost was the favourite. There were surprisingly few fallers on the first circuit. Freddie had got the favourite in the middle. Second time around the open ditch claimed two victims, but there was not the ensuing scrummage there had been in the Fox Hunters.

As they crossed the Melling Road down the back straight for the second time, the field was down to eighteen. Freddie had moved up and was going easily in seventh place. The open ditch was negotiated safely by the pair, and soon they were approaching Bechers for the final time. Freddie took approximately the same course as Amanda had, and the famous obstacle was negotiated safely and with ease. Turning towards Valentine's, Freddie looked to be going as easily as any of the runners in front of him.

Approaching the fence, for some inexplicable reason, the horse put in an extra stride, got far too close to it, hit it, and ended up doing a complete somersault. Freddie was fired off the horse and was soon standing. The horse wasn't. It was clear that the horse had broken its neck. Jay had mixed feelings. He was delighted that Freddie was well, but sad that his great friend was not going to win the National. As always he felt a great sorrow at the death of a good horse, and sympathy for its connections. At the same time he felt slightly ashamed that he had breathed a sigh of relief that Harry Solomons had not won the £400,000 available for the winner. By the end of the afternoon it was left to Sandown to decide the Trainers' Championship.

In the ensuing days Jay decided that he would have no runners other than Splendid Warrior. Many of his horses were young and had had busy seasons. Much though he wanted to win the Championship, he had to look towards their long term future, rather than just the selfish objective of being the top trainer.

A number of new arrivals were broken in, and some of the bumper horses were given plenty of schooling over hurdles. The stable staff were kept busy as there was a lot of maintenance work to be done in the quiet period between the two seasons. Jay had taken the view that he would not be running any of his horses at the summer jumping meetings. This was not because he had any objection to them, but rather he felt that his horses and staff deserved a break.

Every morning and evening he went to see Splendid Warrior, with a dreadful fear that his great horse may have contracted some sort of injury which might prevent him from running. By the evening before the big race Jay could breathe a sigh of relief that the preparations had gone without a hitch.

Chapter Thirty-Three

Speculation surrounding the outcome of the steeple-chase at Sandown was huge. All the racing columns were covering the news that it was a head to head between Harry Solomons and Jay Jessop for the Trainers' Championship. At the same time the French horse was a major threat. As the day dawned it became clear that the going was going to be on the fast side of good, which would suit all three runners. The bookmakers were having difficulty in deciding who to make favourite. Duc D'Avignon, Splendid Warrior and Harry Solomons' Blue Havana were all less than five to one. Blue Havana was the least known quantity. Still being a novice over fences, she had gone from strength to strength culminating in a hugely impressive win at Cheltenham.

In view of the previous circumstances Jay had engaged Benny's team to add additional security. They had stayed the night before at County View and travelled up with the horse in two separate cars. They had now mounted guard outside the stable block.

Although the prize money went down to sixth place, the calibre of the three main contenders was such that, by the morning of the race, there were only five runners left to dispute the £87,000 winner's prize money. Giles Sinclair of the Jockey Club assured Jay there would be additional security inside the stable block and this would be centred not only on his horse but on the other contenders as well.

Seeing his horsebox on the way Jay and Eva waited for the helicopter which Howard had arranged to pick them up. Chris and Amanda were also going and Jay had offered them a ride.

Eventually they landed at Sandown, and walked across towards the stands of one of the most challenging and exciting steeplechase courses in Britain. It had many happy memories for Jay, including the first time he sat on Pewter Queen in a National Hunt Flat Race there, and started to realize what huge potential the mare had. Arriving in the owners' and trainers' bar he immediately spotted Howard, Bubbles and Victor in earnest conversation, reading the race cards and the *Racing Post*. Howard was his normal ebullient self, but Victor seemed somewhat edgy. For once he didn't mention the Trainers' Championship, but he did ask Jay how well he thought the Warrior was.

Maintaining his normal affable, slightly laid back stance, Jay assured everybody that the horse was in the splendid condition echoed by his name, and he was confident he would give a good account of himself.

The preliminary races seemed to take forever, but eventually the time came for Jay to saddle his stable star. Not only did Benny's men accompany the horse from the stable block to the saddling area, but Giles Sinclair had seen to it that a number of Jockey Club security people were keeping an eye open. There was a tangible air of expectancy as the horses entered the parade ring. Even Freddie seemed slightly nervous at the prospect of how much was riding on this race.

After several circuits the horses were soon on their way down the rhododendron walk and on to the racecourse.

With a roar from the crowd the starter sent them on their way. Blue Havana set the pace in the same way she had at Cheltenham, and was jumping with the fluency of a seasoned chaser, rather than one in her first season over fences. Passing the stands with a circuit to go she was still in the lead, and by this time the French horse seemed to be struggling.

Climbing the hill away from the stand, jumping the one fence on the bend, her jockey increased the pace of the race. All but Splendid Warrior started to lose ground, but Freddie let his fantastic horse creep up to two lengths behind this sensational mare.

The fences down the back straight at Sandown are amongst the most challenging in British racing. Both the mare and the previous Gold Cup winner took them with ease. By this time, barring a fall, it was a two horse race. They had increased the advantage over the other three runners to fifteen lengths. Turning for home and approaching the Pond Fence, Freddie got within two lengths of Blue Havana. With two fences to jump it looked like it was going to be a nail biting finish. Clearing the penultimate fence Freddie took Splendid Warrior alongside Blue Havana. The crowd was roaring and Jay could hardly bear to watch. They jumped the last together and Splendid Warrior started to edge past the still strongly galloping mare. Jumping the last Freddie gave the great horse a slap on the shoulder and he surged into the lead. It looked to be all over, when Splendid Warrior swerved violently to the right giving his jockey no chance to stay in the saddle.

There was a silence of disbelief as the crowd

watched one of their racing heroes gallop riderless past the post.

Jay could hardly believe his eyes. He rushed from the stand, met the horse which had been caught and was being led in by his loving groom. Blue Havana had won the race, and in so doing had presented her trainer with the Trainers' Championship. Although deeply disappointed Jay was relieved that there appeared to be nothing wrong with his wonderful horse. Barry Davies came panting up to ask what had happened.

'I have no idea,' replied Jay. 'I've never seen anything like it.'

Fifteen minutes later an announcement was made asking Mr Jessop to go to the weighing room where he was met by Giles Sinclair, who took him into the Stewards Room. He was asked to sit down and have a look at the recorded footage. Jay could see nothing that accounted for his horse's extraordinary manoeuvre. Giles Sinclair asked for the tape to be run again and to be frozen.

'Look on the rails there,' he said. There standing on the rails was a man with a huge pair of binoculars. 'I think that's the answer. A few years ago at Royal Ascot, Greville Starkey was thrown off a horse which had been "beamed" by what appeared to be a pair of binoculars. The case got considerable coverage, but no prosecution was ever brought because the perpetrators were arrested and convicted on another charge. I believe that the same device has been used today. The police are out there trying to catch the man.'

The stewards were sympathetic but there was no suggestion that Jay had in any way been a party to this extraordinary event.

A very subdued Eva and Jay arrived back in the helicopter at County View, not desperately unhappy at the result of the race, but completely devastated by what was happening around them. They had barely sat down in the kitchen when the telephone rang. It was Harry Solomons.

'It's not the way I would have liked to win the championship,' he announced. 'I don't know what's been going on but it's quite clear that with any luck at all you would have won it.' Jay paused for a moment.

'That's very gracious of you, Harry, I appreciate it. As you can imagine I'm not in a very talkative mood, but we both live to fight another day,' he concluded.

'You bet!' was the response. 'I don't suppose it's going to get any easier for me.'

Once he had ended that conversation the telephone rang again almost immediately. This time it was Harvey Jackson.

'We caught the guy who is a small time crook, and the binoculars are exactly what Giles thought they were. He has told us that he was given the device via a left luggage locker with £2,000 up front, and a promise of another £3,000 if he stopped your horse winning. We hope to gain more information.'

Chapter Thirty-Four

Jay was just going to bed when the phone rang. It was a very tense Hal at the other end of the line.

'Jay, I will be with you by midnight tonight. You can imagine that it is not for the good of my health. I'd like to see you and Eva alone, and what news I have is extremely disturbing. I'll not say anything now, I'm on my way.'

Jay sat in a stunned silence for a few minutes before going upstairs to tell Eva the brief message from their friend and partner. He suggested that she try to rest until the American arrived. Jay promised he would get her up in time.

Going downstairs he sat pondering what this news could be. Hard as he tried he couldn't think of an answer. An hour and a half later he saw the headlights of a car coming towards the house, so he called up to Eva that Hal had arrived.

Eva and Jay met a very terse-looking Hal at the front door.

'I presume I can stay the night?' he asked Eva.

'Of course,' she replied. 'There's always a spare bed made up here.'

'In that case, can I have a very large scotch?' he asked, slumping into one of the comfortable chairs. Jay poured generous measures for himself and Hal, knowing that Eva would help herself to something lighter. As soon as they were settled Hal looked over at both of them.

'Do you know somebody called Vince Rafter?' he asked. Eva and Jay both shook their heads.

'You bloody well do, you know!' he said. 'But you know him as Victor Rainsford. Rafter has a South African passport. He has extensive interests in South Africa, other than the construction business we all know about. He apparently runs an extortion racket, and also a string of high class call girls. In the US he owns a controlling interest in two small casinos, one in Las Vegas, and the other in Atlantic City. Again he has control over a high class call girl racket. He is wanted by the police in both countries, but they have never been able to find enough evidence to prosecute him.'

'There must be a mistake. There really must be,' Eva said.

'I wish to God there was,' replied the American. They all sat in silence whilst the two men took a pull at their whisky. Eventually Jay asked the obvious question but one to which he was dreading the answer.

'Do you think he's behind what's been going on here, and if so, why?'

'I don't think there's any doubt. The motives are a bit more obscure. He's clearly got the facilities and contacts to command access to gangsters such as Kruger, and from the reports we have, he is totally unscrupulous. The mere fact that he has never given you any idea of his dual identity is sinister in itself.'

The three sat in silence, each pondering on the implications of this news. Jay eventually stood up and said that he thought this was so serious that Jackson ought to know. Dialling the policeman's mobile number he was put through to voicemail. He left a message with his name, saying that there was an urgent development he needed to report. Less than ten minutes later his phone rang.

'This had better be good,' growled Jackson. 'It's nearly one o'clock in the morning!' Jay passed on the information turned up by Hal's investigators.

'You were right to call me. I'll be in touch first thing in the morning.'

'I could do with some fresh air,' announced Jay.

'I'll come with you,' said Hal.

'If you don't mind I think I'll go back to bed,' said Eva.

The two men walked around the yard. It was peaceful and soothing, and the only noise was the occasional shuffling of a horse, or a steady munch on a little hay left over from earlier in the day.

'It's all like a nightmare,' said Jay. 'A really bad dream that's too bad to be true.'

'I know,' replied Hal. 'I wonder what Jackson will do.'

Strolling back to the house they both sat down and had another drink before going to bed.

'See you in the morning, you know your way?' asked Jay.

'Yes. I'll just go and get my bag. By the way, I've cancelled all tomorrow's appointments.'

Eva was fast asleep and didn't stir as he crept into bed. After only fitfully sleeping, at five o'clock he got up, dressed quietly and went downstairs without even shaving. He was on his third cup of coffee when Hal joined him in the kitchen. They sat in a brooding silence before walking over to the yard together, where activity was just starting. Finding Danny, Jay explained that he and Hal had some urgent matters to discuss, and would he and Jed please organize the work for the day. Danny responded with a smile and a vigorous nod of his head.

'I'll bet you two are up to no good!' he said. 'You're skiving off, aren't you?'

Jay smiled and thought to himself, if only that were true. He and Hal walked round the yard stopping now and then to look at one or two of their favourite horses before returning to the house. They had just sat down when Harvey Jackson rang.

'I'm afraid what your friend told you is true. I've been on to my South African contacts and to Interpol. Our friend Mr Rainsford has been incredibly clever. His dual identity has been a brilliantly kept secret.'

'What happens next?' asked Jay.

'The first thing I will do is talk to Kruger, then I think we have no alternative other than to talk to Rainsford. Is he in England at the moment?'

'He was yesterday morning. I spoke to him regarding the Tang situation.'

'Right. I'll be in touch,' concluded Jackson.

Having nothing better to do, and wanting to kill time, the two men jumped into the Land Rover and went up to watch the horses working on the gallops. By the time they had returned Eva was up and busy in the kitchen. Jay brought her up to date with his conversation with Jackson.

The next day the *Racing Post* had banner headlines covering the story of Splendid Warrior and of Jay's horses being doped. This time without being too specific, they linked the extraordinary events of the past few months together, including the three murders, the suspicion that a trainer had been paying other trainers to withdraw their horses against his runners, and the odd swings in the betting patterns on the Trainers' Championship.

Jackson phoned Jay later that same morning and insisted on a meeting with him and Sinclair.

'You do realize you will be hounded by the media?' he said. 'I think we need to try to make the meeting discreet.' Jay thought for a moment.

'Let's have it here at County View tomorrow morning.' He then rang Howard and Hal to get them up to date with recent developments. The meeting was set up and at Jay's request Hal was also invited as he had provided most of the background information.

Every newspaper in the country carried the headline of Victor's arrest. They were careful not to be too specific, but the fact there had been criminal activity surrounding County View invoked comment. What was significant was that there were suggestions that Victor had a double identity, along with references to possible South African and American connections. It was clear that the whole story was going to break at any moment.

Eva was distraught and having had a chat with her mother who was now back in South Africa, told Jay that Fiona was returning to give what help she could – even if it was just moral support. It was at this stage that Jay got a completely unexpected telephone call from Hamish Tang.

'I'd like to have a few words with you in private, and I am prepared to come down to County View and discuss it.' This was the last thing Jay needed, but he felt he owed Tang the courtesy of agreeing, as he was about to become a partner in the business. He asked if it was acceptable for Hal to be present, and was given an affirmative answer.

After a few telephone calls it was decided they would all meet at County View at six o'clock that night. Tang and Hal must have talked directly to each other, because at twenty past six a chauffeur-driven Lexus pulled up outside Jay's house and the two men got out. Eva had cleared the dining room. She had put out writing pads, a bottle of sparkling mineral water, a bottle of whisky, and a bottle of chilled white wine.

'Would you like to join us, Mrs Jessop?' asked Hamish Tang.

'I rather think I would,' replied Eva, and all four were soon sitting around the table with various drinks in front of them. Hamish began: 'Jay, a few weeks after you and I first started to talk about a possible partnership between our organizations, and after the initial plans had been laid down, I received a surprising telephone call. I was asked if I would like to go into partnership with an international consortium who would be happy for me to have a major interest in County View. At first I was deeply suspicious that some sort of leak had come from within my own organization. To my personal embarrassment I feared it might be my son-in-law. I therefore had a stringent security check carried out on anybody in the organization who could have been aware of our discussion, or anybody who might have known about the negotiations we were conducting with other studs. Then a new name appeared, and one that I had never heard. A man called Rafter. Through some lawyer he said he would like to join me and take a controlling interest in County View. My informants told me that he was a business man with a somewhat dubious reputation in South Africa and North America. I was advised to have nothing to do with him. In view of the fact that we had not even signed a deal at that stage, I found the situation rather worrying, but it seemed to be something which was a problem for me rather than for you. I now realize how wrong I was.'

There was a stunned silence around the table.

'Thank you for letting me know,' said Jay. 'Would it be very rude if I say I have nothing more to say at the moment, but I will be back in touch with you very soon. As far as I'm concerned, this does not change our proposed agreement.'

'I'm delighted to hear it,' said Tang. Shaking everybody's hand he went out to his car. Hal had already announced that he would hang on for the next morning's meeting.

'Why the hell would he want County View? How does strange betting for and against Jay winning the Trainers' Championship fit in?' asked Eva.

It was the following morning. Jackson and Sinclair had arrived and been filled in on the latest developments, and now they were all sitting round the kitchen talbe drinking coffee.

'I've been thinking about that,' said Sinclair. 'I believe it was an effort to discredit you. All the initial activities pointed the finger at you being so unscrupulous that you would stop at nothing to win the Championship. The fact that the bets were on the whole anonymous added to the intrigue, and made it even more likely that it would be you, or people placing bets on your behalf.'

'Why the sudden swing against me winning?' queried Jay.

'Because huge sums of money had by now been

put on for you not winning at very attractive odds. The fact that there were drugs involved in your yard and your horses suddenly ran out of steam, all added to the fact that you were not a trustworthy person.'

'It seems almost unbelievable that anyone would go to these lengths to get hold of Country View,' exclaimed Eva. 'We are successful, but not that successful.'

'I think there may be another dimension to this story,' Hal interjected. 'I remember that Jay told me years ago that when he was still a jockey Victor tried to con him over a horse that Jay had found him in Ireland. Victor went behind his back, Jay found out, and sent the horse to another owner and trainer. The horse turned out to be a superstar. Victor doesn't like to be beaten, and this has smouldered in his mind for years. He saw the opportunity of being on the inside of County View as a chance to plot his revenge. This man is a complete loner. Has no real friends as you know, and for years he was rejected and viewed with suspicion by both the racing and the business fraternity. County View and his association with you and Howard gave him the opportunity to regain respectability and acceptance. But we have seen enough of Victor to know that money is his god, and the only person he cares for is himself. He pretends he doesn't gamble, and he certainly doesn't have small bets on at racecourses, but a huge part of his organization and his considerable wealth is built on gambling.' Jackson sat back listening to this whilst Giles Sinclair nodded his agreement.

'Why on earth did he resort to murder?' Jay asked.

'It seems that the three victims had all been approached by our South African friend. In fact, the

364

young jockey had spoken to the journalist. The journalist then approached the National Trainers Federation, and as you know, Matt Jenkinson had refused to withdraw his horse. The combination of the three of them with such a respected journalist in the lead, was too dangerous a mixture. Hence the decision to eliminate them all,' Jackson informed them. Eva was aghast.

'I can't believe this has all happened,' she said. Jackson looked at her sympathetically.

'Some of the worst crimes are committed by those who appear to be the least likely,' he said. 'Human nature, on occasions, fills me with despair. Fortunately these are the rare and genuinely evil or sick people, rather than the majority.'

'What's going to happen now?' Jay asked Jackson.

'Rainsford will be tried for murder in this country and will go to jail for a very long while. As indeed will Strauss. Various other people who were involved in the kidnapping and attempted kidnapping etc, will all get long prison sentences. You will all get on with your lives. The media excitement will be huge, but strangely enough, you will probably come out of it with sympathy and understanding, rather than anything else.'

'I can guarantee that,' said Giles Sinclair looking around the table. 'At no time since the very beginning of this strange and convoluted series of events have we ever thought that County View, and in particular Jay, was involved in any wrongdoing. That will be made clear in the statements we will eventually make.'

'Well,' said Hal, 'I've got a very simple proposition. I think the two of you should go and have a good holiday. Have a look at Hamish Tang's studs, and then come to the States and have a good rest at my ranch. It's fairly close to Camp David, but I promise you, you won't have to meet the President. I can assure you we won't go anywhere near Las Vegas or Atlantic City.' There was a bellow of laughter around the table. Jackson stood up.

'I know I ought to be working now, but I've got a suggestion. Why don't we give our kind host a good lunch, and we can all look forward to a rather less exciting future.'

'Hear hear to that!' said Jay in a heartfelt tone of voice.

'Let's hope next season is a little more tranquil than this,' said Eva. 'I'm not sure any of us could stand this sort of stress again,' she added.

'Don't be so ridiculous!' exclaimed Hal. 'You're going to be fighting for the Trainers' Championship again next year, and you can't tell me that any of you would prefer an easy life!'

Later that evening Eva and Jay were relaxing in a pair of comfortable chairs in their living room. Jay was smoking a cigar and Eva was indulging herself in her new passion for knitting baby clothes. She stopped and gave her husband an affectionate smile.

'You know, darling, I think we ought to pause and think about all the wonderful things that have happened to us since we met. The last few months have been hell, but even they haven't been all bad.' Jay looked at her. He got up and kissed her gently on the forehead, before going back to his chair to continue his cigar.

They sat and reminisced about how they first met at Fiona's, the fight to save Danny from the clutches of The Friend, and Jay's riding successes at Cheltenham including winning the Gold Cup on Splendid

366

Warrior. Then there was the planning and setting up of County View and the almost instantaneous success that went with it, Eva seducing him in the Savoy and their wonderful holiday in Tobago, helping Howard to get his revenge on the bookmaker who had cheated him when he was a young man, the unswerving friendship and support of Jed and Danny, and Jay's surprise in Cape Town when Eva and Fiona revealed to him that they were mother and daughter.

The evening sped by as they remembered all these good times and in a thoroughly relaxed and much more cheerful frame of mind they climbed the stairs to bed where they made tender love.

The next morning Jay found contentment in the normal routine of the yard. There was still much to do even though the season was over as far as they were concerned. There were still horses that had to be exercised, and staff to be encouraged.

Although he would never run again, The Conker's leg was beginning to settle down. Howard was thrilled that Jay was going to use the horse as his hack in due course. As he said at the time, 'He'll beat a Land Rover any day.'

Halfway through the morning Jay went indoors for coffee with Eva. Whilst there the telephone rang and Harvey Jackson was on the line.

'Don't worry,' he said, 'I've got a bit of news for you. As it's my day off I wondered if I could come over and we could all three have lunch at the Shepherds Rest. I've got a driver so I would be able to have a couple of glasses of wine with you.'

'Excellent,' said Jay. 'See you later.'

'Again, it's nothing to get worried about,' insisted the policeman.

Sure enough, a little after twelve thirty, an immaculate black Rover drew up in front of the house. Out stepped a distinctly casually dressed Harvey.

'Come on, let's go up to the Shepherds Rest and I'll bring you up to date on my news,' Harvey suggested. 'You come with me and I'll drop you back after lunch.'

They were soon sitting at a discreet corner table in the comfortable dining room of the ancient pub. The wall was already getting covered with photographs recording many of the more memorable moments of County View's relatively short history.

'What are they going to do by the time you have been training for ten years?' asked Harvey looking around.

'Build an extension!' was Eva's smiling reply.

They ordered their food and sat sipping their wine. Harvey looked at both of them across the table.

'There has been a really interesting development. My contact in South Africa rang me last night to tell me that Harry Clough had turned himself in. It seems he had been a business partner with Victor Rainsford or, to be more accurate, Vince Rafter, in South Africa and America for a long while.' Turning to Eva he continued, 'That would be why he appeared to be a lot richer than your father could understand from his relatively modest diamond business. As soon as he heard that Rafter had been arrested he panicked. He has admitted he knew about the bribing and kidnapping but swears he was not involved in it. He was terrified that once Rafter had been arrested he would spill the beans and implicate him in the murder, hence his decision to tell all.

'It seems they worked closely together for many

years, but kept it secret. As soon as Victor Rainsford was invited to join County View, they saw this as an opportunity to possibly make money out of inside knowledge on gambling, and at the same time Clough also saw the chance to hurt Jay who we know he was always hostile towards. He insists that things got out of hand and he started to lose his nerve. However, he also explained that Kipper Fish was responsible for placing a large number of the bets and he himself, using an assumed name, was responsible for the others.' Harvey paused to take a sip of wine.

'He assured his interrogators that Howard knew nothing about that, and I imagine he'll be horrified when he hears that his long time friend was operating behind his back.'

Jay and Eva looked at each other. 'God,' she exclaimed, 'this is a never ending drama!'

The policeman gave her a sympathetic look. 'I honestly think this is the end of it, Eva. Obviously the whole thing is going to get a huge amount of publicity when it comes to trial, but I don't think we will find anything else crawling out from under the stones. I think you should tell Howard rather than him learn it in some other way.'

'Of course,' agreed Jay. 'I honestly think he will be gutted.'

With that they turned their attention to different topics of conversation. Eventually Harvey looked at his watch. 'Right, I've got to be on my way. I've got a game of golf to play this evening.'

He dropped the others off at County View and got out of the car to shake their hands. 'It's been a great pleasure to meet you both. I only wish it hadn't been under such difficult circumstances. You've given me a new interest in horse racing, and I hope something of an understanding. Obviously we shall meet from time to time as the prosecutions get under way, but apart from that I hope we shall keep in touch as friends.'

'That goes without saying,' replied Jay. Eva leaned over and gave him an affectionate kiss on the cheek.

'You've been an absolute brick,' she said.

'Well, you two have shown amazing strength and resilience throughout an extraordinary chapter of events,' Harvey replied. With a cheery wave he was back in the car and on his way to his evening game of golf.

Walking back into the house Jay looked at Eva. 'I think I'll get it over with,' he said. Five minutes later he was on the phone to Howard and relaying Jackson's information to him. His long time friend and partner was completely shattered.

'I don't fucking believe it!' he said, using a word which very seldom passed his lips. 'He and I were kids together at school. Has he done anything illegal?'

'We don't know yet. Jackson is obviously going to investigate that. Maybe he was just being greedy. Although he must have had a pretty good idea of what was going on after his conversations with Benny, it doesn't mean to say he was directly implicated.'

'One thing I can tell you is that if this comes out his reputation in the East End will be in the pits. Nobody will touch him with tweezers, and I'll make bloody sure that bookmaking business is either closed down or he is out of it.' There was a pause. 'You don't think I had anything to do with it, do you?' he asked.

'Howard, if I thought that would I be talking to

370

you now?' the young trainer answered. 'You're my friend and I've trusted you since the first time we met. I am not going to change my opinion now.'

'What happens now?' the older man asked.

'We are going to do exactly what Hal suggested yesterday. We are going on a really good holiday. Cathy and Jed are going to some of the studs, and we are going to be looking at the French one, and the one in the States. By the way Hal has promised we won't have to meet the President!'

There was a chuckle at the other end of the phone. 'Have a good time and I'll see you when you get back. Just tell Danny that if he's got any problems and he thinks I can help, all he has to do is give me a call.'

'I'll certainly do that, and look forward to seeing you on our return.'

Hand in hand, the young couple walked into the living room and sat down in their customary chairs. Eva gave her husband a wicked little grin.

'Where are we going to have our first runners next season?' she enquired. Jay hurled a cushion at her.

'I think I might make this trip by myself!' he cried.

'You wouldn't last five minutes without me!' she announced.

'Probably not,' he laughed.